By a Lady

By a Lady

BEING THE ADVENTURES OF
AN ENLIGHTENED AMERICAN IN
JANE AUSTEN'S ENGLAND

AMANDA ELYOT

THREE RIVERS PRESS · NEW YORK

Published in the United States by Three Rivers Press, an imprint of the
Crown Publishing Group, a division of Random House, Inc., New York.
www.crownpublishing.com

THREE RIVERS PRESS and the Tugboat design are registered trademarks of
Random House, Inc.

Library of Congress Cataloging-in-Publication Data
Elyot, Amanda.
By a lady: being the adventures of an enlightened American
in Jane Austen's England/Amanda Elyot.—1st ed.
1. Austen, Jane, 1775–1817—Appreciation—Fiction. 2. Master and
servant—Fiction. 3. New York (N.Y.)—Fiction. 4. Women
domestics—Fiction. 5. Bath (England)—Fiction. 6. Time travel—Fiction.
7. Actresses—Fiction. I. Title.
PS3603.A77458B9 2005
813'.6—dc22   2005007410

ISBN 10: 1-4000-9799-1
ISBN 13: 978-1-4000-9799-9

Printed in the United States of America

Design by Lauren Dong

10 9 8 7 6 5 4 3 2 1

First Edition

In Memory of Howard Fast

In late 1996, I had the great good fortune to be cast in the role of Jane Austen in Mr. Fast's two-character romantic drama, *The Novelist*. It was a "what if" story, opening with the premise that as Miss Austen began to write *Persuasion*, a dashing sea captain fairly barged his way into her life, sweeping her off her feet and insisting that she marry him. Mr. Fast was one of the twentieth century's most prolific novelists himself, but he cherished his lovely little stage play like a favorite child, and I was honored beyond all measure when the author attended, and then complimented, my performance. My experiences working on *The Novelist* were the best I've enjoyed thus far during my theatrical career, unparalleled in their professionalism as well as their reward. *By a Lady*—and in fact my own career as a novelist—was born of those experiences, and for that I remain forever grateful to the two fellow travelers who so greatly changed my life: Miss Jane Austen and Mr. Howard Fast.

I could not sit down to write a serious romance under any other motive than to save my life; and if it were indispensable for me to keep it up and never relax into laughing at myself or other people, I am sure I should be hung before I finished the first chapter. No, I must keep to my own style and go on in my own way; and though I may never succeed again in that, I am convinced that I should totally fail in any other.

JANE AUSTEN
Letter to the Prince of Wales's Librarian

The novels which I approve are such as display human nature with grandeur—such as show her in the sublimities of intense feeling—such as exhibit the progress of strong passion from the first germ of incipient susceptibility to the utmost energies of reason half-dethroned—where we see the strong spark of women's captivations elicit such fire in the soul of man as leads him . . . to hazard all, dare all, achieve all, to obtain her. Such are the works I peruse with delight, and I hope I may say, with amelioration. They hold forth the most splendid portraitures of high conceptions, unbounded views, illimitable ardor, indomitable decision—and even when the event is mainly anti-prosperous to the high-toned machinations of the prime character, the potent, pervading hero of the story, it leaves us full of generous emotions for him; our hearts are paralyzed.

JANE AUSTEN, *Sanditon*

Book the First

Prologue

*I*T'S BEAUTIFUL," C.J. murmured, examining the curiously pockmarked amber cross. She held up her hand to shield her eyes from the glaring sunlight, then ducked under the vendor's makeshift white canopy, which protected his merchandise from the exigencies of the elements but blocked his enjoyment of a cloudless postcard-blue Long Island sky.

"It's very old," the vendor advised, in a lilting Indian accent. He handed the young woman his business card.

"Aki Singh," C.J. read. "Exactly how old is 'old'?"

The edges of the cross were worn away, having lost some of their definition over the decades. "Was this ever set in silver, or something?" C.J. asked, noting the uneven honeycomb pattern that covered the bottom half of the cross. She could not imagine that it had always looked so rough. It owned a homemade quality, most certainly crafted by hand.

"It is very difficult to say," the vendor replied, adjusting his turban. "Erosion is natural. Amber is a fossil, essentially a living thing."

"I always thought fossils were dead things," C.J. muttered under her breath.

Mr. Singh continued. "Over time, the edges have probably

worn away so that they are as you see them now. Once, there may have been a setting, and you are right; it probably would have been silver. But it is very hard to tell."

C.J. was prepared to buy the cross anyway, as long as the price was reasonable. After all, this was a local crafts fair with the odd antique thrown in; how expensive could it be?

Mr. Singh shrugged his shoulders. "I tell you what: I give you a very good price. I will sell it to you for thirty-five dollars. If you desire a chain, I will make it forty." He displayed an array of generic-looking metal chains.

"Thank you, but I'm sure I have a chain at home. Do you take credit cards?" C.J. fumbled through her voluminous purse for her wallet. As a frequently unemployed actress, she was perennially strapped for cash.

"Cash or checks." The vendor rummaged behind his stall for a little cardboard jewelry box, into which he nestled the amber cross.

"Oh boy," C.J. sighed. She counted the bills in her wallet. Twenty-three dollars, and she still had to take the train back to Manhattan from Bridgehampton. "A check it is." She made out a draft for thirty-five dollars payable to Aki Singh, Estate Jewelry.

The vendor noted the antique gold paper and the writer's name and address printed in formal script at the top of the draft. "Thank you," he said, reading the name on the check, which he then placed inside a slightly dented green strongbox.

"Thank you very much, Miss Cassandra Jane Welles."

Chapter One

Wherein our heroine expresses an affinity for an earlier era,
and a series of events irrevocably alter her destiny.

WILL YOU JOIN ME for the first set?" C.J.'s friend Matthew asked as she perched on the wooden folding chair at the perimeter of the gym, changing her shoes.

"I'd be delighted," she smiled. C.J stood up, in her soft-soled dancing slippers. "You tower above me," she laughed, looking up at her new friend. "Are you sure you don't want to dance with a lankier lady?"

"I've been coming to the English country dance sessions every Tuesday night for four years, and you are my favorite dance partner ever."

C.J. looked about the room at the other dancers, most of whom were in their forties and fifties, and smiled to herself. If they had all been living during the actual periods of the dances—the Georgian and Regency eras—most of them would be considered rather ancient, if they reached that age at all, thanks to poor diets and limited medical knowledge. No penicillin. No prophylactic fix-ups.

Wow! she thought, if they had been Georgians, Matthew

would be in the prime of life, and she—*goodness!*—pushing thirty, would be an absolute on-the-shelf spinster. Her prime would have been over by the time she reached her early twenties. Forget kids; she would have had very little chance for a husband at her age.

C.J. had never considered herself wholly at ease in the twenty-first century. The constant barrage of images and noise, the relentless pace, the seemingly unlimited rudeness of some people. Hip-hop. Cell phones. All of that set her teeth on edge. Oh for a truly kinder, gentler world where quiet and a sense of delicacy and respect—of fellow feeling—were the norm.

Barbara Gordon, one of the workshop callers, took her place in front of the microphone at the far end of the gym. "Okay, if everybody could form sets longways—I think we have enough people for three lines—'old' people, invite some of the 'new' people to dance. Get ready for 'Apley House.' " Barbara nodded to the trio of musicians—piano, violin, and flute.

The musty church basement was not exactly atmospheric for anything but a sock hop, but once the musicians struck up their centuries-old country melodies, everyone seemed to forget all but the dances. In the dancers' imaginations, their Keds became kidskin slippers, and eclectic cotton T-shirts magically meta-morphosed into Empire-waisted sheer muslin gowns and tight chamois trousers.

Matthew bowed to C.J. "Miss Welles, would you do me the honor of joining me?"

C.J. placed her small hand in Matthew's, wishing she were wearing elbow-length gloves. She rose and made a slight curtsy, allowing Matthew to lead her to the top of the set. "Are you crazy?" she whispered. "I'm not sure I know enough to lead!"

"Didn't you study English country dancing at Vassar?" The music had begun; the dancers were honoring their partners and opposites, and listening intently to Barbara's instructions as she began to call the dance.

C.J. looked down the set at some of the dumpier dancers, in their T-shirts and sweats, who were very game but hopelessly twenty-first century. "No, I didn't. I studied period movement styles. The theatre program was very thorough, but English country dancing wasn't even an elective." She flashed Matthew a warm smile.

"Another reason I like to dance with you, apart from your grace," Matthew said, while they set to the right and then to the left, light on their feet. "You love to play as much as I do." He took her hands and they spun, giving themselves completely to the momentum of the music.

"That's true enough," C.J. agreed, and nodded at Matthew's barrel chest encased in a perfect replica of a double-breasted vest, circa 1800, constructed of French-blue brocade. "Nice waistcoat. We're such period geeks, aren't we?!"

"I prefer the term *aficionado*."

C.J. did a figure with her neighbor, a dour-faced matron who put her in mind of a vicar's wife in a small Regency hamlet.

"Do you ever look at these people," C.J. whispered softly to Matthew as they executed a back-to-back figure, "and think of them in period costumes, as townspeople in a Jane Austen novel?"

"All the time," he grinned.

"Imagine the same faces—the same bodies, even—in cape collars and starched cravats!"

The dance ended. "Promise me the supper waltz," Matthew pressed C.J.'s hand before he went in search of his next partner.

"Forgive me," C.J. said as she made eye contact with Paul, another one of the callers, "but I love that they call it the supper break when we go into the kitchen for lemonade and Oreos."

"Don't you think they had Oreos in the early nineteenth century?"

"Of course they did. Even earlier, in fact. Poor Richard referred to them as one of the basic food groups in his *Almanack*." C.J. winked, and curtsied to Matthew to thank him for the dance.

"May I have the honor?" Paul Hamilton asked.

"The honor would be mine, sir," C.J. smiled demurely. Paul was a historian and a stickler for proper carriage and execution.

"You should never be looking at your next partner," Paul had cautioned the assembly as part of his weekly litany. "It is the height of rudeness. Treat each partner as though he or she were the most important person on earth and give him or her your fullest attention. This is about flirting. For the three hours a week that you spend in this basement, you are not only *allowed*, but you are *encouraged* to flirt." When Paul was on the floor, he was in great demand as a partner. His grace and manner seemed timeless. "May I give you a tiny correction?" he murmured in C.J.'s ear as he led her into the set. "You have such natural exuberance that you are a joy to watch as well as to dance with."

"Thank you." C.J. felt her cheeks go pink.

"But, if I may—you must execute your traveling steps more smoothly. Think of gliding. You have a tendency to bounce a bit, which is not as out of place in some of the more energetic dances, but it sticks out when you are cutting the more stately figures."

"Does it make my bosom heave too much?" C.J. joked.

Paul's gaze strayed to the ripe fullness of her chest. "As a man, I of course have no problem at all with the—er—buoyant movement of your body. But I thought that given your affinity for the correctness of period detail, you might want to practice the proper form. Always remember to keep your back straight and your chin lifted."

After the supper waltz ended, C.J. and Matthew bowed to each other and braved the crowd in the kitchen, chatting away over the junk food and fruit punch. This was the time when the dancers exchanged information on other events: concerts, weekend English country dance conferences in New England, and other bits of information and gossip. Flushed from the waltz, C.J. squeezed past a knot of dancers to get to the lemonade, downing three Dixie cups' worth in rapid succession. She sidled past a cluster of women gathered in front of the week's notices and flyers and immediately lit upon a rose-colored leaflet announcing auditions for a Broadway production of a new play called *By a Lady*. C.J. had already clipped the casting notice out of the current edition of *Back Stage*, the professional actors' most popular trade paper. *By a Lady*, a two-character drama set in 1801, depicted the ill-starred romance between the young Jane Austen and a distant relation of hers, Thomas Lefroy. They had hoped to marry, but Tom lacked the funds to support a wife, in addition to which, Jane was considered a poor relation. Tom's protective aunt, Anne Lefroy, was adamantly opposed to the match, so Tom returned alone to his family's village of Athy, in Ireland, where he read law and eventually became the country's chief justice. Jane never wed, of course.

"You should go to that tomorrow," a voice crunched in her ear.

"No kidding! I can't miss it! Between the *Back Stage* ad, this flyer, and your encouragement, the rule of three is now fully in effect. I can't *not* go, now. And . . . Matt . . . ? You're dropping Oreo crumbs down my neck!"

Matthew brushed off the offending bits of chocolate cookie. "Nice necklace, by the way."

"Matthew Bramwell, I thought you of all people would recognize it," C.J. teased, "since you're as big an Austen buff as I am. One of her naval officer brothers—Charles, I think—brought back topaz crosses and gold chains as souvenirs for both Jane and Cassandra from his tour of duty in the east during the Napoleonic Wars. Jane fictionalized the event in *Mansfield Park*, when William brings back an *amber* cross from Sicily for Fanny Price, and she has nothing but a ribbon to thread through it."

"So it's a keepsake for a reasonable Price." Matthew winked.

The musicians struck up a lively tune, heralding the recommencement of the evening's exertions. "Well, my friend," Matthew said, "if you promise not to do so out on the dance floor . . . break a leg!"

THE FOLLOWING AFTERNOON, C.J. found herself standing in a colorful, densely populated audition line that snaked its way through the winding streets of Greenwich Village.

By the time there were only twenty-three people ahead of her,

C.J. felt in her heart that the role of Jane Austen had to be hers. It was more than the visceral connection she felt to the time period. Getting a leading role on Broadway was the holy grail of any stage actress. She fiddled with her amber cross. Somehow, the simple act of touching the antique talisman, of memorizing its rutted topography, centered her in a way no form of meditation ever could.

"Hey there, folks, we're moving right along now. Okay, if I could have the next three men and the next three women step inside the hallway, please. And please have your pictures and résumés ready." The announcement came from a bearish-looking man with a kindly face set off by wire-rimmed glasses. He ushered in the next group of performers with the air of a jovial train conductor. "Have a seat in one of these chairs in the order in which you were standing in line. I'll take your headshots now."

"Who are you?" asked one of the actresses.

"Me? I'm Ralph Merino, the assistant set designer." He patted his belly. "We have a stage manager, but I need the exercise. On behalf of the *By a Lady* staff, thanks to all of you for coming." He handed each actor a photocopied set of "sides," the pages from the script with which they were expected to audition.

"Okay, listen up, folks. If you don't know anything about this show, here's the scoop," Ralph said. "This is a two-character play—a hypothetical love story set in 1801 that focuses on Jane Austen the woman, rather than Jane Austen the novelist. The playwright, Humphrey Porter, is exploring what made The Woman become The Writer. Beth Peters, the director, is an Englishwoman. She's a bit of a wunderkind over there, but she's never directed in New York, and, therefore, *yes*, she is seriously interested in seeing everyone. I won't lie to you: famous names might be important to the producers, but Beth genuinely wants to see new talent. A U.S. national tour and a West End run are not out of the question after the Broadway run closes. *Yes,* Miramax is a coproducer of the Broadway production, which means that they own film rights to the show, should that become a viable option. Nothing is set in stone at this point, including the casting, so you are *not* wasting your time by showing up this afternoon." His presentation completed, Ralph made a little theatrical bow and his rapt audience applauded. "Back in a few to pair you up."

"C.J. Welles?" C.J. looked up when she saw Ralph come out of the auditorium a minute or two later. "C.J., you'll be paired with Bernie Allen. Bernie?" An Archie Bunker type, who was not exactly C.J.'s idea of an English hunk, looked up from his script. "So, Bernie? C.J.? We're ready for you."

C.J. rose from her folding chair and took a deep breath. Bernie squeezed her hand and whispered in her ear, "Let's do it, kiddo." He smelled faintly of cigarettes and beer.

The interior of the Bedford Street Playhouse looked like a Wedgwood box, with white sculptures standing out in relief against a background of china blue. A long folding table set up stage left was littered with stacks of actors' headshots, scripts, and the ubiquitous paper coffee cups.

Ralph introduced C.J. and Bernie to Humphrey and Beth, then seated himself behind the table and pushed an open box of cookies toward C.J. "Before you jump into the scene, have a ratafia cake," the designer said, with his mouth full. "Beth baked them. Sort of to get us all in that 1801 mood."

"What are ratafia cakes?" C.J. asked the director.

"Sort of like little meringues made with ground almonds, egg whites, and orange-flower water. They were a very traditional dessert back then."

"But," Humphrey chimed in, "in 1801, they used to make them with bitter almonds instead of grinding sweet ones. Bitter almonds contain prussic acid."

C.J. frowned. "Sorry, guys, I flunked chemistry. Enlighten me."

"Poison," Beth and Humphrey responded in tandem. They looked at each other and laughed.

Beth smiled. "Prussic acid is hydrogen cyanide. Poison."

"I think I'll pass," C.J. said.

The audition was almost as painful as prussic acid poisoning.

Poor Bernie was a hopeless actor, and C.J. left the stage feeling defeated and robbed of the opportunity to have done her best work. So much for karma. She was in the corridor putting on her coat when Ralph emerged from the theatre. "C.J., they'd like to see you do the scene again with a different actor."

Back onstage, C.J.'s second chance was going terrifically. Beth was highly complimentary of her work and made particular mention of C.J.'s flawless English accent, praise indeed coming from a true Brit.

As she was preparing to leave the playhouse, C.J. felt a tap on her shoulder. Ralph again. "They'd like to bring you in for a callback, C.J. So you'll be hearing from us within the week about the specifics. Congratulations."

As it turned out, there were nine grueling rounds of callbacks before C.J. made it to the final cut. Personally as well as professionally, her nerves were raw.

Two weeks after her first *By a Lady* audition, she stood on a chair in the backstage area, being fussed over by a professional costumer brought in by the producers. The people from Miramax wanted to see the final casting choices in full costume, by appointment, one at a time, as if they were being screen-tested. C.J. caught her reflection in the dressing room mirrors. "Wow! Except for the zipper in the gown, I really feel like I'm back in 1801."

"You look exactly like one of those pre-Regency portraits. It's amazing," commented Elsie Lazarus, the assistant stage manager.

Milena, the costumer, handed C.J. a straw bonnet decorated with simple yellow ribbons. "I can't wait to see how you look in this." C.J. tied a bow under her chin, edged it just off to the side as she'd seen in illustrations of the period, and regarded herself in the mirror.

"Don't forget to accessorize," Elsie said. She gestured to a coquelicot shawl and the cream silk reticule and ecru lace mitts that hung in a net bag on the costume rack. "All set?" C.J. nodded. "Then let's go! Break a leg!"

Fighting the manifestations of stage fright, C.J. stepped out onto the stage. In accordance with the lead designer's mandate from the producers to deliver a rehearsal version of the eventual Broadway set, Ralph had constructed a pair of freestanding frames with brass-handled doors, which now added definition to the space, creating the boundaries of Jane Austen's parlor in Steventon.

Beth's voice echoed from the audience. "*Right*, then, would everyone please humor me and put your Starbucks cups down for the next five minutes. Let's settle. Thank you. All right, C.J., I'd like to hear the monologue toward the end of Act One as if we've got Lefroy onstage with you, and take it all the way through to Jane's exit, please," Beth added crisply.

Infused with something out of the ordinary, C.J. began the speech she had been asked to memorize for her final audition. Perhaps it was the addition of the costume and accessories, but she had no trouble believing that on that stage in Greenwich Village, she was stepping back in time more than two hundred years.

"I will think on it, Tom," C.J. said resolutely, nearing the end of the scene. "And accord the utmost consideration to your proposal." She crossed thoughtfully to the doorway, stopped, and turned as the lights began to fade. "Bath," she said, her voice tinged with ambivalence. "I'm going to Bath."

As she closed Ralph's door behind her and exited the stage, C.J. found herself enveloped in complete and impenetrable blackness.

Chapter Two

The beginning of a most unusual journey in which our heroine
soon learns that Merrie Olde England isn't always.

SEVERAL MOMENTS ELAPSED before C.J. was able to adjust her vision. She surveyed the breadth of the polished oaken floor of the stage, her gaze lighting upon an arcaded area at the back of the house. Through the musty gloom she discerned elaborate boxes trimmed in wine-red upholstery on either side of the intimate theatre above the pit level. The rest of the theatre—including the galleries, which were divided into smaller loges—was decorated primarily in a rich shade of malachite green.

Where am I? C.J. wondered aloud, her voice greeting her in echo. She had just exited the stage at the Bedford Street Playhouse—had stepped off the makeshift set of *By a Lady* into the familiar backstage darkness—or so she thought. But now she was not backstage—either in Manhattan or anywhere.

She peered into the dim cavern illuminated only by renegade slivers of daylight seeping in from outdoors. The small, shallow orchestra stalls were furnished with hard wooden benches rather than individual seats, and the balconies encircling the interior of the auditorium on three sides were considerably close to the stage.

Apart from the hushed, almost reverent, quiet of the darkened empty theatre, there was something else out of the ordinary, if C.J. could only pinpoint it. The playhouse looked like many she had seen in prints and photographs of some of the older theatres in European cities, but something . . . if she could figure it out . . . something was very different from anything she had ever seen. She looked up and was astonished to discover that no lights whatever were visible—no network of grids, pipes, and cables. The ceiling boasted an elaborate mural ringed in gilt, where lissome nymphs and chubby cherubs à la Boucher appeared to join several of Shakespeare's most recognizable characters in a pastoral frolic. The sight of Shylock cavorting with half-clad dryads provoked a sly smile from C.J.'s lips.

Curiouser and curiouser, she thought, although her heart was pounding within her chest. *What the* hell *is going on here?* Was further exploration a grand idea or a dreadful one? C.J. walked downstage—literally—as the floor was significantly raked and sloped toward the audience. A quaint little prompter's box was nestled just below the lip of the stage. Yet here no light was affixed to the wooden podium that nearly filled the shadowy, cramped space.

It was surreal. C.J. rescanned the playing area for clues, wondering when she might wake from her elaborate daydream. High above the center of the stage, at the apex of the proscenium arch, a familiar emblem stood out in gold relief, topped by a crown and trimmed handsomely with a carved ermine drape. It was a version of the English royal crest, bearing several lions couchant, as well as the rampant red lion C.J. recognized as the insignia of Scotland and a golden Irish harp on a field of blue. C.J.'s pulse raced with alarming rapidity. Perhaps she had ended up on another set, one for some period classic. But where? Curiosity trumping fear, she elected to inspect the backstage area.

Through a musty gloom C.J. fought her way past huge painted flats that sat in a track, or rut, allowing them to be slid on and off the stage like pocket doors. Amid the maze of stored scenic elements were stained glass windows, elaborate thrones encrusted in gold and studded with gemstones, a hedgerow fashioned entirely of silk leaves, and several enormous walls interrupted by high, Gothic arches.

Once free of the forest of flats, C.J. resumed her offstage foraging, which finally led her to an imposing door at the stage level. She pushed against the heavy wooden portal, which swung open onto a narrow alleyway paved in uneven cobblestones, then negotiated her way to the street, where she was greeted with a wash of bright sunlight. She found herself as dazed as Dorothy upon her first eyeful of Munchkinland and blinked several times, attempting to adjust her vision.

She turned back to view the façade of the building she had just exited, on which had been painted the words *Orchard Street,* and struggled to make sense of her surroundings. A young lady in a capacious straw bonnet elbowed C.J. as she passed, nearly knocking her to the ground.

Slack-jawed with amazement, C.J. stood in the middle of the street and gaped at the framed sign prominently displayed outside the elegant stone edifice: EASTER SUNDAY! APPEARING TONIGHT AND TOMORROW EVENING! COURTESY OF THE THEATRE ROYAL AT DRURY LANE. MRS. SIDDONS IN *DE MONTFORT* BY JOANNA BAILLIE. And beneath it: TUESDAY NIGHT: SHAKESPEARE'S TRAGEDY OF *MACBETH*, WITH MRS. SIDDONS AND MR. KEMBLE.

Brother and sister costars as the Bard's bloodiest couple; now that would be an interesting production indeed, especially with the greatest tragedienne of the . . . C.J.'s heart fairly stopped. *Mrs. Siddons?* Sarah *Siddons?* And what in heaven was Joanna Baillie, an unknown—to C.J.—female playwright, doing sharing the bill with William Shakespeare? Where *was* she?

The rest of the notice did much to enlighten and, even more, to intrigue her. FRIDAY NIGHT, DUE TO POPULAR DEMAND, MR. KEMBLE WILL REPEAT HIS PERFORMANCE AS HAMLET, PRINCE OF

DENMARK. Her heart nearly leapt out of her chest when she read
the date at the top of the announcement: APRIL 5, 1801, THEATRE
ROYAL, BATH.

Bath? 1801?

A stupefied C.J. looked across the road, arrested by the sight
of the lacy Gothic architecture reaching toward the sky from behind a cluster of low, narrow buildings. Her gaze was drawn
heavenward, tracing the fantastic height of the stone spires and
the graceful, yet impressive, flying buttresses. The church bell
tolled twelve, its chiming reverberations lingering in the air like
a melodic gray cloud. It was all too sudden, too new, and too
wondrous an experience to instill panic—yet. She had recently
read an article about conscious dreaming: because she'd been
eating, sleeping, and breathing *By a Lady* and everything she
could get her hands on about the time period, perhaps she was
somehow willing this strange and thrilling journey to occur.
*Whatever trick my mind is playing, how can I not keep going to see
how it all ends?* thought C.J.

Wending her way up a slender, curving lane and through a
claustrophobic alley that obligingly trapped the intoxicating fragrance of freshly baked bread, C.J. threaded past women with
delicate fichus crisscrossed over high-waisted, lightweight
Directoire gowns, lending their wearers a slightly pigeon-
breasted appearance. She narrowly avoided a trio of bawling
children who resembled their modish parents in costumed
miniature, and practically tripped over an aging macaroni in his
dandified Sunday best, with impeccable cravat and high black
Tilbury hat.

Her investigative perambulations took her along the aromatic Stall Street, undoubtedly named for the vast profusion of
vendors purveying their various wares: everything from piping
hot currant muffins to milk, from fragrant fresh-cut flowers to
remarkably unappetizing unplucked fowl suspended by their
feet from horizontal wooden poles. C.J.'s nostrils were further
assailed by the smell of sweet rolls wafting through the air, the
fragrant aroma of apples being baked to order on a small coal

stove, and the earthy odor of ordure. She soon found herself in a crowded public square, facing a low, shaded colonnade.

"Shall we step inside the Pump Room, your ladyship?" asked a well-dressed passerby of his elderly companion.

The somberly clad dowager attired in a full-skirted ensemble more befitting to the late eighteenth century nodded curtly, closed her parasol, and allowed the younger man to escort her inside.

The Pump Room?!

How had this happened? Minutes earlier—or so C.J. thought—she had walked off the set of *By a Lady* into the darkened backstage area of a Greenwich Village theatre in New York City in the United States of America, which, if the Orchard Street theatre poster had proclaimed the proper date, was only twenty-five years old!

C.J. stood in the middle of the flagstone square as a tide of humanity swept past her very much confounded person. A watercress-laden cart built like a giant wheelbarrow rumbled by, pulled by two small boys who paid no heed to pedestrian traffic. Jumping back to avoid being trampled by the pair of ragamuffins, C.J. backed into the bow-shaped window of Pelham's Bookstore, just opposite a corner of Bath Abbey.

Bath Abbey?!

She turned back to look at the Abbey, which was indeed the church she had glimpsed from the Orchard Street theatre. Across the square, several fashionably dressed men and women strolled in and out of the Pump Room, the women wearing voluminous bonnets or wielding delicate parasols to shield their fair complexions from the sun. Momentarily seized by vanity, C.J. glanced about her to see if any other ladies sported fringed coquelicot shawls like the one she had been given by Milena, the *By a Lady* costume designer, who'd insisted that Austen herself wore one in 1798. None did. Oddly enough, she felt hopelessly out of date amid the scantily clad women in their revealing white Directoire gowns. If she had worn a frock like that under the bright stage lights—particularly the backlighting—the entire audience would have been able to tell how much she'd eaten for breakfast and whether she'd had a bikini wax.

It fleetingly occurred to C.J. that she had stumbled onto a film set. *Boy, those people at Miramax work fast,* she thought. But no camera equipment was in sight, and no one was dressed in a fashion other than that which seemed appropriate for 1801. This seemed much too lengthy for one of those conscious dreams. Had she hit her head when she left the stage in New York? She could not be going mad. She looked down at her feet to see if her delicate kidskin pumps had metamorphosed into a pair of ruby slippers.

No one seemed to take notice of her. Could they see her as she could see them? C.J. rubbed her rear end, which felt slightly bruised where she had bumped into the lead framing of the bookstore windowpanes. Well, she could certainly feel pain.

At first, the thunderstruck revelation that she might actually *be* in Bath, England, in the year 1801 felt like a fantasy come to fruition. This acknowledgment was almost immediately followed by a pang of anxiety that zigzagged like lightning through her body upon the sudden realization that she had absolutely nothing with her, save the clothes on her back and what was in the small reticule dangling from her wrist. She slid open the drawstring, hoping to locate some cash, then realized that it would have been useless had she indeed discovered dollars, the coin of an as yet infant realm. Imagine finding a penny or a five-dollar bill bearing the likeness of a man who would not achieve immortality for several decades to come! A small tortoiseshell comb and a white linen handkerchief edged in lace were all that she found inside the prop purse, and they had been placed there back in a twenty-first-century New York City dressing room.

Full of wonder, C.J. left the square to further explore her surroundings. Bath Abbey looked much the same to her as it had when she'd visited it in the twenty-first century, its unusual fan vaulting still reminding her of the wings of giant swans or, if you spent too much time staring up at them, a kaleidoscope. But instead of the weather-worn, honey-colored stone buildings she'd recalled, C.J. was fairly blinded by the gleaming whiteness of the eighteenth-century façades, made even more resplendent in the glaring sunlight. *So this is what Bath looked like in its heyday!* Now she began to understand why the spa city—the playground of the aristocracy—was considered one of the brightest jewels in the Georgian crown.

She journeyed through the town, keeping the river Avon at her right elbow; and with an uncanny sense of memory she found Great Pulteney Street, as long as three football fields and the widest thoroughfare she'd seen thus far. Stepping off the curb to cross the avenue, C.J. suddenly became overwhelmed; and when a wobbly and uneven stone caused her to lose her footing, she stumbled to the pavement. A rush of thunder filled her ears, and glancing up she saw four black chargers pulling a shiny burgundy-colored carriage about to bear down upon her prostrate frame. An attempt to scramble to her feet resulted in another minor catastrophe as she became tangled in the hem of her narrow skirt, sending her back to the ground. Never before had C.J. felt so terrified.

The enormous coachman on the box bellowed out a warning, tugging on his team's reins to restrain their flight. C.J. caught a glimpse of his deep green greatcoat and high black hat before flattening her body against the road and rolling away from the thundering hooves.

The spectacle raised quite an alarm among the onlookers. A rail-thin lady in an overdecorated bonnet gasped in fright and clutched the arm of her companion, an elderly gentleman of ruddy complexion who still favored the cockaded tricorn, now some twenty years out of fashion. "Oh, I do hope the young miss is all right," she murmured, eyes closed, fearing the worst.

Still dazed, C.J. lifted her head and wiggled her legs, thus verifying their ability to function. After a moment or two, she concluded that she was more affrighted than injured, but her pale yellow muslin had taken quite a dusting and appeared to be beyond reasonable repair. She tried to speak, but no sound would come out. After several more moments passed, she began to catch her breath. How lucky she was to be alive, and apparently in one piece. Still, words deserted her.

"The poor lambkin. And she never even raised a cry for help. Not so much as a whimper. Do you think she's a mute, Sir Samuel?" The birdlike woman glanced anxiously at her companion. The gentleman extended a gloved hand to C.J., who shakily placed her palm in it, allowing him to lift her to her feet.

"Th-thank you, sir," C.J. stammered, groping for her best British accent. "I shall be all right in a moment or two."

"You suffered quite a dreadful panic, miss," the good Samaritan said. "Will you allow us to fetch you anything?"

"No, thank you, sir. You are too kind."

The Samaritan's lady whispered something in his ear, to which the gentleman nodded and smiled. "Here you go, miss," he said, drawing a silver flask from the deep pocket of his coat.

"What is it?" C.J. asked hesitantly, inspecting the container.

"Just a dram or two of brandy to set you on your feet all right." The man offered the opened flask to C.J., who brushed her nostrils over the top, tentatively inhaling the spirits. The stinging aroma was so pungent it nearly made her eyes water.

"It's no trouble. Just take a big swallow," the man encouraged. "It'll set everything to rights. Go ahead now, dearie. There's naught to fear; it'll not harm you."

C.J. put the flask to her lips and took a huge swig of the alcohol. Not having anticipated its degree of potency, she coughed and spluttered as soon as it reached her tongue, practically releasing all of it into her gloved hand. "Holy—good God!" she exclaimed. The brandy was undoubtedly the strongest stuff she had ever ingested. What little she had actually swallowed seared her throat as it made its journey toward her innards. "Thank you, kind sir. And you too, madam," she said hoarsely, managing a faint smile as she returned the silver flask to its owner.

After insisting that C.J. demonstrate to them that she was steady enough on her feet to require no further assistance, the Samaritan couple bid her a happy Easter, leaving C.J. to continue the exploration of her new and strange surroundings.

She continued to walk the length of Great Pulteney Street, her steps taking her to Sydney Place, at the apex of the road, just across from where the formal gardens began. Finding herself in front of number four, C.J. stopped and stared at its façade with the reverence of a pilgrim who has reached his destination. Recalling the research she'd done on Jane Austen before her *By a Lady* auditions, C.J. knew that the Austens had moved to this address sometime in 1801. The house seemed dark and still. Perhaps the novelist was still a guest of her aunt and uncle, the Leigh-Perrots, in the Paragon.

Hoping for a glimpse of her idol, she decided to locate the town house at One Paragon, but realized she hadn't the faintest idea where it was. C.J.'s memories of modern Bath provided a familiarity with some of the most famous locations and streets, but she could not remember ever having come across the Paragon, except in biographies of Jane Austen and Sarah Siddons. But by the time she reached the Royal Crescent, she was exhausted and equally unsuccessful in her attempts to find the Paragon, not even certain whether she was hunting for a street, a square, a close, or a crescent.

It was dusk when she returned to the main square by the Abbey and the Pump Room. The lamplighters in their dun-colored coats and black knee-length breeches had begun the swift completion of their appointed rounds, their illuminations lending the night air a strangely pungent and unfamiliar odor. Here, now, in 1801, Bath was ahead of London in civil engineering. As the mecca for the *ton*, the influential Georgian glitterati, the spa city's streets were fully paved and illuminated, and the sewers had all been placed underground, owing to the tremendous volume of pedestrian traffic in such a small area.

C.J.'s feet felt brutalized after spending so many hours navigating unforgiving stone walkways in her fragile slippers. A stinging pain accompanied each subsequent step she assayed. Her back ached and she felt grimy and exhausted. If the opportunity had made itself known to her, she would have seriously considered bartering her body for a soft bed and a hot bath.

By now the streets were quiet, save for the occasional rumble of a carriage. There was no open coffeehouse or shop in which to seek shelter, no bench on which to rest, and she had not realized until that moment just how hungry she was. C.J. reached into her reticule, half hoping again that some miracle of fate would have placed an English coin or two in the small drawstring purse so that she could purchase something to eat; but of course she found only the comb and handkerchief. She slid to the ground in the shadow of the Ionic colonnade by the Pump Room, wondering how—or if—or when—she might ever be able to return to her own century. It had been an extraordinary day trip, but the novelty was now wearing thin. She was tired, scared, and alone.

Tightly wrapped in her coquelicot shawl, C.J. huddled against the base of the stone colonnade, the magnitude of her predicament resulting in a flood of hot and baleful tears. She was hungry. She was hopelessly broke. And she was homeless.

Chapter Three

In which an act of desperation leads to dire consequences resulting in a taste of English justice, whereupon our heroine is delivered into the hands of a crafty rescuer.

C.J. WAS ABRUPTLY AWAKENED by the rustle of vendors wheeling all sizes and manner of carts into the square, laden to brimming with their several wares. She hadn't the vaguest idea of the time. As she tried to stretch her knotted muscles, endeavoring to ignore the painful cramps that resulted from sleeping outdoors in a crumpled heap, she heard the church bell strike six times. Squealing pigs and squawking fowl joined the ecclesiastical tolling, creating a cacophonous choir.

I must look a fright, C.J. thought as she rose and shook her legs, wincing at their soreness when she placed her feet solidly on the pavement beneath her. She limped over to Pelham's Bookstore, hoping to view her reflection in the emporium's convex window. Her makeup had worn off, and glancing about at the ribbon vendors and bakers, the milkmaids and flower sellers, she realized that perhaps it was for the best that she bore no traces of rouge and eyeliner. She managed a self-mocking snicker. Yeah, she *blended.*

C.J. slid her tongue over her teeth. Her mouth felt as though it were filled with cotton, and she was sure her morning breath was foul. Using Pelham's window as a looking glass, she removed the delicate linen handkerchief from her reticule and wiped the grime from her face, then took off her bonnet and availed herself of the little silver-backed tortoiseshell comb in an effort to make her hair as presentable as possible.

Muscle spasms in her neck and shoulders shot slivers of pain into her temples. Not only had she slept all wrong, C.J. hadn't eaten since the night before she'd left the twenty-first century. Her head throbbed from hunger as well as fatigue. *This is a hell of a way to lose weight,* she thought. In her lightheadedness, she was barely aware of taking an apple off of a heaping pile of fruit from a Stall Street cart. Turning to walk toward Cheap Street, she had all but finished devouring her meager breakfast when she heard a distinct cry of distress.

"Stop, thief!" a man shouted. Barreling toward her was a husky costermonger in a coarse white apron worn directly over his shirtsleeves, which were shoved up past hairy, muscled forearms. Startled out of her confusion, C.J. realized that the apple seller was referring to her as the lightfingers. The coster's accusation engendered a substantial commotion among the other purveyors, who immediately made a grand show of surveying their wares to ensure that they had not been pilfered as well.

Although a small boy encouraged her to "run!" C.J. was too stunned to take off. Within moments, a shadow was thrown across her path and her upper arm was seized by one of the largest men she had ever seen. The blood drained from her face as she beheld with all the terror of a trapped hare an enormous brute menacing her with a truncheon.

"Take her in, Constable," the fruit seller cried. His fellow vendors joined the angry demand in a chorus of belligerent catcalls.

Just as she had reacted on the previous afternoon when she had nearly been trampled into pudding by a coach-and-four, C.J. fought to find her voice, unable to either whisper or scream.

Finally, she managed to ask how the man in mufti could possibly represent the strong arm of English common law.

The constable laughed, showing irregular, worn-down stubs of tooth, some of which were sepia toned from tobacco stains; others were black with decay. C.J. had forgotten how dreadful the state of dentistry was in Britain in those days. "Uniform?" the barrel-chested brute guffawed. "His Majesty's officers need no uniforms to discharge our constabulary duties." He puffed up with pride. "I'll have you know, missy, I was one of the finest Robin Redbreasts in my youth; you've not come across some untrained country-parish idiot."

"Thank heavens!" C.J. replied, her irony lost on her accoster.

"Name's Silas Mawl. I was a Bow Street Runner before I decided to seek greener pastures. Yes, indeed, I was quite the sight in my scarlet waistcoat." Constable Mawl laughed again, displaying his decrepit choppers.

C.J. cast about helplessly, hoping some chivalrous soul or social reformer would come to her rescue. This was no pastoral fantasy, but rather an ordeal of frightening proportions, even for a nightmare. Mawl refused to relinquish his grip. "You're bruising me, sir," C.J. protested meekly, but she was greeted with a grin of remarkable self-satisfaction.

"You're lucky you didn't get greedy and filch yourself a sackful of apples or you'd be looking at a hemp necklace for sure."

C.J. shuddered. Could she be *hanged* in England in 1801 for stealing a peck of apples? What then would the punishment be for taking only one piece of fruit? Shouldn't she merit merely a stern admonishment not to repeat her thievery—or at the very worst, receive a slap on the wrist?

"I'm very sorry I took the apple, Constable Mawl. I was hungry, and I had not eaten for nearly two days—"

"Tell it to the magistrate," Mawl gruffly replied. He softened momentarily when he noticed C.J.'s look of abject terror. "I'm only discharging my civic duties under the law, miss. Let's move it along now." The behemoth commenced to haul her across town, creating a public spectacle as well attended as any perambulation by the Pied Piper. Clearly, the constable was a well-known figure in the city, and the rough treatment of his prey was not only humiliating and painful, but proclaimed to all who witnessed C.J.'s predicament that she was a wrongdoer.

The route they took was an oddly familiar one. When they reached the Guildhall, the enormous official-looking stone edifice that also housed the grand Banqueting Room in all its gilded Georgian splendor, C.J. remembered that the last time she had visited this building, it was as a curious twenty-first-century tourist, eager to soak up as much "period" atmosphere as possible. She had scarce dreamed that someday she would be presented with a far greater taste of eighteenth-century justice than she had ever expected.

Once inside the Guildhall, Mawl led C.J. down several flights of steps whose surfaces progressed from marble to polished wood to limestone as they descended deeper into the bowels of the building.

Mawl lifted a substantial iron key ring from a hook affixed to the stone wall beside the door and escorted the frightened apple filcher down another curving, narrow flight of steps. The gloomy corridor smelled of stale urine, and C.J. was compelled to steady herself by placing her right hand along the damp stone wall. As she realized that her right wrist was equally free, permitting her to maintain her balance as she descended the spiraling stairs, it occurred to her that she had not been placed in irons when she was apprehended, although Mawl's demeanor—and his truncheon—left no guesswork as to what a thief's reward might be should he or she try to bolt. Perhaps, C.J. surmised, her own diminutive stature gave him little reason to imagine that she might be foolish enough to attempt escape.

The jail appeared to be quite an informal arrangement. Four cramped and airless cells, perhaps only six or eight feet across in either direction, were arranged opposite one another like figures in a country dance. The atmosphere, however, was anything but convivial. C.J. was nearly overpowered by the odor of human waste; her hand flew to her mouth to stifle her gag reflex.

The narrow, matted straw pallets that took up roughly half the floor space of each cell appeared to serve as both bed and bathroom. There was no evidence of a washbasin or bowl. Indeed, the only water to be seen was a puddle of rusty seepage in one corner of the divided room.

Maintaining his unyielding grip on the upper portion of C.J.'s left arm, Constable Mawl selected another skeleton key from the large iron ring and inserted it into a flat padlock, unlocking one of the cells, then thrust his young prisoner into the tiny room. "Your quarters, your ladyship," he grinned mockingly. "You won't find any apples down here, but if it's hungry you are, you'll be fed soon enough."

She bit her upper lip. "How long will I be here?" she asked the constable.

Mawl released a sardonic cackle, which gave C.J. no hint of optimism. "Why, you're a lucky girl, you are, miss."

"I? Lucky?"

"Assizes tomorrow. The circuit judge is on the bench this week, missy. If you was to be filching apples *next* Monday, you'd be our guest here until he came riding back to Bath."

"And when might that have been?" C.J. questioned.

"Half a year. Maybe more. Maybe less. If you're acquitted—which you won't be, as they've got more witnesses than spectators at a cockfight to testify against you—you'll be released on your own re-cogni-zance. If you're convicted and sentenced, you might consider making yourself comfortable down here."

"For stealing an apple? *One apple?*" C.J. asked, appalled.

"Thievery's against the law. There's those been hanged for not much more."

C.J.'s hand flew reflexively to her throat.

"Jack Clapham will be bringing you your dinner tonight, missy," he said, leaving her alone. "On behalf of His Majesty, I hope you enjoy it."

C.J. slumped down, hugging her knees to her chest so that she might put as little of her person as possible in contact with the cold and slimy slate. It was impossible to tell the time of day as there were no sconces on the walls to hold torches or candles, and there was certainly no window. Once night fell, it would be dark indeed. This realization was father to another set of fears. As if her dread of whatever germs or diseases might lurk in the fetid dungeon wasn't enough to occupy her thoughts, C.J. shuddered at the contemplation of the other living things that no doubt infested her new lodgings—none with fewer than four legs—and all of them more accustomed to calling her new surroundings home.

She longed for the creature comforts of her own world: a nourishing meal, her own bed—however lonely—and the safety and security of knowing what the next day would bring. She would no longer rage against the fickle vagaries of her chosen career, nor become impatient when her dial-up connection wasn't fast enough or her computer took forever to reboot.

That evening a hunchbacked twig of a man entered the cellar with a rotting wicker hamper. He appeared to be well into his sixties, and his small paunch, combined with the hump, lent him the appearance of a wizened camel. His cheeks and chin were stippled with a coarse red and gray stubble. "Silas said you were a fine one," he uttered through a harelip. He opened his basket and removed an earthenware jug. "Supper time!" he announced. Clapham poured the thin beige gruel into a rough-hewn trough and regarded C.J. with amusement. "Silas said you were a hungry little lightfingers." He turned up his nose, as if to scoff at her. "Well, never let it be said that Jack Clapham didn't look after his guests."

The rancid odor of the unappetizing fare caused C.J. to gag, her gullet already prepared to reject it. If she threw up, she'd have to sit there in her own vomit; if she managed to digest it, she'd be expelling it sooner or later, with nothing but the straw mat for a toilet. But hunger had already felled her, and her stomach was crying out for sustenance, however meager, however mean.

C.J. passed a sleepless night, listening anxiously to the squealing and scuttling of rats as they scurried about the cellar in search of food. She prayed that none would come near her and feared falling asleep, afraid the rodents would find her a worthy appetizer.

She assumed it was morning only when the solid door to the cellar was thrust open and Clapham entered bearing a pair of leg irons. C.J. blanched and the skin on her arms pebbled from fear. Surely the ancient turnkey did not mean to bring her in chains before the magistrate. If her memory served, the American system of justice derived from English common law. Could such barbarism exist for the theft of a single piece of fruit? Irons? She had not even been handcuffed when she was apprehended.

A new terror now overtook C.J. In an age when the sight of a woman's ankle was reputed to cause a calamity, she hoped against hope that the jailer would have too much propriety to lift her skirts in order to affix the leg shackles. But already as good as convicted, prisoners were apparently accorded no such decency, she soon learned, as Clapham knelt and roughly slipped his hands under her gown. C.J. flinched at his touch.

Perhaps it should not have surprised her that the jailer took every advantage of his opportunity to explore her anatomy. His gnarled hands closed around C.J.'s ankles as he applied the heavy cuffs, his palms slid upward and kneaded her calves. She was sickened by his touch. When she attempted to pull away, she was astonished at the weight of the irons, and found herself as much a prisoner of the shackles as she was of the roving miscreants that trembled as they inexpertly plied the stockinged flesh beneath them.

After fastening the shackles, Clapham proffered his palm to C.J., who looked at it uncomprehendingly. "Don't tell me you've got no money, miss," he said in evident disbelief.

"I've got no money, sir. If I'd had any, I would not have needed to avail myself of that apple."

"No need to get bold in your breeches with me, young miss. Now, how do you expect to pay my fee for turning the key for ye?"

"I have to *pay* you for letting me out of prison?" C.J. replied, nonplussed by the entirely alien concept. "I'm not even *free*."

The jailer cocked his head. "How do you expect a man to earn an honest living, missy? I'm no elected official. It's garnish that puts bread on my table and clothes on my back," he said, drawing attention to his misshapen anatomy. Clapham ran a wrinkled hand through his stringy white hair. "But then, I must be going daft in me dotage—expecting a thief to understand a thing about honesty!"

"I should think it would be ransom enough for you to be running your hands along a lady's legs," C.J. retorted.

The turnkey's expression quickly conceded defeat. Clapham led his shackled prisoner up the clammy winding staircases and remanded her into the custody of Constable Mawl, who escorted her down a wide corridor thronged with curious onlookers and rumormongers who halted their conversations midbreath to comment upon the unfortunate malfeasant being led toward the courtroom.

"The young lady looks like quality to me," an older woman whispered to no one in particular.

"Hardly," a female voice sneered. "Why, just look at her shawl. Coquelicot went out of fashion three seasons ago," she tittered, and received a handful of corroborative nods and murmurs.

At the end of the hallway, two scarlet-uniformed officers of His Majesty's army standing sentry at either door swung them open with military precision as C.J. and Mawl approached.

"Oyez, oyez," C.J. heard. She was thrust forward by the enormous constable into the Banqueting Room itself, transformed into a temporary courtroom for the assizes. As she shuffled along, C.J. noticed an impeccably dressed dark-haired gentleman and wondered what had compelled him to attend the proceedings. A bewigged, black-robed bailiff stood at the far end of the high-ceilinged room, his booming voice resounding off the plaster walls and high ceilings as he announced, "All rise for the magistrate."

There was a noisy scuffing of feet and shuffling of chairs and benches as two hundred or so souls of all stamps of society rose expectantly, including the spectators in the small upstairs gallery who responded with jeering enthusiasm at the entrance of the defendant.

With a flourish, another redcoat opened the door at the far end of the pistachio-colored room and the magistrate entered, clearly pleased with the pomp accorded him. Reaching up to adjust his flowing white periwig, he mounted the platform to the judge's bench.

For the briefest moment, as C.J. marveled at his ermine-trimmed crimson robe, she forgot that her life was in this man's hands. They were plump hands, almost like a baby's, and looked unaccustomed to any manner of manual labor. *Okay,* she thought, *I can wake up now. I got the reality check and I'm sure it will better enable me to play someone from this era.* But when nothing changed, C.J.'s fear of being placed on trial in this strange and terrifying world returned with a vengeance, and she fought to keep her wits about her.

"Court is now in session," the bailiff thundered. "His Worship, Magistrate William Thomas Baldwin presiding." The gavel landed with a crack as sharp as a gunshot and the day's proceedings—civil as well as criminal suits—commenced apace.

Alongside the bailiff sat a young clerk who squinted over a pair of bifocals. The magistrate asked the clerk to read the name of the first case. The young man read aloud the name of one Hiram Goodwin, charged with beating his wife, Susan. Mrs. Goodwin cowered in a corner of the courtroom while her husband's hired serjeant-at-law was able to convince the court that although his client had indeed assaulted his spouse, he had done so with an open hand and had never taken a stick to her that was thicker than the width of his thumb, and while not strictly codified, enough judicial precedent had been set to support the legality of Mr. Goodwin's actions.

A sobbing Susan Goodwin stood as the magistrate issued his verdict, dismissing the case based upon the rule of thumb—the determination that the weapon used to discipline the plaintiff did not exceed the dimensions commonly accepted as lawful.

The derisive chorus of catcalls that issued from the mouths of the distaff spectators in the small balcony drowned out the resounding cheers of their masculine counterparts. C.J. was appalled by the verdict.

"Call the next case, Master Masters!"

The young clerk read C.J.'s name from the official docket. She shuffled forward and approached the bar. "I am she, Your Worship," C.J. replied.

"Of what is this young woman accused?"

Constable Mawl stepped forward, having eagerly awaited his moment in the sun. "Your Worship," he began with great authority, "on the morning of April the sixth—the day after *Easter Sunday*, I might add, the holiest day of the year to us God-fearing Christians—"

"Come to the point, Mawl!" came the command from the bench.

"The suspect was seen by several witnesses to take an item of fruit, to wit, a ripe red apple from a pile of the selfsame fruit which sat innocently atop the apple cart of the equally innocent fruit seller, one Adam Dombie by name. The guilty—I mean the *allegedly* guilty—party was immediately apprehended by yours truly, to wit, myself—a former Robin Redbreast of some renown, I may add—and taken posthaste to the prison, where she was placed in the custody of the jailer, one Jack Clapham by appellation."

"Your Worship, might I be permitted counsel?" C.J. piped up. The entire courtroom erupted in spontaneous titters. She tried to appear as unemotional and composed as possible under the circumstances, but every fiber of her being comprehended the gravity of her predicament. If someone did not speak for her, not a doubt lingered in her mind that she'd be a dead woman for stealing an apple.

C.J. continued her plea, striving to keep the desperation out of her voice. "Is not every defendant, no matter how low or mean, no matter how poor, entitled to representation from qualified counsel? A serjeant-at-law? A barrister?"

Magistrate Baldwin was highly entertained by the request. In fact, the young woman's naïveté was providing the most entertainment he'd had in all his thirty years on the bench.

"I was hungry, Your Worship. I had just arrived in Bath the day before I was apprehended, and found myself with not so much as a farthing to my name."

The magistrate banged his gavel on the table, the sound reverberating throughout the room. "Silence!"

C.J. looked utterly bewildered. "Your Worship?" she said meekly.

"I said 'silence,'" repeated the judge. "The prisoner is not permitted to speak for herself."

"But if it is not the custom to afford me counsel, then who shall take my part if I am not allowed to appear pro se?"

Her proper use of the legal term for self-representation was the charm, taking the officers of the court completely by surprise. "Where in Beelzebub's bollocks did you come from?" asked the stunned judge.

C.J. took a moment to gather her wits. "Very far from here, Your Worship. And to tell the truth, I cannot say exactly how I arrived . . . I mean, I *know* not. It is not an attempt at impertinence, sir, I assure you."

"I did not expect you to be familiar with all of the post roads, young lady. However, ignorance of the law is no defense." C.J. prayed that he would pursue his line of questioning no further. "You are a most remarkable young person," the magistrate continued, wringing his fleshy hands as if the act would better enable him to arrive at a verdict. "And I would ask Constable Mawl why he wasted the assizes' time with such a trifling matter. Theft of a single apple is precisely the sort of transgression that a country constable himself is charged with hearing. He is perfectly within the scope of his duties to determine the merits of the case and to mete out punishment where appropriate. I am excessively disappointed in your judgment, Mawl."

The policeman look duly chastened. "Yes, Your Worship."

"Yet a theft, no matter how minor, is still a criminal offense.

If the defendant is an indigent, then she must seek gainful employment or be remanded to a workhouse. Your communicative faculties have astonished this court. Perhaps you can find a suitable position as a governess or lady's companion. What skills do you possess, Miss Welles?"

Somehow, C.J. had the presence of mind *not* to say that she could act, which she knew in this era would be considered another blot on her already damaged character. She racked her brain to think of appropriate pursuits for a young lady of the time, activities that she might actually be able to accomplish if called upon to do so.

A matron clad in an outmoded ensemble of black taffeta rose to her feet with the aid of a silver-handled ebony walking stick. Her reedy voice pierced the air. "Lady Wickham, Your Honor."

"The court is well acquainted with you, Lady Wickham."

"I find myself in need of a lady's companion to read to me and to handle my correspondence. My eyes are not what they once were. If it please the court, I will accept responsibility for the young woman and offer her a position in my establishment in Laura Place."

"Miss Welles, do you admit to the crime of stealing an apple?"

There had been witnesses to her actions. "I do, Your Worship, and I plead my hunger and my penury as the cause, for I have never before taken anything at all—ever—in my entire life." It was the truth.

"Do you repent your criminal action?"

"I do indeed repent that it was necessary to resort to criminal activity in order to feed myself. I am heartily sorry to have deprived Adam Dombie of his hard-won wares, and hope to have the means in future to repay him tenfold."

"Right, then. So be it. The defendant is released into the custody of Lady Wickham, where she is guaranteed gainful employment as a lady's companion." The gavel descended with a bang. "Case dismissed."

Constable Mawl unlocked the shackles incarcerating C.J.'s

ankles. She was free to go. Lady Wickham, hobbled by a club foot, led the way out of the Banqueting Room, motioning for a trembling C.J. to follow her. Under ordinary circumstances, it would have been an easy stroll from the Guildhall to Laura Place, but Lady Wickham's infirmity precluded walking there. When they reached the street, C.J. was astonished to learn that the noblewoman didn't possess her own carriage. Instead, her ladyship begrudged a young boy a farthing to fetch a hackney for the short distance to Laura Place.

Lady Wickham's town house was surprisingly spartan for so fashionable an address. As C.J. passed through a narrow hallway papered in a rather depressing shade of ocher, a pockmarked young man in plain brown livery elbowed a mousy housemaid. "Lookee, Mary, we've got a new one," he snickered.

Chapter Four

Concerning life among the servant class, where our heroine finds a most unlikely friend and ally.

YOU WILL RECEIVE eight pounds a year and an allowance for sugar and tea," Lady Wickham explained as she gave C.J. a tour of the town house. "You will not receive the customary allowance for beer. I do not believe women should consume spirits." Everything was in good taste—though a bit on the ascetic side—and the house was spotless, but C.J. was unprepared for the shabby appearance of Lady Wickham's furnishings.

"Under ordinary circumstances, Miss Welles, the annual wages for a lady's companion fall within the range of twelve to fifteen pounds per annum—depending upon qualifications and references, of course—as well as an allowance. However, all of my servants consider themselves highly fortunate to have employment at all, given their unsavory histories and the manner in which they came to my attention. I expect that you'll agree that eight pounds is vastly preferable to a penal colony in Queensland."

With great difficulty, Lady Wickham mounted the stairs, her club foot landing with an embarrassing thump as she negotiated each riser. She showed C.J. to her room at the very top of the building, just under the eaves. The sloping roof took up a good third of the cramped, dark quarters and the hearth was considerably smaller than those in the rooms below. Still in all, compared to the prison, it was paradise.

In the airless chamber, C.J.'s nostrils were assailed with an unpleasant aroma, and she realized with tremendous mortification that it was her own person that smelled so vile. Sleeping on the street—followed by the overnight incarceration in the cellar of the Guildhall—had compounded the fact that she had been unable to bathe since her arrival. Anyone with whom she had recently been in contact either must have smelled almost as bad or else was exceedingly polite or particularly felicitous of temperament, for she seemed to leave the stink of a cesspool in her wake.

"Wait here, Miss Welles," Lady Wickham commanded. "Mary will be up momentarily with a hip bath and a bucket of water so that you may wash yourself. I shall see about procuring you some appropriate attire." She departed the garret and clumped back down the narrow staircase.

C.J. was afraid to sit on the only bed in the room, a narrow cast iron affair with a thin and lumpy mattress, not to avoid discomfort, but to refrain from infecting it with her stench. There was nothing else in the room but a wooden chest of drawers, moderate in size; a shabby folding dressing screen about five and a half feet high; and a metal trunk at the foot of the bed. Curious, she pried open the trunk, which contained two or three coarse woolen blankets. No personal effects were anywhere to be seen. The walls were bare.

She debated whether or not to remove her dress then and there. When she laid aside her shawl and reached to scratch an itch in the middle of her back, she was suddenly reminded that there was a very twenty-first-century fourteen-inch zipper stitched into the back of the garment. She removed all of her clothes, leaving them in a heap shielded by the screen from the rest of the room, then lifted one of the coarse green blankets out of the trunk, enveloping herself as though it were a Turkish towel.

There was a terrible clatter outside the chamber, and the mousy maid with the dull expression in her eyes appeared in the doorway carrying a large oaken bucket. "God in heaven, you gave me a fright!" she exclaimed, water sloshing onto the floor. "I thought you was an apparition. Bein' wrapped up like that and all." Her jaw slack with wonder and fear, the girl was actually trembling, although her twitching may have owed more to the weight she had somehow managed to transport up four narrow flights of stairs.

C.J. suddenly realized that women of the era bathed in their shifts, and quickly sought a way of disclaiming her social gaffe. "I admit that my appearance is a bit . . . unconventional . . . but my dress and linen gave off such an objectionable odor that I could not stand wearing them a moment longer than absolutely necessary." C.J. wondered if the little maid was cognizant of how she came to be in Lady Wickham's employ. She did not wish to divulge any intelligence the maidservant might not otherwise possess. "My name is Cassandra," she said, extending her hand to the maid.

"Mary. Mary Sykes," the girl replied, realizing that she could not reciprocate the courtesy.

"Good God, Mary, put that bucket down! It must weigh a ton!"

The maid obeyed immediately, then bent and unbent her forearms to relax her aching muscles. The girl's palms were red from rope burn. Then, red-faced, she excused herself with a series of mortified curtsies and went back downstairs to fetch the hip bath. Minutes later, Mary dragged the hip bath into the center of the room and emptied the bucket into it, apologizing for being such a ninny not to have brought the tub before the water, then produced a ball of soap from a pocket in her muslin apron and handed it to C.J., who brought it to her face, inhaling deeply of the delicate lavender fragrance.

C.J. shed the blanket and stepped into the shallow hip bath, settling into it. With her bent legs pulled close to her chest and the water just reaching her hip, she felt like a fairy nestling into a nutshell. Now, in the process of experiencing such a contraption, C.J. understood why the enameled metal tub was called a hip bath. This gave rise to another thought: with the number of obese and gouty people she had seen in just forty-eight hours, however did they manage to squeeze themselves into a basin better suited to hand laundry?

The liquid was only lukewarm by now, but it was crystal clear. She would have preferred a washcloth, but was given none. Nevertheless, it was a joy to be able to get clean, yet another opportunity she'd always taken for granted until now. She almost laughed to think how incommoded she had felt on the few occasions when her landlord needed to shut down the boiler in her apartment building.

"I live here too," Mary finally ventured shyly.

"Do you?" C.J. asked, having once learned that a maid of all work such as Mary usually didn't live on the premises but instead dwelled with her family in a poor and unsavory section of the city. "Which room is yours?"

"This one," answered the maid, her open countenance displaying no sign of jest or merriment.

"But Lady Wickham told me this was to be *my* room."

" 'Tis your room, Miss Welles. But 'tis mine too. I don't mind. I'm happy to have the company. I was very lonely after Fanny left."

"Oh," C.J. said, making polite conversation. "What happened to Fanny, then?"

"I can't say. That is, I don't know, miss. She got herself in the family way and Lady Wickham tried to beat the devil from the blackness of her ruined soul and then she turned her out."

C.J. was aghast. "With nowhere to go? Pregnant?"

Mary's hand flew in front of her mouth to cover her shocked expression. "Oh, you mustn't use that word. That's a vulgar word, that is. Lady Wickham expects her servants to behave genteel."

The word *pregnant* was considered uncivilized? They had decades to go before the eminent Victorians would take it upon themselves to sanitize the English language. Good thing C.J. hadn't blurted out the phrase *knocked up*. Perhaps she should try *enceinte* from now on, although she doubted that Mary Sykes possessed a keen grasp of French.

"She lays great store by gentility, and yet she turns a preg—, a young woman about to be a mother into the street. I suppose Fanny was unwed as well."

"Of course she was, Miss Welles. That's why she was turned out. Lady Wickham said she was a disgrace. I'll never forget how hard Fanny cried when it happened." Mary turned away and C.J. noticed a reddish mark upon the girl's left cheek. She was about to make an inquiry, but something made her change her mind.

"I am sorry that you lost a friend in Fanny as well, Miss Sykes."

"Oh no," the mousy girl gasped. "Mary. You must call me *Mary.*"

"Then you must call me Cassandra."

"Oh no, Miss Welles," said the maid in a hushed voice. "That would never do."

"Why not? We are both in servitude, assigned to sleep in the same room, even expected to share the same bed."

"Miss Welles, *you* are a lady's companion," the girl explained, as though she were teaching catechism to a heathen. "I am a scullery maid. Sometimes, when Lady Wickham needs us below-stairs servants to serve the meals or tea in the parlor, or to sweep and dust . . . which is almost all the time," she added, blushing, "we get to mingle with the gentlefolk; and when I'm above stairs, her ladyship sometimes refers to me by my family name—Sykes—as befits an upstairs servant. But ladies' maids and companions are more genteel-like. It's not proper to call them by their Christian names."

It was quite an education. C.J. had read what she thought was a great deal about the English class system, and she knew, even from watching years of *Masterpiece Theatre* programs and numerous Merchant-Ivory films, that there were different strata of servants, but it had not occurred to her that among the servants themselves there were proper forms of address for each individual station.

C.J.'s existence in the infant nineteenth century was most certainly an enlightening, albeit rather nightmarish, one thus far. At every turn, she acknowledged with much dismay that she was much further removed from this world than she had once imagined she might be. If she could make such a gaffe with a serving maid, what might happen if she slipped up among their betters, an incident that was certain to occur at any time? Not for a moment could she relax her guard, and yet no matter how vigilant she was, it was equally certain that her ignorance could betray her. Every aspect of her daily life would be affected, from the laws of the land to the minutest personal details, and no end of embarrassment might be in store for her. What would she do when she got her period, for instance? She would feel so foolish asking Mary about what was such an obviously routine custom. Even the most private matters of personal hygiene posed the threat of exposure. How could C.J. explain, let alone discuss, why she lacked any familiarity with such a normal ritual?

She wondered what was going on in her own era back home. Had her disappearance been noted at all? Did they miss her? How would she be able to return—and what if she couldn't? What then? If she *was* able to return, how much time would have passed? Would she find, like Rip Van Winkle or the hapless Oisín in the legend of Tir-na-Nog, that generations were born and had died in her absence?

"What are you doing to me?" she asked Mary when the girl knelt beside the hip bath and began to inspect her scalp.

"Looking for lice, Miss Welles. Were you in the jail?" C.J. shivered and nodded, not keen on where this exchange might be leading. "If I find lice, her ladyship will toss you right back into the street. But if Tony can manage to distract her for an hour, I can run to the chemist for some tea tree oil to wash your hair.

That will kill them for sure . . . although we might need to chop off your pretty locks."

"No!" cried C.J., protectively bringing her hands to her head.

" 'Twould be a pity for certain, but leastways the hair will grow back in time and no one will be the wiser if you keep your cap on."

C.J. heard footsteps on the stairs and gave Mary a look of panic. The scullery maid handed her the itchy woolen blanket and C.J. held it before her, creating a shield between herself and the intruder.

The pockmarked youth entered without so much as a request for admission, a bundle of brown fabric under his arm. "These was Fanny's livery," he said, tossing them indifferently to Mary. "Lady Whip-'em wouldn't spend so much as a shilling on a dress for the new one," he added, nodding in C.J.'s direction, "while these was still in fine condition."

"Mind your stupid tongue, Tony," Mary scolded. "You'll scare Miss Welles away."

Tony grinned, ignoring the poor maidservant. "Did Whip-'em get *you* from the assizes too? It's where she gets all her servants. No paying fees to the statute halls for her, no sir. And if she hadn't needed a man to do the heavy work, she never would have forked over the guinea tax to His Majesty for the hiring of a male servant."

C.J. opened her mouth to speak but was interrupted by her new protector. "Never you mind where she came from. Stick to your own business."

"And which business might that be, Mary?" the young manservant asked mockingly. "Would that be tending the coal fire, or fetching her ladyship's parcels from the shops on Milsom Street, or polishing the silver, or sweeping the chimney, or serving the guests what come for supper, or sticking together the bits of candle what burn down in the parlor so as you and Cook and me can have some light in the evenings, because Lady Whip-'em is too cheap to let us buy tallow? Which business would that be, Mary?" Tony scratched open a pustule on his chin, releasing a quantity of viscous yellow fluid, which he wiped away with the back of his hand.

"Just wait 'til you've got to scrub the greasy pots and pans, girl. Or clean out the jakes when they clog. Or get on your hands and knees in the street with a wire brush and scour the sidewalk in front of Lady Whip-'em's doorstep. You'll wish you'd been convicted instead. In the jail, at least you're the one being served—not doing the serving yourself. Now that Fanny's gone, you'll be given her duties for sure."

C.J. swallowed hard. Had she not just been reminded of each servant's compartmentalized tasks and restrictive station? "Lady Wickham said in open court that she was taking me to be her lady's companion, so I doubt that she will be expecting me to fulfill the obligations you have mentioned." Tony's derisive laugh sounded like the wheezing of an asthmatic horse. Even the timid Mary covered her mouth with a grimy hand to stifle a giggle. "Tell me something, Tony," C.J. continued. "Why do you refer to the mistress of the house as Lady Whip-'em?"

Mary shot the manservant a desperate look, as though she feared C.J. might bolt posthaste if he answered, but the pock-marked youth ignored her warning. "Fond of the lash, she is. And her walking stick. And the back of her hand . . . if she can reach you. Once climbed up on a wooden crate to box Fanny's ears."

"Mary! Tony! Cease dawdling this instant!" Lady Wickham's voice caused even her swaggering manservant to jump to attention. Mary's face paled. "Now we'll be whipped for sure," she whispered to Tony. He scrambled down the stairs with Mary scurrying after him. Suddenly itchy, C.J. wondered if she had in fact been infected with head lice. Mary had been interrupted before she could render a verdict on the state of her scalp.

After lifting herself up out of the hip bath, C.J. slid the dead-bolt across the door, then grabbed her yellow figured muslin, the red silk shawl, and all of her period-accurate undergarments, and plunged them into the tub, scrubbing them with the ball of scented soap.

When she finished washing her costumes, C.J. wrung them out as best she could, and re-donned her damp underthings. The heat of her body would have to finish drying them, but the garret was drafty and at first she shivered a little from the wet clothes. She spread the shawl, which now resembled a wrinkled rag, over the top of the folding screen and pressed the yellow gown between the woolen blankets in the metal footlocker. If she could have been sure that no one would find the dress, she would have laid it across the iron bed rail to dry properly, since she was worried about mildew ruining it, but she had no choice. It was better to dry it as much as possible and then hide it, rather than risk its discovery. She'd be hard pressed to explain the zipper to people who were still fastening their clothes with cotton ties.

ONE RAINY AFTERNOON, C.J. tried to count the days she had been in Lady Wickham's employ thus far. One week? Two? She was worked so hard that the days blended into one another. Mornings began at five-thirty with lighting the coal fires and heating the ovens, then she and Mary scrubbed the town house from top to bottom. Silver was polished twice a week. Linens were changed daily and washed in tubs filled with boiling water filtered through sand—a system that also rendered water potable for tea. A five-legged wooden contraption that was cranked by hand functioned as an agitator. Never had C.J. so missed a washer and dryer.

On the rare occasions when Lady Wickham had guests, Tony, Mary, and C.J. were expected to serve the food and help Cook wash up. The fine china was kept in a cabinet off the pantry, away from direct light, as it was hand painted with lead-based colors that were subject to fading. C.J. wondered what all the lead might be doing to their health. If she remembered her ancient history studies correctly, lead pots and pipes were once suspects in the decline of the Roman Empire.

In the afternoons, C.J. would read to Lady Wickham until it began to grow dark. Her ladyship was a miser even with her own candles. In her parsimony she preferred the tapers soaked in animal fat, which emitted a suetlike odor, but even those were rarely lit. Most often, when the light had fully waned, her ladyship pronounced it time to retire. Otherwise, C.J.'s responsibilities as an amanuensis were relatively infrequent, although the mistress of the house corresponded with a sister in Manchester. C.J. was indeed a lady's companion, but the scope of her duties in Lady Wickham's employ was by no means limited to the tasks required of that station.

The only pleasant part of the week was Sunday morning, when the old lady expected her servants to follow her to church. The staff was not accorded a second set of clothes, and, of necessity, found small ways in which to make their humble garments fine enough to celebrate the Lord's Day. Cook, Mary, and C.J. removed their aprons and caps. Tony's livery, such as it was, looked enough like a tradesman's clothes for Lady Wickham to determine that he did not even require another coat for church. The manservant never paid much mind to honoring the day of the Lord: Tony used the sermons as an opportunity to sleep. Mary followed the service like a dumb animal, joining in the hymns when the congregation was asked to lift their voices in song, but she never picked up a hymnal or Bible. Lady Wickham was also too penurious to purchase a pew, the common practice among the gentry, so despite her station, she shared seats with her servants at the back of the Abbey, places that were set aside for the lower orders of society.

C.J. cherished the rare opportunity to dwell in her thoughts while the sermons and homilies were given, often by visiting preachers. While they nattered on in self-important, stentorian tones, she studied the magnificent stained glass and the ceiling's uncommon fan vaulting, and mused upon the astonishing fact that the atmosphere, rather than being devotional, seemed more like a marriage mart, where meaningful glances and billets-doux were routinely exchanged among the congregants.

For a woman who reportedly took to beating her servants at the slightest provocation—although C.J. had yet to witness such vile behavior—Lady Wickham was quite the devout Christian on Sunday mornings.

Sunday afternoons were another occasion altogether. While Lady Wickham most frequently dined alone, she did receive guests for Sunday dinner, an event that entailed the entire staff's participation. Turtle soup was all the rage in the best households, but the mistress of number twelve Laura Place was of the decidedly stinting sort; therefore, mock turtle soup was prepared.

C.J. was horribly squeamish the first time she, along with Mary, helped Cook prepare the soup stock. Rather than shelling, chopping, and potting a terrapin, which C.J. admitted would probably have caused her to lose her appetite forever—delicacy or no delicacy—they used leftover mutton on the bone, from meals eaten during the early part of the week, which had been stored in an ice chest in a cellar twenty-five feet below the kitchen.

Depending on what the butcher was selling more cheaply, either a boned calf's head or veal knuckles were placed in a saucepan and simmered with the mutton stock along with some lemon juice and vegetables.

To C.J.'s mind, the most disgusting part of the preparation—at least as nauseating as decapitating an actual turtle—fell to Cook herself, who, after straining the stock, trimmed and diced the gelatinous meat of the calf's head, setting it aside. Meanwhile, C.J., who had become quite adept at separating eggs with naught but her cupped hands, whisked two egg whites in the calfless saucepan. When the egg whites boiled, they formed a thick scum, the mere sight of which made C.J. queasy.

Cook then lined a sieve with a heavy cloth, and Mary and C.J. hefted the saucepan and strained its contents through the sieve into a bowl, thence transferring it back to the saucepan. That task accomplished, Cook, who was the only one of Lady Wickham's servants permitted the key to the liquor cabinet, unlocked a chest and withdrew a bottle of Madeira, which she poured into the stock, grumbling all the while that a proper mock turtle soup called for at least a cup of the Portuguese fortified wine, but that Lady Wickham's parsimony prohibited her from adding a drop more than *half* the recommended amount. Apparently, as C.J. observed, Cook had long ago decided that such prohibition did not extend to fortifying *herself* from the cut-crystal decanter, and she supposed her stingy mistress would be none the wiser.

After Cook scraped the diced meat back into the saucepan and tossed in some fresh parsley, she would taste it, proclaiming each week that the soup would be vastly improved with the additional half cup of Madeira.

Usually, after the Sunday suppers, the servants had the chance to retire earlier than on the other days, although Lady Wickham frequently asked C.J. to accompany her to the parlor and read to her after the meal. The old woman had a fondness for Dante and for Shakespeare's epic poetry, such as *Venus and Adonis*, which afforded C.J. the chance to read that particular work for the first time. A woman who appreciated Shakespeare, particularly his lesser-known efforts, couldn't be all bad, C.J. reasoned.

C.J. infused her readings with drama and passion. After all, it was her only chance to do anything remotely like acting, and it gave her some comfort to know that Lady Wickham did appear to enjoy the performances. Her ladyship would sit straight as a ramrod in a high-backed chair, her misshapen appendage resting on a footstool covered with a petit point tapestry she boasted of stitching herself in the days when her eyesight was as keen as a razor. "I am seventy-six years old, and I have *never* leaned back," she told C.J. triumphantly when the younger woman had compassionately asked why, given her infirmity, did her ladyship not believe in more comfortable furniture.

"SHE LIKES YOU, Miss Welles," Mary confided one night as the young women slipped out of their simple brown dresses and into the muslin nightshirts that Lady Wickham constantly reminded them she had so generously provided.

Mary blew out the stub of a smelly tallow candle, and they both slipped into the narrow bed.

C.J. remembered that the first time Mary ignited one of the small gunpowder pastilles commonly used to mask the odor of the burning tallow, she had fairly jumped out of her skin from the explosion. She doubted she'd ever become accustomed to such detonations, but Mary cautioned her not to complain to the mistress, or Lady Wickham would surely put a stop to her generosity. "The servants weren't never permitted whole candles, even tallow ones, before you came, Miss Welles," Mary had told her.

In the darkness of their cramped bedchamber, the long day's exhaustive tasks finally at an end, C.J.'s mind would turn to thoughts of home. Although she was not alone, this was the time when she dreamed she could not get back to the twenty-first century, no matter what or how hard she tried. Had her landlord slapped an eviction notice on her door? Had another actress been hired for *By a Lady*? Had everyone there forgotten her?

Tonight her fears got the better of her, and C.J. was unable to control the hot tears that flowed silently down her cheeks. She choked back the sobs so that her bedmate might not hear.

" 'Tisn't just her ladyship what likes you, you know. *I* like you too, Miss Welles," Mary said softly, draping a thin arm across C.J.'s recumbent body. "This house hasn't been so terrible since you came here. Lady Wickham is much nicer to me now." But C.J. was too immersed in her own thoughts to accord her full attention to Mary's stream-of-consciousness rambling. "I hope you stay here forever," the scullery maid murmured, and drifted off to sleep.

"MISS WELLES, you will accompany Mary on her errands this morning," Lady Wickham announced as C.J. finished polishing an elaborate silver candelabra. "It is time you learned how to make the household purchases." C.J. followed her employer into the parlor and retrieved paper and quill with which to make a list. Lady Wickham began to dictate. "Wax candles—six in the pound. I should like two pounds. The candles should last about six or seven hours apiece. The nights are getting shorter; therefore, we will shift from the four-to-a-pound candles to the six. There will still be ample light to read by, Miss Welles."

C.J. wrote out her ladyship's instructions in the penmanship she had mastered during the past few weeks of practice with quill and ink. Her first forays had been a disaster and resembled Rorschach tests rather than correspondence. Lady Wickham had been quite sharp with her for wasting good parchment and blotting paper. Still, C.J.'s fingers bore telltale ink stains that she feared would never completely wash off.

"Fish is too dear, so we shall dine on mock turtle soup again on Sunday. You shall purchase two pounds of mutton for the week, and a calf's head for the stock. Game is scarce, as the hunting season is long over. You should be able to locate pigeon or sparrow, though. I prefer the pigeon as there is more meat on the bones. Purchase four birds. We shall forgo the chicken this week. Ask Mary to show you where to pick up a fine hare."

C.J. dropped the quill, thus creating an enormous ink blot on the sheet of cheap foolscap. She had forced herself to stomach the mock turtle soup and the pigeon pie, even after learning of the ingredients, but eating bunny rabbit was one concession to Georgian cuisine that she was ill prepared to make. She couldn't—wouldn't—do it, although harmless woodland creatures were regular fare in 1801. And people were grateful to get it.

Lady Wickham regarded C.J.'s sloppiness with evident distaste. "I have asked Cook to make a rice pudding, so you will need to fetch rice, of course, and eggs. We will need a sugar cone as well. I am told that we still have butter, and I do not wish to make excessive expenditures."

C.J. finished her list, and after waiting for her to securely close the brass inkwell, Lady Wickham rapped her sharply across the knuckles with her fan. Had the inkwell been open, the writing desk would have been ruined, as the blow caused C.J.'s hands to fly up from the surface and fall back against it with some degree of force.

"What was that for, your ladyship?" C.J. asked, her eyes welling with tears. She kneaded her sore knuckles.

"For handling your quill in such a slovenly manner. I confess that I continue to remain astonished at how a young lady with such an evident sensibility for literature can be so inept with its essentials. Paper and ink do not come cheaply, Miss Welles, and you squander my materials like a drunken sailor!"

Lady Wickham handed C.J. a small purse. "I know to the far-thing how much money is in this reticule, Miss Welles. And I have calculated the cost of each item you have listed. I expect you to return the purse to me with one pound, six shillings in-side. Anything more, and you will receive my thanks for being an astute shopper. Anything less, and I will punish you for the thief you revealed yourself to be on the day that I found you and so magnanimously offered you a position in my establishment."

C.J. descended into town with Mary trotting along like a spaniel at her heel. One item on Lady Wickham's list had caused her particular distress. "Wherever can we find a sugar cone?" she asked Mary, searching in great puzzlement for an ice-cream vendor and wondering why Cook would require such an item in order to make a rice pudding. "And what's so amusing about it?" she added, in response to her companion's sudden peal of laughter.

"Why, Miss Welles," the scullery replied, pointing at a foot-high white obelisk in a shop window, "you're looking at it!" C.J. winced. She had never heard of a cone *made* of sugar and there-fore had yet to recognize one in its pristine form, despite some experience in Lady Wickham's kitchen. "I am so glad of your acquaintance, for I had no cause to smile before you came to Laura Place. If you are not havin' a joke on me, you must be an angel visiting straight from heaven and have lived on naught but ambrosia to know so little of baking ingredients."

C.J. made a pretense of sharing the joke, but despaired of what might happen should she make a similar slipup in front of a less devoted audience. Rather than call further attention to her ignorance, she elected to change the subject. After purchasing the sugar cone for Cook, C.J. removed the smudged list of grocery items from the deep pocket of her dress and reviewed its contents. "I suppose we should get the candles next, then, as they are nonperishable," she suggested.

Mary stopped dead in her tracks. "Where did you get that?!" she asked in dumbfounded amazement.

"Does not Lady Wickham dictate a list to you when you go for her purchases?"

"Oh, noooo. She just tells me what to get, and I try best as I can to commit it to memory. If I get distracted and forget to bring somethin' back, she beats me. But how did you come by a list?"

"I wrote it," C.J. replied simply.

"I thought it was just somethin' Lady Wickham made up so the magistrate would give 'er someone cheap to replace poor Fanny. You really can *write?*" the girl marveled, even more awestruck now.

"Can't you?"

"Cor, no!" the scullery maid replied. "Can't read neither. Same as Tony. Servants like us—we're not expected to know our letters, though most of us know our numbers, seein' as how we have to make purchases for the masters and mistresses. Besides," she added, tugging at a lock of hair that had tumbled out from under her white mobcap, "who would teach us?"

Chapter Five

*Wherein a secret is confided, cruelty exposed, evil confronted,
and our heroine creates quite a stir.*

AT MARY'S TENTATIVE REQUEST, C.J. began teaching her the alphabet. The latter was pleased to be able to accomplish something truly useful, and the former displayed a livelier mind and quicker aptitude for retention and comprehension than C.J. ever would have guessed, owing to the dull vacancy of the girl's usual expression. Mary might never be clever in any extraordinary way, but since C.J.'s arrival, there was a brighter aspect to her eyes. The unfortunate turn of events that had brought C.J. to Lady Wickham's spartan home on Laura Place had produced quite an unexpected result: for the first time in her life, C.J. felt responsible for another human being. A bond had been forged between the twenty-first-century actress and the illiterate nineteenth-century scullery maid. Through it, Mary was blossoming; and in some respects, so was C.J., and for this unusual renaissance, they were both grateful. If C.J. had made a conscious decision to look after Mary, she could not recall the moment it was fixed. In many ways, Mary fascinated C.J. The girl, most likely still in her teens, had never been encouraged or even expected to have an independent thought in her head and had not a bone in her body that was not the property of her employers, whereas C.J. came from a world where women had fought hard through litigation and legislation to be treated as free-thinking, equal members of society. Yet as each day passed, it became clearer that it was the unschooled Mary, and not C.J., the privileged and educated woman, who better understood the nature of their universe.

C.J. was mulling this over one evening as the two young women readied themselves for bed. Mary had slipped off her shift, and C.J., not meaning to watch her, couldn't help but notice the thinness of the girl's arms. How she could handle her menial drudgery with so fragile a form was remarkable, for she seemed to pick at her food whenever the servants gathered in the kitchen for meals.

"You should put some meat on your bones, girl," C.J. said, trying to make light out of her worry that the maid might in fact be ill.

"Oh, I don't like meat, Miss Welles."

"You mistake my meaning, Mary. I mean you should eat more. You eat less than a gnat and you're as thin as a rail."

"But I *did* understand you, Miss Welles," the girl replied obstinately. "I'm not plump like my sisters, and I know I'm not pretty like you. I shall never be otherwise unless I have a stronger appetite, but I never could bring myself to eat the flesh of the birds of the air and the beasts of the field. I look in their dead sad eyes when I'm sent to market and I can't bring myself to take them home with me so they can be our supper." C.J. listened quietly, wondering how many Georgians dared to be vegetarians by choice, as opposed to the happenstance of abject poverty. "That's why I can never eat the mock turtle soup. Were you born in the countryside, Miss Welles?"

"No . . . I'm from a city . . . a very big city." She was tempted to add, "ever so much bigger than Bath," but feared becoming responsible for further elaboration.

"If you could see the mournful look in a calf's brown eyes and see how gentle he is, and as innocent as a newborn, you would never stand for him havin' his head chopped off just to make some nasty old noblewoman a tureen of mock turtle soup!" Mary had driven herself to tears. "And when she sends you out to fetch a chicken, and the poulterer takes it from its cage—clucking and squawking like the dickens because it knows what's about to happen to it—and you watch the man wring its neck right there in front of you . . ." The scullery maid's sobs racked her slender body. "What did a chicken ever do to Lady Wickham that it should deserve to lose its life?"

C.J. tenderly draped an arm over Mary's bare shoulder and drew her close. Side by side they sat on the edge of the bed. "It's all right, Mary," she soothed. "It's perfectly reasonable for you to feel this way."

"No. No, it's not," Mary wept. "You don't understand, Miss Welles."

C.J. noticed an angry-looking mark on Mary's upper arm where her fingers had been resting. "Mary, what's this? How came you by this bruise?"

"Oh . . . I bumped into the . . . a . . . hanging cupboard in the kitchen when I was fetching a . . . I was rushin' too fast you see, because Lady Wickham asked . . ." Mary's untested imagination failed her. She was no good at dissembling.

"My poor Mary," C.J. said softly, stroking the injured area with her thumb.

"I'm such a clumsy girl. I've always been clumsy . . . everybody says so . . . that's why I'm usually in the scullery instead of bein' an upstairs maid, except that Lady Wickham's too stingy to engage a separate upstairs maid, now that she's turned Fanny out. There's not much I can break in the scullery. And I'm too ugly to work upstairs and serve the guests. That's what my other employers said."

C.J. was at a loss for words. "Mary—"

"I got myself turned out of my last position for disobedience. They put me on the street and I had nowhere to go. Constable Mawl arrested me for vay . . ." The girl searched for the correct word.

"Vagrancy?"

"Yes, that's it," Mary sniffled. "That's how Lady Wickham found me. I was brought before the judge. Just like you."

Disgusted, C.J. shook her head. "Mary," she murmured gently, "let's try this again. How did you get this bruise?"

The girl dissolved in a flood of tears. It was useless to try to maintain the deception. Miss Welles could see through her as clearly as if she were a windowpane. "L-L-Lady Wickham," she sniffled in a hoarse whisper.

"Why did she do this to you?"

"Because this mornin' I would not bring back the rabbit she asked me to buy for supper. I could not force myself to do it this time. Miss Welles, it breaks my heart to see God's defenseless creatures strung up like highwaymen at a butcher's, and when she asked me why I returned empty-handed . . . well . . . it's a sin to tell a lie, Miss Welles. It's the devil himself whisperin' in your ear. So I told her the truth."

"And she struck you."

"First she grabbed my arm here, so I could not run away," Mary began, displaying her bruised upper arm. "Then she swung her stick at me and hit me in the same place with it. Fairly lost her balance, she did. In-sub-or-di-na-tion," the girl said, her voice still choked with sobs. "She said she'd have Tony take the lash to my back if I ever tried anything like that again."

C.J. tried to conceal her boiling rage. The child had the sort of open heart that would no doubt have expressed more concern for her friend's anger than for her own mistreatment. "Poor Mary," she murmured. She drew the maid to her and rocked her in her arms, stroking the girl's dull brown hair. "Sleep now. In the morning, we shall set things right."

Mary was too exhausted to protest or try to convince her idol of the inadvisability, not to mention impossibility, of ever affecting a change in their circumstances. If Miss Welles wanted to indulge in dreams, who was Mary Sykes to cruelly dash them?

THE FOLLOWING MORNING C.J. began her crusade. "How dare you, you bitter old crone?" she bravely demanded of her employer. "Striking a defenseless scullery maid! Some civilized nature you've got—you, who consider yourself superior because you admire Dante and Shakespeare! A fine example of Christian charity! You sit smugly in church every Sunday believing yourself a better representation of humanity because you can read and write and comprehend the bishop's lofty sermons. But do you ever *practice* what he preaches?"

Mary lurked in the doorway to the parlor, dust rag in hand, trembling like a leaf in an early November wind.

"Your insubordination astonishes me, Miss Welles! The manner in which I treat my servants is no concern of yours, and I would advise you to keep about your own business or you will mightily regret the consequences."

"I cannot stand idly by while you beat them," C.J. insisted stubbornly, completely unaware of how punishing such "consequences" would be, despite her knowledge of Lady Wickham's cruel reputation.

"Come here!" C.J. obeyed, head held proudly, almost defiantly, in the face of Lady Wickham's admonishment. "Never, in all my seventy-six years—*never*—have I experienced such impertinence from a servant. I regret the day you came to my attention, Miss Welles. You are an ungrateful chit who does not deserve the excellent considerations I have afforded you. This house has been turned upside down and inside out since your arrival. You have encouraged others in my employ to contradict and countermand my orders, to slack their duties and shirk their responsibilities. I have even done you the kindness of purchasing candles for the domestics to enjoy in their quarters in the evenings. Never has such generosity gone so unappreciated."

"This does not concern *me*. Mary Sykes is a human being, your ladyship. She is not a slave."

"You are correct, Miss Welles. Mary is a domestic servant who earns a wage for her labors. She was born to be one and shall remain one for the rest of her life if she does not end up in the jails or on the streets, which is what she deserves for her defiant behavior."

From her position in the doorway, Mary gasped and paled. Realizing she had just given herself away, she turned to leave, in an effort to pretend that she was just passing by.

"Stay where you are, Mary," Lady Wickham snapped. "I am not going to blame you for your recent transgressions. I am fully aware that Miss Welles has put inappropriate notions of grandeur into your thick head—ideas which a girl like you is incapable of acquiring on her own. Therefore, I am willing to overlook yesterday morning's disobedience, and give you another chance to reform your ways rather than turning you out on the spot, an act which, I confess, was my first inclination."

Mary dropped a grateful curtsy to Lady Wickham.

C.J. was appalled. "Mary—," she began, but the scullery maid shook her head and stifled her tears. "You don't understand, Miss Welles," she said shakily.

"Place your hands on the table and bend over, Miss Welles," Lady Wickham commanded. C.J. obliged fearfully. "Come closer, Mary, and take your hands away from your eyes. You will watch what happens to rebellious serving girls who question their betters. Even a lady's companion remains subject to punishment." At the first crack of the ebony cane on her backside, C.J. cried out in pain. "This reprimand injures me more than it does you," the old woman scolded, punctuating her words with heavy wallops that landed on C.J.'s back and thighs.

"You'll break her spine, your ladyship!" Mary cried, as the blows rained harder down the middle of C.J.'s back.

"Regrettably, Miss Welles, your independent spirit and defiance will deprive me of your services, and I shall be unhappily required to sacrifice my reading and my correspondence until you have learned the error of your ways. You will go to the scullery and will not be permitted above stairs, except to sleep in your chamber, until further notice."

Lady Wickham was visibly exhausted from exacting C.J.'s punishment. "Come forward, Mary." The maidservant approached her employer with no small degree of trepidation, her cheeks stained with tears from witnessing her champion's punishment. The crack of a slap rang out against her damp flesh.

"But Mary didn't do anything, your ladyship," C.J. protested through her own tears. Her temerity was rewarded with an equally sharp blow to her own cheek.

"I do not have to explain my actions to my servants!" Lady Wickham snapped. "But as I am a munificent woman, I will enlighten you, Miss Welles. Mary was chastised just now as a reminder to curb her attempts at independent thought. *You* were disciplined for daring to question the actions of your employer." Lady Wickham waved her hand dismissively. "I expect this to be the end of the matter. You are both excused."

C.J. WIPED THE GRIME from her brow with the back of a sticky hand. Flecks of soot flew into her face, stinging her eyes as she used a bellows to fan the flames of the small coal—the portion commonly used to start the coal fires before more lumps were added to the grate. It was miserably hot and her lungs burned from smoke inhalation. Had she been pressed into service on a chain gang, the labor could not have been more arduous than the exigencies of a Georgian kitchen.

Mary sat nearby, scrubbing rust from the bottom of a pot that Lady Wickham was too penurious to place on the rubbish heap.

"Why don't we just bolt?" C.J. whispered. "We could sneak away in the dead of night. Anything would be better than this." She nearly choked on another mouthful of smoke.

"Are you daft, Miss Welles? If they catch us—and they will, make no mistake—they'll beat us for sure! Maybe worse." Her eyes widened with fear. "They could hang us!"

Stretching her cramped arm muscles, C.J. nearly knocked over the rat shelf suspended above her head. Mary had explained that the shelf's position rendered it impossible for the rats to get to any food placed upon it—hence the nickname.

"For the life of me, I cannot make it past my third day down here," C.J. bitterly replied, wiping her hands on her greasy apron. "I can't imagine how you do it every day."

Mary shrugged resignedly. "It's my place, Miss Welles. One must accept their lot, and it's no good tryin' to change things."

Mary was too ingenuous to indulge in exaggeration. If servants who went AWOL might really be subject to death by hanging, there appeared to be no alternative but spirit-crushing servitude. Admittedly, C.J. did not know enough to elude either her employer or the authorities; and Mary was equally ill equipped, for different reasons. It was both sobering and depressing for C.J. to acknowledge that Mary was probably right: to survive in this world, she, too, would have to adopt Mary's resignation to her "lot." C.J. began to regret having agreed to help Mary improve herself. Perhaps the poor girl had been better off in her previous state of defeated complacency. A little knowledge could indeed be a dangerous thing sometimes.

Lady Wickham was expecting a guest for afternoon tea, so Cook ordered the two young women to make the "new tea." "Like the voice of a little bird, her ladyship is: cheap, cheap, cheap," scoffed Cook. "She even makes her own new tea 'stead of buying it off the vendors." She noticed C.J.'s uncomprehending expression. "You must have been quality once," the thickset woman remarked, "not to know about new tea." She showed C.J. how they took the used tea leaves and dried them over a heated plate. "For green tea, we add copper dye," she told a horrified C.J., who wondered what the copper was doing to their systems when they drank the doctored beverage. "When her ladyship wants black tea, which she prefers, we add logwood dye to give it the right color. She even serves her guests the smouch."

"Smouch?" C.J. asked.

Cook enjoyed being able to teach the girl who could read and write a thing or two. "It's what you call the black tea what's been adul-te-rated. Tea is very dear, and poor folks can't afford better. The stingy old gimp upstairs has no excuse but her greed."

Bold enough to inquire what other potables and comestibles

were routinely doctored, C.J. learned that the practice was wide-spread—quite a surprise for someone who had thought that nineteenth-century food and drink was much purer and health-ier than the processed and packaged food of the twenty-first. Cook and Mary were proud to show off their superior knowl-edge, explaining to C.J. that if logwood dye was unavailable, black lead would be used to counterfeit Indian tea.

C.J. learned that gin was often faked with turpentine and sul-furic acid. The "preservatives" found in beer included a number of poisonous substances masquerading as "spices," and it was frequently adulterated with treacle, tobacco, or licorice in order to achieve the desired color. Port was made to appear aged by the addition of supertartrate of potash.

As far as foodstuffs went, C.J. was revolted to hear that the pickle sellers' wares owed their bright emerald hue to tincture of copper; the vibrant orange of a good Gloucester's rind was achieved with red lead, and commercially baked bread was loaded with alum. Big Macs now seemed positively organic by comparison. C.J. reasoned that her Georgian counterparts must have developed constitutions of cast iron. What a miracle they lived to adulthood at all with such a noxious diet: if the co-mestibles themselves didn't kill them, the copper cookware surely would finish them off!

This was the first time her ladyship was to entertain a visitor since C.J. had been banished to the kitchen. Lady Wickham had no choice but to order her upstairs to serve the tea, since she made a better appearance than the unfortunate Mary. Ac-cordingly, C.J. scrubbed the coal dust from her face and hands, removed her filthy apron, and tried to make herself look as pre-sentable as possible.

She entered the parlor with the heavy silver tea tray and placed it carefully on the sideboard. Lady Wickham's guest was a well-dressed woman whose plump, dimpled countenance, framed by a profusion of gray sausage curls that poked imperti-nently out of her white lace cap, lent her an air of jollity—a stark contrast to her prune-faced hostess.

"I am pleased to see you out and about again, Euphoria," said Lady Wickham as C.J. spread a white linen cloth on the tea table, then set down the teapot, sugar bowl and creamer, and a plate of lemon halves wrapped like bonbons in cheesecloth. "Miss Welles, Lady Dalrymple does not take cream. When you have finished serving the tea, you will return the pitcher to the kitchen before it turns."

C.J. discreetly nodded in acknowledgment, laying the delicate cups and deep saucers from Lady Wickham's best china service before each of the women. The hand-painted floral pattern was worthy in itself of admiration, but the aspect that C.J. admired most was the way the deep saucer allowed for the setting of a finger sandwich or biscuit right beside the cup, thereby eliminating the need for an additional plate on an already crowded tea table. How clever! And why were modern tea services not so configured?

"It does one good to take the air after such a lengthy period of mourning. Though I cannot say what you have ever done to merit preferential treatment, Eloisa," replied Lady Dalrymple, her twinkling eyes indicating that she was speaking partly in jest, "you are my first social call since Alexander's death. Were it not your natal day, I should have remained at home amid the comforts of my parrot, my pekes, and my grief."

C.J. set out the three-tiered stand upon which sat two freshly baked currant scones, a few tiny finger sandwiches, and a meager plate of sweets—a lavish display indeed for Lady Wickham, although it would not constitute a proper meal for one person, let alone two. She eyed Lady Dalrymple, a generously proportioned, furbelowed woman, perhaps a generation younger than Lady Wickham. The caller's full quilted skirt with its deeply flounced hem lent her a somewhat upholstered appearance. C.J. thought of Mother Ginger from *The Nutcracker*.

"You must forgive my curiosity for gaining the better of my civility, Euphoria. I never learned how the young earl met his end. Miss Welles, you have forgotten the plates!"

C.J. endeavored to cover her confusion, not to mention

shock, apologizing profusely to Lady Wickham for her inattention. But did not the deep saucers serve the same office?

Lady Dalrymple released a weighty sigh and reached for a watercress sandwich. "I should have thought it was the talk of the *ton*, Eloisa."

"I do not often visit the Pump Room for the latest gossip," Lady Wickham replied, pointing to her gimpy leg with the tip of her walking stick.

Imagine C.J.'s astonishment when the two elegant noblewomen dumped their tea from the cups into the saucers! What sort of proper table manners were these?! Lady Wickham made a second demand for the tea plates, reprimanding C.J. for her lack of alacrity in the fetching of them. The plates' most obvious necessity had now illuminated itself. C.J. beat a hasty retreat to the pantry cupboard for the proper dishes, returning to overhear the following conversation.

"Of course, ever since the trouble began on the Continent, it has been inadvisable for Englishmen to visit France on the Grand Tour," Lady Dalrymple began. "My good friend, Lady Oliver, who has always had a rather impregnable opinion of the French, which naturally does not extend to the selection of her modiste, persuaded me to insist that my son visit the East instead. It has become all the fashion, you know, since the birth of the French Republic. One never knows what might happen to an English nobleman on French soil nowadays."

Lady Dalrymple took a sip of the new tea and made a dreadful face, although she elected not to comment on the brew. "Alexander was visiting India, and at the invitation of the rajah, was riding atop one of their sacred white elephants." Her eyes dimmed with tears. "The earl was perched in one of those howdahs when something spooked the beast, and it reared up, dislodging the howdah from its back. Alexander fell to the ground and was trapped in the small compartment. He could not free himself in time before . . . the elephant . . ." Lady Dalrymple extracted a dainty handkerchief from a large reticule of apple-green watered silk. "Imagine, the last thing the earl—my Alexander—

saw was an enormous wrinkled foot, or do they call it a hoof? I never . . ." She broke off her narrative and blew her nose loudly.

"How frightful!" C.J. exclaimed.

Lady Wickham looked up from her tea, aghast at her servant's interruption.

Lady Dalrymple inserted her monocle and peered in the girl's direction. "Who is the young lady, Eloisa? I have never seen her here before."

"You were always an original, Euphoria," sniffed Lady Wickham with evident distaste. "I must confess that I have never comprehended your eccentricities, in particular your fascination with members of the lower orders of society."

"If that be the worst of my faults, Eloisa, I am prepared to face my maker with a clear conscience," replied the visitor, continuing to inspect C.J. through her glass. "The English—not God—created the class system." A cloud of concern dimmed Lady Dalrymple's otherwise pleasant countenance when she spied the fading mark on the girl's cheek, the telltale evidence of where Lady Wickham had slapped her three days earlier.

"I found Miss Welles at the assizes a few weeks ago. She had stolen an apple and was brought before the magistrate for her misdemeanor. She quite stunned the court and the spectators by displaying uncommon intelligence for a wayward indigent, whereupon I decided to engage her as my companion; and I hasten to add that she has caused nothing but trouble ever since her arrival. I have no qualms about repeating in her presence that Miss Welles is the most impertinent person I have ever had the misfortune to encounter."

C.J. poured more tea, forcing herself to hold her tongue. The visitor reached for a small white macaroon.

"An excellent selection, Lady Dalrymple. Cook makes superior ratafia cakes," remarked Lady Wickham, nibbling at a fresh strawberry tartlet.

Ratafia cakes? "Pray don't eat that!" C.J. exclaimed, virtually wresting the meringue-like cookie from the guest's bejeweled hand. "It's poison!"

Chapter Six

In which the sudden acquisition of an eccentric benefactress is accompanied by a painful farewell.

ON HEARING THIS DIRE WARNING, the rather portly Countess of Dalrymple fairly leapt from her seat.

"Miss Welles! What the deuce are you about?" An infuriated Lady Wickham rose in high dudgeon to her full height of about four feet seven inches. "Are you suggesting that I am poisoning my guests?"

"Not deliberately, Lady Wickham," C.J. hastened to add. "But Cook uses bitter almonds in the recipe, does she not?"

"Where is your overactive imagination headed, Miss Welles?"

"The proper way to make ratafia cakes is to grind bitter almonds," C.J. pressed on, remembering what she had learned at the *By a Lady* audition. "Bitter almonds contain a chemical—" She was met with two uncomprehending stares. "The bitter almonds themselves contain an ingredient called prussic acid. Any chemist will tell you it's the same thing as cyanide, but in a much milder form."

Lady Dalrymple was curious. "Then why have we not all met our maker from taking afternoon tea every day?" she asked whimsically.

C.J. wondered the same thing. "I expect that one would have to devour an unfathomable number of ratafia cakes in a lifetime in order to die from them. But even in small amounts, the prussic acid can have an adverse effect."

"Miss Welles, you have enlightened us quite enough!"

"Let the girl speak, Eloisa," the countess contradicted. "I should very much like to know what this prussic acid can do to one's constitution."

"I believe that it makes the heart race faster than it properly should, Lady Dalrymple."

"How fascinating!" replied her ladyship. "Eloisa, I have often wondered why I am met with palpitations in the early evening hours. Perhaps my fondness for ratafia cakes is the author of such experiences. Your knowledge of science is quite remarkable for a young lady, Miss Welles. I am curious to learn how you came by it."

Fortuitously for C.J., who had begun to scramble for a sensible reply, Lady Dalrymple was more interested in her own narrative thread. "My brother, Albert, dabbled in alchemy as a hobby," the countess continued. "Even as he gambled away his inheritance, the marquess sought methods of turning hazard punters and betting slips into gold. What are your Christian names, girl?"

Lady Wickham released an indelicate snort, wishing more than anything to put a stop to this conversation, but even she was above being overtly rude to a guest.

"Cassandra Jane, Lady Dalrymple."

"Good heavens!" The dowager countess withdrew a large fan from her reticule and snapped it open dramatically. She fished amid her brocaded bodice and drew forth a locket, which had been resting on her ample chest. "How astonishing!" she exclaimed, comparing the miniature portrait in the silver capsule to the young serving woman who stood before her. "There is no other answer for it."

"No other answer for what, your ladyship?" C.J. asked.

"You are the *image* of the late marchioness," Lady Dalrymple marveled. "And of course your Christian names are those the marquess gave his only daughter . . . and now, for the love of heaven, I see the *cross!*" C.J. touched the rough amber pendant hanging around her neck, surprised that Lady Dalrymple could see the cross without her monocle, since its color was nearly the same brown shade as was her livery. Lady Dalrymple appeared to be on the verge of tears. Had she lost her wits? What was the eccentric woman about? "Where did you come by this cross, Miss Welles?" her ladyship asked in an astonished whisper. Although C.J. attempted to formulate a response, she was immediately interrupted once again by Lady Dalrymple, who provided the answer to her own question.

The countess ran her thumb and forefinger along the cross's pockmarked underside. "When you were born, Lady Cassandra, this cross was given to you by your mother and father. You never had the chance to remember your mother, and more's the pity on't. She died giving you life. Such a beautiful woman Emma was. Your father was monstrous heartbroken by her death. The marquess lost everything at once; after his young wife was carried off, he tried to drown his sorrows in gambling and drink, and was in no fit condition to look after a babe. One day, shortly after your birth, your father removed the silver setting from your cross and pawned it to satisfy a tradesman's bill."

C.J. endeavored to follow the countess's narrative. Did her ears deceive her or had Lady Dalrymple addressed her as *Lady* Cassandra?

"Euphoria, what meaning am I to extract from this mawkish display of sentiment over a servant?" queried a stunned Lady Wickham.

"Eloisa, I have you to thank for reuniting me with my niece."

"*What?*" chorused Lady Wickham and C.J.

"Now I understand why you came to Bath—alone and incognito." Lady Dalrymple leveled her gaze at C.J. in an effort to communicate to the young woman that she had never been mentally healthier in her life. "Albert's unfortunate downfall is well known in our circles, and without a proper introduction some of our set would wish to cut you ere they made your acquaintance. Small wonder that you had to invent a new name for yourself. And to call yourself Welles when you are new-baptized, as it were—in a city renowned for its waters—is quite clever indeed." Lady Dalrymple restored her fan to the capacious reticule. "Eloisa, I shall take my niece home with me immediately. Fetch your things, Lady Cassandra."

"Please, your ladyship—call me Miss Welles."

The countess pursed her lips. "As you wish. No doubt you have already endured enough pain since your arrival," she added, with a rebuking glance toward Lady Wickham.

"You will leave your livery behind, Miss Welles," Lady Wickham commanded.

"Yes, your ladyship," replied C.J., who entertained no notion of absconding with it. Her fate had taken such a sudden turn that she had no time to untangle the jumble of thoughts that had entered her head. If Lady Dalrymple was truly raving mad, Lady Wickham would never have entertained her at Laura Place. A new adventure had landed in her lap—one that was clearly preferable to a life of servitude for Lady Wickham—and C.J. seized her opportunity to see where it would lead.

"I shall wait for you in the vestibule, Cassandra," said Lady Dalrymple.

C.J. returned to the airless garret she shared with Mary and retrieved her yellow muslin gown from its hiding place in the metal trunk. She dressed herself, making sure that the (now rather shrunken) fringed coquelicot shawl concealed the zipper from view, then slipped the strings of her reticule over her wrist, donned her bonnet, and descended directly to the scullery.

From her friend's expressive countenance, Mary immediately ascertained that Miss Welles was leaving her for good. "Don't cry, Mary," C.J. murmured, holding the sobbing girl in her arms. "It seems I have been presented with an astonishing reversal of fortune. I *promise* you I will do whatever is in my power to get you away from here as soon as possible."

"I daren't ask you not to go, for I know you must . . . and you'd be a foolish goose indeed if you did not, Miss Welles. But I shall miss you dreadfully. And as long as I live, I will never be able to thank you enough for what you've taught me."

"I can express no less, Mary," C.J. confessed.

"I never loved anyone before, Miss Welles." Mary sniffled.

C.J. stroked the girl's hair. Poor child; even her tresses lacked luster. She kissed Mary's moist forehead and broke the embrace, her cheeks stained with tears, her heart unable to articulate the words within it.

Lady Dalrymple escorted C.J. to a gleaming burgundy-colored coach, which seemed somehow familiar. When the green-clad coachman swiveled from his perch to regard her, C.J. realized that it was Lady Dalrymple's carriage that had nearly run her down on Great Pulteney Street.

"Willis!" chirped the countess. A young, periwigged footman in forest-green livery hopped down and opened the carriage door for his mistress. "Help the young lady into the carriage, Willis, and tell Blunt to drive home immediately."

"Yes, your ladyship." The white-gloved Willis turned the brass latch and handed C.J. inside, followed by Lady Dalrymple. She rapped upon the inside of the roof with the head of her walking stick and the coach began to lurch along the cobblestones. Suddenly, C.J. wondered if she had made a wise decision. Feeling trapped, and fearful of becoming engaged in further conversation, C.J. pretended to faint, but her new-found benefactress swiftly came to the rescue with a cone-shaped ivory vinaigrette, waving the vial under C.J.'s nostrils.

The sharp scent of the distilled smelling salts made her eyes water, and she pushed aside the older woman's plump hand, which was adorned with several heavy rings studded with semi-precious stones. She felt her stomach churning with anxiety, remembering Georgian novels—and even erotica—where young ladies of no verifiable parentage were kidnapped by well-fed, well-accoutred matrons such as the one seated beside her, and

thence condemned to lives of prostitution in high-class bor-
dellos.

Perhaps the countess was reading her mind. "Have no fear,
my pet," Lady Dalrymple soothed. "I am a lonely widow who has
recently lost her only son. You are clearly a young woman of uncommon intelligence." She patted C.J.'s wrist with a fleshy
palm. "You must be aware that many girls of your age don't even
have their alphabet."

"But, I'm not . . . ," C.J. began, and was hushed by her patroness.

"Are you an honest girl, Cassandra?"

"I should like to believe so, your ladyship," C.J. replied carefully, completely aware that her daily existence in 1801 was
based upon a series of lies that seemed to grow more elaborate
by the hour.

"Then all I ask of you, in return for your lively companionship, is to indulge an eccentric old woman. My schemes may be
fond and foolish, but I crave your trust."

C.J. fingered her amber cross as though it were a string of
worry beads. "You know next to nothing about me," she
protested. Were Lady Dalrymple ever to hear the truth, the
countess would be hard pressed to discern which one of them
had the wilder imagination.

"You appear to me to be a young person of quality. That sat-
isfies me for the nonce."

The coach-and-four rumbled up a hill and ground to a halt in
front of a huge town house at the edge of the Royal Crescent,
the magnificently designed semicircle of elegant residences built
by John Wood the Younger only a couple of decades earlier. To
reside here was to be in the very pink of fashion.

A uniformed manservant preceded them up a short flight of
steps and opened the bright red lacquered door to the entryway.
Lady Dalrymple nodded to her footman. "Thank you, Folsom.
How is your new son faring?" Even C.J. knew that gentry did not
converse with their servants as though they were equals. Either

the Countess of Dalrymple was indeed the very avatar of equality or else she was a counterfeit noblewoman and had managed to deceive even the hawkeyed Lady Wickham.

Folsom made a polite bow. Like Lady Wickham's beleaguered Tony, this man, too, bore the marks of having survived the pox, his pitted face making him look considerably older than she guessed he might have been.

"Jemmy is quite healthy now, your ladyship," the servant replied in a thick Scots burr. "A touch of the whooping cough, the wife and I were given to understand. Fair racked his little body with convulsions. It was so kind of you to send for your own doctor. The wife and I are greatly in your debt. Your 'umble servants always." Folsom bowed again to Lady Dalrymple as she passed.

"Saunders," her ladyship said, addressing the dour-looking maidservant in the process of making every effort to appear as though she were not eavesdropping, "ask Cook to make us some tea. We shall be in the drawing room."

The maid dropped a quick curtsy and disappeared in a flash of starchy white efficiency. C.J. had never seen an apron quite so bright, and so crisply pressed, and she wondered why Saunders should look so gloomy when the rest of Lady Dalrymple's staff seemed as content as anyone would be who had been relegated to a life of servitude.

The countess motioned for C.J. to follow her into a large, sunny room. The pale yellow-gold walls were set off by white plaster cornices and elaborate triple moldings, lending the salon the appearance of a Wedgwood vase or—to C.J.—a Sylvia Weinstock wedding cake.

It was all she could do to maintain her wits, for she sensed that she was about to be cross-examined. *This is really acting without a net,* she thought to herself. Her improvisational abilities were about to be severely tested.

"Is it true that Lady Wickham discovered you, as it were, in the prisoner's dock?"

C.J. was careful to choose her words, speaking slowly as she formulated her response. "I am afraid so, your ladyship. I had traveled very far to come to Bath, and found myself all at once penniless and friendless. Upon my arrival I wandered the city and slept under a colonnade that night, as I had neither a place to lodge nor the means to pay for it. The following morning, my hunger got the better of my wits, and I plucked an apple from a fruit seller's cart to satisfy my stomach's siren song." *Was this a bit too much drama?* she worried. C.J. lowered her eyes, genuinely ashamed. "Believe me, your ladyship, I have never stolen anything—ever—before this single transgression, which I freely own I regret mightily."

"You poor child. If you had only been familiar with our city, you might have known that every morning a public breakfast is offered in Sydney Gardens. I am certain that some charitable soul would have seen fit to feed you." Lady Dalrymple reached out to touch C.J.'s hand reassuringly. "But good heavens! I daresay the punishment did not fit the crime." She adjusted her skirts and arranged herself on a settee upholstered in pale green striped silk, patting the seat beside her.

C.J. warily sat. "I suppose I should be grateful to Lady Wickham. After all, if she had not taken me in, I have no idea what might have become of me. Perhaps I would have been sent to a workhouse. Or worse. She treats her servants abominably, though. Can nothing be done about it?" C.J. had indeed been monstrously appalled by Lady Wickham's cruelty, and her question served very well to deflect attention from herself.

"Eloisa's methods are deplorable," Lady Dalrymple concurred. "But her domestics consider themselves fortunate to find a roof above their misbegotten heads. Situations are scarce, particularly in the finer homes, and since Eloisa uses the courts of law as a statute hall, her staff are unlikely to locate such opportunities elsewhere. No respectable servant registry will accept a convict, leaving the poor souls no alternative but to survive by their wits on the streets upon gaining their release." Lady Dalrymple rose and paced the large, airy room. C.J.'s eyes followed her, affording the opportunity to more fully take in her new surroundings.

A rather large brass telescope faced the south window of the room. In one corner C.J. spied a vividly colored parrot in a gilded cage, and opposite it, a Chippendale-style curio cabinet of brilliant flame mahogany that appeared to be filled with an assortment of exotica from the natural world; odd-looking mechanical instruments, which she could not readily identify; and several crystal balls of varying sizes, displayed on cunningly fashioned tripods.

The parrot cawed as his mistress passed his perch. "Here you go, Newton," Lady Dalrymple cooed, offering the bird a small, square biscuit. For a fleeting moment, C.J. wondered if this was when Fig Newtons were invented. She marveled, open-mouthed, at the countess's unusual possessions and at the elegance of her home, a substantial contrast to Lady Wickham's ascetic tastes. Thus far, C.J.'s nineteenth-century experiences had been viewed through the eyes of the defeated, choiceless, and impoverished. What a fresh adventure she was about to embark upon! Now it appeared that she would learn to become a lady of quality in order to fit the mold into which she had been newly cast. But how long would favor smile upon her, C.J. worried, before her deception would be detected and cruelly exposed? And what then? She had learned the hard way that for those who had been cursed with the misfortune of having neither title nor means, it was a harsh world indeed.

Lady Dalrymple marked not her new protégée's wonderment, nor did she observe the fearful expression that clouded the young woman's otherwise lovely countenance. Having arrived at what she considered a fitting plan of action, her ladyship came to roost once again on the edge of the upholstered settee. She drew a deep breath, no doubt for dramatic emphasis, and her face dimpled into a mischievously triumphant smile.

"As I told you in the carriage, I am a lonely old widow, Miss Welles. My late son, Alexander, was unmarried and left no issue—that I am aware of, in any event—and consequently, there is no heir apparent to his title. Were you indeed my brother's only living child, you would be the heir presumptive in the absence of a male heir. You are evidently a young lady of breeding and intelligence, despite your unknown birthright. You will learn in time, Miss Welles, that I have singular views on the inbreeding of the English aristocracy. One has only to look at the Prince of Wales to see the unfortunate result. It would give me unalloyed glee to manufacture a noblewoman according to a mold of my own invention."

C.J. gasped in disbelief, not quite knowing what to make of the madwoman seated beside her who would single-handedly transform the English ruling class into a meritocracy. "But this is too much! Your ladyship is more than kind."

"Nonsense! There is no alternative. I make situations as I find them. You are of age, of course?"

"Yes, ma'am."

"When did you attain your majority?"

Certainly C.J. could not confess that in fact she would not even be *born* for another hundred and seventy-five years or so! She did some quick calculations and shaved a number of years off her true age. Could she pass for a young woman of prime marriageable years? "I came out two seasons ago, your ladyship. I am twenty now," she fibbed. Another lie. And here she had represented herself as a young person of integrity.

Lady Dalrymple seemed pleased with C.J.'s response. "Twenty. A perfect age, my dear. And I shall see to it that you are advantageously matched before the end of the season." Her gray eyes twinkled at the prospect.

C.J.'s acting training had been thorough, her education comprehensive, and her aptitude quick, but never could she have imagined being thrust into such an elaborate charade. At any moment she might unwittingly reveal herself to be the adopted daughter of a deceased New York businessman from another century! How was she to manage the correct etiquette of a gently bred Georgian, and who would believe that she was the daughter of a marquess—however disgraced—and the niece of a countess? Still, Lady Dalrymple's astonishing offer merited serious consideration. Besides, C.J. reasoned, until she might contrive a way to return to the twenty-first century, it was difficult to imagine a more pleasant alternative.

Chapter Seven

Suspicions are aroused; a garment presents surprising challenges of its own; and we meet two persons of extreme importance to our story.

"YOU ARE CONFOUNDED, my pet," Lady Dalrymple remarked. "It does not astound. I have given your young head quite a shock. I'll allow that my somewhat original behavior has been often remarked upon, even by those whom I hold dear, but I assure you, Cassandra, I am quite in my proper mind."

They heard footsteps approaching, followed moments later by the opening of the enormous double doors at the far end of the room.

A distinguished older gentleman liveried in green and black stopped at the entrance. His very presence demanded silence.

"Lady Oliver and her nephew, the Earl of Darlington, your ladyship."

"Heavens, Collins! It had completely gone out of my head that we were entertaining Augusta and Percy for tea this afternoon. I have already had a nibble—such as it was—when I called upon Lady Wickham to wish her many happy returns of the day, but the sudden arrival of my niece has put me completely out of sorts."

The butler discreetly arched an eyebrow.

"My brother Albert's child. Lady Cassandra Jane."

Collins missed nothing. He cast an appraising eye on the sorry state of C.J.'s yellow muslin and seemed to arrive at his own particular assessment of the situation. "Very good, mum. Shall I ask them to wait while her ladyship—"

"You will call her Miss Welles, Collins. We will continue to avoid my brother's name for the nonce."

"Very good, mum. While *Miss Welles* is afforded the opportunity to . . . put on her tea gown."

Taking Collins's meaning in an instant, Lady Dalrymple's hand flew to her mouth. No, it would never do for Lady Oliver and her nephew to meet Cassandra in her present state of disarray. "Precisely, Collins. The very thing. Perhaps they might like to view the Gainsborough before coming up."

"I believe her ladyship has seen the Gainsborough—when she last called. And on the half dozen visits before that," the butler calmly responded, indicating that it would provide neither distraction nor subterfuge.

"Well, she may have the pleasure of enjoying it yet again. Her nephew can discuss the brushstrokes with her, or compare it to the classical style," Lady Dalrymple retorted. "Heavens! I don't give a fig what you tell them. Just keep them downstairs."

"Very good, mum," replied the butler, the enormity of his assignment evident in his lined face. He bowed slightly and closed the heavy double doors behind him.

"Heavens! Whatever am I to do about your wardrobe? I do not suppose you have a trunk somewhere?"

"I'm sorry, Lady Dalrymple—"

"Call me Aunt Euphoria. It's time you started getting used to it."

"I have nothing but the clothes on my back, Aunt Euphoria. Such as they are."

The dowager clucked her tongue. "I thought as much, of course. Oh, if only the wish were father to the deed." Lady Dalrymple tugged at an embroidered bellpull.

C.J. surveyed the deplorable condition of her gown and, re-membering the zipper, drew the now-shabby coquelicot scarf about her. "Can we not simply tell them that I caught my heel in a stone and took a fall in the road?"

"Augusta Oliver is a perceptive woman, Cassandra. Her two most positive attributes are that she employs an incomparable modiste, and that she eschews cream in her tea. She is also the most powerful tabby in Bath. Needless to say, Gustie is my dear-est bosom friend. No, my dear, we must have a proper remedy, albeit a temporary one."

In response to the summons, Saunders appeared through the double doors.

"Stand next to my niece, Saunders." The maid gave Lady Dalrymple a look of perplexity. "There is no other young female person in the room, Saunders. Back to back with my niece, Cassandra Jane, if you please."

The lady's maid eyed the newcomer with suspicion but has-tened to obey her mistress. She and C.J. were roughly the same height, although Saunders was a good deal less curvaceous.

"Yes. It will have to suffice," her ladyship sighed. "There is nothing else to be done at such short notice. Saunders, you will be so good as to lend Miss Welles your Sunday frock for the du-ration of the day. Tomorrow we shall pay a call on Mrs. Mussell to have some new gowns made up. No expense will be spared. And Saunders?"

"Yes, your ladyship?"

"My niece will be staying with us from now on. You are not to address Lady Cassandra as 'your ladyship,' but will refer to her as 'Miss Welles.' Please see Miss Welles to the blue room, and take care that she is provided for as she may require. I will make in-quiries for young ladies in search of situations so that Miss Welles may have her own lady's maid in future." The countess smiled, once more revealing her deep dimples. "I would not wish to tax your good nature any more than my own personal needs demand."

"Yes, mum," responded the maid, curtsying to her mistress as she beckoned C.J. to follow her.

Even when Saunders appeared to crack a smile, C.J. thought the woman looked grim. While Lady Dalrymple was possessed of a definite playful streak, her lady's maid was a mirthless creature entirely lacking a sense of humor. A rather odd match, that. She refused Saunders's assistance, terrified that the already suspicious domestic would discover the zipper in her costume. C.J. took her cue from the countess, asserting that she could not abuse the maid's good nature by overtaxing her, and that as her ladyship no doubt required her services, C.J. would willingly dress herself.

Saunders, who was not particularly eager to increase her duties, nonetheless departed with a degree of hesitation. For a gently bred young lady to dismiss a servant in favor of dressing herself was irregular behavior indeed. There was something about this newfound "niece" of the mistress that did not tally. The girl was a parvenue, perhaps, or a fortune hunter who preyed on good-natured elderly women of uncommon wealth and generosity.

Saunders inclined her head and listened for a moment outside the closed door of the blue room, certain she heard "Miss Welles" lock something away. Not customarily prone to the peregrinations of a fanciful imagination, the lady's maid resolved to learn the truth about the soi-disant Miss Welles and to maintain a vigilant aspect where the visitor was concerned.

After locking the distressed yellow muslin dress in the uppermost compartment of a mahogany highboy, C.J. slipped the small iron skeleton key into her reticule. Having dismissed the servant, she had no alternative but to dress herself. Saunders's simple "round gown" was deceptively difficult to don, infinitely more complex than Lady Wickham's ugly brown livery. C.J.'s own lightweight petticoat sufficed as an underpinning, but as she and Mary had always helped one another to dress, it had never occurred to her how hard it was to fasten a garment while she was corseted, however lightly, by her wrap stays, which resembled a modern sports bra.

At least the small bustle pad that puffed out the back of her gown just below the shoulder blades was secured to the stays' ties by two long strips at the back, just the way her *By a Lady* accessory functioned. But the easy part was over. C.J. now regarded the gown as though it were a Rubik's Cube, engaging in several sallies of trial and error before successfully dressing herself. She finally determined that the narrow bands from the front waist passed through worked loops at the center back bodice and had to be held in position there before being tied at the center front under the bodice itself. Her arms ached from trying to hold one part of the dress while tying another. No wonder people had ladies' maids! C.J. struggled to button the high stomacher. Although it was snug, she was grateful to be fastening something in front of her chest, rather than straining to reach her back. She made a mental note to eventually thank Milena, should she ever see her again, for the anachronistic zipper.

It seemed like hours before C.J. reappeared in Lady Dalrymple's drawing room, reattired in Saunders's church dress, with its modest neckline and nondescript hue. She felt like a pregnant wren. The seams at the bodice strained to contain her full breasts. At least her sprigged muslin had been tailored to fit her figure.

"Well, niece, at least you look healthy," the countess sighed.

"I feel very much like a poor relation, Aunt Euphoria."

The dowager's face broke into a dazzling smile of revelation. "Heavens! Yes—the very idea. You *are* a poor relation, of course! And we do not discuss my brother Albert in polite company, so I will not trouble you at present with any more alarming facts and circumstances than you have already been privy to. Not with Augusta and her nephew about to join us at any moment. The person of Lady Oliver presents enough of a challenge. You shall have to call upon all your powers of imagination, child." Lady Dalrymple chattered on. "You must think the way those actresses do. Perhaps you would not know . . . but then, of course, we shall say that you have lived in London. Have you indeed been to the theatre?"

"Oh yes, many times, your ladyship," C.J. replied, remembering to keep all her answers as honest as possible.

"Well, I shan't discuss my brother's abilities—or absence of them, according to the critics—but perhaps someday we shall compare our views on Mr. Macklin and Mr. Garrick. You are far too young, of course, to have seen Garrick on the stage, but his fame lives on, to be sure."

C.J. was rescued from the necessity of fabricating a response by the interruption of Collins announcing Lady Oliver and her nephew, Owen Percival, Earl of Darlington.

Surely the stately matron sailing into the room was Jane Austen's Catherine de Bourgh in every imposing ounce of flesh. Her impeccably tailored iron-gray redingote, satin gown, and plumed bonnet matched the color of her hair, lending her the appearance of a battleship.

Lady Oliver's nephew, on the other hand, presented rather a different impression altogether. With a start, C.J. recognized him as the handsome aristocrat she had marked in the courtroom on the day of her trial. Her stomach plummeted. Did the earl remember her? How she wished for a fan with which to hide her face! He looked to be about thirty-five years old, perhaps a bit older, with merry, deep blue eyes; and even before he uttered a syllable, she could plainly see that it was the gentleman, rather than his forbidding-looking aunt, on whom Lady Dalrymple truly doted.

Was it C.J.'s imagination, or did the man's eyes sparkle even more when he focused them on her? "Aunt Euphoria" was not insensible to the earl's reaction, and motioned for him to sit opposite C.J. so he could better admire the view. C.J. was relieved that he did not appear to recognize her from the assizes.

"I see you have a guest, Euphoria." Lady Oliver retrieved a gilded lorgnette from her reticule and scrutinized C.J. as though she were a microbe. *"Qui est la jeune fille habillée comme une domestique?"*

"My niece, Cassandra Jane. Goes by the name of Welles." Lady Dalrymple lowered her voice. "Albert's child."

Her guests nodded in complete comprehension. "Of course," Darlington agreed softly. "Ah yes . . . and her choosing to be known by another name. It is better that way."

"Better, Percy? Of course it is *better*," Lady Oliver erupted, laying aside her lorgnette and opening an ivory-handled fan fashioned from Chinese silk. "*Il fait très chaud, ma chère.* Are you not stifling as well, Euphoria?" Lady Oliver wrinkled her nose as though she smelled decaying fish. "The eighth Marquess of Manwaring is a notorious wastrel who gambled away his fortune and was forced to earn a living as an *actor*," the battleship sneered in a rather theatrical tone herself. "Albert has always been a most unattractive combination of the bombastic, the cantankerous, and the unwise."

"You are nevertheless speaking to Lady Dalrymple and her niece of their own flesh and blood, Aunt Augusta," interposed the earl in a tone that signified an end to the matter, and left his aunt pursing her lips in evident distaste.

"I'll allow that my father is not without his faults, but I would wager he is not the only person in England who is 'bombastic, cantankerous, and unwise,' your ladyship," C.J. found herself saying.

Lady Oliver snapped her fan shut in a most indiscreet gesture.

"Lady Cassandra appears to have inherited *your* spiritedness, 'Aunt Euphoria'," Darlington remarked, evidently pleased by the lovely newcomer's intrepid reproval of his formidable aunt.

"You must remember to call her Miss Welles, Percy," Lady Dalrymple replied, her twinkling eyes conveying the endorsement of her headstrong "niece's" behavior. "*Elle est arrivée cet aprèsmidi. Mais oui*—just this afternoon. All the way from London," she continued, aware that Eloisa Wickham would be too embarrassed by her mistreatment of the girl to ever contradict Lady Dalrymple's version of the truth. Her warm smile illuminated the room. "How remiss of me not to make a proper introduction! Cassandra, may I present my dearest friend, Lady Oliver, and the Earl of Darlington—her nephew, Owen Percival."

The earl approached C.J. and bowed gallantly. The glossy dark hair that framed his handsome face smelled of a spring morning. Yet among Darlington's immediately agreeable qualities, it was the intelligence in his eyes, which danced with an incomparable sparkle, that rendered him most compelling.

It occurred to C.J. that it might be better to volunteer nothing more to the conversation, and to avoid speaking unless expressly spoken to. It would be an exercise in restraint—ordinarily not one of her strongest suits. Thus, it was both a blessing and a curse when the older women retired to a corner of the room, at the prompting of Lady Oliver's disdainful sneer in the direction of C.J.'s bodice.

Her voice pierced the air like a cold poniard through warm flesh. "My dear Euphoria, the girl looks like a street urchin, perhaps worse, in that unfortunate gown. You cannot possibly be considering her introduction into polite society unless she is taken well in hand. Well in hand, I say! Perhaps her appearance was acceptable to Albert, but it simply will not do here. I cannot imagine what you were thinking in allowing her to be seen looking like a tradesman's wife."

Polite society, indeed! With half an ear to the women's conference, C.J. deemed Lady Oliver's denunciation of her appearance as anything but polite. In fact, in what C.J. had always imagined was a world of excessively good manners, her ladyship's shocking rudeness came as a great surprise. C.J. knew a couple of fine old Anglo-Saxon words to describe a woman of Lady Oliver's stamp, but with some effort she restrained herself from voicing them. She also wondered why the women peppered their conversation with French when they were both English bluebloods. *And their nation is at war with France!* There must have been a reason for such pretensions, but to inquire seemed inadvisable.

"I have every intention of sending her to Mrs. Mussell at the first opportunity, Gustie. However, the girl arrived today, so shortly in advance of your call that I had not the chance to properly groom her."

Groom her? C.J. felt like a horse.

"Mrs. Mussell," Lady Oliver sniffed. "A second-class seam-stress. Send her to *my* modiste, Madame Delacroix. Clearly, the girl has a figure worthy of admiration, if my nev-you (for that is how she pronounced the word *nephew*) is any indication."

The older women discreetly turned to see the earl and Miss Welles engaged in animated conversation.

"Percy has always had an eye for the ladies," Lady Dalrymple remarked, silently noting that they had not always been ladies of quality and gentle breeding. When Darlington had finally cho-sen a wife, he was nearly disinherited for selecting so poorly. Marguerite de Feuillide was not only a Frenchwoman, she was also an actress—herself shunned by her noble family for pursu-ing a life upon the stage of the Comédie-Française. In Lady Oliver's estimation, the only crime worse than appearing on a public stage was being French.

It would be an uphill climb for Lady Dalrymple to bring her dear friend around to accepting Cassandra in any guise as a suit-able wife. By styling her as the child of the black sheep of the family, Euphoria ensured that little would be expected of the girl. No one in polite circles spoke aloud of her brother Albert. Lady Oliver's characterization of the dissolute nobleman-turned-actor was unfortunately a rather accurate one. But these proclivities rendered the Marquess of Manwaring no better or worse than a dozen of his contemporaries. Among the Georgian nobility it was a badge of honor to be deeply in debt, and many a man who had been ruined at the gaming tables was still received in the best circles and was always welcome at his clubs. It was his ill-fated decision to pursue a stage career that had made Lord Manwaring a pariah among his peers. Euphoria was fully aware that some of her ilk would be reluctant to accept the girl in society. The tack to adopt was that Miss Welles could not help her lineage. After all, the marquess's reversal of fortune and sub-sequent adoption of the thespian's mantle had occurred while the unfortunate girl was still in swaddling clothes.

Chapter Eight

In which an otherwise enchanting nobleman discloses his prejudices, somewhat marring a blissful afternoon; our heroine's idol, Miss Jane Austen, pays a visit; and a most unusual time-travel conveyance is discovered.

C.J. WAS FINDING the earl to be a witty and well-read conversationalist. Educated at Eton and then at Oxford, he was of course well versed in Greek and Latin but had read history at Magdalen College—a secular shift from an earlier inclination toward theology. Of course, as a first son he would never have entered the clergy, but he was interested in the subject of all religions, most particularly the pantheistic ones practiced in ancient Greece and Rome. When he was branded a pagan and a Philistine by his don, Darlington decided to focus his interests instead on the classical world, relishing the poetry of Homer and Virgil in their respective original tongues. He had even enjoyed some modest success as a translator but was rather retiring about what he allowed were only modest accomplishments. "I daresay, the only reason any of the translations sold was that people were dead curious to see what a nobleman dabbling in such scholarly pursuits might publish."

They shared a laugh. "I am quite sure, your lordship, that you are undervaluing your achievements."

"If I were to tell you then, Miss Welles, that there was no call for a second printing, you might revise your good opinion of my efforts." He smiled, then leaned toward her and in a very confidential manner spoke a few words of a foreign language.

"What is that?" she questioned admiringly. "It sounds lovely, whatever it is."

"The first line of *The Aeneid*. Impressed?"

"Indubitably, your lordship!" More laughter.

"My classical leanings I admit to have come by honestly, owing to my father's keen interest in archaeology, but I have not divulged my true passion, Miss Welles."

It was a comfort to realize that the nature of flirting had changed so little over time. "May I express the hope that you will reveal it to me?"

"I confess it is not so mysterious nor as prurient as I have made it sound. Nowadays it is fashionable for the better educated of my class to profess an appreciation for Shakespeare . . . but for me it is so much more than that."

C.J. favored him with a look of pure radiance. "I, too, have a passion for Shakespeare, your lordship, although, in the numerous productions of his plays that I have had the opportunity to . . . view, I would have wished for 'more matter with less art.'"

"However do you mean, Miss Welles?"

She realized that she had nearly divulged the secret of her true profession and was about to say that she was something of a purist, preferring interpretations that placed the Bard's glorious language over production concepts like putting *The Tempest* on Mars or setting *Romeo and Juliet* in Miami's South Beach. "It does not signify. Merely an attempt to be clever, which fell far short of the intention. Do go on, your lordship. You said there was so much more . . ."

Darlington's expression was one of pure rhapsody. "Ahh . . . the golden age of England, Miss Welles . . . the Renaissance . . .

the flowering of literature . . . art for art's sake. I have so often wondered what it would be like to travel back in time to have such an experience, sharing a bumper with Kit Marlowe in a Deptford tavern . . ."

"In that case, your lordship, you would be hobnobbing with the marginally rich and posthumously famous. Would you still wish to be a nobleman if you were to travel back two hundred years?" C.J. quizzed.

"Given the choice, I firmly believe that no one would elect to live in squalor, even if he is a poet. And for the briefest window of time, Miss Welles, if I may disagree with your assessment of Marlowe's literary achievements, he was the most celebrated dramatist of the day. 'Aunt Euphoria,' " he called to the dimpled dowager entertaining his blood relation, "will you make a loan to me of your crystal ball so that I may travel back to the Renaissance?"

"Absolutely not, Percy!" his hostess retorted. "The *Renaissance* the golden age? Pish-tush! Now *my* salad days were the golden age of England: the *Enlightenment*—the Age of Reason. Discoveries. Inventions. Art for *man's* sake."

"And the world has gone to the devil ever since," Augusta concurred. "Look at France."

"You are sufficiently enlightened then, Lady Oliver?" C.J. asked charmingly.

"It is unwise to bait her," Darlington warned in a whisper, but his merry expression indicated that he quite enjoyed the young lady's boldness. "However, on the subject of the French Republic, Aunt Augusta is well aware that we tread common ground."

"How so, sir?"

"Miss Welles, we have spoken of my predilection for antiquities and touched upon the subject of my pastimes. It is not appropriate for me to venture into a discussion of politics in the presence of a young lady."

"And why, pray, should I not be entitled to learn more about you, especially on the issue of something which so clearly strikes to the core of your beliefs as a man?"

"Suffice it to say," Darlington said stiffly, his skin coloring a deep red against the stark white of his starched cravat, "that the French learned everything they know about revolution from the Americans!"

The earl's jingoistic ignorance both shocked and surprised her. "I don't believe they ever used guillotines in America, your lordship!" C.J. countered. He had been right. One passionate political remark and a barricade had been erected between them that threatened to unduly mar an otherwise charming acquaintance.

"It was not enough for them to take up arms against their sovereign," Darlington continued hotly. "But the infant nation of heathens and savages had to pour their democratic pestilence into the ear of England's other enemy . . . dispatching traitors like Jefferson and Franklin to Paris with the hope of winning converts to their perverted brand of government. And they found them—in Marat, Danton, Robespierre!"

C.J. drew in a slow, measured breath and counted to five before speaking, the better to control her temper. "I think . . . perhaps . . . it is an exaggeration on your lordship's part to intimate that Thomas Jefferson played Claudius to the French monarchy's Old Hamlet. In fact it was Jefferson himself who said that when you consider the character which is given America 'by the lying newspapers of London and their credulous copiers in other countries, when you reflect that all Europe is made to believe we are a lawless banditti, in a state of absolute anarchy, cutting one another's throats and plundering without distinction,' how can a reasonable person expect a European to know that in truth, 'there is not a country on Earth where there is greater tranquility, where the laws are milder or better obeyed, where everyone is attentive to his own business, or meddles less with that of others, and where strangers are better received, more hospitably treated, and with a more sacred respect'?"

The earl allowed the young woman to deliver her defense of

America by proxy before issuing his challenge. "Have you been *in* France, Miss Welles?" Darlington asked, his voice rising.

"Well . . ."

"I was! And I saw innocent people—dozens if not hundreds of innocent men, women, and young children . . . *babies* ripped from their mothers' arms—taken to the Place de la Concorde and bloodily dispatched with one stroke of a falling blade!"

"Have you ever *met* an American, your lordship?" C.J. demanded.

"I hope if ever I do, I am wearing a sword or carrying a pistol."

What colossal bigotry! "You would kill an innocent, and perhaps unarmed, stranger simply because you do not like his kind or his countrymen? And yet you have the audacity to accuse others of barbarism?" C.J. thought the Englishman would spit in disgust right on Lady Dalrymple's pastoral Aubusson. "Ah yes, 'Rule Britannia! Britannia rules the waves!' " she added in a lilting tone intended to lighten the tenor of the conversation. It occurred to C.J. that her particularly impassioned defense of her own nation was predicated upon wounds inflicted to her homeland that were as fresh as France's atrocities were to Lord Darlington and that they approached the subject from a chasm more than two hundred years wide. In this world, the Reign of Terror was a recent event, not something consigned, as it was for C.J., to the dusty pages of a distant history.

"Heavens!" Lady Dalrymple exclaimed. "The pair of you! I knew there was a reason gentlemen did not discourse on politics at tea. Percy, you'll frighten my poor niece out of her wits with talk of heathens and pistols and Frenchmen."

Offering a polite bow, the nobleman apologized for his outburst. "Forgive me, Miss Welles. It was entirely imprudent of me to allow you to draw me into a discussion of international proportions. I should not be surprised to discover that you have a bit of the Yankee rebel in you, yourself."

Oh yes, you should, C.J. thought. *If you only knew how much.* But she replied simply, "Pooh! If ladies and gentlemen discussed nothing but the weather and the state of everyone's collective and individual health, we should never begin to learn one another's true natures. However distasteful."

"That is what marriage is for, my dear," the countess beamed, ignoring C.J.'s last remark.

"But by then, it is often too late, Aunt Euphoria." She looked to his lordship for a reaction.

Darlington studied a biscuit. "I have a witty cousin who believes that a young lady should never know too much about her husband before marriage, as she has the rest of her life to devote to acquainting herself with his habits."

Lady Oliver peered at her teacup as though she were inspecting it for germs. "Speaking of our cousin, where is she, Percy?"

"I understood Miss Jane had first to pay a call upon an acquaintance. You must excuse her tardiness, Lady Dalrymple. I fear she has been delayed."

As if on cue, Collins opened the large double doors to the drawing room.

"Ah, there she is." Darlington rose to greet the new arrival, who fairly blew into the room with a palpable energy and poise.

The slender brunette who appeared to be in her early or midtwenties handed her straw bonnet to the manservant and touched her hand to her dark curls. "Faugh! Open carriages are nasty things. A clean gown has not five minutes' wear in them. You are splashed getting in and getting out, and the wind takes your hair and your bonnet in every direction." The young lady grasped the train of her simple muslin frock, pulling it toward her, the better to inspect her hem.

The earl greeted his cousin and the young woman presented herself to Lady Oliver, receiving an indifferent kiss on the cheek.

"Allow me to introduce the young ladies, Aunt Augusta. Miss Jane, I should like you to meet Lady Dalrymple's niece, Lady Cassandra—although she goes by the appellation of Miss Welles. Miss Cassandra Welles, I give you a cousin whom I hold in fondest esteem. Miss Jane Austen."

C.J. nearly swooned. Luckily, a fortuitously placed armchair helped restore her equilibrium.

"Beware of fainting fits," the newcomer cautioned, retrieving a vinaigrette of smelling salts from her reticule. "Though at the time they may be refreshing and agreeable, if too often repeated and at improper seasons, they may prove destructive to your constitution. Run mad as often as you choose, but do not faint."

C.J. was flummoxed. "I beg your pardon. I . . . am . . . *truly honored* to make your acquaintance," she stammered, causing Miss Austen to wonder at the effusion of her reception.

"You are never sure of a good impression being durable," Jane demurred, as she took C.J.'s trembling hand. "Everybody must sway it. Yet having never met me, you seem quite assured in your opinion, Miss Welles."

Her senses at sixes and sevens, C.J. suggested that she and Miss Austen retire to the settee. Jane reached for the teapot, but Lady Dalrymple shot her niece a look that conveyed the inappropriateness of a hostess permitting a guest to serve her own tea. "Let me be 'mother,' Miss Austen," C.J. said, as she prayed to all the gods in heaven to help her correctly pour tea for Jane Austen. "Cream?" she asked. Miss Austen declined, preferring lemon. It was all C.J. could do to contain her giddiness. How impossible not to be able to reveal her genuine excitement!

Lady Dalrymple politely asked Miss Austen if her prior engagement had been a pleasant one, to which she received an assessment of the young lady's discourse with her friend Mrs. Smith, who, newly wed to a country squire, was endeavoring to become the perfect wife. "She was doomed to the repeated details of his day's sport, good or bad: his boast of his dogs, his jealousy of his neighbors, his doubts on their qualifications, and his zeal after poachers."

C.J. was fascinated. "But did Mrs. Smith know nothing of her husband's rather narrow pursuits when she married him?"

"Where people wish to attach, they should always be ignorant." Miss Austen sipped her tea. "To come with a well-informed mind is to come with an inability of administering to the vanity of others, which a sensible person would always wish to avoid." From the way Miss Austen's eyes sparkled, C.J. wondered if Jane was having a joke on the lot of them.

So Darlington had been right about his cousin's opinion of relationships. "Then, Miss Austen, I have no sense and even less sensibility, for I learned of your cousin's prejudicial political preferences—which he proclaimed most earnestly—all in the space of a single afternoon's acquaintance."

Darlington's lips curved into a tiny smile. "Let it be said that Cousin Jane and I disagree on the matter of matrimony where prior knowledge of each other's faults and foibles is at issue. *I* believe in fully knowing what one is letting oneself in for, so to speak. The learning should be an enlightening experience in the most positive sense."

He turned to Jane. "Call me insensible, cousin, but should I decide to wed Miss Welles, for example, I trust that every day in her company would yield many singular and delightful discoveries, and I should have no difficulty administering to her vanity. Undoubtedly, I should find many occasions to offer an honest compliment."

Lady Oliver, appalled by her nephew's merest mention of the notion of marriage to Lady Dalrymple's oddly attired and altogether too unreserved poor relation, sought to change the topic of conversation. "Percy—," she began to rebuke, but was checked by Miss Austen, who was quite keen to learn how C.J. had come to Bath. C.J. found wisdom enough to hold her tongue and let Lady Dalrymple, who was eager to entertain, deliver a highly edited rendition of her "niece's" travails.

Jane expressed the hope that despite her early tribulations, Miss Welles would grow to enjoy Bath and furthered the wish with the desire that they should become fast friends. She enumerated the pleasures which they might savor together: the social whirl of the Pump Room, the Assembly Dances, the shopping—for Jane admitted she could not pass a milliner's without stepping inside—and of course the delights of the theatrical season. C.J. could scarcely believe her good fortune.

"Speaking as you had been, Percy, of Shakespeare, Mrs. Siddons is to play Lady Macbeth this month," Lady Dalrymple interjected swiftly. "Right here in town."

Without thinking, C.J. jumped in. "I hear her performance is quite . . . modern . . . so they say."

"It is quite the object, Miss Welles. She does the most extraordinary thing in the sleepwalking scene." Darlington rose to his feet and crossed over to the doors. "She enters from a grand staircase with a lighted candle," he began, offering his own dramatic interpretation of Siddons's somnambulance. "Then . . . *she puts her candle down!* And she wrings her hands, thusly," he demonstrated, "as though to wash Duncan's blood away!"

"Simplicity, indeed, is beyond the reach of almost every actress by profession," Miss Austen interjected, whereupon C.J. allowed that she should like to trod the boards and perhaps assay Lady Macbeth herself one day. This elicited a horrified gasp from Lady Oliver, and Lady Dalrymple began to wonder if Miss Welles was not somehow related indeed. Jane studied her teacup thoughtfully. "I have no wish to be distinguished, and I have every reason to hope I never shall. Thank heaven I cannot be forced into genius and eloquence." C.J. bit her lip, for she knew that Miss Austen's secret passion for "scribbling" would one day place her in the pantheon of English novelists.

Darlington addressed the countess. "Lady Dalrymple, with your kind permission, I should like to escort Miss Welles to the theatre to witness Mrs. Siddons's extraordinary performance for herself."

Jane laughed merrily. "See! Shakespeare gets one acquainted without knowing how. It is part of an Englishman's constitution. His thoughts and beauties are so spread abroad that one touches them everywhere, one is intimate with him by instinct."

Lady Dalrymple was about to offer her consent to the proposed excursion, when she was briskly interrupted by Lady

Oliver. "Highly inappropriate, Percy. Highly inappropriate. To bring a young lady to the theatre unchaperoned."

"Then perhaps Cousin Jane will accompany Miss Welles," Darlington offered.

Jane nodded her head. "I should be only too glad. I am an indifferent card player and I much prefer the theatre to a dreaded evening of whist."

"The *theatre*," Lady Oliver continued dismissively, addressing her nephew directly. "As if the theatre had not brought you enough ruin in your lifetime. And to the family of Miss Welles too. Euphoria, is it not true that your niece is too embarrassed to be known by her proper name, and to use the title which she should be accorded, because of her father's theatrical connections?"

Miss Austen fixed her gaze on Lady Oliver, then regarded C.J. with tremendous sympathy. "There is someone in most families privileged by superior abilities of spirits to say anything."

Lady Dalrymple and C.J. exchanged a look. "To be sure, Augusta. Of course, Percy, *Macbeth* is notorious for being an accursed play. All that pagan mumbo jumbo. Although I am rather fond of the tragedy myself—"

The countess received a sharp reproof from her steely contemporary. "Highly inappropriate, Euphoria. For my nev-you to escort Miss Welles to the theatre, regardless of the performance. I will not allow it."

Is he not a grown man? C.J. wondered. *Why does he not rebuke the old bat?*

"Ah, well." Darlington accepted his defeat with equanimity. "The theatre is sure to be crowded and warm, and there are scores of people who enjoy perfectly fulfilled lives without ever deriving the pleasure of watching Mrs. Siddons play Lady Macbeth. Are you fond of *dancing*, then, Miss Welles?"

Jane smiled slyly at C.J. and whispered over her teacup. "I have often observed that resignation is never so perfect as when the blessing denied begins to lose somewhat of its value in our eyes. And fine dancing, I believe, like virtue, must be its own reward."

"Oh yes, I *love* dancing," C.J. responded enthusiastically— and perhaps a bit too energetically. She had to keep reminding herself that, as Shakespeare said, a low voice is "an excellent thing in woman." Lady Oliver looked up from her tea and narrowed her slate-gray eyes.

The earl leaned toward C.J., the better to speak more intimately to her. "Then when I see you at the Assembly Rooms, I hope you will save a dance for me."

"To be fond of dancing is a certain step towards falling in love," Jane added with a wink at her cousin.

"Percy?" his aunt quizzed sharply. "What are you discussing with Miss Welles?"

"Miss Welles has promised to honor me with a dance at the Upper Rooms on Thursday, Aunt Augusta."

Aunt Augusta wasted no time in indicating her immediate disapproval of the revised proposition. "Percy," she sneered, "you will not be seen in public with someone dressed like a scullery on Sundays."

"Nonsense, Aunt Augusta," her nephew deftly countered. "I am sure that Miss Welles possesses everything she requires. No doubt she did not wish to call attention to her wealth when traveling, and deliberately dressed in a humble and appropriately modest gown."

If only that were true. Then it struck C.J. that the gentleman sitting opposite her—an *earl*—did not care two figs what she wore, or so it seemed. How refreshing! Not only that, after a full afternoon's discourse he still evinced no recognition of having seen her before. C.J. smiled to herself, immensely relieved.

Lady Oliver placed her teacup on the ebony tray and rose to her feet. "Come, Percy. I must stop at Travers's to inspect a new bonnet before we reach home, and the hour grows late." She bestowed a kiss on Lady Dalrymple's cheek and donned her dove-gray gloves before offering her hand to C.J. "It has been an enlightening experience to meet you, *Miss Welles*. Percy, you will join me now. Miss Jane, are you accompanying us? My carriage will drive you home."

Jane set down her cup. "The sooner every party breaks up the better," she responded, the irony lost on Lady Oliver.

Lady Dalrymple rang for Collins.

The earl was appraising Lady Dalrymple's relation. *Quite a lovely and charming creature,* he thought to himself, *and uncommonly—delightfully—intelligent. Truly an original. Particularly her interest in politics. Highly unusual for any female.* Bluestockings never irked him the way they did other gentlemen of his ilk. Darlington allowed that he was looking forward to the next opportunity to enjoy the young woman's company. His hope was that he would not have to wait too long. He bowed to Cassandra and with a gloved hand brought her own hand to his lips and kissed it.

"Percy! You have the manners of a Turk!" His aunt was aghast. "What the deuce can you be thinking to kiss that girl's hand? Ungloved and unmarried! And not the hint of an understanding between you."

The earl ignored her. "I outrank her," he whispered to Cassandra with a twinkle in his eye. He leaned down to Lady Dalrymple and kissed her rouged cheek. After all, he had known the countess practically all his life, so his aunt had no cause to carp at any lack of propriety in that connection.

"I am honored to have met you, Lady Oliver. And your lordship," C.J. said as Darlington bent down to kiss her hand once more, if only to further appall his aunt. "And to have had the extreme pleasure of meeting *you,*" she emphasized, bidding Miss Austen good-bye.

Such an intimate exchange did not pass undetected by that most astute of observers. Jane clasped C.J.'s hand in hers and drew closer, tipping a conspiratorial wink in the direction of her handsome cousin. "With men he can be rational and unaffected," she whispered, "but when he has ladies to please, every feature works."

IT WAS STILL DAYLIGHT when their visitors departed, and C.J. persuaded Lady Dalrymple to permit her to take an unchaperoned constitutional. She embraced her benefactress as tightly as the older woman's girth would allow, an expression of thanks that even Euphoria found excessive. What the dowager did not know was that C.J. had every reason to believe that they might never see each other again. Her ladyship had been remarkably munificent in rescuing her from what might have been a lifetime of misery with Lady Wickham; but delightful as the afternoon had been, C.J. had resolved to somehow find the way back to the twenty-first century.

This would be her first opportunity to return to the Theatre Royal since her Easter Sunday arrival in Bath. During her weeks of servitude on Laura Place, she had never been left alone. Even in the dead of night, she could not have left her bedchamber without waking Mary. And perhaps, too, there was a part of her that had been unwilling to abandon the girl, feeling acutely responsible for her welfare.

C.J. regretted leaving those who had shown her kindness—and forgoing the pleasure of making the further acquaintance of the Earl of Darlington, not to mention relinquishing the opportunity to befriend Jane Austen. But she needed to return to the life she had been leading more than two hundred years ahead. There lay the possibility of the perfect job—everything for which she'd studied, sacrificed, and strived for years to attain. How ironic that what lay ahead of her was what she had so unexpectedly—and perhaps irrevocably—left behind.

C.J. returned to the blue room, unlocked the highboy, and redonned her yellow muslin, using her palms to press out the wrinkles and smooth away the smudges as best she could. Extricating herself from Saunders's gown was mercifully simpler than putting it on. Grabbing the dilapidated red shawl, her bonnet, gloves, and reticule, she locked the door to the blue room and placed the key inside the little purse. She left Lady Dalrymple's gleaming white town house and began the descent toward the Theatre Royal on Orchard Street. If she'd found herself in the middle of its stage upon her bizarre arrival in 1801, perhaps she could somehow return the same way. It was certainly worth a shot. What had she to lose in the effort?

She managed to slip in through the theatre's side door—the one that opened onto the alleyway. Hearing voices coming from the stage, she hid in the wings behind a heavy black curtain.

A handsome woman in elaborate medieval costume was waiting backstage to make an entrance; and from the extravagance of her gown, it was no doubt the play's leading lady who was standing atop the huge staircase descending from the upstage wing. C.J. clapped her hand to her mouth to stifle her excitement. *Good God!* She was looking at the great tragedienne herself. Tonight, Siddons was back in *De Montfort,* the same production that had been on the bill the day of C.J.'s supernatural appearance.

C.J. peered around the velvet curtain to see what was happening onstage. Crowds of supernumeraries dressed in long cloaks milled about, creating atmosphere. A young boy dressed as a page addressed one of the actresses onstage.

"Madam, there is a lady in your hall who begs to be admitted to your presence."

"Is it not one of our invited friends?" the actress replied.

The page shook his head. "No, far unlike to them. It is a stranger."

"How looks her countenance?" the actress onstage questioned the boy.

C.J. sidled along the curtain like a crab, trying to get closer to the stage.

"Is she young or old?" the lady asked the page.

"Neither, if I right guess," came the reply. "But she is fair. For Time has laid his hand so gently on her, as he too had been awed."

C.J. watched the actors clad as servants crossing the stage as the conversation progressed and looked about for a spare costume that she could simply slip over her head.

"What is her garb?" asked the lady of the young boy.

"I cannot well describe the fashion of it. She is not deck'd in any gallant trim, but seems to me clad in the usual weeds of high habitual state."

C.J. nearly snickered, since Mrs. Siddons was dressed in a garment that must have cost a king's ransom. No "gallant trim" indeed! A supernumerary rushed past C.J.'s hiding place, dropping a robe and a silken cord at her feet as she dashed off to don another costume. Nearly invisible amid the hubbub in the dark, C.J. stooped to retrieve the saffron-colored shift. It was a simple garment, almost like a cassock, constructed of two pieces of cloth with an opening for the head and long, dolman-style sleeves. It slipped easily over her own yellow muslin, covering both it and the red shawl completely. She hid the bonnet under the robe and secured it with the cord.

It was now or never. Wishing to draw as little attention as possible, she stepped into the light, and—although she yearned to revel in the experience—scuttled across the stage like a golden beetle.

"Thine eyes deceive thee, boy. It is an apparition thou has seen," the lady declaimed.

C.J. slipped through an architecturally resplendent medieval archway into the blackness, the reverberations of a man's resonant voice echoing behind her. "It is an apparition he has seen, or it is Jane de Montfort."

The last thing C.J. remembered hearing was the thunderous ovation that greeted the entrance of the great Sarah Siddons.

Book the Second

Chapter Nine

An attempt to return home is fraught with frustration; an
unnerving encounter backstage in Bath; another slipup, this
time in a bakery; and we learn a little more about the
intriguing Lord Darlington.

C.J. COULD HEAR VOICES and just about make out some shadows on the stage. An argument was taking place.

"Look, Beth," a man was saying. "The woman disappeared. She did her final audition, walked through that door, and no one ever saw her again. You put out a call and she didn't return it. We've got to continue the casting process. We've booked the Shubert because you wanted a jewel box theatre. The marketing plan is already underway; the advertising is all but completed, minus the names of the cast. All you've got to do is pick *two* of them. You're not casting *Hamlet* here."

"Maybe she's considering our offer before she gets back to us," Beth reasoned. "Maybe she's speaking to her agent. Maybe she's hoping for more money. Who knows? Look, she's not the first actress not to answer her phone the day we offer her the role."

"And she's not the last actress in New York either. Or LA, for that matter."

C.J. could smell cigar smoke through the gloom, although she couldn't see who was talking. Most likely Mr. Miramax.

"Since you weren't crazy about the final callbacks of the other two women we saw, I told you who you could go with, Beth. I've got a list of names as long as my right arm."

"You can have Koko's list for all I care. C.J. Welles is my first choice for the role of Jane. She has a certain *je ne sais quoi*. She's not mannered."

"Plenty of actresses aren't mannered. One phone call and I could get you . . ." The male voice lowered to an unintelligible murmur.

"I don't want to star-fuck, Harvey. I told you that when you brought me in on the project. I can see the adverts now: 'J-Lo *is* Jane Austen.' The reason I don't want a celebrity in the role is that I don't want audiences to equate Jane Austen, who ought to be enough of one in her own right, with some Hollywood flavor of the month. One reason my stage production of *That Hamilton Woman* won so many Olivier Awards last season was because my leads weren't stars whose personal wattage eclipsed the vibrancy of the characters."

"Beth. Oh, Beth," Harvey intoned. "Your job is to direct the show. A producer's is to write your paycheck. Also, my job is to put the butts in the seats, to sell lots of full-price tickets so that I *can* write your paycheck. Three days. I'm more than generously giving you three days to find the actress who did a Cinderella number. Then we go into rehearsal with someone else as Jane."

"Harvey . . ." Beth said gently.

"I really *don't* have more money than God; people just *think* I do. Renting an entire theatre for twelve weeks to cast and rehearse this show costs a helluva lot more than booking a studio in the Minskoff Building, even if it *was* my idea. If I can't see from the outset how it'll look onstage, I can't picture it on the screen. And it's costing us extra money just to arrange this additional day of callbacks, after you told us the actress never returned your phone call."

"Hey, guys! I'm here!" C.J. cried out. "Beth! I want the part!"

"I'm only humoring you, Beth, because you've won two Olivier Awards in as many years," the producer warned.

"And because Gene, Jerry, Sam, Stephen, Mike, Sir Peter, and Julie all had prior commitments," the director replied wryly.

C.J. was desperate to get their attention. "Hey, folks! The red shawl Milena gave me *is* out of fashion," she called out. "By three seasons." It was infuriating. Frustrating beyond belief. They couldn't see her through the dark void that separated the centuries, and although she could not see them either, she could hear them. And evidently, no one could hear her. C.J. impatiently shifted her weight from foot to foot, trying to make more noise, but the stamping seemed as ineffective as a child's temper tantrum. They were all talking about her and there she was, speaking up but unable to be heard. Apparently, she was on the threshold of the past and the present, and for whatever reason, she couldn't get her body all the way into the twenty-first century.

They must have been taking a break from the audition process because there was so much chatting going on. She tried to match the voices with the speakers.

"What is so remarkable to me, as a writer," said Humphrey Porter in his inimitably patrician and slightly pompous cadences, "is that Austen had written more than half her mature oeuvre by 1801, yet with *Pride and Prejudice,* for instance, she couldn't get a publisher to look at it, much less offer to print it."

"It makes you wonder how many other works of great genius were rejected by those who claimed superior knowledge of the profession—or of the market," Ralph Merino concurred.

Humphrey continued his dissertation, pleased to have an audience. "But while Jane kept her writing a secret from the outside world, scribbling in private and sliding her pages under a placemat whenever anyone walked in the door, her father believed in her work. Amazing, isn't it? Jane was only twenty-two years old when Reverend Austen brought the manuscript of *P and P* to a publisher, who rejected it before he'd even read it."

"I was reading about the Austen home when we were re-searching designs for the set," Ralph said. "In 1801, before they retrenched, I suppose, their library boasted more than five hundred volumes."

C.J. continued to listen to their fragmented conversations, not knowing whether she'd been hallucinating the recent events of her life, or if she had indeed somehow traveled through time; whether her journey to 1801 had been a singular phenomenon, or if she could repeat it at will. Her attempt to return to her own century had not proven entirely successful. What if she could not penetrate the blackness that lay between her and the people in the Bedford Street Playhouse? It had to be done!

As she assayed another step toward the *By a Lady* staff, a gust of wind tinged with the pungent odor of cigar smoke blew toward her, filling her nostrils and stinging her eyes. C.J. cried out in pain when she slammed her shin into an immovable ob-ject. She blinked several times in an effort to refocus her eyes.

Wait! She was here! She had done it! Returned to her own place and time. C.J. stifled a squeal of discovery when she real-ized that her leg had come into contact with an enormous gilt throne. But . . . she remembered seeing nothing like it backstage at the Bedford Street Playhouse. C.J. poked around, looking for familiar furniture—and to her dismay, she found it: the stained-glass panels from the Theatre Royal, Bath's production of *De Montfort,* and the unwieldy silk hedgerow. She looked down at her body and realized that her saffron-colored *De Montfort* cos-tume had somehow evanesced.

There has to be something supernatural about this theatre, C.J. reasoned. Or else she would not have ended up here in the first place. Should she poke around and see if there was another "open sesame" that would lead her home . . . a wardrobe, for ex-ample? It had worked for C. S. Lewis. The taste of failure lin-gered bitterly on her lips. She had to try again to return to her own place and time. The notion that she might be forever trapped in the nineteenth century was not one she was willing to accept, let alone embrace. C.J. rummaged backstage, seeking trap doors and secret passages, but her search was cut short by the sound of voices close at hand.

She followed the acrid aroma of tobacco smoke that wafted through the open door leading from the backstage area into the alley just outside the theatre. Two powerfully built men with muscular forearms stopped in midconversation when they saw C.J. leave the building and try to sneak past them. An awkward standoff ensued as C.J. and the stagehands exchanged glances.

"What do you think you were doin' snoopin' around in there?" demanded one of them, crushing the stub of his cheroot beneath his boot heel. "There's no performance today, miss." C.J.'s heart palpitated like a pair of castanets and her mouth went dry, all sense of improvisation deserting her.

The other man drew a small tin from his pocket, took a pinch of brown snuff between a dirty thumb and forefinger, and inhaled it with a quick snort, his gaze never leaving C.J. as he addressed his companion. "Did you hear what Mrs. Siddons did last night, Turpin? Almost refused to go on as the Thane's wife—seems she'd mislaid her lucky rabbit's foot, and she didn't want to set foot on the stage without it—seeing how it's 'The Scottish Play' and all."

Wait! If Siddons was performing *Macbeth* last night, according to the stagehands, and C.J. had tried to return to the future during *De Montfort,* then how much time had elapsed between her attempt to get home and the present? How long had she been struggling in the void between the centuries before she was bounced back to 1801? How might she find out without appearing daft?

The two stagehands stood like street toughs blocking C.J.'s path to the safety of the avenue beyond the alleyway. "You haven't told us what you were about in a dark theatre, young lady," Turpin said.

Her brain was already addled from trying to account for the

time lapse; now her heart was pounding more heavily as she fought to think fast on her feet. "I . . . work for Mrs. Siddons," C.J. fibbed in a flash of inspiration. "I was just bringing her rabbit's foot back to the theatre to leave it in her dressing room. She had . . . taken it home by mistake." A dreadfully lame alibi, but she prayed it would work.

The stagehands eyed C.J. suspiciously, then must have decided that she was telling the truth and that her despair was born out of fear of being sacked by the great Siddons. Warily, they let her pass. She walked quickly through the alley and out into the street, whistling an English country dance melody she remembered to mask her panic.

"I *knew* she was no actress!" the shorter man remarked to his confederate, as though he'd just won a wager. "If she'd whistled like that inside the theatre, she'd catch a canvas drop on her head before she knewed what hit 'er. Just like the old days in His Majesty's navy, eh, Turpin? They whistles and you unfurl the sails."

"I must say as I do miss that life," Turpin sighed wistfully. "Bein' cooped up in a dark theatre don't compare to the open sea, do it, Mr. Twist."

"No, it don't indeed," agreed Twist, rubbing his tobacco-stained thumb and forefinger together. "Maggoty hardtack and stinkin' wages a convict would take as an insult," he added, mocking Turpin's elegiac tone. "To be sure, those were the days."

C.J. hurried away from the Theatre Royal, pausing to glance at a copy of *The Bath Herald and Register* being hawked by a ragamuffin no older than nine or ten, but she failed to catch the date printed at the top of the broadsheet. Paper was dear, so the few large pages were covered margin to margin with print so fine it was nearly impossible to read without spectacles. "Pay, pay, or go away," the boy scolded in a childish singsong. The church bells tolled three times, their reverberation lingering in the spring air like a perfumed angel.

A warm and glorious scent prompted C.J. to follow her nose toward its source. The smell of fresh baking led her not far from the Abbey to a bow-windowed stone building in the North Parade Passage, which, C.J. recalled from her twenty-first-century travels to Bath, was billed as the oldest house in the city.

Sally Lunn's refreshment house was doing a brisk business for mid-afternoon, and C.J. could not suppress her craving for one of the eponymous famed rolls, a slightly sweet giant brioche, ordinarily served hot with butter. What a lovely treat they would make for her "aunt" Euphoria. She patiently waited her turn, amused at how the elegantly attired ladies and gentlemen elbowed and jostled their way to the counter, clamoring for the bread like a bunch of starved peasants or—closer to her own experiences—like the Sunday-morning crowd at Zabar's appetizing counter.

C.J. found herself admiring to the point of covetousness the gown of one of the young ladies, a fashionable light blue sarcenet. Gazing about her as she waited her turn, C.J. was rather surprised to see so many women, not all of them in the bloom of youth, attired in so much white. The Directoire neoclassical, or Grecian, look, so popular in 1800 and 1801, did little to conceal any imperfections in one's figure. Some of the gowns were alarmingly sheer even for evening wear, but many ladies were attired thusly in mid-afternoon.

"May I help you, miss?" A cheery voice from the other side of Sally Lunn's counter politely inquired if C.J. required assistance with her purchases.

"Oh yes, thank you. A half dozen of the Sally Lunns, please."

The rosy-cheeked, strawberry blond shopgirl was only too eager to help. C.J. marveled at how the girl managed to maintain such a sweet disposition amid the crowd of patrons jockeying for position each time a freshly baked tray of buns was brought up from the ovens.

"Over here, Lucy," a man's voice called, brandishing a note as though bidding at an auction.

"At your service, Mr. Churchill, as soon as I help the young miss."

C.J. thrust her hand into her reticule, and finding no money, of course, was struck by the horrifying realization that she could not pay Lucy for her purchases.

The shopgirl was about to hand over the wrapped parcel of warm rolls when she noticed C.J.'s ashen expression. "Something the matter, miss?"

A long arm, clad in a deep cranberry-colored sleeve, reached past C.J.'s face. "Here you go, Lucy," spoke a quiet baritone voice. "For Miss Welles's cakes."

C.J. turned around to see the Earl of Darlington completing the financial transaction on her behalf. He must have offered Lucy a generous gratuity for her services, for she reddened and bobbed up and down a number of times, profusely thanking the handsome aristocrat.

Lord Darlington took the package of warm rolls and proffered his arm to C.J. "Miss Welles, allow me to express my pleasure at seeing you again. I trust the past two days have found you in tolerably good health?"

"Then *two* days, and not one, have passed since the day we met?" replied C.J., puzzling it all out.

"Today is Wednesday, Miss Welles. You missed Mrs. Siddons's Lady Macbeth last night." C.J. frowned. Her expression did not pass undetected by her companion. "But I tread upon rocky terrain. Forgive my momentary lapse; I had quite forgotten my aunt's directives regarding your attendance with me at such a performance."

"Wednesday," C.J. repeated. Had she been trapped in the void between centuries for two 1801 days? Was it truly possible, then, that from the time of her inexplicable departure from the Bedford Street Playhouse all the way through every event in 1801—her homeless state, her incarceration and subsequent trial, her weeks under Lady Wickham's brutal thumb, and the brief time she had spent in Lady Dalrymple's protection—only twenty-four hours or so had elapsed in the modern era?

"I suppose my lengthy journey from London has addled my wits a bit, and I am more fatigued than I had anticipated," C.J. hastily added, remembering Lady Dalrymple's revised version of her history and desperately hoping to conceal her mystified bewilderment from her admirer.

Darlington gazed down at her with a hopeful gleam. "And if I am not pressing my luck too far, tomorrow evening is the date I had fixed to expect to see you at the Assembly Ball in the Upper Rooms."

C.J. smiled gratefully. "I *have* been out of sorts since my arrival in Bath," she added truthfully. "My little escapade at Sally Lunn's is a fine example of my muddled mind. You saved me from dreadful embarrassment," she confessed. "I had thought to bring my aunt a treat, but discovered, right in the middle of the transaction, that I lacked all means to pay for it."

The earl studied her face for a moment. "Think no more of it, Miss Welles. I am glad to have been able to be of service." Darlington boldly slipped his arm through C.J.'s own. Mercifully, he was too polite to make a comment on the state of her ratty yellow muslin.

C.J. glanced at their linked arms. She felt immensely—and surprisingly—at ease in his company, as if she had known him far longer than the duration of an afternoon tea. "Are you not taking liberties with me, your lordship?" she asked anxiously. First, arrested for thievery; now, for all she knew, she might be branded a whore for such brazen behavior. Every time C.J. thought she had gotten a handle on their mores or manners, these Georgians threw her a curve. A proper lady did not address the servants as equals, and yet she drank her tea out of a saucer!

Darlington inclined his head toward her and said softly, "I confess, Miss Welles, I have developed a rather intense curiosity about you, which I am in perhaps too great a haste to explore."

C.J. suddenly realized that observing what she imagined were the maidenly proprieties of the early nineteenth century was going to prove the hardest acting assignment of her life. Oh, why couldn't she have ended up in an era where libertinism among women was perfectly acceptable?

Darlington's arm was warm and protective and even through

his sleeve, she could feel his well-formed musculature. She enjoyed their proximity. No wonder women went mad back then; they had to stifle all their sexual urges, and even when they married, they were expected to grit their teeth and think of England rather than enjoy themselves. C.J. had always imagined that such women were dreadful prudes. Now that she was actually in their world—with such lax attention to personal hygiene and the inability to bathe frequently and fully—she allowed that prudery probably had little to do with the matter. All the teeth gritting might have had a lot more to do with stench than sensuality.

"Do not mistake my meaning, your lordship. I thought perhaps . . ." *from reading Jane Austen novels*, ". . . that you and I would have to have some sort of . . . understanding . . . between us for us to so publicly promenade."

Darlington immediately withdrew his arm and regarded his companion with grave concern. "Believe me, Miss Welles, it was never my wish to cause you either anxiety or apprehension. Bath can be quite sophisticated or quite narrow-minded, depending upon the observer of the behavior. Lady Dalrymple, who has rather singular views on human nature, might be included in the former category, whereas my aunt Augusta is most decidedly in the latter."

They continued to walk toward the Royal Crescent, maintaining a foot or so of distance between them. "If the truth be told, I had not given the taking of your arm a moment's hesitation. I do not view myself as merchandise for the marriage mart. Regard me in an avuncular light if it sets your mind at ease, Miss Welles. I am an old widower of thirty-seven, well past my prime, with far too much leisure time on my hands; and to avoid being labeled a useless layabout, I have offered my services to your aunt to guide you about the city should you wish to see any of its sights. My cousin Jane, of course, who was quite glad of your acquaintance, would be happy to chaperone."

Now that *would be something!* C.J. thought, but was quite sure that the earl would wonder should his innocuous comment elicit from her such an excited reaction. Instead, she replied to his lordship's most surprising, and ridiculous, confession. "Old? *You,* your lordship? If you will forgive my saying so, that is absolute rubbish! And might I be so bold to add that I could never be persuaded to see you 'in an avuncular light,' were you to swear you were as old as Methuselah!"

"You flatter me, Miss Welles," Darlington replied with the utmost sincerity. "My dear girl, there are men my age who are marrying off their sons and daughters. Country balls resemble circuses nowadays. But I did not desire to impugn your reputation when I took your arm just now. I crave your apologies."

He looked so earnest and so unhappy that he might be the cause of any consternation on her part. "Think nothing more of it," C.J. said, afraid he might never touch her again. "I was concerned for your reputation as well, your lordship."

"You are behaving quite correctly, Miss Welles. But it makes me feel so sober when you speak to me with such formality. I have no wish to keep you at arm's distance."

"Arm's distance?"

"I speak metaphorically, Miss Welles."

"I knew that—I mean, I thought so," she responded under her breath.

Darlington cocked his head toward his companion. "Beg pardon? I could not hear you just now." He gestured toward his left ear. "A swimming accident when I was a boy."

C.J. regarded him quizzically.

"In Brighton. When I was a lad. Every summer my parents would return to England from their Continental peregrinations, and the family would enjoy a seaside excursion." The earl's voice grew soft. His eyes became misty with reminiscence. "One afternoon . . . the season my younger brother was eight years old, Jack swam out too far—farther than we had ever planned, or had been allowed to venture. The current becomes rather swift fifty yards or so from the shore . . . and I heard his desperate cries for help as he began to be pulled out by the tides."

C.J. paled.

"I did reach Jack, but it was barely in time, and by the time we were both lifted from the water and hauled up on the deck of a small fishing boat, I had caught a frightful chill. An infection developed in my head that spread to my left ear, and although twenty-seven years have passed since the unfortunate incident, my hearing in this ear has never fully returned."

C.J. placed her hand sympathetically on Darlington's arm. "I am so sorry. What became of Jack?"

"At present he is a very healthy vicar in Sussex with four noisy children and a silly wife who dotes on him. He could not be happier. And he has just slaked his thirst for adventure by becoming the partner on a business prospect in the Americas—a mahogany plantation in Honduras—where I imagine he'll be expected to journey from time to time to inspect his investments."

At the foot of Union Passage, Darlington stopped abruptly. "I offer my apologies in advance, Miss Welles, for insulting your intelligence, but I confess that even among my set—perhaps *especially* among my set—gently bred young ladies are . . . how shall I term it? . . . less well read than you appear to be. I have been thinking on our conversation about Shakespeare and Marlowe."

"I confess I am indeed a great reader. Should you wish to brand me a bluestocking, I would not quibble. And after all, my . . . father . . . quoted Shakespeare to me while I was still in the cradle," C.J. added, improvising wildly.

"I am a man who relishes discoveries. I consider them one of life's chiefest pleasures. As an example of my theme, ever since I was a youth I have had a passion for archaeology, Miss Welles. On the rare occasions when I saw my father, his notion of a proper excursion for a father and son was to join in the excavations at Pompeii—certainly not the usual pursuits for earls and their young offspring—although I prized every chance I was afforded to roll up my sleeves and dig deep into the earth of ancient times. The old earl gave Thom Huggins, our steward at Delamere, a head full of thick white hair before poor Huggins turned thirty. My father, the second Earl of Darlington, knew more—and cared more—about amphorae than farmers. He entrusted Huggins with the entire management of Delamere, but the steward was ill at ease with my father's frequent and lengthy absences. Huggins had a kindly, albeit weak, disposition. He always wanted to please everyone, and he let too many of the tenants gain his advantage. They abused his munificence."

Darlington glanced at C.J., who had become fully absorbed in his story, and he checked his inclination to reveal even more of his past. "But I fear I bore you with the details of Delamere's mismanagement," the third earl said. "I merely thought to explain to you my predilection for the past."

C.J. found it odd that a man of this era would openly discuss his finances with anyone other than his bank managers, and more particularly a young woman who was scarcely an acquaintance. Perhaps he'd felt the same immediate ease in her company as she had in his. "Then we have a good deal in common," she exclaimed, spontaneously touching his hand. "A great affinity for the past, I mean." Their eyes met in mutual understanding. Instinctively, C.J. took his hand in hers. Each could feel the other's quickening pulse; each noticed the other's hand was soft and warm.

"You were about to say something, Miss Welles?"

How prescient he could be. The sincerity of the earl's manner caught C.J. unawares. He was no casual flirt, no light cad like Austen's Willoughby or Frank Churchill. "I was about to . . ." The catch in her throat surprised her. How could she possibly be considering divulging her greatest secret? "It doesn't signify, your lordship. Merely a remark on the innocuous delights of the day's weather." She let go of his hand.

Much to C.J.'s astonishment, the countess evinced no surprise at C.J.'s reappearance, other than to remark that she was pleased to see that her "niece" had finally elected to take a constitutional after two days spent behind a locked door sleeping off the ill effects of her arduous journey from London. No doubt her ladyship genuinely did believe that C.J. had indeed been exhausted enough to sleep for so long after such arduous servitude for Lady Wickham!

"Ooh, lovely, Cassandra, I see you have found each other!" she exclaimed, her two Pekinese yapping at her heels as soon as she rose to greet her "niece." The pups immediately scampered toward the earl when they caught the scent of the fresh buns, for which they received a stern rebuke from her ladyship. "Fielding! Swift! Behave this instant!"

The two small dogs ceased their clamor at Darlington's feet and looked profoundly repentant. C.J. knelt to receive their affectionate greetings.

"Aunt Euphoria, we thought you might like some fresh Sally Lunns. They were to be a treat from me, but his lordship rather graciously stepped in, so you must accept them as his gift." C.J. rose and bestowed a kiss on Lady Dalrymple's cheek.

"Percy, it warms my heart to see you so kindly disposed toward my dearest of kin. Come child." The countess beckoned C.J. with a bejeweled finger. "Handsome devil, isn't he?" she whispered to C.J., adding with an impish grin, "You make an old woman very happy."

"You are a wise and wonderful woman, Aunt Euphoria." The dowager Countess of Dalrymple reminded the young actress very much of her late adopted grandmother. Too often, in the apartment they had once shared, C.J. had lain in bed at night missing the guidance, comfort, and support that had been such a stable element in her life until Nana died. Death had come to Mr. and Mrs. Welles when C.J. was very young, and so she was raised by the mother of her adoptive father, as though she were Nana's own child. "It's not the blood that makes you family," she was fond of saying. "It's the love." And here C.J. was, more than two hundred years *earlier*, finding the same stamp of goodness in Lady Dalrymple, a robust personification of the bountiful Georgian era.

How increasingly impossible it was becoming for her to straddle two worlds. C.J. had to get back to the twenty-first century within the next three days or lose the role of Jane in *By a Lady*. As she grew closer to Lady Dalrymple—and even to Darlington—where much was beginning to be expected of her presence, how could she continue to manage the relatively strife-free life of a gently bred young lady in Bath without drawing attention to her urgency of finding the way back home? Permanently remaining in 1801 was an option she refused to consider; and yet the more acquainted she became with her new surroundings and the era's manners, mores, and pastimes, the more they fascinated her, though she would have been the first to admit that the rosy illusions she had once so innocently—if not ignorantly—harbored had been decidedly dashed.

Chapter Ten

Of period pastimes, a portrait, planets, and a pretentious parvenue.

C.J. WAS RELISHING the quiet, candlelit evening at her "aunt's" prior to their departure for the Assembly Rooms. Although the music commenced at seven, balls rarely got underway until nine; and as it was not the fashion to be one of the first arrivals, the early hours of the evening were spent in other social pursuits.

Apart from the occasional yapping of Fielding or Swift, who craved a treat from their indulgent mistress, or Newton calling out bids while Lady Dalrymple's visitors played hands of écarté, the tranquility of C.J.'s new surroundings both calmed and energized her. For a young woman accustomed to the clamor and cacophony of a twenty-first-century metropolis, a lifestyle where nothing was demanded of her beyond a cheerful countenance, a pleasant disposition, and witty discourse, while otherwise left to her favorite activities—reading, needlework, the taking of fresh air, and shopping—presented itself as a paradisiacal holiday.

Mr. and Mrs. Fairfax, the evening's callers, were amiable enough, decent sorts, although Mrs. Fairfax was something of a parvenue. Throughout the evening she continued to lament to Lady Dalrymple how sorely disappointed she was by what she considered the "leavings" in Bath. As far as she was concerned, anyone who was anyone had deserted the town earlier in the season, and only the nouveaux remained. Bath, she bemoaned, was no longer what it used be in her day. Mrs. Fairfax held every hope that her adversaries at cards would assist her in securing proper husbands for her two eligible daughters, Harriet and Susanne. The one had a predilection for soldiers; the other a propensity toward Scots, and Mrs. Fairfax proclaimed that for the life of her, she could not rightly discern which was worse.

Through a quick reading of Mr. Fairfax's expression during his lady's energetic discourse, C.J. judged that the gentleman most distinctly wished that he were somewhere else—anywhere else perhaps—than across the table from his prattling wife and in the company of the most feared dragon of the *ton*. Lady Oliver did little to conceal her disdain for the nattering drivel of Mrs. Fairfax, as well as the person who uttered it, and had even less use for the husband who was fool enough to have married the woman.

Lady Dalrymple was all for playing ombre but received a derisive scolding for choosing a game that was hopelessly old-fashioned. The hostess was outvoted when Mrs. Fairfax, who took great delight in being able to trump her aristocratic evening companions with some precious tidbit of arcana, asked if she might introduce a new game to them, which she had taken the liberty of bringing with her, ordering the beleaguered Mr. Fairfax to fetch her satchel. She had even persuaded Lady Oliver to join in. Pope Joan, the convivial combination card and board game, was named for a ninth-century pontiff, and the board was illustrated with such provocative demarcations as "Intrigue" and "Matrimony," as well as "Pope Joan," "Ace," "King," "Queen," "Knave," and "Game." What distinguished the deck was that the eight of diamonds had been removed, which, to C.J.'s mind seemed a completely arbitrary excision.

An indifferent card player herself, C.J. watched the proceedings comfortably from an ormolu-mounted mahogany window seat upholstered in apple-green silk. Besides, had she elected to participate, she would have hazarded embarrassing herself to no end in the present company, certain she would be expected to have some familiarity with several of the more popular card games. When Lady Dalrymple helpfully informed her that ombre was played much like whist, it meant nothing to her. C.J. pleaded ignorance of cards, claiming quite honestly that she much preferred to embroider or bury her nose in books. So she had asked her "aunt" for a piece of needlework to stitch while she enjoyed her solitude, and Lady Dalrymple was only too happy to provide her young charge with a bit of crewelwork intended to be the cover for a footstool. The countess complained that nowadays, in the candle glow, the close work hurt her eyes, and her hands were becoming too stiff of late to ply the needle as she had done with such dexterity in her youth. She had provided C.J. with the most cunning contraption: a lit candle placed behind a globe filled with water, the effect of which was to magnify as well as illuminate the needlework.

Before the card party began, Lady Dalrymple had proudly shown C.J. the set of curtained bed hangings in her chamber. C.J. had marveled at the yards and yards of creamy duchess satin that the sixteen-year-old countess-to-be had spent months intricately embroidering as a wedding gift for her husband, the Earl of Dalrymple. The old earl's portrait still hung in a gilt frame opposite the heavily canopied four-poster, and his widow wiped away a tear as she described her freethinking, progressive husband.

"He was such a helpmate, Cassandra, and I was the envy of the *ton*," she had said, mopping her brow with a plump hand and tucking a pewter-gray curl back into her lace cap. "Of course, to look at me now, you would never think that I could have turned heads—I was a slender little creature then—but I had eyes for none but Davenport Camberley. 'Portly,' I used to call him—fondly, mind you.

"When all the gentlemen would retire after supper to

brandy and cigars, Portly would insist on my accompanying him. It raised many eyebrows, I can tell you, Cassandra, and several times we were nearly cut for his eccentricities. Men might include their mistresses among such company from time to time, but never their wives. I used to return to the drawing room, my garments reeking of tobacco smoke; my maids pleaded with me for mercy," she laughed. "They detested airing my gowns after such outings. Some of my friends would fairly beg me to tell them what their husbands conversed about outside their presence. Others, of course, were just as glad to be rid of them for an hour or two. Among our set were dozens of aristocratic ladies, legally compelled to share their husbands' beds in loveless marriages and bear them lawful heirs, but who knew nothing about them, nor did their spouses care to learn what interested their wives. Such concerns were not the way of the world when I was a young girl. Of course, not so much has changed. True love, my dear, is the exception in high society, rather than the rule. The upper classes are expected to forge alliances of money and property—not passion. For passion, one takes a lover—providing it is discreetly done—unless of course you're a member of the royal family, in which case one dares not question your behavior. But I adored Portly. I used to dance for him, Cassandra. Not the sort of dancing one does in the ballroom, which of course we both enjoyed immensely. But late at night, in the privacy of our bedchamber, I . . ." She broke off her narrative when her voice began to break. "One day, I hope you will know the kind of love I had. And you will want to dance for your husband." The countess reclaimed her emotions and gave her "niece" a wink. "It puts a little ginger in a marriage."

C.J. returned her focus to her tapestry. She had been daydreaming again, an easy feat when Lady Dalrymple became engrossed in one of her card games. No one thought to trouble her, and she found it rather refreshing to be left alone.

"Miss Welles."

C.J. glanced up from the embroidery hoop and saw Lady

Oliver beckoning her with a jeweled finger. There was something about this woman that truly unnerved C.J., although she did her best to try to conceal her apprehension. She felt as though Darlington's aunt could see right through her new sarcenet gown and her cambric undergarments, straight to the marrow of her bones, whereupon the dragon would publicly denounce her as a fraud.

C.J. dropped a quick curtsy before her judge. "How may I be of service, your ladyship?"

Lady Oliver recited the facts in a steely voice. "My nephew has invited you to dance at the Assembly Ball this evening in the Upper Rooms. You have accepted his invitation."

"Heavens!"

The entire party was startled by this rude interjection. C.J. turned to face the speaker and stifled a laugh. The culprit, now feigning disinterest, gnawed on a bit of biscuit at the bottom of his gilded cage. C.J. smiled at Lady Dalrymple, who assumed a sober countenance and nodded to Willis to place a cloth over Newton's residence.

Lady Oliver elected to ignore the parrot's editorializing. "It is most improper. Most improper indeed. You have come from nowhere, child. You may have just as well dropped down from the sky. Your father was—nay, *is*—such an objectionable creature that we do not even speak of him in polite society."

"And yet this is the second time I have heard your ladyship mention him in as many encounters," C.J. replied boldly, adding, "And as this evening has been pleasant and genial thus far, and I may allow that I *have* been passing it in polite society, it would be proper indeed if neither my father's name nor mention of his unfortunate circumstances—nor even, by extension, my own—should pass from our collectively respectable lips."

Lady Oliver refused to permit herself to be discommoded by the placid look on C.J.'s face and found a new focus for her disdain by remarking upon C.J.'s pale blue silk gown.

"Euphoria, I trust that your niece will have a more suitable frock to wear to a ball in the Upper Rooms."

Lady Dalrymple beamed triumphantly at her bosom friend. "My dear Augusta, on your own recommendation Miss Welles is wearing one of the day dresses Madame Delacroix designed. It so artfully becomes her, does it not? It was delivered this afternoon along with one evening ensemble. The rest of my niece's gowns will be ready in no time."

Lady Oliver wrinkled her nose in evident disapproval. "Euphoria, I wish to make it quite clear in front of the young lady that I shall not permit her to dance more than once with my nephew, and even *that* I will consider to be an act of charity toward the poor relation of my dearest friend."

Mr. Fairfax evinced some discomfort at his being privy to such a conversation. His wife's pink ears perked up, however. The grand behavior of the upper crusts of society into which her nouveau riche status accorded her the privilege of mingling never ceased to impress her. "Such condescension," she exclaimed approvingly to her shuddering husband, who attempted to shush her lest her remark be overheard.

"How kind of you to express such concern, Augusta," Lady Dalrymple said sweetly. "If Percy were to dance more than three sets with my niece at her very first ball, the entire city of Bath would expect him to offer for her." She laid the ace of hearts on the felt-covered gaming table.

"Ha-ha, I do believe she has trumped us," Mrs. Fairfax giggled, whereupon her husband motioned for the footman to remove his wife's sherry glass from the table.

THE FAIRFAXES HAD DEPARTED for the Assembly Rooms, and Lady Oliver had insisted on following in her own barouche, hoping to have the occasion to speak privately with her stubborn nephew before the festivities began in earnest.

Lady Dalrymple was in her front drawing room, gazing into the dusky sky through her telescope, when C.J. came downstairs to model her new ball gown.

"What do you see, Aunt Euphoria?"

The dowager turned around, startled. "Heavens, child! You gave me a fright." She appraised C.J. in the gauzy white dress. "Aphrodite herself would be jealous; that is what I see. Come, give your aunt a kiss."

C.J. obeyed, taking care not to trip on the slight train at the back of the fine muslin gown as she tested her delicate new shoes. What a shock she had received when Saunders, while dressing her, had remarked that for her first ball, her young ladyship was certainly "putting on the dog" with her dancing slippers. C.J. was familiar with the expression but thought it was a quaint colloquialism from the Jazz Age. She had nearly gagged when the sour-faced lady's maid curtly remarked—or so it sounded to C.J.—that the "dog" she referred to was one that had given its skin to make the finest of dance slippers, wondering aloud if the poor victim had been a spaniel or a terrier. Clearly there were some things about her present situation to which C.J. might never become reconciled.

"I meant, what do you see through the telescope?" C.J. asked her "aunt."

The countess smiled. "The future, I suppose. One imagines that there must be so much out there that we can never know. Have you ever seen such an instrument?" Lady Dalrymple asked, referring to the telescope.

"Never in person," C.J. answered truthfully.

"This one was given to me by William Herschel, a dear, dear friend of mine . . . and Portly's, of course. Such a clever man. Brilliant. I think he may be a *Jew*," she said, lowering her voice. "A handmade telescope very much like this one was the instrument he used to discover Georgium Sidus from his house right here on New King Street, in 1781."

C.J. gave her ladyship a look of total incomprehension. "Discovered who?"

"Georgium Sidus is a planet, my dear. There are seven of them . . . maybe fewer . . . I can never remember. Most are named for Roman deities, of course. Venus and Mars, Saturn, Jupiter, Mercury . . . then there's Georgium Sidus, to be sure, and my favorite, although I don't believe it's a planet—the moon."

C.J. wondered which planet Georgium Sidus was. "Roman planets, and an old Roman city," she said. "I wonder how the earliest astronomers decided to name so many of the planets for Roman gods. Why not name them after the Greek ones? Or the Hebrew prophets? Or the kings of England?"

"Well," the countess answered, "Sir William *did* decide to name his discovery, despite its being accidental, after our monarch, who, naturally, was his royal patron. *Georgium sidus* is the Latin for 'star of George.' Heavens! Such a clever question. Portly would have been a great admirer of yours, child. Oh yes, he placed great store in an inquisitive mind, especially in a young woman. In time you will learn that there are those, like Augusta Oliver, who have little or no use for what they cannot immediately see, smell, and taste, although she was not always as you see her now. Her grief—not to mention the scandal that ensued—has embittered her for many years."

C.J. perched delicately on the footstool, prepared to hear the shameful tale of woe. "But that is another story for another time," Lady Dalrymple added definitively. "My dearest Portly believed as the Hindus do, in the reincarnation of the soul. 'The eccentric earl,' he was called. And I do believe in my heart that *his* spirit still very much resides with us." Her eyes were moist with tears.

"I daresay you are right to believe that, Aunt Euphoria," C.J. added, her own eyes misting over. "Perhaps souls do indeed live forever—they only inhabit different bodies along the way. But even if that might not be the case, I think it is a duty of the living to maintain the memory of the departed so that their spirits do indeed live on in our recollections and our thoughts. In that way do they achieve an immortality."

Euphoria gave her "niece" a warm hug. "I had never thought to find anyone else who did not think my notions mere folly. You are very like him in many ways." Suddenly, Lady Dalrymple clutched her bodice.

"What's the matter, your ladyship?"

"My heart," she gasped huskily.

"Did I upset you? Goodness—are you in pain?" C.J. endeavored to conceal her genuine alarm. She dashed over to the embroidered bellpull hanging near the huge double doors and gave it an energetic tug, setting off a bell in the servants' quarters belowstairs.

Lady Dalrymple shook her head. C.J. could not decipher whether it was to be interpreted as a yes or a no.

"Can I loosen your stays?" C.J. regarded the dowager's evening dress to see where she might be able to give her some breathing room. Although the narrow-skirted Directoire gowns were all the mode, many fashionable women of Lady Dalrymple's generation dressed in an earlier style, in what was commonly regarded as the Georgian fashion. Lady Dalrymple's stiffly boned bodice, or "stomacher," was like an insect's carapace, armoring its wearer and providing little range of motion or flexibility to her rib cage. No wonder women were always in danger of hyperventilating.

Collins entered the drawing room with a pitcher of water and a crystal goblet, which C.J. asked him to leave on the small table beside the striped divan. She poured a glass of the cool liquid for her "aunt," then spilled a bit of lavender water onto her lace-edged handkerchief and applied it to Lady Dalrymple's brow.

The countess attempted to dismiss C.J.'s ministrations. "There, now you've gone and spoilt your nice linen square, and you will need it for tonight."

"Nonsense, Aunt. Madame Delacroix had more than a dozen delivered this morning with my dress." She squeezed Lady Dalrymple's hand. The countess was breathing heavily, increasing C.J.'s concern.

Lady Dalrymple took a dainty sip of water. "It was but a brief pang," she assured her "niece." "Dr. Squiffers says I must avoid anxiety whenever possible."

"I am so dreadfully sorry, Aunt Euphoria. I had no idea that you were afflicted with a delicate medical condition." C.J. took her ladyship's hand in her own and gave it a gentle kiss. She couldn't help admiring the countess's large emerald ring. She'd never seen a real gem quite that large, and the fire emanating from the green stone gave it an exceptional depth and luster.

"Think no more of it," the dowager urged, her voice a weak command. She forced a smile. "Now tell me what you are thinking—as long as the state of my health is not the subject of the conversation. I can imagine nothing more tiresome."

C.J. straightened Lady Dalrymple's lappeted cap, then leaned in to bestow a kiss upon her forehead. "I suppose," she began hesitantly, wondering if there would ever be an appropriate time to tell her benefactress the truth about her arrival in Bath. "I confess . . . I am a bit anxious myself about my first ball. I'm dreadfully afraid I shall make a mess of things and cause you no small degree of mortification." C.J. furrowed her brow.

"That is a very unbecoming expression for a young lady," chastised the countess. "It leads to wrinkles before their time. Look at my face. I am threescore and two. Augusta is two years my junior, and looks like my stepmother. Why? Because frowns create more wrinkles than smiles and turn a peachy countenance to a prune. If there is one thing an old woman can hope to teach a young lady, it is to recognize happiness and to embrace it freely. Life will always be full of the inevitable sorrow and loss, but I have indeed been fortunate: I have lived to love a man very deeply with every fiber of my being," she said with a little sigh.

C.J. knelt beside Lady Dalrymple, and the two women held each other. After a couple of minutes passed, C.J. could feel her ladyship's breathing grow stronger and steadier. She did not look up for fear of causing her embarrassment, but she was sure she heard Lady Dalrymple choke back a sob.

"Come now, child, you mustn't get mussed up before your very first ball," the countess chided gently, nudging C.J.'s torso from her ample lap.

Chapter Eleven

*Our heroine's first Assembly Ball, whereat her English country
dance experience proves a godsend in that she starts off on
the right foot, but with the wrong arm, leading to a highly
embarrassing faux pas; and her rosy view of the aristocracy
is cruelly shattered.*

C.J. FELT AS THOUGH she had stepped inside a
pistachio-colored confection when she and Lady
Dalrymple entered the grand hall of the Assembly
Rooms.

In a modern postcard, the straight-backed walnut chairs that
ringed the empty ballroom's perimeter stood like so many silent
sentinels, waiting to be used by the phantom dancers who
graced the well-polished wooden floor with quadrilles and
polkas, the occasional mazurka, and eventually—though not formally until 1812—the waltz. One was left to imagine how the
room might have appeared in its heyday. Now that C.J. was getting an eyewitness account of its glories, she had expected to
find a crush of people, owing to their fashionably late arrival; but
only five or six couples were dancing a longways set, their small
number dwarfed by the majesty of the room itself.

Lady Dalrymple did little to conceal her disappointment.

"There is a paucity of revelers because it is so late in the season," she informed her young protégée, sotto voce. "A pity you did not arrive in Bath sooner."

Taking in the scene, C.J. noticed several young ladies gowned nearly identically in filmy white muslin, escorted by their doting mothers dressed in deeper tones. The chairs, by their very lack of comfort, were conducive to dancing, and fortunately, several of the tunes were recognizable to her ear. Still, to watch some of the couples executing intricate maneuvers nevertheless generated flutters of anxiety that should the inevitable invitation to make one of a set arise, she would risk exposing herself as an impostor.

The strident voice of Mrs. Fairfax could be heard well above the music, thus Lady Dalrymple had no trouble reconnoitering with her acquaintance in one corner of the room. The parvenue, eager to dispose of her two marriageable daughters before the season's end—and with time rapidly running out—raised her quizzing glass to one eye and surveyed the eligibles across the room.

"What think you of the way Mr. Essex dances?" she said, scrutinizing a young pup in a leaf-green coat and formfitting white breeches energetically executing a hay in the middle of the floor.

Her good husband found it difficult to maintain his pretense of ignoring her when he felt such an adamant tug on the cuff of his sleeve.

"He bounces too much," Mr. Fairfax replied laconically.

Mrs. Fairfax returned the quizzing glass to her right eye and squinted. "Upon re-examination, I quite agree with you, my dear Mr. Fairfax. Yes, you are invariably such an excellent judge of character. Too much exuberance on the dance floor undoubtedly connotes a juvenile temperament."

"And Lord knows, our daughters are silly enough without encouraging their suitors to share their frivolity," her husband drawled.

Two young ladies approached the older couple with glasses of negus, the sugar-sweetened, mulled, and watered-down wine customarily offered at such gatherings.

"Quite a dear you are, Harriet." Mrs. Fairfax patted the hand of a very pretty girl, her face framed with golden curls. She took a sip of the negus and handed it to her husband. "Mr. Fairfax, do taste this and tell me whether they have used port or sherry this evening. I can never discern. Lady Dalrymple, I believe you have met my eldest daughter, Harriet; and this," she added, indicating the strawberry blonde hovering near her opposite shoulder, "is my younger, Susanne." The young women curtsied to the countess, and turned to gaze upon the newcomer in their midst.

"Ah yes. The poor relation," Mrs. Fairfax announced a bit too loudly and with an entire lack of tact. "Girls, allow me to name you Lady Dalrymple's niece . . . Miss Cassandra Jane Welles."

The young ladies curtsied daintily and acknowledged the poor relation's presence in a tandem of soprano voices. "Miss Welles."

"Miss Fairfax, Miss Susanne. It is a pleasure to meet you." C.J. wondered if in this light her own gown was as nearly transparent as those of the Miss Fairfaxes. Even at twenty-first-century parties, where young women clearly in the marriage market displayed deep cleavage and long legs, one still didn't wear diaphanous attire and pretend it was a hallmark of modesty. C.J. surveyed the room once again. Good heavens! A ballroom filled with virgins (surely she was the only one in white who did not qualify), whose garments left nothing to the imagination. She ventured that a gentleman could place a wager on the calculation of a lady's weight, just by eyeing her in her white muslin.

"Aunt Euphoria, allow me to fetch you some punch," C.J. offered, hoping to avoid being within earshot when Mrs. Fairfax gossiped behind her fan to her two daughters, tut-tutting over poor Miss Welles's misfortunes.

She wended her way across the gleaming parquet floor and out into the Tea Room, where enormous silver epergnes dripped with fruit: plump, fresh grapes in three different colors, plums, figs, and fragrant Seville oranges. With two kinds of cold punch, lemonade, and the warm negus in huge urns filled near to overflowing, the table, groaning under its weight, resembled refreshments at a bacchanalia.

The display was just shy of perfection, however; and C.J., not wishing to call attention to the problem, and not having an inkling whom to hail for assistance in any event, thought it would be best to tackle the issue alone. Just as she had steeled her nerves to do the deed, an exceptionally elderly couple, nearly blind and ambulating only by the grace of God and sturdy walking sticks, approached the punch table. The couple probably would have noticed nothing, were they to swallow the offending object, but C.J. could not content herself to stand idly by.

"Stay back!" she warned. The urgency of her tone and the volume of her voice instantly drew a curious crowd. At least she had the presence of mind not to ruin a brand-new, buttery-soft kid glove. While keeping her spectators at bay, C.J. struggled to tug the skin-tight, elbow-length glove down the length of her arm. Having succeeded, she plunged her right arm—all the way up to the elbow joint—into the punch bowl, jumping back so as to avoid splashing herself and ruining her new gown. But the object of her consternation, a common housefly, was not as easily trapped as she had initially thought. Its wings were not beating as though the mite were drowning, so C.J. assumed that the poor bugger had drunk himself to death and she was merely to play the role of undertaker. The shadows in the liquid danced and her target bobbed up and down upon the waves created by the intrusion of her arm as she struggled to capture the cadaver.

Meanwhile, Mrs. Fairfax was furiously semaphoring her husband to locate a chair, so that Lady Dalrymple could make herself comfortable, when a flurry of movement at the entranceway caught her eye. "Harriet, Susanne, stand up straight. Lady Oliver and her nephew have arrived. Make yourselves presentable for the Earl of Darlington." She seated herself with an exaggerated show of gentility and lowered the quizzing glass to her lap.

But the earl was not advancing toward Mrs. Fairfax and her party. His steps took him in an altogether different direction. "I would dare to kiss your hand in greeting, Miss Welles, but it seems to be . . . occupied at present."

"Gotcha! Good heavens!" C.J. jumped when she heard the voice behind her. Her arm flew out of the deep punch bowl, and the assembly ducked for cover. "I apologize, your lordship. My very first ball, and I seem to have gotten off on the wrong foot."

"Oh, I wouldn't say that, necessarily. The wrong arm, perhaps," he added, appraising her bare appendage and clutched fist. "What have you got there?"

C.J. inclined her head, indicating that he should come closer. "There was a fly in the punch!" she whispered. "And I thought it best to surreptitiously remove it on my own, rather than call the majordomo, or whomever I must alert in such circumstances. Alas, I ended up with an audience." She opened her fist and looked curiously at the wet black spot nestled in her palm. "That's funny. It has no wings."

"That is because it is not an English fly."

"What the devil do you find so amusing, your lordship?"

"It is a French fly. A *mouche*. And in Italian, should you be curious to know, the word for fly is *mosca*."

C.J. blanched. What a fool she had just made of herself! "Thank you for the education in romance languages, sir. All that for a *mouche*?" C.J. said, scarcely able to disguise her mortification.

"Come, Miss Welles. Let us take a turn about the room and see if we can spot the real perpetrator of this heinous hoax. We shall put the first man or woman with a glaring red pockmark to the rack to see if they confess." Smiling, he glanced down at her bare limb.

" 'Twas nothing more than a *patch*, then." C.J. shivered and sighed and searched about for a linen towel with which to dry her arm. She would have to wash it before attempting to replace her glove, and without her glove, she would not be permitted on the dance floor. "Please excuse me, sir," she said, and found a liveried servant, who arranged to have a basin of water and a clean cloth brought posthaste.

Her impromptu toilette completed, C.J. sought out the rest of her party. She tried to ignore the cutting glances of the well-accoutered assemblage but was unable to stop her ears from the insidious buzz circulating around the room apropos of her hoydenish behavior.

"Countrified manners," sneered a handsome woman in a jeweled headdress, glinting over her peacock-feather fan. "But then what can one expect from a poor relation."

"I daresay my horses are better schooled," guffawed a yellow-toothed, odiferous elderly gentleman. He removed his gold-rimmed spectacles to dab a rheumy eye with the edge of his ruffled cuff.

Myriad comments of a similar nature filled C.J.'s ears, and she tried to hold her head high despite the sting she felt from the *ton*'s assault, but before she reached Lady Dalrymple at the perimeter of the ballroom, there was a collective gasp from all and sundry.

Could her gaffe have been of such epic magnitude?

When C.J. realized that this particular communal intake of breath was not directed at her, and that all of the patrons had turned toward the door, she, too, paused to regard the cause for such commotion.

A young woman, attired from head to toe in lemon yellow, had just made her entrance on the arm of a dapper escort. They had eyes only for each other and feigned obliviousness to the effect they had produced amid the gathering throng.

Just as the couple had located a pair of chairs, and the gentleman had seated his lady and was about to make for the negus table, Mr. King, the Master of Ceremonies, approached them and announced in stentorian tones, "You are not welcome here, your lordship, your ladyship."

The murmurs began anew.

"She is carrying his child," remarked a sweet-faced blonde. "And her, barely out of mourning for her father."

"I hear," smirked a dandy so coated with cosmetics that he resembled a china doll, "that it was at the earl's funeral that the deed was done . . . while the guests were partaking of the mourning meal. The funeral meats were cold, but our young Lord Featherstone's was smoking. Just past the hedgerows, I hear it happened—on the old earl's own property. He was always so fond of his rose garden."

"And now it seems that his Rose's bush has been well pruned," his older companion snickered.

"Nay, not so much pruned as *pricked*," the dandy laughed.

"It seems Featherstone could not wait for the banns," whispered a haughty matron who pointed a gloved finger at Lady Rose's ever so slightly rounded belly.

"You are to leave the room at once and are not welcome at future public assemblies," Mr. King proclaimed, audible to all.

There was no opportunity to protest and no court in which one would be entertained. Lord Featherstone offered his hand to Lady Rose.

The collective reaction of the *ton* could not have been more powerful had it been choreographed. As the loving couple exited the room, depriving their detractors of the satisfaction of watching them depart at a hasty pace, it seemed that almost every aristocrat, regardless of age or gender, made a great show of turning his or her respective back on the pair. The silence during this exhibition was deafening. Once the illicit lovers had departed the Upper Rooms and were enveloped by the night air, the cats indoors resumed their merriment.

Shocked by this display, C.J. made her way over to her "aunt" and seated herself beside her. Lady Dalrymple read the young woman's expression and patted her hand sympathetically. "I do not condone the behavior you have just witnessed, nor do I agree with it, but my dear, that is the way of the upper crust. We are expected to set an example for those considered to be in the inferior classes, and when decorum is so flagrantly violated—paraded even—well, you see the degree to which it is tolerated."

"Is that what it means to be 'cut'?" C.J. asked.

"It is indeed," replied the countess. "To endure the censure of one's peers in such a fashion has quite effectively and publicly rendered Lord Featherstone and Lady Rose societal outcasts. Their presence will not be tolerated at public gatherings such as these, and any hostess who would presume to entertain them in her home or on her estate risks similar censure herself for the very act of defying this unwritten decree."

"But what if Lord Featherstone were to marry Lady Rose?"

"No doubt he will, my child. Any fool can see that they are very much in love. It doesn't signify, however. The indiscretion has been committed and no matter what pains are taken to rectify the situation, the act of censure remains the same."

"How dreadful. And ridiculous. I noticed that Lord Darlington did not turn his back, nor did many of those seated around the perimeter of the room."

"Percy has always been his own man, and for that reason, I have always doted on him. Now," the countess explained, gesturing with her fan, "the others you remarked upon are not of the same strata as the *ton*. They have no call to cut their betters, whatever their behavior. Their circles rarely intersect with ours, except at public assemblies such as these."

"I cannot imagine *wanting* to be in the same room as those who would so universally condemn my actions."

Lady Dalrymple squeezed C.J.'s hand. "Ahhh . . . but a life of ostracism can become a very lonely one. It will be interesting to see whether or not Lord Featherstone and Lady Rose can endure such an existence without inciting rancor between themselves."

Mrs. Fairfax, who had been struggling to overhear the conversation between C.J. and the countess, admitted defeat and broached a subject of her own. Aiming her closed fan at Lord Darlington, she said, "The earl is one of the most eligible bachelors this season, your ladyship. Perhaps he will suit one of my girls. It will take their minds off of His Majesty's officers."

"But, Mama," Susanne lamented, "he is a widower and over thirty-five years old. Thirty-seven or even thirty-eight, some say. That is nearly more than twice Harriet's age, and assuredly more than twice my own."

"Imagine being married to a man twice one's age," interjected Harriet. "If I were twenty, he would be forty. And by the time *I* reached that age, he would be *eighty!*" C.J. had to remind herself that she was dwelling in an age where it was popularly held that female children had no need to learn mathematics. "Besides," Harriet continued, "I hope that Captain Keats will be here this evening. He looks so splendid in his uniform," she confided to C.J.

"Captain Keats is a poor officer with nothing of substance to recommend him," her mother said dismissively.

The pretty blonde sighed petulantly over her mother's ignorance. "He has a medal for valor, Mama, which is more than any man of our acquaintance can boast."

As if on cue, a tall young gentleman, resplendent in his scarlet coat with its gold braid and shiny silver buttons, and decorated with an item that Mrs. Fairfax was quick to discredit as a mere tin trinket, approached their party.

Harriet blushed. "Captain Keats! We were just discussing your merits. Do join us for a glass of punch."

"I should be only too happy to oblige," the dashing captain replied, as he stood beside the infatuated Miss Fairfax. "I could not help overhearing as I approached, mum, your daughter's mention of my medal for distinctive service."

Mr. Fairfax presented Captain Keats to Lady Dalrymple and her "niece," and the officer explained to the little group the history of his decoration. "I was one of Sir Ralph Abercromby's expedition to Egypt this past March, you see, and each of us was granted the distinction of the Sphinx. If you inspect the order more closely, you will see that it is inscribed with the word *Egypt*."

Miss Fairfax was only too happy to oblige. "Oh, bless me!

Goodness if it does. Egypt," she mused. "That must be terribly far away."

"Indeed it is, Miss Fairfax. And a rather more arid climate than we are used to in England."

Quickly losing interest in a discussion of North African weather, C.J. scanned the room, noticing the earl and Miss Austen in the company of Lady Oliver and an older couple. Darlington was glancing in her direction as they sought chairs, none of which appeared to suit his esteemed aunt.

After a few moments, the earl approached their party, greeting each of them warmly. He allowed that he remembered the Miss Fairfaxes, yet there was not a hint in his manner of anything beyond cordial recollection. Mrs. Fairfax would have to wage an aggressively persistent campaign on behalf of her nubile offspring if she wished the earl to entertain even the slightest inclination toward espousing either of her daughters.

Darlington surreptitiously leaned forward to speak to C.J. "I should like a word in your ear, Miss Welles, if you can spare me a moment this evening."

"You have piqued my curiosity, your lordship."

"I should be quite honored if you would join me in a set." He inclined his head toward the center of the room. "As you are no doubt aware, propriety prohibits me from engaging your company more than twice this evening—and my aunt's wishes are rather adamant in my halving that number—which will not afford me nearly as much opportunity as I should like to enjoy your delightful company. Perhaps the supper dance would be best, and then we may talk more freely afterward."

C.J. was learning something else about the inhabitants of this society. Nearly everyone here danced around his or her intentions, cloaking them in nuance, riddle, and understatement. Would she ever become used to it? "I should be honored, your lordship," she replied, and dropped a respectful curtsy.

"My cousin would like to say good evening to you, Miss Welles, if you will allow me to separate you briefly from your companions." Darlington nodded to the Fairfaxes and to Lady Dalrymple and begged their indulgence while he spirited away Miss Welles to greet his cousin, his arm lightly guiding C.J. by the elbow as they crossed the room to address the other party.

"Miss Jane's cousin's first husband and my late wife were brother and sister—if you can follow that rather knotty family tree," the earl informed C.J., who did not recall hearing about Darlington's first marriage from his own lips. She supposed that among the *ton* everyone knew one another's business regardless of whether or not the source of the intelligence was firsthand.

They reached the opposite side of the ballroom, and his lordship made the introductions all around. "Miss Jane Austen, with whom you are of course acquainted, Miss Welles. And Miss Jane's uncle and aunt, with whom she is staying in the Paragon, Mr. and Mrs. Leigh-Perrot."

C.J. offered them shallow curtsies and tried to express her pleasure in the opportunity to make their acquaintance. She felt woefully inarticulate and socially inept.

"This is Miss Welles's first season," prompted the earl, surprised at her unusual muteness.

Fortunately, C.J. was rescued by the articulate Miss Austen. "It is a pity you were not here earlier in the year." Jane surveyed the room, and shook her head. "The crowd is shockingly and inhumanly thin for this place, though there are people enough, I suppose, to make five or six very pretty Basingstoke assemblies."

"Yes, Jane never tires of poking fun at poor little Basingstoke's countrified remoteness," Mrs. Leigh-Perrot agreed, then excused herself and her husband to join another couple in one of the few country dances requiring a square.

Darlington held out a chair for C.J. "You would not think it to know her, for her manner is always so gentle, but my cousin has an exceptionally wicked predilection for gossip," he commented. "You were treated to a taste of that at tea the other day, Miss Welles. Cousin Jane, do share with our companion what you were just telling me."

Miss Austen slid her chair closer to C.J.'s and spoke in a confidential tone. "I have a very good eye for adulteresses," she whispered, glancing toward the opposite end of the room at a highly rouged woman wearing a handsome striped silk turban with a large topaz at the center, from which an enormous egret feather sprouted. "Though I have been repeatedly assured that another in the same party was the *she*, I fixed upon the right one from the first." Jane looked pleased with herself.

"You have great powers of perception, Miss Austen, to be able to detect the slightest foible of character at fifty paces," C.J. murmured to her new acquaintance.

The young women shared a laugh, and Jane, sensing a kindred spirit, took hold of C.J.'s hand. "I do believe we shall become great friends," she pronounced with assuredness.

Chapter Twelve

*A chapter fraught with incident, in which Miss Austen shares
her opinions on the follies of both sexes; Lady Dalrymple puts
on a show; our heroine gets kissed in the moonlight, followed by
a stunning, though not altogether unexpected, proposal; and
Lady Oliver's checkered past is disclosed.*

RETURNING FROM THEIR EXERTIONS, the Leigh-
Perrots asked Darlington if he would kindly fetch
them some punch. Lady Oliver wished for a full report on all of the available refreshments before she would commit to a preference for a single one of them, and insisted that
these days all the best assemblies served orgeat water, a nonalco-
holic beverage made from barley and orange-flower water.

Miss Austen directed C.J.'s attention to two members of the
adulteress's party. "I cannot remember being so amused at a
ball," she informed her companion with a gleeful smile. "Mrs.
Busby is abandoning the two young women whom she is obliged
to chaperone to run 'round the room after her drunken husband.
His avoidance and her pursuit, with the probable intoxication of
both, has provided the most convivial entertainment I have had
this past hour." Jane urged C.J. to quickly turn her chair, as the

objects of Miss Austen's pointed censure were headed their way. They swiftly rearranged their positions so as to avoid the addresses of Busby and wife.

The earl rejoined their party with glasses of punch for the Leigh-Perrots and for his aunt, despite her earlier directives. No orgeat water, or ratafia liqueur either, was to be had this evening.

Lady Oliver missed nothing of her nephew's interest in Lady Dalrymple's poor relation and squandered no opportunity to issue a rebuke. "If I had wished to spend my evening in the company of a salivating male, I should have brought my best Pointer. Percy, you are perfectly aware of the impropriety of the situation. To give Miss Welles such undue attention is not becoming to your status as a gentleman, and it will undoubtedly cause embarrassment to the family, not to mention damage to your already blemished reputation."

"Then a further blot will pass undetected, Aunt Augusta," the earl replied.

C.J. smiled complaisantly. "Lady Oliver, forgive my rudeness. Although we are seated five persons apart from each other, I could not help overhearing your remarks to your nephew, which I am sure were intended to be in confidence. Surely, if my presence is intolerable to his lordship, he is free to direct his attentions elsewhere."

Her ladyship's rather audible grunt connoted her defeat as well as her displeasure. She adjusted her position with the aid of her ivory-handled walking stick.

"She likes *you* well enough," C.J. whispered to Miss Austen.

Jane looked up and smiled placidly at Lady Oliver in case the old bat should misjudge the young women's gentle conversation for internecine plotting. "Her good nature," she said sardonically, "is not tenderness." Miss Austen lowered her voice to a whisper and raised her fan. "All that she wants is gossip, and she only likes me now because I supply it."

Darlington cleared his throat, which had the intentioned result of interrupting the tête à tête. "Ladies, I do believe it is time for the supper dance. Miss Welles, if I am not mistaken, you have promised this one to me." He offered C.J. his arm and helped her from the hard wooden chair.

An agreeable-looking young man with a fair complexion and reddish hair approached Miss Austen and requested the dance. The escorts led the young ladies out to join the longways set that was forming in the center of the room.

Now that she was on the dance floor, C.J.'s anxieties about dancing all but dissipated and she began to feel herself on a surer footing. Owing to her twenty-first-century workshops in English country dancing, she was somewhat practiced at the kind of repartee exchanged among the gently bred men and women as they faced one another, traded partners, entwined under a raised arm, or took hands.

She overheard Jane, down the set, engaged in an animated discussion with her russet-haired partner, a vicar's son named Mr. Chiltern. The latter, who did not wish to share his witty partner with others in the set, was emphatically arguing, "I consider a country dance as the emblem of marriage. Fidelity and complaisance are the principal duties of both; and those men who do not choose to dance or marry themselves have no business with the partners or wives of others."

Miss Austen twirled away from him as they moved one couple down the set. "But there you are wrong, sir. People that marry can never part, but must go and keep house together. People that dance only stand opposite each other in a long room for half an hour."

C.J. and Darlington laughed. "I daresay, your lordship, your witty cousin is getting the better of the poor vicar's son. He may wish to switch partners after all, despite his views on the parallels between making hays and holy matrimony."

Jane was clearly enjoying herself, pressing her point that a difference indeed existed. "You will admit that in marriage the man is supposed to provide for the support of the woman, and the woman to make the home agreeable to the man. He is to purvey, and she is to smile." Jane beamed triumphantly. "But in dancing, their duties are exactly changed. The agreeableness and compliance are expected from him, while she furnishes the fan and the lavender water."

C.J. found it difficult to maintain her gaze on her partner and still keep up with the exchange between Mr. Chiltern and Miss Austen, not wishing to miss a word Jane uttered. "Were I to have the opportunity to know your cousin well," she told the earl, "I should become fast friends with her. There is already much to admire."

"Miss Austen has expressed the same desire to better acquaint herself with you, Miss Welles. But do not deny your own ability to fascinate. There is an unquenchable energy to your spirit, a strength of character, and—if you will forgive me—a certain contradiction in your nature that compels me to discover the cause. Forgive my bluntness, Miss Welles, but from the moment I made your acquaintance, you have never ceased to haunt my thoughts. I am but a poor suitor in your thrall."

"You give me far too much credit, your lordship," blushed C.J. "Were your countenance not so earnest, I should scarce believe such pretty words!"

"Oh but you must, Miss Welles! You may apply to your aunt as my character witness should you doubt my integrity on the matter."

The tune ended and the musicians laid down their instruments. The couples parted, moving toward the gilded doors of the ballroom to take advantage of the break in the dancing by enjoying whatever light repast was available.

"I do love dances," Jane told C.J. as they joined their families and the Fairfaxes at the perimeter of the room. "And, as for gentlemen," she added whimsically, "all I want in a man is someone who rides bravely, dances beautifully, sings with vigor, reads passionately, and whose taste agrees in every point with my own."

Not such a bad aspiration, when all is said and done, thought C.J.

"And you have met him, Jane," the earl teased. "But fortunately—for Miss Welles's sake—he is your cousin!"

THE FOYER WAS A CRUSH of people rushing to crowd into the Tea Room to locate glasses of cold punch or warm negus, depending on their age and preference. As the evening progressed and the ballroom grew increasingly more populated, the temperature rose, causing many of the ladies in particular to require a cool refreshment. Apparently, the warmer the ballroom, the greater success the ball. The smell of sweat and of well-tanned leather, commingled with the aromas of various perfumes—from hyacinth to jasmine to rose to honeysuckle—was overpowering and not entirely pleasant. In fact, the odor did much to dampen C.J.'s appetite.

Mrs. Fairfax, with Miss Austen in tow, fairly elbowed her way past those who had recently been on the dance floor and were flushed from their terpsichorean exertions. The parvenue's husband was nowhere to be seen, having decided to avoid the crowd by remaining sedately in his chair along the wall of the ballroom, and trusting that his good wife would no doubt bring him his glass of wine soon enough. To endure her complaints about his complaisance was an acceptable barter for the punishment he would have had to suffer packed among hundreds of other patrons in a hot, stuffy anteroom.

"If there is anything disagreeable going on, men are always sure to get out of it," Miss Austen slyly remarked.

The two smaller parties had joined, and now C.J., Lady Dalrymple, and the Fairfax family brought their chairs over to where the Leigh-Perrots, their remarkable niece, Darlington, and the redoubtable Lady Oliver had positioned themselves earlier in the evening. The dragon was doing her best to create distance between her noble nephew and the object of his inappropriate fascination. Whenever Darlington attempted to maneuver himself closer to C.J., his aunt managed to insinuate herself between them or impede his advance by discreetly adjusting the angle of her chair.

Miss Austen seemed to derive a wicked little pleasure in bait-ing Mrs. Fairfax, who had not the slightest inkling she was a subject for the writer's gentle raillery. C.J. listened to Miss Fairfax prattle on about some inconsequential nonsense to Captain Keats. The girl appeared to have very few subjects, and a discussion of the merits of her military beau seemed to be the chief topic of any conversation she began. C.J. would have much preferred to spend the tea break enjoying the clever observations of Miss Austen. "I can never fathom why so many gentlemen seem to prefer such empty-headedness in women," she remarked to her new friend.

Jane squeezed C.J.'s hand and smiled beatifically in the direction of her handsome cousin. "A woman especially, if she have the misfortune of knowing anything, should conceal it as well as she can." Miss Austen then turned directly to the earl for confirmation of her assessment. "To the larger and more trifling part of your sex, imbecility in females is a great enhancement of their personal charms, and there is a portion of them too reasonable and too well informed themselves to desire anything more in woman than ignorance."

Darlington, however, was ready for the riposte, and C.J. was developing the opinion that the two cousins relished their banter as a sort of sport. "I will allow that a good deal of men may share the sentiment you have just expressed, Miss Jane, but as I have informed Miss Welles, I am not one of those gentlemen who disdains the company of intelligent women. To be sure, I often find greater stimulation in the sharing of ideas with one of the brighter members of the fairer sex than I do in the company of men, all of whom have been schooled to believe the same credos and frequent the same clubs."

C.J. smiled. "Then you are sui generis, your lordship."

He blinked at her use of a Latin phrase. It may have been in common usage, but issuing from her lips, it sounded uncommon indeed. What an extraordinary specimen of womanhood! The earl saw his opportunity to take advantage of his aunt's occupation in animated conversation with Lady Dalrymple. "Miss Welles, could you kindly spare me a moment or two of your time?" He rose on the pretext of obtaining another round of refreshments for their party, indicating with the merest inclination of his head and an intense expression in his eyes that he wished to speak to C.J. alone. The young lady rose as well, and the couple withdrew a few feet from their companions.

"Your lordship?"

"I shall come straight to the point, Miss Welles. I have already compromised you too much. That is what I desired to speak to you about."

"Compromised? How do you mean?"

"It was both forward and thoughtless of me to walk with you unchaperoned to your aunt's home a few mornings ago."

"But you assured me that every propriety was observed." Feeling wounded, C.J. looked up at Darlington, worrying that this might signify an immediate end to their acquaintance, which, brief as it had been, she had found exceedingly enjoyable. "I was not offended, nor did I feel in any way violated," she hastened to add.

"Your forgiving nature, Miss Welles, does not excuse my impertinence and my heedlessness. My waggishness could have caused you—an innocent and trusting party—irreparable harm. You are blameless of course, but it will not cease any censure. I am entirely at fault. If you and your aunt will permit me to call upon you, I shall take care in future to see that you are properly chaperoned. Miss Austen has but recently arrived in town and has lamented her lack of friends and companions here. She enjoys long walks and shopping expeditions as well as any young lady, and as you have expressed the wish to know her better, I shall endeavor to enlist her company so that you will not become exposed to idle gossip and speculation. And no doubt, her aunt, Mrs. Leigh-Perrot, who is equally fond of shopping, would also welcome an opportunity to show you the sights along Milsom Street."

"Percy." Lady Oliver's command had the effect of cold water on a wintry morning. "I should like some punch. Surely there must be some refreshments remaining."

"Happy to oblige, Aunt Augusta," Darlington replied as pleasantly as one might between clenched teeth.

The exchange did not pass unnoticed by Miss Austen. C.J. drew Jane aside to ask, "Whatever might I have done that Lady Oliver should so fear my association with her nephew? Surely I have never given her occasion to be displeased with me."

Jane took her new friend's hand. "Where there is a disposition to dislike, a motive will never be wanting." She shook her head and agreed that a specific objection might offer some degree of consolation. At least one knew where one stood, and why.

Mr. King opened the second half of the evening's dancing. According to Lady Dalrymple, he was ordinarily the Master of Ceremonies in the Lower Rooms. None of the young ladies in C.J.'s party wanted for a partner during the remainder of the evening; and in one instance, a red-faced but amiable gentleman led C.J. to the top of the longways set. She felt somewhat nervous in so prominent a position but summoned her theatrical training to overcome her anxiety. Thank goodness, the tune was "Apley House," one she had the good fortune to know well from her New York English country dance workshops. When it ended, the ladies, rosy-cheeked and giddy, made their way across the crowded dance floor to their chairs, although in the crush, Harriet Fairfax's gown was trod upon by a gentleman displaying the staggering effects of too much mirth.

"Sister, look!" cried Miss Susanne, pointing to Harriet's tattered hem.

"Oh dear!" Miss Fairfax surveyed her gown. "Mother! My best frock!"

Mrs. Fairfax rose to inspect the damage. "What a boor of a partner to tread so clumsily on my daughter's finest muslin. Don't you agree, Miss Welles? Still, had the offending gentleman been a man of means, it would have been a lucky turn of events," she loudly declaimed, and turning to her husband, who was looking upon his good wife's ranting with a degree of mild bemusement, added accusingly, "It's thanks to *you*, Mr. Fairfax, that a suitable class of gentlemen shies away from our girls."

"Mama, I should like Miss Welles to accompany me downstairs so that my gown may be repaired."

Miss Fairfax took C.J.'s hand and pointed the way to the retiring room where a few seamstresses remained on call, employed expressly to remedy such unhappy occasions. While her hem was being mended, Miss Fairfax treated C.J. to an enumeration of Captain Keats's finer attributes, not the least of which was his stunning scarlet coat with its buttons as shiny as newly minted coins.

When they returned to the ballroom, the earl was being presented by his aunt to a pretty young heiress identified by Miss Fairfax as Lady Charlotte Digby, and to an elegant couple in their forties who must have been Lady Charlotte's parents. Lady Digby, tall, with an angular face, was expensively gowned in seafoam-green silk. Her fashionable turban, striped in shades of pale green and rose, accentuated her regal cheekbones. The daughter, though fairer complected, clearly took after her rather than Lord Digby, a slightly florid gentleman with thinning auburn hair. The earl appeared to smile quite favorably upon Lady Charlotte, his manner nothing like the cool formality he had exhibited when he was introduced to the Miss Fairfaxes earlier in the evening.

C.J. suddenly felt sick to her stomach and doubted that it was the negus that was making her queasy, although she was admittedly unused to drinking the warm wine. Perhaps it was nothing more substantial than her intuition, but something about the picture before her made her heart sink. Preoccupied by the discomfiting scene, she returned to the Fairfaxes in the company of their elder daughter. Lady Dalrymple, who was pretending to listen to Mrs. Fairfax express her displeasure regarding the latest fashion of bonnets, was nevertheless keeping an interested eye and both ears on the conversation between Darlington and the Digbys.

It could not have been more than a minute later that the countess began to fan herself furiously. "Cassandra! I am having a pain!" she announced loudly, her hand flying to her heart.

C.J. paled. "Aunt—"

"Our carriage is not to arrive for another half hour at the earliest. I must return home as soon as possible so that I may loosen my stays and lie down in comfort." C.J. bent over her "aunt" to assure her that she would do everything in her power to see her home swiftly and safely. "Here, Niece," Lady Dalrymple exclaimed, pressing C.J.'s hand to her chest. "Feel how my heart palpitates."

In the fuss that ensued as the other members of their party scrambled to give the countess some air, her ladyship's hand firmly encircled her "niece's" delicate wrist, pulling the young lady toward her. She winked at C.J.

The young woman gasped. "I beg you never to do that again! You gave me such a dreadful fright," she whispered. The countess was embarking on another performance equal to her elaborate improvisation in Lady Wickham's drawing room. Miss Welles was beginning to wonder which of them was the greater, or more prolific, play-actor—herself or her eccentric benefactress.

Darlington had hastily excused himself from the Digbys and now approached C.J. and the countess, a study in solicitousness. "Miss Welles, may I be of some assistance?"

C.J. looked up at him, her eyes swimming with gratitude, until something in his expression made her realize that the earl seemed somehow in on the game. What, C.J. wondered, had transpired between his lordship and Lady Dalrymple when she had repaired downstairs with Miss Fairfax?

"Lady Dalrymple, may I offer the use of my carriage? I find that I, too, must leave the assembly posthaste, and it would grieve me terribly should anything happen to you while you were waiting for your own equipage to arrive. It is but a small distance from the Royal Crescent to my town house in the Circus, so you will not be putting me to any hardship."

The countess gratefully clasped Darlington's hands in her own. "Oh, your lordship," she gushed. "I am most grateful for your kind generosity. Are you absolutely certain you will not be too much incommoded by the aches and pains of an old woman?"

C.J. thought that perhaps her "aunt" might be hamming it up a tad, but the rest of their party did not seem the slightest bit suspicious, or even remotely aware, of the charade being enacted before their eyes.

The Digbys and Lady Oliver, several yards away on the opposite side of the ballroom, appeared unconcerned with Lady Dalrymple's discomfort. Evidently, claims of bosom friendship notwithstanding, Darlington's aunt elected not to join the others in expressing concern for the countess's health. Whatever subject she was discussing with the Digbys evidently took precedence.

Her ladyship was graciously helped from her chair by her "niece" and Lord Darlington, who supported her on either side as they made their way to Darlington's handsome black and burgundy barouche. His exit went unnoticed by his ordinarily hawkeyed aunt. Darlington exchanged a few words with his coachman, then handed in Lady Dalrymple and offered an assist to C.J. before ascending himself, taking the seat facing the countess and her niece.

Indeed, it was not a long ride to the Royal Crescent. The coachman halted at Lady Dalrymple's door and rang a bell produced from a pocket in his voluminous coat. Folsom came out of the house to open the carriage door for his mistress and assist her descent, handing C.J. down as well.

C.J. looked back at Darlington, who had joined them on the pavement. "I am most grateful to your lordship for your kindness toward my aunt," she said softly.

The night air smelled of jasmine. How wonderful to discover that it bloomed in Bath! Lady Dalrymple surveyed the young people before her. "Cassandra, it is quite musty inside the house. I have not been airing the rooms as often as is my wont, due to my condition. Perhaps you should like to take an evening constitutional before retiring. You are no doubt fatigued from dancing and enduring the crush and the heat in the Assembly

Rooms; the night air will renew your spirits. I shall have Cook make a tisane for me. You may bid me a good night at your leisure."

The coachman gave a short command, and the horses advanced several paces, creating a discreet distance between the carriage and the couple.

"Your aunt is a better actor than her brother was," remarked Darlington slyly, as the dowager entered her town house. He gave C.J. a searching look as if to ask, "May I?" before he reached for her hand.

In an instant she was enfolded in his arms, inhaling the heady combination of the perfumed night air and the earl's own musky scent. This was not the time to play the surprised virgin. "My lord," she whispered, as her lips met his with the same eagerness, her tongue performing the same ardent dance as his. Yielding and pliant to his desire, she felt Darlington's body, hard and muscular against hers, enveloping her softness.

His hands expertly roamed from the small of her back, tracing the curves of her supple torso, up through her hair, sending tingles down her spine, while he pocketed a handful of tortoiseshell pins that had secured her upswept curls. His tapered finger twirled a glossy tendril. C.J. felt no regrets about succumbing to her hunger for his touch, for the taste of his mouth on hers, or for the craving his body inspired in her. She was masquerading as the daughter of a dissolute marquess, but she didn't also have to pretend she was coy about sex. Not now.

Darlington tenderly kissed each eyelid, allowing C.J.'s soft lashes to flutter against his lips. "Percy," she whispered, addressing him in the most familiar way. It flouted all rules of decorum to use his nickname, but to do otherwise under the circumstances would have been ludicrous. At that moment she would have surrendered herself to him entirely without any hesitation.

"Sweet, sweet Miss Welles." Darlington's hand traced a path down her cheek. "So soft," he whispered, "like the petal of a rose. Sometimes, I admit, you confound me, but Mr. King—the Master of Ceremonies—was right. You *are* an 'original.'"

"I can assure you, sir, that Mr. King and I have never embraced like that," C.J. teased. "Nevertheless, I shall take your remark as a compliment."

And then it was as though a cloud had passed between them and lingered in the air. The earl became quite formal, stepping back a pace or so, leaving C.J. utterly confused by such a profound shift in his manner. "Miss Welles, in my position in society there is only one way that I may consider it proper to address you more familiarly, and for that I must speak to your aunt."

"More familiarly than that kiss? And I am of age, your lordship." C.J. smiled. "Were there any doubt in your mind."

"In that case, I shall advise you of the nature of the conversation I intend to have with Lady Dalrymple." He seemed to pause for emphasis. "While I allow that we have known each other for only a brief space of time, I have spent enough hours in your company to have been able to arrive at an informed decision. I may appear to you, Miss Welles, to be a propertied man of leisure. That is certainly true in many respects; nevertheless, I also pride myself on being a man of action. And as I mentioned to you in one of our prior conversations, I am one who derives immense pleasure from acts of discovery. Therefore, tomorrow morning I shall ask your aunt if I may pay my addresses to you."

Why not. Why the hell not?

He was answered with a spontaneous cry of joy and a passionate embrace. What followed were many kisses and sighs and the promise of a pastoral promenade the following day. C.J. hated to part company with him and stood outside Lady Dalrymple's town house watching the earl's barouche traverse the modest length of Brock Street until it rounded the Circus and disappeared from view. Had she been capable of becoming airborne, she would have giddily floated all the way to Lady Dalrymple's beloved moon.

Yet not a half hour later, C.J. paced the floor of her chamber trying to figure out how, or even whether, to tell Owen Percival the truth.

AT TEN O'CLOCK the next morning, C.J., who had passed a sleepless night, was taking breakfast with her "aunt" in the sunny front drawing room when Collins entered, bearing a cream-colored note on a silver salver. "This just arrived for you, Miss Welles," the butler announced.

"Thank you, Collins." She gingerly lifted the folded note from the tray and turned it over to inspect the seal. Lady Dalrymple instantly recognized the Earl of Darlington's burgundy and black crest embossed and outlined in gold leaf at the top of the sheet of vellum. After scanning the note to see if it contained anything of an exceptionally personal nature, C.J. shared the missive's contents with the countess.

> *Miss Welles,*
>
> *I regret to postpone our engagement to parade in Sydney Gardens this afternoon; however, Miss Austen remains delighted to accompany you and I hope to join the two cleverest young ladies in Bath, albeit at a later hour than I had anticipated. Please accept my apologies if I have caused you even a moment's disappointment.*
>
> *With fond thoughts,*
> *Darlington*

C.J. refolded the note and looked at Lady Dalrymple.

"Perhaps I should have signed it 'Percy,'" a warm baritone voice teased, as the earl himself entered the room.

"Why did you send Collins in with a note?" C.J. asked.

"I was afraid you might turn wrathful at the prospect of a temporary setback in our plans," he smiled. "I must make certain arrangements today that interfere with our appointed hour of rendezvous, but the morning's most pressing engagement of all could not be postponed." Darlington then greeted Lady Dalrymple, depositing a kiss on both of her cheeks. "May I say, Aunt Euphoria, that you are indeed the picture of health. I am greatly encouraged to see you so fully restored in so short a time."

Lady Dalrymple blushed. "Fie, Percy, only you have this effect on me. And under the present circumstances, I think you should consider an alternative term of endearment for me. I cannot have both of you calling me Aunt Euphoria, can I?"

"I don't see why not. But if I may be so bold, I can only hope that it will soon be acceptable for Miss Welles to address Lady Oliver as Aunt Augusta."

C.J. spluttered into her coffee. The delicate Wedgwood cup teetered on its saucer. "I do not think your aunt fancies me," she said, recovering her poise and hoping his lordship had not observed her unmannerly reaction.

"Nonsense," Darlington smiled slightly. "She fancies no one." He was only half joking. "Aunt Euphoria, I have come to pay a call of a particular nature upon you this morning—and perhaps it is proper for your niece to absent herself from—"

"Felicity?" C.J. interjected sweetly, unable to resist the Shakespearean reference.

"—the *room*, so that I may speak to you privately."

"Don't be silly, Percy. Cassandra is not a child. Unless you plan to say something that would surprise one of us, I see no reason not to throw custom to the hounds. Let my niece continue to enjoy her eggs and porridge before they become cold and inedible; otherwise you will also incur the wrath of my cook!"

"Since you phrase it so delicately," Darlington began, "last night I gave Miss Welles an inclination of what I intended to say to you, in case she should not feel kindly disposed toward me . . . and it appears to be the case that Miss Welles is quite . . ." Darlington twisted his signet ring. "I feel like a schoolboy. Here I am, a widower, closer to forty than thirty, and I have become tongue-tied. I confess to both of you gentle ladies that I had not anticipated being at a loss for words, even under the circumstances."

"Shall I make it easy for him, Cassandra? Come, Percy, I

trust I am not mistaken in the hope that my niece and I have a rather good notion of what you wish to say to me."

C.J. drew herself up into as elegant a posture as possible, a playful sense of triumph in her dark eyes, and regarded Lady Dalrymple. "Oh no, Aunt," she insisted impishly. "All my life I have waited to hear such words. I daresay every woman feels quite the same way. You would not *deprive* me of that pleasure?"

The countess looked at Darlington. "Speak, Percy. 'Tis your cue."

"The paces you women put us poor menfolk through," he sighed.

"Aunt" and "niece" exchanged a mischievous glance.

Darlington affected an elegant bow. "Lady Dalrymple, although I have known her a comparatively short time, I should like to pay my addresses to your niece, Cassandra Jane Welles, with your kind permission and the fervent hope that you will do everything in your power to encourage my suit."

"Heavens, Percy! Why did you not say so before?" The countess emitted a full-throated laugh. Darlington and C.J. joined in.

When he recovered himself, the earl apologized to his hostesses for his need to depart their mirthful company, and promised that he would endeavor to meet up with Cassandra and Miss Austen in Sydney Gardens as soon as his plans would allow. There seemed to be a spring in his step as he left Lady Dalrymple's lemon-yellow drawing room.

"I did do the right thing, yes?"

"Yes, you did, Aunt," C.J. acknowledged softly. "And I am very, very happy. But has it not been your design from the first?"

Lady Dalrymple sighed dramatically. "And here I thought that for all my years, I was still a woman of mystery."

C.J. gave her "aunt" a warm hug. "Have no fear in that regard, your ladyship."

The women resumed their repast. C.J. much admired the countess's "lady pamper" table, purpose-built so that two ladies could cozily breakfast and gossip across from one another in their respective chairs while enjoying all the comforts of a more commodious piece of furniture, owing to the table's shelves and crannies. What a pity, C.J. thought, that such a table—and the custom—would one day go the way of the dinosaur. Somehow, Lady Dalrymple's cook had procured a melon—a most exotic addition to the meal. How different it tasted from the bland hot-house fruit that was all C.J. had known in her other life. The ripe melon drizzled its juice down her chin, and she caught it with her finger, then licked it off, savoring the sticky sweetness. C.J. took another spoonful of melon and paused, midbite. "Aunt Euphoria, if I have indeed entered into an understanding with Lord Darlington, I should like to know everything about his family and connections, for curiosity's sake if nothing else. You referred to Lady Oliver as the subject—or perhaps the object—of some dreadful scandal. I have often wondered about her, since, for all her thorniness, you still esteem her and claim her for a bosom friend."

Lady Dalrymple stirred some cream into her coffee with a delicate silver spoon, dramatically replacing it on her saucer before she began to speak. "Augusta Arundel had the misfortune to be the firstborn into a family where beauty was prized above all else." The countess nibbled the edge of a rout drop cake. The currant-studded cookies infused with rosewater and sherry were an especial favorite of hers.

"Gustie was serious and thoughtful; and even then, as girl-hood friends, she admired me as much for my mirthful nature as I envied her seemingly endless capacity for pragmatism and practicality. Abigail and Arabel, her inseparable twin sisters—dark-haired, blue-eyed beauties two years Gustie's junior—were lively and loud, quite the opposite of their older sibling. Gustie became a handsome woman, though she never had the delicate prettiness of her twin sisters, nor was she the darling of every ball and the delight of every male, suitable or otherwise, within a fortnight's journey of Sussex. Naturally, it was a tremendous surprise to all when Oliver offered for her. He was a notorious rake and the devil's own gambler. Oliver could win and lose an inheritance all in the same night. Many a rascal wondered what he could possibly have found to fancy in Augusta Arundel, but there was wide speculation that Oliver's father had threatened to disinherit him if he did not sober up and settle down by his twenty-fifth birthday."

C.J. pursed her lips. "Did Augusta know about Oliver's reputation?"

"If she had, it would not have made a bit of a difference. Arundel was a strict adherent to the custom of the firstborn to be the first wed, and, in fact, he was tremendously relieved to be rid of an aging spinster who was neither a beauty nor a wit. Both fathers had agreed upon the match. The wishes of the future bride and groom were not a matter of consideration. What just transpired in this room, Cassandra, is not the customary manner of courtship. I had a sixth sense, if you will, that you and Lord Darlington would suit, and it did not take long to prove my intuition correct. Percy has endured a great deal of unhappiness and upheaval in his life and, of late, has finally begun to regain the humor for which he was once so admired. Your mirthful outlook upon the world, your strength, compassion, and capacity for quick comprehension, in addition to your obvious grace and beauty, make you an ideal match."

"I shall do everything in my power, Aunt, never to disappoint his lordship," C.J. said, painfully aware that if she could manage to return to her own century, it would be inevitable for her to go back on her promise. In the most literal sense, it was only a matter of time.

Chapter Thirteen

In which we learn more of Lady Oliver's misfortunes, our heroine takes a stroll through Sydney Gardens with Miss Austen and has a delicious encounter in the maze, and Lord Darlington admits that his past contains a secret.

Despite her private misgivings, C.J. tried to take comfort in her "aunt's" complete certainty and pressed her for further details about Darlington's misunderstood distaff relation. "Then what happened with Augusta and Oliver? Clearly, they did marry, since she is Lady Oliver."

"It was the wedding of the season," Lady Dalrymple explained. "But the embers on the marital hearth were barely banked when Oliver bolted, abandoning his new bride. If the match had been purely for pragmatic purposes, Augusta might have been better able to bear her burden, but she had become quite smitten with the rake and truly believed his fervent declarations of love. Having never received the ardent attentions of *any* suitor, Gustie was completely taken in. To compound the betrayal, Oliver had absconded with *both* of Augusta's younger sisters."

"Well, you did say that Abigail and Arabel shared *everything*,"

C.J. commented, attempting to conceal her shock. She had read a good deal about the Georgian era being a licentious time, compared with later periods, but a scandal along the magnitude of the aftermath of Lady Oliver's nuptials would have even shocked Hollywood.

"I suppose, Cassandra, that this was their last act of sharing. The day after the wedding, the three of them fled to Switzerland, leaving Augusta to mourn her loss and face the censorious world alone."

"And her sisters?"

"Scandalized. Entirely ruined."

C.J.'s eyes widened.

"And Oliver had his father to rights regarding his inheritance," the countess continued. "He had indeed wed before his twenty-fifth birthday; the ceremony was legal, and there was nothing the father could do to renege on the bargain he had made with his renegade son. So Oliver inherited the land and the title, and his bride of one night earned the right to be called Lady Oliver."

C.J. shook her head. "And Owen Percival—Percy is . . . ?"

"Abigail's son. His mother sent him back to England to be raised by his austere aunt so that he could take his place in society. His younger brother, Jack, later earned the same privilege."

"But Percy is the Earl of Darlington. Then he was not Oliver's son?"

"For the briefest space of time that was thought to be the case. However, soon after the Arundel sisters arrived in Switzerland, Oliver tired of Abigail and concentrated his attentions on Arabel. She lived as his paramour after Lord Arundel successfully petitioned the Consistory Court in London for a divorce *a mensa et thoro* on behalf of his eldest daughter. The twins never spoke to each other again. The bohemian Abigail recovered from her broken heart with astonishing alacrity and married Peregrine Percival, Lord Darlington, the adventurer who had gotten her with child a few months after her departure from Oliver's *ménage*. Percy was born legitimate, though conceived as a love child. His parents permitted him to join them on their archaeological excursions in countries as far-flung as India, believing the experiences there would expand his educational horizons better than any tutor might do. During Percy's early childhood, both Peregrine and Abigail, possessed with a certain wanderlust, traveled the world over while their eldest son was afforded the finest opportunities and an English education under the exalted eye of his abandoned aunt."

C.J. assayed one of the rout drop cakes, which she discovered tasted more of fragrance than flavor. Perhaps it was the rosewater. She lifted the heavy silver coffee pot and poured for her "aunt," filling the cup only halfway.

The dowager topped off her cup with cream. "Like Portly and me, the elder Percival was one of those aristocrats who enjoyed flouting convention. Some considered him merely eccentric, but most branded him outrageous. Yet Peregrine never laid store by what others thought of him. You must know, Niece, it is endemic to the Percival men that once they fall in love—no matter what unfortunate circumstances may have befallen the object of their affections—rabid dogs could not dampen, diminish, or dissolve the desire to woo and win their ladyloves. It's quite medieval!" Lady Dalrymple said gleefully. "To my memory, every Lady Darlington has had a 'past,' and nonetheless, the Percivals have pursued each of them like the Holy Grail."

"Where is everyone now?" C.J. asked curiously, thinking that *her* past would trump them all.

"Gone. All dead, except for Augusta and Percy. Arabel died of ague in 1791. A year later, Oliver took a nasty fall down a flight of stairs and never recovered. Abigail and Peregrine both perished during a devastating monsoon in India. The old earl—Peregrine—left his estate, Delamere, in quite a shambles too."

"What kind of divorce did you say Lady Oliver won?"

"*A mensa et thoro.* One can only obtain a divorce by petitioning the ecclesiastical court assigned to handle such matters. Lord Arundel's solicitors appeared on behalf of him and his daughter at the Consitory Court in Doctors' Commons in

London. Neither spouse may testify, and only the aristocracy has access to such a procedure. It is extremely costly, but as Arundel was quite close to the Archbishop of Canterbury, who sat just a few feet away from him in the House of Lords, several special dispensations that are 'not on the books,' as they say, were granted him."

Lady Dalrymple smiled slyly. "Nothing, of course, should be inferred by his lordship's sudden and extreme generosity to the Church by way of a rather large land grant. The nature of Augusta's decree permits neither spouse to ever remarry, but effects a separation that is legally recognized by the Church of England."

C.J. could not stop shaking her head in wonderment at the magnitude of the scandal. "I suppose Augusta never spoke to her sisters after that fateful day?"

"Only as concerned Abigail's son. She never again exchanged a word with her estranged husband. Everything was settled by the legal representatives on either side." Lady Dalrymple placed her coffee cup on the large silver tray. "Which reminds me. I must make arrangements to speak with my solicitor."

"And I suppose I should dress for my promenade with Miss Austen," C.J. proposed. She beamed in anticipation of her adventure.

C.J. REGARDED HER reflection in the gilt-framed mirror as she remade her toilette. She was accustomed to wearing considerably more makeup than was thought appropriate for young ladies, particularly in this era of naturalism where women were expected to resemble either country lasses or classical statues, neither of which were known for their overuse of powder and paint. The cosmetics now available to her were lead based anyway, so it was probably a good thing to avoid them as much as possible. But oh, my kingdom for a few modern tubes of lipstick and mascara! she thought. Pinching her cheeks as a substitute for a pot of rouge had thus far resulted in more bruises than blushes. As she studied her image, she replayed the morning's events. "Heavens!" to quote Lady Dalrymple's outspoken parrot. She went to her writing table, unable to resist the temptation to see what "Cassandra Jane Percival, Lady Darlington" would look like in print, then sanded the signature to hasten the drying of the ink and prevent its smudging. Smiling, she noted that her penmanship had vastly improved. Would that she could flaunt it under Lady Wickham's nasty beak.

"MY IDEA OF GOOD COMPANY is the company of clever, well-informed people who have a great deal of conversation," Miss Austen sighed extravagantly, as she walked arm in arm with C.J. under a bright sky punctuated with fluffy, cumulus clouds. They strolled past Sydney House, a hotel within the beautiful Sydney Gardens boasting a ballroom, card rooms, coffee and tea rooms, as well as a taproom in the cellar where weary chair carriers and coachmen could while away a spare hour in leisurely pursuits. How many trusting souls, C.J. wondered, had imperiled their lives at the shaky hands of chauffeurs who had been tippling away the afternoon?

Miss Austen was enjoying her first outing in her newly made round gown, which she fancied so well that she was considering having the same pattern made up in a lighter color. C.J. was amused to discover what an eye for fashion her companion displayed. She empathized completely when Jane lamented that her financial constraints ill afforded the opportunity to present herself to the world in as stylish a fashion as she would have preferred, still owning, for example, an outmoded accessory she was now loath to wear in public: a three-year-old coquelicot shawl!

C.J. unsuccessfully suppressed a grin. This afternoon was the fulfillment of one of her lifelong fantasies. To be alone in the company of *Jane Austen* (and, of all things, talking with her about shopping on a budget!) and, better still, to form a part of the novelist's circle of relations, friends, and acquaintances! It was sheer, unalloyed ecstasy.

On observing the amber cross that C.J. wore about her neck, Jane was given to remark that she had just received a letter from her brother Charles, who, as a naval lieutenant on the *Endymion,* was entitled to a financial share of the prize money from the capture of *La Furie,* a French privateer. She expressed the hope of conveying this information in a letter to her sister, who, she remarked, shared the same Christian name with Miss Welles.

They strolled past the maze, a labyrinthine construction of hedges, which, for C.J.'s edification, Jane identified as one of Bath's most notorious spots for assignations, illicit or otherwise. C.J. wondered if an assignation could be anything *but* illicit. "I confess that the merest mention of the word *illicit* makes me desire to venture forth," C.J. confided, and elected to explore it immediately. Jane declined to join her, preferring to sit quietly on a nearby bench, as she wished to make some notes to herself and perhaps compose that letter to her sister.

C.J. entered the web of foliage and journeyed deeper and deeper toward its center. The hedges were so high that one could not see over them, reminding her of the mazes at Hampton Court and Leeds Castle; and within a matter of minutes, she had completely lost her way. As everything looked the same, her sense of direction had become entirely unbalanced. Frustrated, she released a vocally trained cry for help that could no doubt be heard well beyond the confines of the leafy configuration.

"Miss Welles, is that you?" a voice called.

"Yes. Your lordship?"

"Stay where you are. I shall come and find you," Darlington announced; and it could not have been more than two or three minutes, though it felt like an eternity, before his arm protectively encircled her waist. "I have always been rather an ace with puzzles," he confided with a twinkle in his eye.

"Miss Austen informed me that this was quite a popular place for romantic assignations," C.J. said, tilting her chin up at the nobleman. "Did you deliberately arrange this with her? I thought she was above such complicity."

"I hope you have no quarrel with my cousin, Miss Welles. The blame rests entirely with me. I merely suggested to Miss Austen that you might enjoy the maze."

"Perhaps it is not the custom for ladies of quality to demonstrate such wanton behavior, but I prefer a good romp to maidenly reserve any day, your lordship."

"I suppose that means you wish me to kiss you."

Actually, C.J. was ready to be tumbled on the ground, right then and there. "If you did not enjoy last night's encounter at my aunt's doorstep, I should be loath to force you to repeat it, your lordship."

Decorum mattered very little to either of them right now. How could she possibly be expected to conservatively revert to a nonsensical modesty? *If God had not wanted men and women to desire one another,* C.J. reasoned, *the world would literally be a barren landscape.*

Darlington needed very little encouragement. One look from C.J. gave license to his hands to explore every curve of her until she felt she would burst the confines of her diaphanous white dress. The sensations he produced when he nuzzled her neck were most delicious indeed, and when he darted his tongue in and out of her ear, then sought her mouth with his warm lips, devouring her with hungry kisses, she was brought, pulse racing, heart pounding, to the very brink of ecstasy.

When they finally broke their embrace, C.J. feared that her inevitably disheveled appearance when they exited the maze might raise some eyebrows. "Oh dear," C.J. sighed contentedly. "What you must think of me, Percy?"

"I think of you as the woman who has accepted my suit and thus evinces a desire to share my bed in future. If you were to reward my embraces with a chilly reception, I should be forced to rethink my good opinions of you."

"I don't suppose many gently bred young ladies behave as I have been acting these past twenty-four hours."

The earl smiled. "You would be surprised, Miss Welles. Your behavior is not only perfectly natural, it is as God intended, or the world would never be peopled. It must be said, however, that what takes place behind hedgerows ought never to be paraded in public assemblies, as you were made well aware last night."

The earl expertly led the way out of the labyrinth, and the couple found Jane on the bench where C.J. had left her, making tiny notes with a pencil on a scrap of paper, which, upon noting their arrival, she immediately replaced without comment in her reticule.

Jane greeted her cousin; and discreetly discerning a blush upon Cassandra's cheek and perhaps a stray curl or two, hinted that if there was an understanding between Miss Welles and her cousin, she would be quite content to remain where she was while they enjoyed the rare opportunity of an unchaperoned stroll through the gardens. Lord Darlington confirmed her suspicions, then offered his arm to Miss Welles. Miss Austen waved them a fond farewell and removed her notes from her reticule.

The lovers traipsed over the sloping, manicured lawns, the earl supporting C.J. as she negotiated the occasional stone or uneven patch of terrain in her fragile leather slippers, stopping to rest when they neared a row of stone balusters. Darlington twisted his signet ring in a display of discomfort. "This is not an easy subject for me to broach, Miss Welles, especially with you, but it is precisely with you that I must share these thoughts and feelings."

They leaned against the carved baluster, and C.J. felt a knot begin to tie itself within her stomach. The earl read her expression. "I hope that my saga of woe will not give you cause for alarm, but rather illustrate certain facts about my past. You may decide for yourself whether or not you still esteem my character after you hear them. Frankly, I had never expected to meet a young lady who so captured my interest. Heretofore, I have long considered that part of my life over."

He sounded like a lawyer. C.J. set her jaw and prepared for the worst.

"Our . . . courtship . . . is proceeding more along the lines of

Cousin Jane's theories of romance, rather than my own, Miss Welles. I have asked and you have allowed me to pay my addresses to you without your knowing very much about me at all. It does you credit, I suppose, to take me at face value, as it were . . . but I cannot avoid feeling that a selfishness on my part in withholding information from you concerning my past places you at a disadvantage, which, I have determined . . . after agonizing over the decision . . . is unfair."

C.J. tried not to appear impatient with his maddening ability to be circumspect, struggling to keep her expression one of placid concern, rather than betray her anxiety. In a way it was hard not to pity Darlington's difficulty in expressing whatever it was he wished to confess to her.

"Miss Welles, it is no secret that I was once married and that I am now a widower. My wife was . . . not the kind of woman who enjoyed a favorable regard among our set, owing to two accidents: one of birth, and one of profession. Marguerite, although a noblewoman—the sister of a count—was a Frenchwoman." He lowered his voice. "She was also an actress."

Chapter Fourteen

*Darlington continues to reveal the details of his own painful
past, followed by a fortuitous interruption, and the rather
sensuous results yielded by a sudden rainstorm.*

C.J.'S EYES WIDENED and she emitted a little gasp.

"I did not mean to shock you, Miss Welles," Darlington hastily interjected. "I had formed the assumption that you were a more open-minded young lady. Forgive me if I was incorrect."

"No—no, it is not that at all," C.J. insisted, wondering if her own secret could be read on her face as easily as if it were emblazoned there. "Go on, please."

"My late wife, Marguerite, was one of two sisters of the Comte de Feuillide, the man who married Miss Austen's relation Eliza. Fiercely independent, Marguerite made a name for herself at the Comédie-Française. I myself was one of the most ardent admirers of her talent, finally screwing up the courage to ask if she would permit me to call upon her one night in her dressing room after one of her luminous performances in *Tartuffe*.

"When the Terror began in Paris, I insisted that she remain with me in England. We were extremely happy together, but

Marguerite missed her life upon the stage. Her command of the English language was not secure enough for her to gain similar employment here; besides which, because she was a nobleman's wife, her profession was severely frowned upon by the British aristocracy."

"What happened?" C.J. asked softly.

"We lived in London for two more years, but Marguerite grew increasingly homesick. In 1794, against all my fervent entreaties, she crossed the Channel alone, as I had affairs to attend to that kept me in England. When news of the bloodshed in France reached me, I chartered a vessel to Calais. In cover of darkness I rode straight through to Paris, for it was known on the Continent that I was Marguerite de Feuillide's husband, and therefore an 'aristo' myself, although the Republic could not officially execute members of the English nobility."

Percy's voice became choked with emotion. "There had been a time . . . long before I met Marguerite . . . when she was little more than a girl, that an idealistic young firebrand, a member of the *sans-culottes*, had turned her head. Emile LeFevre was thoroughly smitten with her, and his Gallic charm was nearly enough to persuade her to abandon her own family and to follow the principles of the new Republic. Marguerite went so far in accepting the merits of LeFevre's beliefs as to flout the aristocratic Feuillide pedigree and pursue her ambition to enter the theatre. Her suitor was pleased with her apparent conversion from aristo to citizeness, but soon his zealotry for the Republican ideals— which were blossoming into a bloodthirsty form of misplaced revenge against the nobility—caused Marguerite to fear LeFevre, and she attempted to bring a halt to the attentions he was paying her."

Darlington anxiously ran a hand through his thick dark hair. Reliving the devastating events of his past was understandably an arduous task. "Marguerite and I met soon after she had requested LeFevre to leave her be. The Frenchman mistakenly believed I had come between them, and he detested me for being an Englishman, for being an aristocrat, and for the alleged theft of his true love. From that time forth, he did everything in his power to destroy Marguerite and me—and by extension, any of her family. When Marguerite returned to Paris to perform at the Comédie-Française, it was Emile LeFevre who gave the names of his former amour and her entire aristocratic family, including her brother—Eliza's husband—to Robespierre's Committee for Public Safety."

"Good God," C.J. whispered, horrified.

"Marguerite and her brother had been taken to the Bastille by the time I arrived in Paris. In 1794, the Terror had reached fever pitch. My efforts to negotiate with—even bribe—every Frenchman from the penurious jailers to the petty officers to Robespierre himself were jeered at. If attempts to secure their release failed, I had plotted an escape for them, but—to the misfortune of all—it was detected. One could not even trust the priests then. On the morning of the execution, I was escorted by armed citizens of the Republic to the Place de la Concorde, where I was forced, at point of bayonet, to watch my beautiful, talented wife and her brother, the Comte de Feuillide, beheaded by Madame la Guillotine, 'guilty' of nothing other than having been born into the aristocracy. Perhaps now, Miss Welles, you can more fully apprehend my revulsion for the French and for the fatal influence of the American rebels." Darlington angrily scuffed a rut into the pebbled ground with the toe of his boot. He found himself unable to look into C.J.'s eyes.

There was a gulf of silence between them.

"I'm so sorry," C.J. said softly. This was not the time to embark on a political diatribe or another impassioned defense of democracy.

"I have not grown so fond of you, Miss Welles, simply because your aunt favors the match. The woman who I feel will give me the utmost happiness has the right to know my past. To embark upon anything more than a friendship with storm clouds of mystery between us is, to my mind, dishonest."

"Why should you have feared that I would find defects in your character owing to what you have just imparted?"

"Perhaps you feel that I should have compelled my wife to remain by my side in England. It would have saved her life," he said bitterly.

"No woman can be truly happy married to a tyrant who keeps her under lock and key, regardless of whether he claims it is for her own good. Trust me, Percy. You *did* do the only proper thing. Marguerite knew the risks, and took them regardless . . . and although I never had the privilege to know her, or to see her on the stage, I am sorry for you both."

The earl took her hands in his. "Thank you," he murmured. As he had hoped, Miss Welles did ease some of his burden. Perhaps it was a form of forgiveness he sought from her, as she was not his first love. Or perhaps it was the freedom to unburden his soul without the fear of her judging him. After he returned to England, it had not been in his plans to ever remarry. His solitude, he felt, was a deserved penance for being unable to prevent the murders of Marguerite and her family. Then Lady Dalrymple introduced him to the remarkable Miss Welles, and he began to reconsider his promise to himself.

The earl continued his discourse, recognizing, as he spoke, how parallel were some of the branches on his family tree. "Miss Austen's cousin, born Eliza Hancock, who is presently married to Jane's favorite brother, Frank, was Eliza de Feuillide, the count's wife, until his execution. She was spared from the blade because she was an Englishwoman. So you see, we mourn, but we move on. If one were only capable of a single great love, it would be a tragedy. For think how many people experience that love when they are very young and, suffering disappointment, spend the remainder of their years alone, grieving or bitter. Take my aunt Augusta, for instance."

Or take Jane, who never moved on after losing Tom Lefroy. She is a tragic heroine such as you have just described. But C.J. could not say the words. It was one story she would never tell. Would that she *did* have the power to alter Jane's romantic history. One of the worst things about her nineteenth-century existence was the possession of knowledge she would be happier not to own. "Lady Dalrymple confided Lady Oliver's unfortunate history just this morning. Your aunt does not approve of me," C.J. observed.

"As I mentioned to you once before, she does not approve of anyone. It is a tone she has adopted for decades to shield herself from further injury. Not knowing her, one would think her impervious, when in truth, the very opposite is the case. She is as fragile as sugarpane. Shall we walk on?" Darlington offered C.J. his arm as they continued to wend their way through the lush gardens. After a considerable distance, the earl halted their progress to admire a half dozen men and women clad in light-colored clothes, thoroughly enjoying themselves on one of the manicured lawns. A gleeful young woman clapped her hands as she successfully knocked away a gentleman's ball, bringing her own black spheroid inches closer to the small white ball at the end of the bowling green.

"Lady Charlotte Digby," Darlington informed his companion, as he nodded in the direction of the giddy young bowler. "Her uncle, Admiral Henry Digby, is a highly decorated officer in His Majesty's navy."

"Yes, I heard her name mentioned at the assembly. You were speaking with her and her parents at the time, I believe."

"The Digbys are especial friends of my aunt's. Lady Charlotte is her godchild."

"Ahh. The black ones look a bit like cannonballs," C.J. remarked, trying to suppress a pang of jealousy as she observed the game. "Do you not think so, sir?"

"Indeed," the earl mused. "I had not thought of it in that way before. And I should be quite content if I never clapped eyes on a cannonball again. Although some explosions can be quite spectacular. Have you ever seen a fireworks display, Miss Welles?"

"Oh yes," she replied enthusiastically, although she would have liked to continue their earlier discussion. But, by degrees, she was slowly getting used to not "pushing." She was becoming less American. Less twenty-first century. This behavioral modification was like wearing a new garment. It pinched and pulled at times in all the wrong places, and she still had trouble deciding if it suited her.

Darlington looked somewhat disappointed with her response. "Silly of me to imagine that you had never seen fireworks. As you are accustomed to life in London, you have surely seen that sort of spectacular pageantry. I confess that I foolishly had hoped to escort you to your very first experience at such an exhibition. They are regularly held on midsummer evenings, right where we stand."

"No . . . I meant . . ." *'Twere well it were done quickly,* C.J. thought to herself. "Your lordship, if this afternoon is a time for us to be honest with one another, then it is only proper that—"

Lord Darlington took C.J.'s hand and regarded her imploringly. "I beg of you not to distress yourself. I know what you are about to say, Miss Welles."

How could he? C.J. wondered. It was impossible. And before she could utter a word, the earl returned to the subject of his stunning admission. "Miss Welles, I have yet another confession to make." His cadences accelerated as though he feared she might interrupt at any moment. "Miss Welles, while it is true that we never met before your aunt introduced us at tea the other day, I admit to having seen you before then. On one prior occasion."

C.J.'s heart sank into the earth beneath her feet. She had expected the worst, even believed she was prepared for its eventual announcement, but never had she felt so entirely bereft. Of words. Of explanations. Of hope.

"Lady Cassandra, I first became fascinated by your remarkable gifts when I glimpsed you before the bar at the assizes. The country proceedings keep me in touch with the concerns of the lower classes." He noticed C.J.'s face, now streaked with tears, and touched a finger to her chin to tip her gaze to his. "You were in such an unfortunate state, accused without benefit of a serjeant-at-law to plead for you. Your transgression was so entirely understandable to any sensible soul." Darlington removed his glove and gently wiped away C.J.'s tears with his fingers. "You may be assured, Miss Welles, that once I discovered your true identity, I endeavored to purchase, and then destroy, as many copies of the transcript of your trial as I could locate; and I offered Mr. Cruttwell a handsome sum to discontinue any further publication. I wished to ensure that no additional damage would be done to your character. The public adores no greater scandal than when a mishap befalls a member of the aristocracy."

C.J. began to cry even harder, partly out of gratitude for the earl's uncommon act of chivalry; partly from amazement that he still believed she was Lady Dalrymple's niece, despite the circumstances under which he had first laid eyes on her; partly from the revelation of how narrowly she had escaped notoriety; and partly from relief that his lordship never came close to suspecting the reality of her state of affairs.

She thought about the fact that there existed published transcripts of her trial. Pausing for a moment's reflection, she recalled learning at some point that scandal sheets containing all the particulars of celebrated trials were published and sold for a few shillings. Miss Austen's own aunt had fallen victim to the procedure only a year earlier, accused of stealing a length of lace by a pair of greedy shopkeepers enamored of the Leigh-Perrot wealth.

Darlington studied C.J.'s face, his own registering a degree of confusion. "Miss Welles, I thought this news would cheer you. Now you need not fear any censure owing to the unfortunate experiences that attended your arrival in Bath."

"I am . . . immensely grateful to your lordship once again," C.J. said, attempting to recover her equanimity. She clasped Darlington's hands. "I wish I could repay you somehow for your kindness . . . and yet, to be entirely forthright, I feel there is so much more I must share with you—"

They were nearly blinded by an enormous flash of white light as a crackle of lightning sizzled through the heavens, slicing through the afternoon sky and scarring the earth just a few feet from where they stood. The couple felt the shock of the electricity snaking up through the dry ground into their bodies. They fell into each other's arms, trembling with relief that, standing so close to the point of impact, they had been mercifully spared.

Above them another clap of thunder boomed with enough force and resonance to be heard from Bath to Brighton. With no immediate thought to propriety, the earl grabbed C.J.'s hand. "Come with me!" he shouted. C.J. struggled to keep up with him as he tore across the open field, hoping to avoid their becoming scorched by the lightning that continued to streak across the sky. Darlington's only concern was for Cassandra's safety, and he refused to relinquish his grasp of her hand.

The rain slashed their faces as they sought sanctuary from the violence of the storm. C.J.'s flimsy slippers were soaking up water like sponges. The ground squished and sloshed under her feet, nearly causing her to lose her balance on a slick patch of grass, but Darlington's strong grasp prevented her from falling. He pulled her, panting, into the shelter of a pavilion, one of the many to be found in the landscaped areas of Sydney Gardens. The little structure was roofed with thatch but otherwise resembled a marble neoclassical temple, encircled with Ionic columns. For a few moments, they struggled to catch their breath as they watched the torrential downpour continue around them.

The earl's hair was plastered to his head in Titus-style ringlets. He removed his deep blue coat and wrung out a heavy silk-lined cuff, then looked at C.J. apologetically, as though he felt personally responsible for the rainstorm.

C.J. regarded the disheveled appearance of the man who always appeared so fastidiously and unaffectedly dignified and could not contain her laughter. "When you get as wet as this, it no longer signifies as a great disaster," she said between silvery peals of amusement. "I am quite sure I look like a drowned rat, and my dress is past salvation, but after the first few drops, I had already resolved to accept its ruination." She looked down at the diaphanous muslin, which clung to her skin in sodden folds, and realized that the effect of the soaking rendered the garment absolutely transparent, her thin stockinette stays utterly useless. Immediately self-conscious, she blushed and folded her arms across her chest.

The unceasing waterfall surrounding them, running in a *shh-hhhhh* off the thatch onto the thirsty ground, created a wash of white sound. It was as though the rush of rain was purifying the air, leaving a sweet, clean fragrance in its wake. In fact, the damp straw gave off the odor of something earthy, freshly transmuted.

In an instant, blushes gave way to desire. C.J.'s arms encircled the earl's neck, and she pressed her body so insistently against his that they melded together as one. She ran her warm hands through his damp locks, massaging his temples, as her mouth met his in a questing kiss. Guided by sheer want, C.J. took the lead, probing the depths of his mouth with her tongue, sucking and nibbling, then running it gently along his teeth and lips.

"Cassandra," Darlington uttered hoarsely, as her hand aggressively slipped between his thighs, touching him through the straining fabric. He slipped her wet gown off her shoulders, lowering the bandeau to bare her breasts as he bestowed hot kisses from the length of her graceful neck across her pale throat and down toward her chest, forcing her to arch her back against the support of his strong hands. He hungrily tasted each of her nipples, gently biting the roseate buds to hardness, exploring the perfectly formed globes of her breasts with his practiced hands. She looked into his deep blue eyes, her expression one of glazed insatiability.

"Good Lord!" C.J. exclaimed when their bodies parted for a moment. "I think my frock has shrunk!" Indeed there did not seem to be quite so much fabric as there had been before the drubbing from the thunderstorm.

Darlington drew her close. "Cassandra Jane Welles, what the devil am I to make of you?"

Her eyes sparkled with mischief, commingled with lust. He felt her breath warm against his lips. "Take me home," she murmured huskily. "Yours."

Chapter Fifteen

Wherein our heroine experiences the pleasures of the Tantra.

THE RAIN HAD DIMINISHED from its almost biblical proportions to a fine drizzle, and the earl thought it best that C.J. should wear his coat until they were safely removed from all possibility of public scrutiny. It was serious business enough that Miss Welles was not properly chaperoned. In his clinging shirt and soggy, wrinkled cravat, the earl's lack of presentability did not signify when compared to Miss Welles's resemblance to the nearly nude Aphrodite at her toilette.

The slick streets were quiet, owing to everyone's exodus indoors to escape the sudden storm, so Darlington and C.J. were fortunate to be able to make the journey from Sydney Gardens to his town house in the Circus without eliciting censorious comment.

"Wood considered the Circus his finest architectural achievement. It was modeled after both the Colosseum in Rome and Stonehenge in Wiltshire, if you can imagine such a combination, Lady Cassandra," the earl remarked to C.J. in a very public voice, meanwhile entirely sensible of the energy crackling between them.

The door to the elegant town house was opened by an aging majordomo, tall and rail thin, with a shock of white hair that looked like a comb had never been able to produce much good effect. He seemed unperturbed by the sight of the master of the house—very much looking as though he had been swimming in the Avon—accompanying a scantily clad young lady whose dignity was preserved only by the master's sapphire-colored superfine coat.

"Good afternoon, Davis," an equally unruffled Darlington said to the majordomo. "I am going to show Miss Welles the salon. Please ask Cooper to have some hot tea brought up for us." The earl's unflappability impressed his female companion to no end. It was all so *Masterpiece Theatre*. C.J. tried to behave with similar aplomb despite her bedraggled appearance.

"Very good, your lordship," the ancient replied, and shuffled off toward the bellpull.

C.J. thought she had detected the slight arch of a bushy eyebrow. "I suppose he is bred—I mean trained—to ignore the eccentricities of the aristocracy, his betters," she snorted. "Goodness, what a world!" The prospect of so elderly a man still having to work for a living appalled her. Davis should be retired in comfort somewhere with a decanter of good port and a sizable pension.

"Davis was majordomo when Aunt Augusta celebrated her first season in Bath," the earl explained. "A spaniel could not be more faithful to a family."

"We are not discussing a dog, Percy!"

"The English class system has been ingrained for centuries, Miss Welles, and everyone knows and accepts his place with alacrity. That is the way of the world."

"*Your* world," C.J. corrected. "Accepting that I am superior to another human being simply because of an accident of birth does not rest easy in my conscience."

"This sceptered isle is far more advanced than other nations, *Lady* Cassandra," Darlington replied, using what he believed to be her proper aristocratic title. "The heathen Americans practice slavery! There's your barbarism right there! Here in England, those of the servant classes receive a wage for their labor. They are not the property of another human being."

C.J. recalled vividly her experiences at Laura Place and what Mary had warned her was the fate of recalcitrant servants or runaways.

Before she could reconsider censoring the words that tumbled from her mouth, she had practically mounted a soapbox. "It is regretful that the freedom of *some*—namely white male landowners—was wrested from King George at great expense to others. I believe slavery should be abolished entirely, but the very principles upon which America was founded are based on the premise that 'all men are created equal,' one that is deliberately antithetical to the structure of English society. Your— *our*—servants are supposed to be free men and women in the sense that they are not enslaved; but many are indentured, which has ever been the case in England. Should a servant misbehave in the eyes of his or her employer, to quote Shakespeare, 'who shall 'scape whipping?' How *dare* the English consider themselves a civilized nation when the little Mary Sykeses are beaten and battered and bruised by the Eloisa Wickhams for the crime of spilling a cup of tea? *You* may find the class system not only necessary, but the natural order of things. *I* find it intolerable."

The force of her argument nearly reduced C.J. to tears. But she was fired up about the injustices she had witnessed in this era and by the hypocrisy, or the blindness, of many of the upper crust to the plight of the working classes. Certainly the experience of being arrested, then possibly deported to a penal colony for fourteen years for stealing an apple, did much to form her opinions on the subject.

Darlington studied her for a few moments. Such an uncommon woman, however difficult she could be on occasion. All the fibers of her being trembled and glowed with her every passion. "Boadicea on the warpath," he said, not unadmiringly. "But you quoted Shakespeare quite out of context, Miss Welles, unless of course you intended to imply that the whipped servants in question were always receiving an undue punishment, rather than their 'just desserts.'" The corners of his mouth curled upward into a warm smile. "Is there such a chasm between us, Cassandra?" he asked softly, slipping his arm about her slender waist.

She looked up into his eyes. "I own that it would be a grave error for either one of us to pretend that we believe the same things in this regard."

"*I* believe that a man owes a duty to honor his word, to protect his family, and to treat other men with the same respect and deference he would wish for himself."

C.J. smiled. "And women? But you are changing the subject, your lordship."

He seemed momentarily puzzled. "Women? More so," he replied, as he gazed into her dark eyes. The earl decided it would be the better part of diplomacy to discuss something else. "Shall I show you how I spent my childhood, Miss Welles?"

She nodded, and he led her through a set of heavy wooden doors into a long, rectangular salon lined on three sides with shelves of books spanning the height of the room. The fourth wall was decorated with a fresco depicting young women disrobing at the edge of what appeared to be a Roman-style bath. C.J. approached it to gain a better inspection.

"Rather appropriate, I suppose," she noted, coloring slightly at the notion that the earl should spend so much time in this room, presided over by these naked, nubile graces. "The mural would be out of place in the modern world anywhere but in Bath."

"Actually, it is not a Roman bath that is illustrated here," Darlington explained. "The fresco is Greek, depicting a Dionysian mystery cult. It is believed to have been painted around the year 50 B.C. My parents had it installed during one of their infrequent return visits to England."

"What does Lady Oliver think of such things?"

"To my mind, it is none of her concern, and her opinion,

good or bad, does not signify. Suffice it to say that although it was my father, and not I, who was the amateur archaeologist, after a certain unfortunate event in my mother's young adult life, nothing she ever did would have shocked Aunt Augusta. Now, look up and make a wish."

The ceiling was painted a deep teal color and upon the resplendent blue-green ground the entire heavens, with the constellations fashioned in fine gold leaf, were laid out. C.J. found no words to express her wonderment at the sight. A deeply appreciative sigh was the most she could muster.

A more careful inspection of the room—with its heavy, patterned Persian rugs in shades of ultramarine, claret, cerise, and cream, and its richly striped silken draperies, which also ran the height of the library—revealed a highly unusual display of antique artifacts.

"And what is that, may I ask?" inquired C.J. of an odd-looking contraption—a studded leather cube on a wooden frame.

"My 'liver shaker,' you mean?" Darlington stepped up onto the box and sat atop the cube. "It has springs inside," he said, grasping the handles and commencing to bounce, the action mimicking a monstrously rough ride on horseback. "It's a gentleman's exercise machine. The perfect solution for a rainy day."

"Is there room for two?" C.J. quipped suggestively. Were his lordship able to read her mind, he might be shocked. An activity for a rainy day, indeed!

Darlington descended from the exerciser and gestured toward a foot-high, rather primitive-looking statue of a male figure with an erect phallus practically as long as the sculpture was tall. "My father unearthed him at Pompeii," the earl remarked of the curio.

"It's so . . . *erotic*," she whispered.

Darlington slipped his coat from C.J.'s shoulders, observing how her drying gown clung to the contours of her luscious body. "Not unlike the figure before me," he appraised, as his fingers gently traced the length of her arms. He raised her hands to his lips, bestowing a kiss in the center of each palm. They could both feel the heat rising in her body.

C.J. cleared her throat. "Would it be untoward for a proper young lady to suggest a glass of sherry to help her ward off the ill effects of the dampness?"

Darlington rang the embroidered bellpull. "Done," he smiled. C.J. was sure she could get lost in the crinkles around his eyes. "I was debating whether or not I would violate your delicate sensibilities by suggesting an alcoholic fortifier."

"Since my own behavior thus far has not been a very good credit to my character, were I you, I shouldn't worry."

"Lady Cassandra, I believe it was you who reminded me that there is no shame in the free expression of one's desires."

"Touché, your lordship."

Darlington returned his coat to C.J. just as Cooper, the butler, entered the room with a pot of steaming hot tea and proceeded to set up a small table for the earl and his fair companion. He was followed into the room by a footman bearing a tray with a cut-crystal decanter of amber liquid and two delicately etched glasses, which he set upon the tea table. With another nod from their employer, the servants lit the beeswax tapers in the numerous ornate candelabras.

After his staff departed, Darlington poured their sherry. He swirled the spirits in his glass as he offered its twin to C.J. "May I show you my most prized possession?" he inquired. She nodded wordlessly. "Have you ever seen a first folio, Miss Welles?"

She gasped when the earl lifted a protective glass pane and removed from one of his bookcases an enormous leather-bound copy of the complete works of William Shakespeare. "I used to read from this to Marguerite," he said softly. C.J. allowed her fingers to trace the length of the volume's spine. For her, the touching of such an icon would remain a highlight of her life, no matter what might follow.

Darlington approached her and entwined his arm with hers, gracefully pulling them both to the floor, where they rested against the large, silken, tasseled cushions.

"'For where your treasure is, there will your heart be also,'" he murmured, tasting the sherry on her lips.

C.J. blushed deeply. "My dress is now quite dry, but these spirits," she remarked, as she swirled the liquid in her glass, "are rendering me rather warm."

"I have a remedy," Darlington whispered, as he slipped both his coat and her own garment off her shoulders, freeing her from the semi-sheer column of white muslin and her undergarments within a matter of moments. The gown puddled about her ankles like the seafoam eddies that swirled around the iridescent shell of Botticelli's Venus. He eased her back against the cushions and stroked her body with a featherlight touch. "So soft," he whispered. "So soft." He ever so gently extricated her feet from the discarded gown and removed each slipper, placing a lingering kiss on her instep before divesting her of her pretty white stockings and ribboned garters.

Self-conscious at feeling so much on display, she strove to pull him toward her, but he resisted the tug of her slender arms. "Shhh. No, love. There will be time for that soon enough."

She was indeed a feast for his eyes. His hands roved expertly across her nude body, bringing into full relief every erotic sensation. C.J. had never experienced such an attentive lover. He aroused her every pore; every fiber of her being became more alive at his practiced touch. Darlington pulled her into his arms, and she felt the soft cambric of his shirt rub against her skin. They were on their knees, and while C.J. devoured his eager mouth with hungry, burning kisses, she sought to remove the fine linen barrier between them, tugging the shirt over the earl's head, tossing it a few feet beyond where they knelt entwined in each other's arms.

Everything was happening in hushed whispers. She smoothed her hands over his chest, noting the perfect contours, how the bronze of his skin tone formed a stark contrast to her own, how the dark patch of hair spread across his pectorals in perfect symmetry. She moved to unbutton his pantaloons, then realized they would be impossible to remove unless certain obstacles were eliminated. "Your boots," she whispered, tugging one of his muscular legs toward her. C.J. placed his heel on her thigh as she struggled to find a posture that would not topple them both.

Darlington's temporary distaste at placing the not-so-sparkling heel of his shiny Hessians on her soft skin was erased by the sensuous sight of the tall black riding boot, such an emblem of masculinity, resting against the creamy suppleness of the young woman's bare flesh. Cassandra in her splendid altogether, deftly removed each boot, sliding the stiff leather shaft down the length of his calf, effortlessly disengaging it from his foot. "I cannot remember when I have had such an engaging valet," he teased softly.

The boots were quickly disposed of and landed with twin thuds, joining the cambric shirt on the colorful Persian carpet.

The earl was immensely enjoying being undressed. In fact, no woman had ever done this for him—not even Marguerite, who had been quite a proficient lover herself.

C.J., who was in the process of skillfully unbuttoning his chamois pantaloons, looked up at him, distressed to catch a dark cloud dimming Darlington's chiseled countenance. God, he was beautiful in the late afternoon half light, augmented by the candle glow; but his troubled look made her cease her progress.

It was not fair to her, the nobleman thought. "Stop," he heard himself say.

"Is something the matter, Percy?" she inquired softly.

"It's not right," he murmured.

"What's not?"

Summoning every dram of willpower, Darlington took C.J.'s hand in his and removed it from his loins, then entirely misread her look of distress. "Cassandra, you fascinate and delight me endlessly . . . but I cannot ask you to compromise your . . . to perform . . . to . . . desire you to behave in a manner . . . to do for me what no gently bred . . ." He had no words. Thought and reason had deserted him under her caress. "For God's sake!" he finally exclaimed. "You are Lady Dalrymple's niece, and here I am expecting you to pleasure me like a . . . like a cyprian!"

C.J. pulled away and rested against one of the large silken cushions. "Forgive me," she said, her eyes brimming with tears. Several moments of painful silence passed between them. To be fully honest with her sexuality meant that she would have to be fully honest with Darlington about her past, and she could never disclose how she came to be so carnally experienced.

"What are you thinking?" he asked her.

"That . . . it cannot possibly be . . . untoward . . . to obey the promptings of nature with the man one loves. Yes, I am Lady Dalrymple's niece. And her ladyship—as well as her late husband—and my . . . and my father . . . are all 'originals.' Given where I came from, I can only be who I am." *God help me for that lie,* C.J. thought.

"You don't think me an ogre?"

"I think you my love!"

"My Cassandra. Come here." Darlington opened his arms, into which C.J. melted with alacrity. Their mouths met in a passionate kiss, which deepened as they recommenced the exploration of each other's bodies.

"What now?" C.J. asked when the earl seemed to shiver under her touch.

"No. N-nothing," he responded, his voice straining as her hand found his most vulnerable spot—apart from his heart—and *stayed there,* learning him, stroking him. He was aching for her, and he knew she could feel it. C.J. drew the length of him through the placket in the buttery soft leather breeches.

Darlington moaned in anticipation when he felt her warm breath against his skin. Her fingers moved in skilled, smooth strokes, and when she placed her soft mouth over him, he fought not to explode immediately from the sheer perfection of the sensation. Concentrating on not succumbing to release too soon, Percy would give her a gift too, he thought to himself, to prolong their mutual bliss—turn each moment into a higher plateau on the journey to complete ecstasy—a total oneness of their bodies, minds, and souls.

C.J.'s tongue was as practiced as her hands as she varied her pressure and speed, sending electric sensations straight through to the core of his being. "Cassandra," he cried huskily, drawing her even nearer as he clutched handfuls of her silken tresses. "My love." He needed her *now*. He had to know, to *feel* what it was like to bury himself deep inside her softness. But he also knew how much more pleasure they could give each other if they took their time. Darlington cupped his hands on either side of C.J.'s face, easing her gently away from him so that he could remove the final fabric barrier.

He slid his skintight yellow-gray trousers over his thighs. *God in Heaven!* This encounter was not his first in the past seven years, Lord knew, but it was certainly only the second time in his life that he had ever cared so deeply for a woman. He owned that he had fallen hard for the extraordinary young lady who was wresting his breeches from around his ankles. Everything she said or did brought a fresh, unexpected, and highly pleasurable surprise. And what she had been doing to him with her soft hands, and her moist lips, and practiced tongue, was one of the most superbly delicious surprises he had ever experienced.

"I have always believed," C.J. whispered, helping Darlington remove the remainder of his clothing, "that if you can get your tongue around Shakespeare's iambic pentameter, you can get it around anything."

He had remained ready for her, despite the almost comical extrication from his trousers. When he clasped C.J. to him, and they had the first opportunity to enjoy such unimpeded warmth, the lovers found themselves moaning in low, short breaths, hungering to explore every contour of each other's body. Darlington's hands cupped C.J.'s full, rounded breasts, feeling their weight and exquisite softness. The suffused light from the candles turned her skin alternately rose and apricot, russet and peach.

C.J. arched her back. "Please," she whispered. "*Please*, Percy. *Now.*"

"Not just yet," he replied softly.

He arranged her body over the cushions so that the two of them could lie side by side. Her hand trailed along the length of his firm, sculpted body, from the tender hollow at his throat, down along his breastbone, past his navel and down to his manhood, where she continued to stroke and tease him. His fingertips lightly played upon her lips, and she opened her mouth to take in first one finger, and then another, expertly sucking on them with the same dexterity she had demonstrated on a lower area minutes earlier.

She felt his hot breath in her ear. "I'm going to teach you something very special, Cassandra." His clever hands played well-practiced arpeggios along her breasts and flat belly, coming to rest at the juncture between her thighs, which had been wet with anticipation from the moment she felt his first caress. "*This,*" he said softly, noting her wetness as he began to explore the deepest recesses of her sex, "is your *yoni.*" He took her soft hand in his and placed it gently on his fully erect sex. "And this is my *lingam.* Look into my eyes, Cassandra, as I touch you. No, don't be ashamed," he urged, when she turned her face away. His fingers began to titillate her until she cried his name, hoarse with desire, craving more. Needing release.

C.J. reached down and gently touched Percy's hand, as if to temporarily halt his progress. "Percy?" she began tentatively. "I think you should know that I am not a vir—"

He slipped one, then two fingers inside her, feeling her slickness and readiness with no physical barrier to impede the taking of their pleasure. "Shhh, love. I know," he replied softly, continuing to stroke her. "Keep looking at me, Cassandra. The rhythm of your breathing will begin to match mine," he whispered. And when Percy excited her most exquisitely sensitive spot, just behind the pubic bone, C.J. cried out as she held his gaze. Tears, formed from the deepest recesses of her soul, coursed like summer rain down her flushed cheeks. It was as though she had lost all control of her own body and was no longer human, but had become color—pure color. First scarlet, then persimmon orange, then vibrant kelly green. "Everything is green," she gasped in an astonished stupor as the tears continued to flow freely.

"It's the *Tantra*," Percy whispered. "The weaving of energy. An Eastern practice nearly four thousand years old. All of the energies of the body are brought into harmony, creating the highest form of pleasure possible. Green is the color of the heart—the *anharta*," he added, tracing circles around her rosy aureoles.

C.J. reached up to wipe away her embarrassing tears. Percy stroked the outside of her sex, teasing her by gently tugging at the downy hair covering her pubis. The slight pinching sensation increased her craving for him. "It's all right to weep," he soothed. "When I touched you deep inside your yoni, your tears released your fears and opened your heart." He continued to rhythmically caress her. "It is the fullest way to experience lovemaking. Your eyes—the windows to the soul—your heart, and your yoni all open to me at once, like a beautiful blossom. You give and receive completely at the same time."

He kissed her eyelids, first with his soft lips, then bestowed butterfly kisses on her lids, cheeks, and lips by fluttering his lashes against her skin, provoking tiny tingles of electricity. Percy nibbled at her lips, drawing her bottom lip into his mouth and deftly continuing a southern migration down her entire body, marking her with tiny bites on her throat, breasts, belly, mons, and thighs. Every time Darlington lifted his mouth from her body, he left C.J. wanting more. Each caesura was an exquisite moment, rich and full, suspended in time; the reward that followed every pause became a revelation.

"I am marking you as mine, Cassandra. In India, these ancient sensual practices were codified in the fifteenth century in the *Kama Sutra of Vatsyayana*. It has never been translated into English. Imagine how much I could pleasure you if I were fluent in Hindi!"

Before C.J. could reply or ask him how he had come to know portions of the sacred sexual text—an answer she was unsure she wanted to hear—Percy had placed his mouth over her nether lips and was exploring the soft folds of her sex with his tongue. He continued to tease her into wave upon wave of ecstasy until she could swear she was floating above her own body.

She continued to come in colors as he brought her with each increasingly powerful orgasm closer and closer to nirvana. Sticky rivulets of *amrita*, her own natural love juices, ran down her thighs, and once again, she no longer felt earthbound.

Now. Now it was time.

Darlington eased himself on top of C.J., claiming her mouth with his as he entered her with a cry of relief commingled with the purest ecstasy.

Rising to meet his rhythm, her body responded to his as though they had been destined for each other. She felt her flesh shudder and explode; and as his hands reached behind her neck to take hold of her hair, she became a wild thing, giving in to an even more primal pleasure as he took her higher and higher. It was as though C.J. had become every element in rapid and rotating succession—first all earthy desire; then an unquenchable fire of unslaked ardor; then air itself as she soared to new heights of rapture; then water as her body turned to liquid, melting into and around him.

Covering her tender eyelids with kisses, honoring her flushed cheeks, her throat, and her searching mouth, Darlington cried his pleasure into her.

It was a celestial experience. C.J. was certain she was seeing stars. In fact, she was. As their lovemaking had progressed, day had become dusk and the slender wax tapers now illuminated the ceiling above where they lay satiated in each other's arms. Where the candlelight captured the luminescence of the gold leaf, the constellations shone, creating a dazzling effect. C.J. released a throaty sigh of sheer contentment. She flexed and relaxed her muscles, gripping him, then releasing; gripping, then releasing. He was still rigid inside her while her gentle contractions squeezed every drop of fluid from him. "*Mulabandha*," he whispered huskily.

"What?"

"What you're doing down there. It's called mulabandha. Very advanced."

Darlington gazed down at his beautiful woman. Did he guess that the thoughts racing through her extraordinary mind consisted of the realization that this was light years better than any amorous encounter she had ever experienced? Not only that, but if there had been any doubt of it before, she was truly sure now that she was deeply, irrevocably, irreversibly in love with Owen Percival.

They lay quietly in each other's embrace, enjoying the warmth their bodies produced. Percy reached for one of the sherry glasses and, dipping his finger into the wine, traced a wet path along C.J.'s lips, then proceeded to kiss the aromatic liquid away. He was without a doubt the most sensuous man C.J. had ever known. Her head was swimming with satisfied desire. Outside, it sounded as though the storm was making another appearance. "A *coup de foudre*," she whispered, stroking his chest.

"What?" he responded, startled.

"A *coup de foudre*," she repeated. "Not just the clap of thunder from the storm this afternoon—and now," she explained, translating the phrase, "but what happened when we met."

"I know what a coup de foudre is," he said softly. "What I never knew . . . until now . . . is the *extent* of your mastery of . . . *French*."

"*Merci*," C.J. replied. She cradled him in her arms and smiled, then kissed his lips. "I have yet to find a better expression to describe what I felt when we were introduced in my aunt's drawing room. It was exactly as though a clap of thunder echoed through the heavens, and in an instant, I believe I was head over heels in love with you."

"I felt it too. The coup de foudre," Darlington murmured, twining a tendril of her hair about his fingers.

She drank in his appearance in the firelight. "Percy?" she began tensely. "I must get back home." Her voice was lower than a whisper. "I have been away for so much longer than I had anticipated that I fear Lady Dalrymple will be anxious for my return."

"I shall have my carriage brought 'round and take you there myself." Darlington pulled her close. "Promise you will come back to me." She stroked his cheek with the back of her hand. He caught her wrist and turned it over to kiss her palm. She held his gaze. In the candlelight, his eyes sparkled like Indian sapphires. He kissed her tenderly. "What is your favorite color?"

"My favorite color? Why?"

"I should like to show you more of Bath, but my route cannot be easily accomplished on foot. Therefore, I propose that we ride out together."

Her eyes shone. "I love to ride."

"Well then, I must speak to Madame Delacroix about having a riding habit made up for you, since I doubt your aunt has seen to it that such an ensemble should form an essential asset to your wardrobe. Lady Dalrymple is not overfond of horses."

"Is it too warm for a hunter-green velvet?"

He stroked her soft cheek, brushing his hands against her lips, for which he was rewarded with a gentle kiss along the back of his fingers. "I shall endeavor to see that my lady is accommodated in her every desire."

"Yes," she whispered. "I am already quite convinced of that."

Darlington held C.J. at arm's length, studying the play of the candlelight across her face. God, but she was exquisite. So yielding and sweet; so willing and enthusiastic a partner. How she came by her sexual knowledge was a matter more of curiosity than concern. Clearly, she was gently bred. And though it was uncommon for young ladies of her ilk even to evince lustful desire, let alone have any experience in connubial practices—in this generation at any rate—such things were not entirely unknown. As Cassandra had reminded him, her family were renowned for following the dictates of their hearts; and from there, he reasoned, it was but a short step before nature took its course. "Well then," he sighed. "You now have something to look forward to." He ran his fingers through her hair, once again creating a shivery sensation all along her spine.

Did he mean the tantric sex or the horseback riding? "You need not have bribed me with the promise of a green velvet riding habit," C.J. teased. "I would freely return to learn more about the *Kama Sutra*."

"I will teach you everything I know . . . with the greatest pleasure."

"I promise to be a most attentive student." C.J. ran her hands through Darlington's soft, shiny brown curls. The gesture produced a sudden thought: "I was wondering if you might allow me a . . . a memento," she said, twining her finger around a tendril or two. To her delight, the earl took her meaning immediately and fetched a pair of fine Toledo scissors. He handed them to C.J. and inclined his head. "Pick one."

The recalcitrant spiral that flopped across his brow when he bent toward her gave the earl an even more tousled appearance. "Would you mind standing up straight, your lordship? I'd prefer a more discriminate 'rape of the lock.' We would not want to cause speculation on the sudden loss of your barber's sense of symmetry."

"What is so willingly bestowed can hardly be construed as rape," Darlington replied as C.J. discreetly snipped one perfect curl. "And you will require a proper place to store your treasure." He went to his escritoire and opened a small chest. "This was my mother's," he told C.J., placing a small silver locket into her hand. "A gift from my father for the selfsame purpose. *Omnia vincit amor,*" he added, reading the inscription to her. "Love conquers all." He took the C-shaped ringlet from C.J.'s palm and placed it inside the locket, then closed their joined hands around the gift.

Ever so softly, C.J. kissed his lips. "It's a price beyond rubies," she whispered. "Thank you, your lordship."

They dressed at leisure, desiring to prolong their parting as much as possible. Then Darlington's barouche carried C.J. back to Lady Dalrymple's town house, the short distance from the Circus to the Royal Crescent being all too brief a drive.

Book the Third

Chapter Sixteen

*This time Lady Dalrymple does not cry wolf; our heroine rids
the household of parasites, and makes a desperate effort to take
matters into her own hands.*

T HE HOUSE ON the Royal Crescent was dark and still
as C.J. approached, and she wondered if she had
been missed when Folsom, who opened the door to
admit her, gave her an anxious look. She slipped inside and tiptoed up the highly polished wooden staircase, removing the skeleton key from her reticule when she reached the blue room. A
cursory glance in the beveled cheval mirror to ensure that there
was nothing suspiciously untoward about her appearance revealed one or two stray curls; but otherwise, her thin muslin
gown, though it had appeared to be a total loss at the time, had
survived the soaking in Sydney Gardens.

It was too quiet. C.J. shuddered. Something was amiss. She
quickened her step as she approached Lady Dalrymple's bedchamber and almost collided with Saunders, who was leaving
the darkened room. "Miss Welles! You gave me such a fright,"
she exclaimed, a panicked expression in her light gray eyes.

"Saunders—whatever has happened?" C.J. asked. She had
learned enough about the dour maid's character to know that

she would not offer any intelligence unless it was demanded of her, though Saunders's countenance—like that of the footman, Folsom—clearly betrayed the fact that a matter of grave importance had transpired within the past few hours.

"It is her ladyship's heart, Miss Welles," Saunders whispered, unable to mask her alarm and distress. "Dr. Squiffers is with her now."

"How . . . grave is her condition?" C.J. asked, already divining an answer from the maid's tearstained face.

At the entrance to Lady Dalrymple's bedchamber, C.J. paused to steady her breath so that her entrance would not further upset her "aunt."

The heavy crewelwork drapes were drawn around the countess's bed. The small, slight Dr. Squiffers, dressed in a somber wool crepe frock coat, stood beside her, illuminated by the flame from a single taper.

Lady Dalrymple looked surprisingly diminutive and alarmingly thin propped up by numerous damask-covered bolsters and eiderdown pillows. It was horribly warm within the confines of the closed curtains, and the odor of illness was palpable. The dowager's white lace cap was askew; a sheen of sweat plastered her gray curls to her glistening brow. She held out her arms to C.J.

"My niece. My dear niece. Come to me."

C.J. obeyed immediately. She took her "aunt's" hand in her own. The older woman's palm felt small, somehow, and slightly clammy.

"Tell Dr. Squiffers to pull the curtains. I want to see Portly."

"It is inadvisable for the patient to have so much light," the medic soberly counseled, kneading his knotted arthritic thumbs.

"Nonsense. Give her ladyship what she wants." C.J. decided to take charge. She placed a kiss on Lady Dalrymple's damp forehead. "Get her a cool, wet cloth," she ordered the doctor, who rang the velvet bellpull; then, drawing him aside, C.J. softly asked the medical man about the countess's condition.

The response did little to cheer her.

"We are doing all we can to make her comfortable, Miss Welles, but your aunt appears to have a greatly enlarged heart," the doctor replied, steepling his fingers together to form a triangle. He found it did wonders to reduce the tremors that had been plaguing him ever since he had decided to reduce his intake of alcohol. How long had it been, now? Two weeks? Two months?

He regarded Lady Dalrymple's young niece and pursed his lips. Like most men of the medical profession, Dr. Squiffers was not overfond of persistent sorts who questioned his authority. Upstarts. "We do not know how long her ladyship will last. It could be a matter of months, or weeks . . . or it may be only a matter of days." What did people expect of him? Death was a matter of course. His patients and their families always demanded miracles that no mere man, even a learned man of medicine, could provide. What would they next insist of him—that he walk on water?

Saunders reappeared with a glass tumbler, several fine Irish linen towels, and a white enamel basin. The doctor retrieved a small metal box from his worn black leather bag and opened the hasplike closure. Then he took the drinking glass from the lady's maid. His hands trembled as he held it over the candle flame to sterilize it, requesting that Saunders part her ladyship's dressing gown to expose the affected area. She picked up the small delftware bowl by Lady Dalrymple's bedstead and turned to the medic for approval.

"Sweetened milk, sir. As you requested." The lady's maid took a fingertip towel from the bedside table and, dipping it into the bowl of sweetened milk—which seemed to C.J. more appropriate for a tabby cat's midnight snack—began to apply dabs of the sticky liquid to her ladyship's exposed *poitrine*. It was certainly an odd ritual. What could Saunders's preparation be for, except perhaps to attract bugs?

Curiosity compelled C.J. to peer into the doctor's little strongbox. She gasped, then nearly gagged. Regrettably, her suspicions about the contents of the box were confirmed. She had never seen leeches up close and never desired to again; and if she had to tackle the doctor to prevent him from bleeding Lady Dalrymple, and then bodily evict him from the premises, by God, she was prepared to do it.

Not only had Squiffers not washed his palsied hands before placing them on the patient, he was about to compound matters tenfold in C.J.'s view by touching the writhing brown-black oblongs beginning to desiccate in the box before him.

"Did you bring the salt, Saunders?" the doctor inquired; and in response to C.J.'s look of questioning horror, he explained, "The leeches must be left on the skin in order to achieve maximum efficacy. Once they fall off of their own accord, one must place them in a dish or plate of salt so they can vomit up the blood."

C.J. was herself about to regurgitate. "And the sweetened milk?" she managed to stammer.

"A little sweetened milk placed upon the affected area stimulates the bloodsuckers to bite. Quite the customary practice, Miss Welles. There is nothing to fear."

Maybe if you were a leech. C.J. threw her body between Dr. Squiffers and the countess, knocking his arm away from Lady Dalrymple. The medic easily lost his grip of the heated tumbler, which fell to the carpet and rolled several feet away. He scrambled to retrieve the glass as C.J. slammed the lid shut on the case of hideous, writhing leeches, closing the clasp. "Out! Out, you parasite!" she shrieked, shoving the doctor from the room while an aghast Saunders stood helplessly by.

The maid attended her ladyship's bedside as C.J. retrieved the doctor's black bag and the box of leeches and followed him from the room, closing the heavy bedchamber door behind her. The physician stood by, shaking with ire.

"Miss Welles, you must let me do everything in my power to heal your aunt. I have taken an oath!" he insisted. Wringing his hands helped stop them from trembling, but only with the greatest concentration could he control his shaking limbs when anger or anxiety got the better of him.

"I absolve you of your Hippocratic responsibilities," C.J. said, her voice tensing.

"Without my expertise, Lady Dalrymple will very likely *die*," the doctor urged under his breath, lest their voices carry through the closed door. He knew the odds of survival were slim in any event. Softening his tone, and taking C.J.'s hand, he consoled, "I understand that you are reluctant to accept that it is nigh your aunt's time, but if you wish to prolong her . . . departure . . . you must not prevent her ladyship from receiving the best possible medical care. I shall endeavor to ease her pain and make the inevitable more comfortable for her. Surely you can derive your own comfort from that knowledge, Miss Welles."

C.J. withdrew her hand. "No, sir, I cannot. And I do not. Nor do I accept that it is Lady Dalrymple's 'time,' as you aver with such ridiculous certainty. Time can be altered, I have learned . . ." She trailed off, realizing that she was failing in her attempt to sway his opinion. Perhaps leeching, or bleeding, was the standard course of treatment at the time for everything from bunions to dog bites to bubonic plague.

What effect cupping and leeching could possibly have on the countess's enlarged heart—short of burning her skin and thinning her blood, owing to the leeches' scarlet extraction—would have to be thoroughly proven to C.J. in order to convince her of the efficacy of the procedure. Although, when she paused to think for a moment, she acknowledged that blood thinners such as aspirin were prescribed for heart patients in her own era.

She looked deep into Squiffers's eyes—pale blue orbs now red rimmed and slightly bloodshot—and then leveled a challenge. "I will offer you a bargain, Doctor. I absolve you of all responsibility—medical, ethical, or legal—with regard to the future health of Lady Dalrymple. From this moment on, my aunt's life is in *my* hands, and I shall accept whatever consequences there may be . . . should she recover"—C.J.'s voice dropped below a whisper— "or not." She took a deep breath and shook the doctor's hand. "If we have further need of your services, I shall have the footman, Willis, summon you." Dr.

Squiffers's gaze was indecipherable. She placed a hand on the medic's back and guided him toward the staircase. "Good night, Doctor. And thank you."

C.J. waited at the top of the stairs until she could no longer hear the physician's receding footsteps. Then she reentered her "aunt's" chamber. "Mary. Mary Sykes would probably know what to do," C.J. muttered half to herself, wishing now more than ever that Lady Wickham's little scullery maid were there to see her through this crisis. Mary was resourceful and pragmatic and understood how to get along in this world. She would undoubtedly know about efficacious and less barbaric home remedies and how one might concoct them. More important, because Mary had an infirm employer, she might know where a better physician than Dr. Squiffers could be located.

C.J. realized that her own brow was damp with sweat. Perhaps she had overreacted. After all, she was comparing her awareness of modern medicine and technology with the state of medical science in 1801—something she admittedly knew nothing about.

She mopped her brow, then wiped her perspiring hands on her hips. The white gown had been through so much today, its condition could not get much worse. Now, what to do about Lady Dalrymple? It was not the time to second-guess her ill treatment of Dr. Squiffers. She did fear that her refusal to allow the medic—who appeared to have a permanent case of delirium tremens—to bleed and cup the countess might actually hasten her demise rather than prolong it. She had acted upon impulse just now, and although she was not ordinarily the praying sort, she hoped that there was an all-knowing divine force somewhere in the universe that had guided her to make the right decision.

Lady Dalrymple's eyes were half closed, her forearm draped over the moist compress that Saunders had made from another delicate fingertip towel. C.J. pulled open the embroidered drapes and secured them to the bedposts, affording the countess a full view of the portrait of her late husband hanging on the opposite wall, then drew up a chair to sit by her side. She re-adjusted the linen compress and stroked Lady Dalrymple's brow.

"Well . . . it would seem that you were right, Cassandra. It appears as though my fondness for ratafia cakes has gotten the better of me after all. And thank you, my dear," the countess whispered weakly, "for evicting Dr. Squiffers just now. I have a horror of leeches."

"I would never have let the doctor apply them; have no fear, Aunt."

"Besides," the patient continued pragmatically, "there is no need to bleed me when I shan't be here for very long anyway." Lady Dalrymple reached for C.J.'s hands and pulled her "niece" toward her. "I am dreadfully sorry, child, that our time together turned out to be so brief. I had wanted to do so much more for you."

C.J.'s anguish tumbled out in a series of sobs that wracked her body. No matter that the stoic Saunders stood by the door like a sentinel. Maybe a show of emotion would encourage the servant to plumb the humanity in her own soul. "*I'm* sorry, Aunt. I should not let you see me like this," she said, trying to restrain the flood of tears. She looked up from the bedside and gazed through the window. The sky was unusually bright—a deep French blue illuminated by a full moon and so dotted with stars, it seemed as though the heavens had been sprinkled with glitter in a sort of celestial arts-and-crafts project.

And then, as they both regarded the pale disk suspended in the sky like a silver medallion right outside their window, C.J. experienced an epiphany. If she could return to the twenty-first century as soon as possible, she might be able to obtain a remedy for Lady Dalrymple's condition. She tried to curb her anxiety so as not to alarm the countess.

"I am going to say good night to you now, your ladyship, but I refuse to say good-bye," C.J. murmured as she smoothed the invalid's lace cap and rearranged her pillows so that she could rest more comfortably. Then she blew out the candle.

As she tiptoed out of the room, dismissing Saunders, C.J. heard Lady Dalrymple's faint voice calling to the portrait opposite the bed: "I'll be with you shortly, Portly." C.J. left the door slightly ajar and waited just outside the bedchamber until she heard Lady Dalrymple's irregular breathing, a sign that the dowager was asleep.

She watched while Saunders retreated downstairs to the servants' quarters, then slipped into her bedroom and bolted the door behind her. Intuition told her the eagle-eyed lady's maid was not to be trusted. C.J. changed into her costume from *By a Lady*, grabbed her bonnet, and descended the staircase holding her breath every step of the way.

Saunders hung back in the shadows and watched Miss Welles leave. Surely the girl was up to no good. Her wardrobe was proof enough. Gently bred ladies, especially titled ones, no matter what names they went by, changed clothes several times a day. There were morning frocks and walking frocks and afternoon frocks, tea gowns, dinner dresses, and ball gowns. Yet for all her new finery, the "niece" had a love affair with that dreadful yellow muslin frock and the equally shabby shawl and straw bonnet. The lady's maid was unsure if such odd behavior was worthy of report to Lady Oliver, but she duly noted the time of night that Miss Welles departed the residence and slipped the note back into the deep pocket of her apron. Perhaps she might merit an even more substantial reward if she could find out for certain what the young miss was up to.

It was C.J.'s initial notion to try the front door of the Theatre Royal in Orchard Street before sneaking into the alleyway. After all, she reasoned, as she tugged at the long elaborate handles to no avail, it would be rather ludicrous to go to all the bother of sneaking about when it might be quite possible to just walk right into the building the way everyone else did: through the front door.

I have just obeyed my first instincts, C.J. thought to herself, admitting defeat. Now she would assay a more familiar route. She glanced about to see if any garrulous stagehands were lurking in her favorite byway in Bath, but there was no one in the alley alongside the theatre. C.J. approached the stage door and gripped the handle. Nothing happened. She pulled it toward her with greater force. The door would not budge. Time for a little modern urban ingenuity. C.J. slid her bonnet off her head and allowed it to hang down behind her while she pulled a hairpin from her coiffure. *When all else fails . . .*

She tried to work the heavy iron lock with the slim tortoise-shell ornament. For some reason, the configuration made her think of the carnal union between an underendowed old man and an ancient madam. Momentarily distracted by her bawdy thought, she urged the delicate accessory too far. It snapped in half, both ends now rendered useless for their intended purposes.

C.J. stifled an agonized cry of helplessness. She had no more ammunition at the moment and no further thoughts on how to get into the theatre. Her grand plan would have to be put off 'til the morning. She could only pray to anyone willing to listen that Lady Dalrymple could hold out that long.

Chapter Seventeen

In which our heroine slyly cheats danger not once, but thrice, and ends up getting an education—and an eyeful—at the notorious Mrs. Lindsey's house.

A DEFEATED C.J. had begun to return to the Royal Crescent when she heard footsteps behind her. Being a native New Yorker, she felt her reflexes quicken, and she flattened herself against a stone façade and waited to see if the person belonging to the footsteps passed by. But she was greeted with silence. Too apprehensive to look back, she elected to test whoever was following her in an effort to ascertain whether it was simply someone taking a similar route or one who might, in fact, be stalking her. To her horror, her impromptu experiment appeared to substantiate her fears.

She accelerated her pace and heard the corresponding steps behind her quickening as well. The footfall, though distinctly audible, was light enough to belong to a woman—perhaps someone from the working classes—for C.J.'s own tread in her expensive kidskin slippers was almost noiseless. She increased her speed, aided by a slight decline in the pavement, and turned a dark corner into a dimly lit street, which she realized immediately was a cul de sac. Her heart began to pound. There was no turning back or she would run straight into the panting being who was now but a few yards behind her. Given the recent events surrounding Lady Dalrymple's illness, C.J. hazarded a quick guess as to the identity of her pursuer, but dared not look back to verify it. Her aim was to elude, not to confront. Breaking into a run, she noticed a door being opened about ten feet away; C.J. shoved past the exiting gentleman like a cat scuttling indoors from the cold.

The heavy oaken door shut behind her, locking automatically and leaving a cursing Saunders on its threshold.

Soaked with sweat, C.J. leaned against the wall just inside the building and clutched her chest to catch her breath. Flames flickered in the baroque wall sconces, casting shadows, like greedily lapping tongues against the red flocked wallpaper. The narrow foyer, tiled in a domino black and white, gleamed in the candlelight.

Leaving the building now was inadvisable. Saunders might be lurking near the doorstep, anticipating her exit. This would be a waiting game that C.J. had to win. Her breathing steadier, she decided to explore her sanctuary and slowly pulled back the deep gold damask drape that masked the foyer from the rest of the town house.

C.J.'s eyes widened. Beyond the golden curtain was a world worthy of Hogarth: colorful, brightly lit, loud, and merry. Gentlemen of all stripes were enjoying brandies in oversized crystal snifters, some wagering at snooker—one lewdly brandishing his cue stick as if it were a priapus—and indulging in amorous play with willing young ladies in various states of dishabille. Far from being shocked, C.J. was fascinated by the exhibitions before her. Bustling about like a mother hen in a gown of purple satin with deep décolleté was a stately looking woman with a pile of extravagantly coiffed silver hair and a violet patch on one of her highly rouged cheekbones.

A besotted client, deep in his cups, prostrated himself before the madam. "Mrs. Lindsey, I am forever in your debt," he said with near-religious fervor before passing out, one arm draped over Mrs. Lindsey's amethyst-encrusted slippers. The madam had only to glance at a large periwigged man and a small African page boy attired in harem pants and a jewel-studded striped silk turban, and the inert patron was noiselessly ejected.

Suddenly, C.J. felt a tug on her arm as the page boy got her attention. He escorted her to a thin, bandy-legged chap approaching middle age. "Yes, that is the she who will be my ladylove!" cried the patron gleefully. "She shall play my virgin tonight! There can be no other!"

Before C.J. could protest that she was not in Mrs. Lindsey's stable of beauties, the sweet-faced, ebony-skinned page led her and Mr. Bandylegs—who introduced himself as Sir Runtcock— down a candlelit corridor, passing a half-opened door through which C.J. spied an odd liaison indeed. An extremely fat gentleman of middling age and florid, baby-faced countenance was dressed as a young schoolgirl in a simple, high-waisted white frock with a wide pink sash. His bare, and corpulent, bottom was being soundly flogged by a doxy severely attired as a governess. The cross-dressed patron, evidently enjoying his "punishment," cried out to be birched with even greater ferocity.

Having reached their destination, the exotic-looking page extracted a ring of skeleton keys from his belt and turned the lock, admitting C.J. and her "client" to a bedchamber of gigantic proportions. C.J. attempted to appear neither surprised nor overwhelmed by her surroundings, all the while scoping out a means of escape that would not lead her directly into the path of the prying lady's maid or another of Mrs. Lindsey's patrons. The enormous canopied bed rested atop a raised platform as though it were an altar to love. Above them cavorted painted nymphs and satyrs, contorting themselves into all manner of elaborate sexual postures, the outsized phalluses of the half beasts tipped in bright red, the faces of the voluptuaries convulsed with ecstasy.

The heavy wooden door closed behind them, and C.J. could hear the ever fainter jangling of keys as the page receded down the corridor.

"Ah, my pretty one," cried Runtcock, rubbing his palms together with delight and hopping from foot to foot. "What are you called, my sweetling?"

C.J. stole a glance at the painted plaster firmament, her eye lighting on a pair of muscled arms stretching up from a shadowy abyss toward a nubile, bare-breasted young woman with flowers entwined through her blond, knee-length tresses: "'Tis Proserpine, sir," she replied, coyly playing her part.

"*Ahh*, thou devilish sweet Proserpine, come to your Hades!" exclaimed Runtcock, deftly unfastening his breeches and dropping them to expose, poking through his linen, the tiniest pillicock that C.J. had ever seen. He wriggled out of his pants, linen, and hose, revealing his pale, scrawny bandy legs. Naked now, from the waist down, he proceeded to chase his prey around the gargantuan bed. "Oh, how fond my Proserpine is of the chase!" he squealed as C.J. leaped up onto the mattress and scampered across its breadth. Runtcock stopped in midpursuit. "Something is amiss," he declared. "Your dress, my precious virgin, is not appropriate to your undefiled temple. My virgin should be attired in purest white!"

Anxious that her "patron" would rush out in his present state of undress and declare to Mrs. Lindsey that he had not been given a true "virgin," thereby exposing her as an imposter, which might cause her to be ejected from the premises straight into Saunders's suspicious grasp, C.J. gathered her wits for a swift defense of her sprigged muslin gown.

"La, good sir," she said airily, "but your Proserpine is garbed as the virgin spring, which befits her name and her nature!"

"Oh, you clever, clever minx!" Runtcock exclaimed, leaping from the bed, while reaching for C.J., who deftly sidestepped the man, causing him to land facedown on a thick bearskin rug.

Runtcock gamely continued to give chase. He was more resilient than C.J. had anticipated. "Those delicious thighs," he cried, grabbing hold of her upper leg when she paused to catch her breath, using one of the lewdly carved bed pillars for support. Latching on like a leech, the skinny bandylegs forced C.J.

onto the mattress, his gnarled, clawlike hand inching higher and higher up her thigh. "Yes, my sweet! It is time to yield your virgin honeypot to Hades!" he panted, his petite member, staunch as it could ever be, flapping pathetically in the air.

C.J. tried to best him, but Runtcock was also stronger than she had assumed. Over and over the mattress they rolled, his lordship tossing a sinewy leg over C.J.'s hip until, at last, she rolled onto the rug and coyly skittered behind the draperies.

"Sweet Proserpine, I must see thy luscious form, those ripe twin globes and virgin forest." Runtcock, who by now had succeeded in removing his upper garments, baring a rib cage sorely in need of a good meal, lunged for his voluptuous, fully clothed target.

Poking her head out from behind the wine-red velvet swags and pulling her red shawl more tightly about her shoulders, C.J. called out to the flagging Runtcock, "You impugn my modesty, sir. Let us devise a pastime: a game of hide-and-seek. You shall conceal yourself somewhere within this chamber, and once in hiding, count to fifty, after which time you may begin to look for me in *my* place of concealment. Should you find me, my virginity is yours to ravish."

The bandylegs rubbed his hands together. "A game! How enchanting! Yes, yes, where can I hide, my little vixen?"

"Sir Runtcock, what about the wardrobe?" C.J. suggested gaily, nodding at a large double-doored armoire large enough to conceal at least two grown persons.

The naked patron appraised the cupboard. "A splendid idea!" he agreed, with more alacrity than C.J. had dared to hope for, and opening the doors, he climbed up into the armoire.

C.J. emerged from behind the drapes. "Now, sir," she reminded him, "I shall close the doors and you shall count to fifty, during which time I shall conceal my supple virgin body within the room."

His proximity to her caused Runtcock's poor excuse for a penis to drool. "I shall count the moments, Proserpine!"

She closed the wardrobe and noiselessly slid the wooden bolt through the loops on each of the gilded doors. A muffled voice counted "one . . . two . . . three . . ." as she picked up her hat and tiptoed across the chamber to the door. As C.J. reached for the cast-iron ring that served as a handle, she heard footsteps and laughter just outside in the corridor and the sound of a body bumping up against the door.

She rushed back to her hiding place behind the velvet swags just in time. A drunken trio staggered into the room, each wielding a jeroboam of champagne from which they swigged large draughts in between fits of hysterical mirth.

Suddenly, the gentleman lurched to a halt in the middle of the bearskin. "I thought this room was empty," he said with a puzzled expression, gazing at the rumpled bedclothes.

" '*Tis* empty, silly," burped a luscious redhead, looking about the vacant bedchamber.

"There's no one here but the three of us, lovey," added the blonde, naked from the waist up. A tad unsteady on her feet, she tackled the gentleman, who had not quite gotten to the bed, and in one motion the pair slid to the floor, dissolving into a tangle of limbs and a heap of giggles.

"Don't leave me out!" pouted the redhead, who pounced upon the supine couple and began to fumble with the gentleman's cravat, while the blond doxy pulled at the redhead's bodice, loosing her full breasts.

"How perfect!" exclaimed the gentleman, who was made naked in a trice, owing to the deft work of his two lovely handmaidens. His left hand groped for the redhead's bosom while his right one toyed with the blonde. "One set of pink," he said, as he suckled the redhead's erect nipples, "and one of brown," as he favored the blonde.

Pausing for air, the gentleman complained of a prodigious thirst, which his voluptuous concubines immediately addressed, the blonde holding his lips apart while her confederate doused his gullet with champagne. "Jennet, my witch," he said drunkenly to the russet-haired beauty, "let's see if yer a real redhead! And you, Camilla," he continued, tugging at the blonde's flimsy frock, "is yer cunny as flaxen as yer hair?"

"Shall we show 'im?" Camilla asked Jennet, laughing raucously.

"It's what 'e paid for," the redhead sniggered. Jennet reached across the gentleman's body and linked arms with Camilla; with astounding and practiced grace, the half-dressed women pulled themselves to their feet. Jennet, the taller of the two, led Camilla to the bed and urged her up onto the mattress and into a supine position. While Camilla languished, her eyes growing heavy lidded and dreamy, Jennet played her bedfellow's body like a fluid arpeggio, her hands fluttering over her pale throat, down to her firm breasts, teasing her nipples with light flicking strokes, playing over her flat belly, then gracefully sliding Camilla's diaphanous gown over her thighs, past her well-turned calves and over her dainty ankles.

C.J., undetected behind the deep recesses of the drapery, watched the scene with increasing fascination, as did the patron of the pair of skilled voluptuaries, his eyes shining with boozy lust.

"No tricks at Mrs. Lindsey's," cooed Jennet. "Camilla's beard's as yellow as August cornsilk." The redhead's tapered fingers twined gently through the blonde's nether curls; and the fair-haired Maja reclined against the Florentine bolster, stretching her arms above her head as she felt Jennet's insinuation within her. Her back arched farther and farther upward as she reached the point of ecstasy.

Reaching for Jennet, Camilla pulled her partner toward her until the redhead was kneeling above the blonde's torso. Camilla made short work of Jennet's flimsy shift, leaving Jennet in her stunning altogether, her thick russet ringlets streaming down the contours of her back as she straddled Camilla's still supine form.

"You certainly are a redhead," the gentleman murmured approvingly.

By now Jennet was perched over Camilla's mouth like a conqueror. The blonde's clever tongue sought its target, darting in and out with enviable dexterity.

It was becoming increasingly warm behind the velvet drapery.

Jennet arched back, grasping onto each of her ankles, her hair reaching the mattress as she lengthened her torso and dropped her head back. Her large breasts stood out in full relief. The redhead's lithe body shuddered with pleasure as Camilla accomplished her mission.

"My turn, ladies!" cried the gentleman, and bounced up onto the mattress.

The trio then engaged in a series of extravagant maneuvers while the gentleman tried to service both of his playfellows at the same time. With the ménage à trois thus preoccupied, C.J. emerged from her hiding place and was tiptoeing across the room when the gentleman suddenly exclaimed, "What have we here?"

Unaware that he had spotted her in a mirror, artfully positioned on the ceiling above the bed, and equally unaware that the wardrobe concealing the now-forgotten Sir Runtcock contained a peephole especially designed for such voyeurism, C.J. stopped still in the center of the chamber.

"One of each!" cried the gentleman ecstatically, angling himself to get a better look at the new girl, with not a care in the slightest as to how she might have materialized. "A blonde, a redhead, and now a brunette!"

His companions appeared equally unconcerned with her provenance. Camilla reached down and retrieved one of the champagne bottles. "Come'n join us, lovey!" she slurred happily.

C.J. found herself taking a step or two toward the bed.

"Umnhnhmn!" came a muffled cry from somewhere in the room.

The four of them looked about.

"Mnuhmnmn!" the voice repeated emphatically. "That's my Proserpine! My virginal Proserpine!"

"It's coming from the wardrobe," deduced the astute Jennet.

"Proserpine. What a pretty name," remarked the friendly Camilla. "When did you start?"

"Perhaps we should release him," said Jennet, stretching her long legs and striding over to the armoire. She slowly slid back the bolt, tossing a lascivious look at the gentleman. Out popped a scrawny little man with a bandy-legged gait, made all the more prominent by his incarceration within the narrow confines of the wardrobe.

"My Proserpine," he gasped and lunged for C.J.

"Oh, my goodness, we were interrupting your sport," Camilla realized.

"Nay, we were quite through," replied C.J.

The gentleman caught C.J. unawares about the waist. "Come and join *us*, then," he insisted, planting a sloppy, wine-soaked kiss behind her ear.

Jennet unwittingly came to the rescue. "Proserpine is Sir Runtcock's for the evening and cannot be released from his patronage until Mrs. Lindsey permits it."

"Jennet is right," C.J. contributed. "I dare not risk my . . . situation . . . until I am at liberty to do so. But if Sir Runtcock is . . . through . . . for the evening, I shall endeavor to see if I may be permitted to come back and join you." *Talk about winging it.*

"Never!" cried the skinny little man, taking his member in his hand. "You are my little virgin!"

"And there you have it," said C.J. gaily, as she pulled open the door and hastily slipped into the corridor.

Sir Runtcock, as bare as a plucked guinea fowl, once again took up the chase. The corridor was not more than forty feet long, with a spiral staircase at the far end of it. C.J. scampered nimbly down the cold marble steps, winding her way about the center pole for several feet. Halting briefly, she glanced up and noticed that her "patron" was nowhere about. His deformity rendered the configuration of the staircase too treacherous for him to follow her.

Having safely reached the foot of the stairs, C.J. took stock of her surroundings. Embedded in the stone walls of the catacomb, tiny slivers of mica glinted in the flickering candlelight provided by thick beeswax pillars in heavy, elaborate iron wall sconces. Mrs. Lindsey evidently spared her patrons no expense if she used such costly candles in her basement.

C.J. traversed another dimly lit corridor and rounded a dark corner. A hand-carved sign above the ebony door before her read STYGIAN CAVES. She pushed against the door and, to her surprise, found it yielded more easily than she had expected. She heard the sounds of lewd laughter and the thumping of pewter tankards and goblets meeting in toasts and then slamming emphatically on long wooden tabletops.

She ducked behind a large stone pillar near the door, praying to remain undetected by the score or so of gentlemen—or so they were by birthright—some attired in modish fashion, with others robed in monkish, hooded brown cassocks tied at the waist with a length of rope. C.J. had read about the Hellfire Club and similar secret societies, which rose to prominence in the middle of the eighteenth century. She thought such brotherhoods had been banned, but apparently, the secret orders were still welcome within the bowels of brothels.

Through the haze of burning frankincense, C.J. watched as the "monks" retrieved black masks from the deep pockets of their cassocks and donned them with utmost solemnity, then with nearly sinister precision, raised their left hands to their hoods and slid them back over their shoulders.

One of the "monks" lifted a ram's horn from a hook on the wall behind him, brought it to his lips and blew one long blast, followed by eight short ones, then another long blast. The rest of the brotherhood stood facing the center of the table. Two women garbed as nuns in habits and wimples of black and white led a female attired as a novitiate in snowy white to the head of the table. The anonymity of the "sacrificial virgin" was ensured by the mask she wore: a white one that covered her face from her forehead past her cheekbones, enhanced with a blood-red teardrop painted to appear as though it dripped from the "virgin's" left eye. The woman's mouth was stained a ruby red.

In a carefully ordered procession, each "monk" had his turn with the newly baptized "virgin," declaiming the phrase "in love and friendship and in Lucifer's name!" before he sought entry, to the loud cheers of his audience. One "brother" who was even more exuberant than the rest, dislodged her mask, pushing it back from her face and over her hairline.

C.J., who had a relatively good view of the proceedings from behind her pillar, gasped when she discovered the identity of the "novitiate" and covered her mouth with her hand to stifle her shock. The young "virgin" who had been enduring such repeated defloration was none other than Lady Rose, whom C.J. had witnessed so cruelly "cut" in the Assembly Rooms for parading the barely discernible results of her illegitimate pregnancy. Could the girl have fallen so fast? What, C.J. wondered, had happened to Lord Featherstone, the babe's father, who had seemed so enamored of his lady?

Having witnessed a variety of lewd displays this evening, the only thing that truly scandalized C.J. was the predicament of Lady Rose, and she was powerless to do anything but stew in her anger about the unfairness of it all and the insensitivity of the society they lived in. For one unfortunate indiscretion, the ill-fated aristocratic beauty was doomed to a whore's destiny. While the individual members of the secret order continued to initiate Lady Rose into their sacred rites, C.J. slipped out the door and retraced her steps to Mrs. Lindsey's noisy parlor, where the revels showed no signs of abating. She opened the establishment's main portal. Peering cautiously down the street and finding it empty, C.J. heaved a relieved sigh and headed home, grimly acknowledging that if someone had set Saunders to spy on her movements, she was not entirely out of danger.

Chapter Eighteen

*A chapter crowded with incident, in which our heroine
eavesdrops on a tidbit of theatrical history and engages in some
impromptu acting of her own; Saunders's suspicious nature is
further piqued; and a dream come true presents some
nightmarish choices.*

AVING SAFELY REACHED the countess's town
house, C.J. considered the ramifications of pen-
ning a note to Lady Wickham the following morn-
ing, asking her to release Mary Sykes. The resolute little scullery
maid was the only person C.J. would trust to care for the countess while she tried to return to her own era to obtain the modern
medicine that could save Lady Dalrymple's life. But after agonizing for several hours, arguing both sides of the issue with herself, C.J. ultimately thought better of sending such a missive.
The less Lady Wickham, or anyone on the outside, learned of
her business, the better.

LATER, EAGER TO RETURN to her own world before it was too
late, C.J. stood at the back of the darkened Theatre Royal watching the mid-afternoon rehearsal, looking for an opportunity to

slip through time. At first she thought she was seeing *De Montfort,* because the supernumeraries' costumes were more or less the same generic medieval garb, but as soon as the leading lady set foot onstage, it was apparent that quite a different play was being acted.

Siddons was wearing the most expensive "nightdress" that C.J. had ever seen—a gossamer, cloth-of-gold confection with a train that trailed behind her like several feet of white cobwebs. Candle in hand, she made an unearthly Lady Macbeth. Although she had little time to waste, how could C.J. not savor this once-in-a-lifetime chance to witness the legendary tragedienne's "innovative" interpretation of the famous sleepwalking scene?

True to Darlington's description, Sarah Siddons did not break stride from her somnambulant state, but hung the long taper in its brass holder on a conveniently contrived crook in the stone walls of Dunsinane, permitting an astonished "doctor" and "gentlewoman" to marvel as she rubbed her hands together in the futile attempt to blot out the remembrance of Lady Macbeth's bloody deeds.

C.J., too, was transfixed. And this was only a rehearsal. What struck her as so extraordinary was not the "newness" of Siddons's stage business, but the woman's undeniable majesty. She had true "star power." Very few stage actresses of C.J.'s own era projected such strength and confidence. Unfortunately, C.J. knew she had to tear herself away to try to sneak backstage. In an effort to avoid calling attention to herself, she stealthily hugged the wall of the orchestra stalls.

The theatre manager himself applauded Mrs. Siddons's brilliant performance in the rehearsal and released her in order to work on the opening scene of the play. The actors playing the three witches were called to the stage, and those portraying Duncan, Malcolm, Donalbain, and Lennox—with what seemed like a dozen attendants—were told to stand by for their entrance.

The prompter called out the words *music,* and *fog,* and *thun-*

der and lightning, so the witches could time their stage business and be properly cued for their lines. They had no sooner begun when an actor attired in tights, deliberately tattered inky robes, and an enormous headdress that severely limited his visibility—and carrying a huge bowl overflowing with disgusting-looking animal parts—stumbled and fell. Like a series of dominoes, the extras waiting to enter with the Scottish nobility toppled over one another in a cacophony of clanking halberds, claymores, and round, target-shaped shields. To C.J., it seemed like a miscue straight out of Monty Python.

"Stop!" roared the manger. "Come out here, you!" he commanded the "evil spirit" busily adjusting his top-heavy headdress, which had gone woefully askew in the melee. "Who is that?" he demanded of the assembled cast. The young man dressed as the goblin stepped forward. "Remove your mask. I can't see your face. I want to remember that face!" thundered the livid theatre manager. With some difficulty, the neophyte undid the leather straps that bound the elaborate headdress under his chin. "Who are you?" his employer demanded.

"Kean, sir. Edmund Kean," answered the stocky young man.

"Time is money, and you have wasted both, Master Kean. Were it not for engaging your services, such as they are, the company would be spending the afternoon at the Black Swan, instead of rehearsing in a beerless theatre."

"I'm sorry, sir. This is the first time I have appeared in a tragedy."

"Well, *Ned*," the manager replied with extreme condescension. "If I have any say in the matter, you will never work in one again! Back to work, everyone!" he commanded.

C.J. would wager that time had erased all memory of the name of the manager of Bath's Theatre Royal in 1801; but Edmund Kean, now merely an inexperienced youth at the brink of an illustrious, though tempestuous, career as one of the great tragic actors of the English stage, was—despite this inauspicious debut—going to prove his employer's prognostication to be dramatically incorrect.

What an amazing place to be . . . right here, right now! And she had to leave it as soon as possible! Was there no justice?

The ruckus following Master Kean's portentous entrance and the attendant histrionics of the theatre manager afforded C.J. the opportunity to slink backstage. She was on the verge of combing the racks of medieval robes in search of an appropriate disguise when she felt a hand clamp down upon her shoulder.

"What 'ave we 'ere?" rhetorically asked the burly stagehand, mercifully neither Turpin nor Twist. C.J. panicked. The first defense that sprang to her mind was to feign total ignorance. And what better way to do that than to appear not to understand a word of English.

"*Pardon?*" asked C.J., widening her eyes. "*Je ne comprends pas l'anglais.*" Pretending to be French might not work, but it wasn't as lame as saying, "This is the first time I have appeared in a tragedy." She surmised that the irony would be lost somehow.

The stagehand scowled. "Listen, Frenchy, I dunno how you got in 'ere, but this ain't a museum."

"*Je suis . . . perdue?*" C.J. replied in her most plaintive voice, indicating that she had gotten lost.

"Well, you just get along now," the stagehand advised as he steered her toward the backstage door that opened onto her favorite alley. "If the manager sees you back 'ere, there'll be 'ell to pay. 'E's already in a snit over that damn clumsy fool Kean causin' such a ruckus."

C.J. nodded and smiled like an uncomprehending idiot, and when she found herself in the narrow lane outside of the theatre, just for good measure she looked about like a confused rabbit, in case the stagehand was watching her. Which he was. "Down the lane, mamselle," he boomed, as though her inability to understand his words was due to deafness, rather than a language barrier. He gesticulated wildly in the direction of Orchard Street when C.J. deliberately began to head the opposite way, which would have landed her smack in the middle of a whitewashed stone wall. Afraid that she might be overplaying her hand, she looked back and, grinning foolishly at him, scampered out to the main thoroughfare.

The handbill posted outside the front of the theatre announced the final performance of *De Montfort* that night. Since this play alone appeared to be the "open sesame," C.J. would have to avail herself of what would undoubtedly be her last opportunity to find some modern medicine for Lady Dalrymple.

Her state of agitation served her well for a change. On the pretext of feeling faint, and with the certainty that the cool night air would do her good, she persuaded the countess to permit her an early evening constitutional. C.J. kissed her "aunt" good-bye and made sure that she had enough money in her reticule to purchase a theatre ticket in case her stage-door shenanigans backfired yet again.

Saunders discreetly noted the time that Miss Welles departed the residence for the second time that day with no stated destination, no call to pay, nor particular errand to run.

THE SIDE DOOR to the Theatre Royal had been deliberately left ajar that evening for the purposes of generating cross-ventilation, so C.J. slipped in unnoticed amid the usual backstage hubbub that occurred during major scene shifts. Elaborate drops were raised, replaced, and lowered, and the louvered flats rumbled into place while dozens of journeyman actors scrambled to change from one costume into the next.

And once again, just in time for Siddons's dramatic entrance as Jane de Montfort, C.J. managed to cross the stage and exit into the dark vortex that she prayed would convey her home.

Emerging from the darkness, she staggered back onto the stage, completely dazed. Ralph, the *By a Lady* assistant set designer, who in C.J.'s absence had made considerable progress on the Steventon parlor, was the first to come to her aid. "Holy shit, what happened to you!" he exclaimed, hammer still in hand. He gave a shout, and the entire production team came running over.

"We've spent the past day and a half considering possible replacements for you; Harvey was convinced you'd fallen off the planet. Haven't you gotten my messages? I've been looking for you from here to kingdom come!" Beth said.

"Where have you been?" Humphrey Porter asked her.

"Kingdom come, I think," C.J. replied, still in somewhat of a fog. The theatre lights were so bright it was hard to see, let alone think, straight. "I . . ." C.J. shook her head, not knowing what else to say that would absolve her of any further inquiry. "Personal business," she murmured.

Beth flipped open her cell phone and punched up a number. She held up a finger to C.J. as she waited for the call to connect. "Harvey," she said after a few moments, "we've found her." Beth moved downstage to enjoy some privacy for the remainder of her conversation with the producer. "Right, then!" she said, rejoining the cluster of production staff still surrounding C.J. "We'll be all set to start rehearsals tomorrow if you—" She stopped speaking abruptly and stared at C.J.'s disheveled appearance. "What the hell happened to you?" she asked, more concerned than appalled. "Wait! Before you tell us, please, please say that you are going to accept the role of Jane Austen before I commit hara-kiri right here in the middle of the stage."

"Well . . ." C.J. hesitated.

"Please don't fuck me over, here," Beth pleaded, "and I mean that in the nicest possible way."

As her thought process became clearer, C.J. felt as though her entire life was hanging in the balance. On both sides of the scale, actually. On one side—the third-millennium side—she was being offered the role of a lifetime and the chance to finally enjoy the career of her dreams. On the nineteenth-century side of the balance, she was *already* playing the role of a lifetime in many ways. More urgently, on the other side of the void there was a dying woman who had been her benefactress and for whom she had developed an immensely strong affection. Perhaps only modern pharmaceuticals could save her, and for that C.J. had to risk sacrificing her twenty-first-century existence to bring the remedies with her across time—if the journey was even possible to achieve. Also on the other side was the blossoming friendship with the real Jane Austen, the woman she had idolized all her life. And then there was Lord Darlington and the powerful mutual attraction between them. She had willingly given her body to him and acknowledged that she had parted with her heart as well. Why was everything happening at once?! And in both of her worlds, time played the leading role.

"You look as if you've been through the mill and back," Humphrey observed. He grabbed a handful of the yellow muslin dress. "It looks like you slept in this."

C.J. looked down at her gown. "I must have done," she replied. "I suppose I'll have some explaining to do to Milena. And the hat and the shawl too. I don't know what happened."

"You've been gone for two and a half days," Beth informed her. "And you're also speaking with an English accent."

Jesus! She'd been using a foreign accent for so long she'd forgotten to switch back to her own. How embarrassing. "Well, you know me," she joked feebly, finding her own American voice. "C.J. Welles, method actress. Oh, and *yes*, by the way. In case I didn't tell you," she added, grasping the director's arm, "of course I want to play Jane. I would *love* to do the part."

Beth looked heavenward, at the proscenium arch. "Oh, thank God. Thank God." She shook C.J.'s hand vigorously, gave her a little hug, and tossed her cell phone to a personal assistant. "Call Harvey back," she said, "and tell him to messenger the contracts over here right away." Physically seating her new leading lady, Beth told her, "You're not moving from this chair, Miss Welles, until you've signed your contract." She tugged at a lock of her flaxen hair. "See this? Gray. I've gone gray while you've gone missing!"

Two hours, two cups of coffee, and one tuna salad sandwich later, C.J. Welles signed her first Broadway contract. It should have been one of the most thrilling moments of her life, but she was thinking about the fate of Lady Dalrymple. The production staff congratulated her, and C.J. weakly accepted her plaudits.

"I'm sorry . . . I know I should act more ecstatic," C.J. said, "and believe me, I am indeed as high as a kite over all this," she hastened to assure them. After all, Beth in particular had really gone out on a limb for her. "But I suppose . . . at the moment . . . I'm too exhausted to seem appropriately elated."

Milena was called down to the theatre to take any further measurements, if necessary, in order to get the ball rolling on the costume construction. She shook her head, somewhat dismayed, when she saw the state of the yellow muslin, the now-ratty and shrunken coquelicot shawl, and the straw hat that looked like it had been a horse's lunch. C.J. apologized profusely. "If you need me to pay you for the damage to the garments, I will," she said, heading back to the dressing room to change into her contemporary street clothes.

"Don't worry about reimbursement," Milena assured her, "but before you get dressed, I want you to try this for me." She pulled a light blue dress the color of a Wedgwood vase from a rolling rack of garments and surveyed it. "This doesn't have a zipper, so it's easier to adjust. If it fits you, I have the pattern back in my studio, and I can work from that for your day dresses." The costumer laced C.J. into the sarcenet gown and made a few minor adjustments.

"This itches a bit," C.J. complained, tugging at the small white ruff at her throat.

Milena looked at the collar and fussed with it a bit. "This is called a Betsie," she told the actress. "Very fashionable in 1801."

"Very ugly," C.J. mused, disappointed and thinking that the blue sarcenet gown that the fashion-forward Madame Delacroix had made for her was ever so much nicer, and only the nerdy girls in 1801 wore Betsie collars. If her destiny was to remain in present-day America, she wanted to look a bit, well, sexy onstage, if it was at all possible with these period dresses that resembled granny nightgowns more than anything else.

"I'm afraid that Jane Austen wasn't much of a fashion plate," Milena sighed.

More than you think, C.J. almost said aloud. Instead she said,

"Do you mind if I wear this during rehearsals? I'm one of those actresses who finds it easier to work on her character when she's got a reasonable facsimile of the costume. Particularly with a show like this where my entire body language is dictated by the garments and the customs of the era."

Milena sighed. "Well, I don't see why not. As long as it's all right with Beth. But please don't bring this one back to me as if it's been in a cat's mouth. I'll give you another reticule and bonnet as well," she added, leaving the dressing room.

Wow. How strange it felt to put on a pair of jeans and a pullover after all this time in flimsy, empire-waisted gowns. Somehow her tight pants felt more restrictive than any of her 1801 corseting had. *Amazing what a body can adjust to*, C.J. marveled as she went back downstairs to the theatre.

Although it was offered, she refused any medical treatment for her dazed behavior. So the *By a Lady* staff sent her home to get some rest and prepare to start rehearsals at ten the following morning. C.J. went back upstairs to the dressing room to claim her cloak and noticed a modest-sized carpetbag on the bottom shelf of the costume rack. Perfect for transporting drugs across time. What was a little petit larceny compared to the life of a dear friend? Tomorrow she would bring some beta-blockers to rehearsal and see if she could somehow get back to Bath and cure the countess. Was it possible to alter someone's destiny? Was it right? Shouldn't saving the life of a loved one come before all else?

It felt very odd to be surrounded by automobiles, trucks, buses, and so much comparative bustle and noise, and to enter a modern high-rise and turn the key in the lock of her apartment. C.J. fingered the amber cross that still hung about her neck and sighed; not relieved, but disconcerted. After such a strange journey, she was back home. Or was she?

Chapter Nineteen

While Lady Dalrymple benefits from a new nurse, our self-proclaimed apothecary does some night crawling of her own, but a nasty surprise threatens to once again alter our heroine's destiny.

WHEN SHE GOT UPSTAIRS, C.J. made a beeline for the medicine cabinet in the master bathroom, her heart pounding as she looked for the state-of-the-art prescriptions that had helped postpone the inevitable for her grandmother as long as modern medicine could.

The interior of the medicine chest resembled a well-stocked pharmacy. C.J. found a large amber-colored plastic bottle of green and yellow nitroglycerin capsules. It was nearly full. She sifted through bottles containing hexagonal Inderal tablets, each penny-candy color denoting a different dosage. Nana's long illness had spurred C.J. to do her own research into the properties of various medications. The Internet had provided a host of information, and the *Physicians' Desk Reference* had become her bible. From the little C.J. had managed to glean from the incompetent Dr. Squiffers, she surmised that Lady Dalrymple was suffering from a form of angina, in which case the nitroglycerin should effectively treat her condition or, at the very least, prolong her life. Best case scenario: the dowager countess was merely the victim of chest pain; worst case: the pills could certainly be no more dangerous than Dr. Squiffers's antediluvian methods of treatment.

If the modern medicines worked, C.J. would have another hill to climb to persuade Lady Dalrymple's cook to completely alter her mistress's diet. Caffeinated tea was probably a bad idea too. It was going to be difficult to convince her ladyship to forgo afternoon tea. Oh yes—and then there was alcohol. No more afternoon dram of sherry or evening glass of port. C.J. wondered if her "aunt" would consider the forfeit of so many of her life's simple pleasures worth the cure. At least the countess kept a positive outlook on life, and that was supposed to be a plus when it came to the anticipation of a full recovery from the condition known as effort angina.

C.J. only hoped that time was on her side. There was no consideration of waiting until the rehearsal. She had to get right back to the theatre. She dumped the contents of each plastic pill bottle into separate paper envelopes, carefully labeling them with a fountain pen. Then she toured her apartment for the last time, shedding several tears over what she was willingly leaving behind. Amid a tinkle of wind chimes, she shut and locked the apartment door, feeling as if her body was being stretched on a rack that spanned more than two hundred years.

LADY DALRYMPLE WAS resting comfortably while Mary Sykes sat vigilantly by, cross-stitching a simple tapestry. "I have not yet seen Cassandra," her ladyship remarked anxiously, accustomed to her "niece's" nightly visit to wish her a good evening and a tranquil slumber.

"I think she was quite fatigued," Mary lied, wholly aware that Miss Welles had not even been home to witness her arrival at the Royal Crescent. "But she wished you a good night before she went—to sleep," she quickly added. "Does it still hurt, your ladyship?"

Her respiring had been labored for the past several hours, during which Mary bravely tried to conceal her alarm. "Only when I breathe," the countess replied gamely.

THE FRONT DOOR of the Bedford Street Playhouse had been padlocked, and as C.J. struggled to open the back door—which appeared to have been locked from within—she was approached by an unshod man who materialized from the alleyway and limped over to her, hand extended, palm up. At first C.J. didn't comprehend what the man wanted, his speech being slurred by drink or drugs or dearth of teeth. The panhandler looked young and tolerably healthy enough to hold down a job, barring the apparent substance abuse.

"Hungry?" C.J. offered him an apple from her shoulder bag. The beggar inspected it closely, then grudgingly decided to accept the gift. After devouring the fruit as though he hadn't eaten in hours, if not days, he stretched out a dirty hand, cocked his head to one side, and regarded his benefactress mournfully.

If only someone had helped me when I first arrived in Bath, C.J. thought, carefully extracting a dollar from her wallet. It was the first time she had ever capitulated to a homeless New Yorker accosting her for alms; but she felt a pang of empathy for the man standing before her, who was, in fact, nothing like herself at all. Nothing like her present self, anyway. The morning she'd stolen the apple off the vendor's cart in Stall Street, she had been just as destitute and nearly as dirty.

There was a tense standoff while C.J. was afraid that the bum might try to attack her person or her purse. She tried to look confident, hoping the man didn't smell her fear. But after about half a minute, the panhandler lost interest and slunk away down the street and out of sight. C.J. watched his retreating figure until he turned a corner.

Back to the playhouse door. She was losing time. C.J. jiggled the well-worn iron handle. No luck. She looked up to see if there was another way. A sliver of light emanated from an upstairs room. Someone had left a window open on the second floor.

If at first you don't succeed . . .

Mercifully, no one noticed the slender brunette giving her best shot at impersonating a Flying Wallenda, trying to climb the rusty, dangling fire escape ladder. *Did it count as breaking-and-entering if you didn't break anything as you ent—oops!* Losing her footing, C.J. slid down a couple of rungs, scraping the length of her right leg. Dots of blood stippling her thigh and calf seeped through her pants, freckling the fabric. In about another five minutes, the long pink scratches on her pale skin would metamorphose into a red weltlike ribbon. Fighting the stinging pain, she repeated her climb.

Goddamn! Decades of paint layers on an already rotting window sash made it nearly immovable. Her hands hurt from trying to force the window open.

Flattening herself like a cockroach, C.J. wriggled through the open window, landing on the linoleum in a makeshift handstand. Her shoulder bag went skidding across the floor.

Who ever thought this little caper would be easy? C.J. asked herself as she slumped against the wall to catch her breath. After cleaning her cuts with some warm soapy water, the next goal was to get into her new loaner costume and go downstairs to the stage so she could try to get back to 1801.

She removed the blue sarcenet gown from the rolling costume rack, donned it, surveyed her image in the full-length mirror, and did a quick sartorial inventory. Underwear, petticoat, dress, hose, shoes, bonnet, gloves, reticule . . . *carpetbag.* C.J. placed the numerous medicine envelopes into the period prop bag, covered them with a folded blue velvet spencer, and raced downstairs to the set.

Shit! Since she'd left the theatre just a few hours earlier, the stage had been altered. It now looked as if a wrecking crew had enjoyed a field day. Set units had been turned around or moved off their tape marks. The Austens' parlor in Steventon was once again a work in progress. The door was gone. *Her* door—the one that had transported her across the centuries and back—had been moved from its position as the gateway to C.J.'s other life.

She found the unit on its side, minus the wooden shims that enabled it to stand freely when secured by sandbags from the backstage side. Nothing remained of the upstage-left exit area except four small Ls made with red gaffer's tape, marking the proper angle and placement of the door frame.

C.J. regarded the disassembled set pieces, tapped into all of her emotions, and re-created the staging for the end of the act that Beth had given her during the audition process—this time with the addition of the carpetbag—walking through the spot on the floor delineated by the red Ls.

After another maddeningly unsuccessful attempt, it was abundantly clear that C.J. was not going to be able to travel anywhere but the backstage area of the Bedford Street Playhouse. Exhausted both mentally and physically, she shuffled off to the green room, collapsed on the sofa, and fell asleep.

AFTER AWAKENING in a wrinkled dress with a stiff neck and a few abrasions from the itchy Betsie at her throat, her hand in a cramp from clutching the handle of the carpetbag as she slept, C.J. showered in her dressing room, ironed the blue sarcenet dress, and, after donning it again, debated what to do next. Ralph would have to arrive at the theatre well before today's first rehearsal to finish putting the set back together—unless, to her horror, Beth just wanted to sit around a table for a read-through of the script. That was the customary way with first rehearsals, although her experiences with *By a Lady* had so far been anything but ordinary.

At half past nine, the production staff began to straggle in, provisioned with coffee, bagels, and Krispy Kreme doughnuts. Sweating like a wrestler and swigging water from a plastic sport flask, Ralph entered the building, hefting his enormous metal toolbox, which he refused to leave in the space overnight.

The designer looked at C.J., then at his watch. "Rehearsal doesn't start for half an hour."

"I know. I thought I might as well get into costume. Save some time."

Ralph mopped his brow with what appeared to have been a royal blue washcloth in another life. "Don't see why you needed to." He gestured to the mess onstage. "I've got all this to deal with and get out of the way before we start," he added, visibly stressed.

"Do you think the door will be put back, because . . . ?"

"Everything will be put back exactly the way it was when you saw it yesterday. I was trying to fix some things—like the shims on the stage-left door and the ones on the fireplace unit—and there's a loose leg on the sofa that has me nervous. I expected to get everything done last night, but then I got a migraine in the middle of using the electric drill, and Beth suggested I give it a rest for the night."

"Because you're running yourself ragged, darling, and I can't afford to lose my assistant scenic designer in the beginning of the rehearsal process." Beth strode down the aisle of the theatre and stepped up onto the stage to hand Ralph an ice-cold can of Diet Coke. "Enjoy your breakfast," she teased.

A young actor with curly blond hair, wearing a denim jacket and black jeans and carrying a knapsack, bounded down the aisle and dropped his pack onto a chair in the front row. Beth immediately greeted him with a hug. "C.J.," she called, "here's your Tom. C.J. Welles, our Jane, meet Frank Teale, direct from the Royal Shakespeare Company."

"By way of the Cleveland Playhouse," Frank added. He was a real Brit. Or else he insisted on staying in character even more than C.J. did. "I was just doing *Hedda* out there."

"C.J. Welles," the actress said, extending her hand to her costar. "By way of office temping and unemployment. I bet you made a lovely Hedda Gabler," she joked.

"Actually, I might have done," Frank replied. He shook C.J.'s hand and gave her a winning smile. "But they cast me as Eilert

Løvborg, alas. Nontraditional casting has not come that far in the American Midwest."

Well, well, C.J. was thinking, wondering why she'd never met this hottie during the lengthy audition process. Should it turn out that she would have to remain in the twenty-first century forever, she had a very cute and charming costar and a few passionate kisses in the script. *Not a bad way to make a Broadway debut.*

When Humphrey finally arrived, perspiring and apologetic, mopping his glistening brow with a handkerchief edged in Harvard crimson, Beth called Frank and C.J. to the apron of the stage for a brief discussion of some script modifications. "Of course it's one of the laws of the Theatre that as soon as you think you've got all your ducks in a row, one of them decides to develop a mind of his own. In this case, we've got some script revisions to go over before we do a first read-through with a—dare I say—*entire* cast. Both of you. I expect the whole rehearsal process will be an evolving and collaborative one." She winked at Humphrey. "But it's the deal you make with the devil, I suppose, when you work with a living playwright." Beth ceded the floor to the dramatist as though she were passing a baton.

"I feel as if we've been neglecting Jane as a *writer*—as the thing that defines the woman," Humphrey urged, cleaning the lint from his tortoiseshell-framed eyeglasses with a specially treated cloth. "It's my fault for writing it the way I did, but I feel that the way things are right now, she's accepting the change in her life too easily."

"Meaning . . . ?" C.J. asked.

The playwright thoughtfully chewed the end of his eyeglass frame. "I would like to cut Jane's lines after Tom's exit—you know, 'Bath. I'm going to Bath'—and not have her leave the stage, but *instead* cross over to the writing table, sit down, and begin to write as the curtain falls. I want to show that she finds *solace* in the writing, despite the enforced move to Bath, because it salves her soul from her emotionally painful reunion with Tom."

C.J. dug her nails into her palms. This revision could present an enormous impediment to her ability to get back to the nine-teenth century. "You mean keep her onstage at the end of the act, instead of exiting?"

"Another duck heard from." Beth immediately recognized her leading lady's obvious discomfort with the proposed new staging. "C.J., you're going to be so good in this role. That's why I went to the mat for you. And I'm sure you can take any direction and play it so that it works beautifully. Let's try what Humphrey suggests when we run through it. Just make a different, but equally strong, choice at the end of the act." She looked visibly upset, as though she was already beginning to regret putting her neck on the line for an actress who was turning out to be an uncooperative diva.

"While you guys futz around, I'll just start putting things back together," Ralph announced to no one in particular. He went upstage-left and began to repair the shim on the door unit.

A first rehearsal for her Broadway debut was not the time to begin acting up instead of acting. But how could C.J. explain things to Beth and Humphrey without their deciding which to do first: fire her or commit her to the Bellevue psychiatric ward?

"I know this may sound like a silly request," C.J. said, punting, "but I like to work organically—put all the elements together from the getgo—so . . . well . . . does anyone mind if I try to see how the whole thing feels in my body, with the blocking and the dialogue?" She indicated her blue dress with a tug. "The costumes too. I'm weird that way. But it just helps me get into character and stay there right from the start. Milena gave me this dress to wear for rehearsals, so I thought—"

Beth heaved a little sigh and rewarded C.J. with an indulgent nod. "Our very own Daniel Day-Lewis. Oh, what the fuck. Why not?"

C.J. gave the director a grateful smile. "Many thanks! Just give me a minute, okay?" She retreated to a dark, quiet corner behind the set where she had placed the carpetbag containing the pills for Lady Dalrymple. The only way to convince Humphrey that his original instinct was the right one was to play the revised scene the way they wanted to see it, thereby demonstrating its reduced effectiveness. "Let's do it," C.J. called out resolutely. "I know there aren't any lines in this new version, but I just want to see how the different blocking feels." C.J. crossed to the writing desk and sat there for a few moments pretending to write, imagined that the curtain was falling, then crossed the diagonal length of the stage and grabbed the carpet-bag as she exited through the same upstage area that had previously opened for her onto another century. But all she found in the gloomy light on the other side of the set was a stack of dusty flats leaning against the brick wall of the theatre. Silently she beat the backstage side of the door frame with her head.

Humphrey came up onstage and sat cross-legged with his face in his palms. "I don't know. In a way I'm glad that C.J. wanted to get right up and try the new ending because, in fact, now that I've seen it on its feet, it *diminishes* the energy that we've been building up through the whole Jane/Tom confrontation. I thought the new way would be a more dramatic moment. But maybe it's not." He sighed theatrically. "I'm sorry if I wasted everyone's time."

"Don't be ludicrous, Humphrey." Beth ruffled the playwright's hair and gave his shoulders a brief rub. "The upside about working with a living playwright is that it's all a work in progress until the curtain falls on the final performance."

Elsie made a production number out of clearing her throat. "Don't you guys go all improvisational on me when we get into the run," she warned, shooting the actors a threatening look. "You'll be a stage manager's nightmare."

Humphrey and Beth bent their heads together for a brief conference.

"Okay," Beth said, emerging from their tête-à-tête. "Humphrey doesn't think that his suggestion worked after all. For the time being, at any rate. And at the moment I'm inclined to agree with him."

C.J. raised her hand to offer a further contribution. "I'm figuring this out as I speak here. You don't want the audience to view the retrenching as forcing Jane to give up her writing. Because she had no way of knowing that she was going to, in effect, suffer writer's block once she got to Bath. So get this," C.J. continued, her urgency to convince the playwright and director increasing with every word. "Tom leaves. I say my line alone onstage, realizing the magnitude of the change in my life as I know it. Then I survey the room, taking a last look at what I shall be leaving. *Then* it occurs to me that I need to pack, and the first things I would pack—because I am, after all, Jane Austen—are my writing implements, which are sitting right out there on the table. So I pick up a carpetbag and cross to the table, open the bag, and place my scribbling paraphernalia—the manuscript, the pens—and the tapestry I'm working on in the bag. I take my deep breath while I'm standing just above the table, say the lines about going to Bath softly instead of resolutely—as though I've made my peace with the retrenching—then cross upstage to the door, and exit."

The writer and director exchanged looks. "Let's try it," Beth announced.

"Can we just run it now?" C.J. asked, trying to sound casual. "I want to make sure the timing is right."

Elsie looked at her watch, then at the director. "Up to you, boss. It's 10:45 and we've got an Equity break coming up in fifteen minutes."

"Let's do it," Beth said. "All right, C.J., let's see your idea in motion."

C.J. checked her props, ensuring that all the medicine envelopes were tucked away into the carpetbag, then brought the bag onstage and placed it on the floor near Jane's writing table. She reinventoried her costume accessories to make sure that she had everything she needed to travel to Bath. Having the last line of the act back was a blessing. Now if she could convince Beth and Humphrey to keep it that way, she might be home free, in a manner of speaking. This time it would be no strange twist of fate, no surreal accident. She was making a considered choice between her own world and 1801. *De Montfort* had closed; the portal from the other side was no longer open to her now. If C.J. did manage to return to Bath, she stayed there. No Broadway debut; no stage career; no rent-stabilized three-bedroom two-bath Manhattan apartment; no toilets, tampons, or television. No Internet, and a permanent farewell to her twenty-first-century friends and colleagues. She was effectively and irrevocably sacrificing everything she had ever known and strived for to try to save the life of the woman who had rescued hers. To remain in this century knowing there was something she might have done for Lady Dalrymple was unthinkable; she would feel guilty about it to her own grave.

C.J. was willingly choosing the waning Age of Enlightenment over the thriving Information Age. But back in 1801 were new friends, a new love, and someone who needed her more than any of them—and more than C.J. needed to be a Broadway star. For Lady Dalrymple, it was a matter of life and death—and because of that, C.J. was choosing life.

She delivered the act's curtain line. And this time, as she exited the stage and passed through Ralph's newly repaired doorway, C.J. found herself drowning in a pool of blackness. *Finally*, she thought, both trembling and relieved. It was working like a charm.

Chapter Twenty

Wherein our heroine returns to Bath in the nick of time and is reunited with an old friend, though spies abound in an enemy camp; Lady Dalrymple enjoys increasingly restored health, but a morning's excursion is marred by a rumormonger.

LADY DALRYMPLE'S BEDCHAMBER was a somber sight.

Good God . . . how long have I been gone?

C.J. elbowed past the dowager's visitors in a highly unseemly fashion for a gently bred young lady. The countess, pale and weak, lay against a sea of white linen, her eyes half closed. But upon seeing C.J. again, she found a renewed energy. "Come here, Niece," she beckoned.

C.J. approached the bedside and gave her "aunt" a warm hug. How much more frail the countess had become; her ladyship's previously plump form seemed little more than a sagging sack that hung about her feeble bones. In her infirmity, her ladyship was beginning to show the signs of her true age. "I promise I will not leave this room until you are cured," she assured her benefactress.

"Nonsense," retorted Lady Dalrymple, her voice as hoarse as a whisper. "You have dances and parties to attend—walks—and shopping with that delightful Miss Austen. Never mind an old lady like me. Life is for the living. Besides," she added, gesturing to a slender figure shyly hanging back amid the shadows, "Mary can stay right at my elbow. I have full confidence in her nursing abilities."

Mary? Mary Sykes?

Lady Wickham's former scullery maid stepped forward into the candlelight. In livery that properly fit her narrow frame, and with clean and shining dark hair peeking out from under her white mobcap, she was not at all an unattractive girl. With no thought of censoring her behavior, C.J. rushed forward to greet her. For a moment, they held each other like long-separated siblings, their faces streaming with tears.

"I've tried to do my best by 'er ladyship," Mary sniffled apologetically, focusing her attention on the palsied medic who was pacing the room.

Dr. Squiffers appeared self-conscious when C.J. cornered him. "At your insistence, Miss Welles, I have not bled her ladyship," he assured her.

She shot him a look of warning. "You had best be telling me the truth or you have only begun to taste my displeasure."

Suddenly, C.J. realized that two more pairs of eyes had been upon her since she'd entered her aunt's room. Lady Oliver sat by the other side of the bed like Cerberus guarding the gates of hell. If she had indicated her disapproval when Miss Welles embraced the new serving girl, C.J. never heard it. Lady Oliver's nephew had positioned himself by the window, where he hung back, alternately twisting his signet ring and anxiously chewing on his thumbnail in a most ungentlemanly fashion.

C.J. had not seen him since the first and only time they had made love.

"I was watching for you, Miss Welles," he admitted as he drew C.J. into his arms. Not even Lady Oliver could object to such compassion during a time of crisis. His warmth and the security of his embrace were a godsend.

"What is Dr. Squiffers doing here?" C.J. whispered suspiciously.

"What he perceives to be his duty, I imagine."

"I expressly forbade his presence." She noticed someone skulking in a corner of the bedchamber trying to appear invisible. *Saunders.* Only the mistrustful lady's maid could have been responsible for Squiffers's return.

"Have no fear," Darlington soothed. "He has done nothing but wring his hands and wear out the carpet with his steady tread."

"I should like everyone to leave the room," C.J. requested of the earl. Her wish became his effectively issued command, and with minimal fuss the countess's visitors were hastily ushered from the bedchamber.

C.J. filled a tumbler with cool water from the ewer by the bedside table. Then she opened the carpetbag, removed the blue velvet spencer that had protected the bag's important contents from discovery, and drew out the various envelopes of pills, placing them on the table by the bed. She had no way of knowing that Saunders had sent Mary down to the kitchen on some pretext and was herself squinting a jaundiced eye through the keyhole. Lady Oliver, refusing to wait in a corridor like a commoner, suggested that Dr. Squiffers join her in the parlor for a glass of her hostess's finest ruby port, declaring, "Neither time nor wine should go to waste."

C.J. extracted a nitroglycerin tablet, electing to give the countess a low dosage of the beta-blocker. "Aunt, I am going to make a highly irregular request of you: I pray you not to ask me what apothecary provided this remedy, nor how I came by it."

Lady Dalrymple looked at her "niece," her eyes as wide and trusting as a small child's. She regarded the colorful object in C.J.'s hand. "It looks quite like a pastille," she said, managing a laugh. "You truly believe that this magical pill will cure me?"

"If you do *not* take it, I cannot promise that you will regain any greater degree of health than you enjoy at present," C.J. counseled gravely.

"Well then," the countess sighed dubiously, "if following your regimen will enable me to feast at your wedding breakfast," she continued slyly, "I see no other alternative. Hand me the glass, Cassandra."

There was a discreet knock at the door. C.J. hid the envelopes, then admitted Mary, who slipped into the room with a cup of tea.

"For 'er ladyship."

"Thank you, Mary. But you did not have to make tea at this late hour."

"But I did," the serving girl corrected. "Saunders told me 'er ladyship required it. And not to dawdle, or I'd get what for, for sure." She placed the steaming cup of fragrant chamomile tea on the table by Lady Dalrymple's bedside.

Saunders again.

"Not to dawdle?" C.J. was appalled. "Mary, I can only surmise by your presence here that you no longer work for Lady Wickham. And you certainly are not to take orders from Saunders. She is out of her part if she is giving you instructions, and I assure you, my aunt will hear of it. And Mary? No one in this house gives anyone 'what for'; do you understand?"

"But I arrived just yesterday morning. And Saunders has been in 'er ladyship's employ ever so much longer than I have," protested the new girl in her own defense. " 'Sides, she's a proper maid, and I'm just lucky to have a situation at all."

C.J. gently drew Mary aside. "You sweet, trusting girl. We do not threaten anyone with eviction or termination here. We are the ones who are lucky to have you in service. Remember that, Mary. Mind you, I have no proof in any way," she whispered to the former scullery. "It's merely a feeling that I have in here," she continued, her hand to her heart. "I do not trust Saunders. Not that she means my aunt any harm, but I believe we must keep a watchful eye on her . . . as a mother bird does her young."

"Gentlelike?" Mary asked.

C.J. smiled for the first time since her return. The girl merely needed a bit of oil on the rusty gears of her untested mind. She had suffered others' low opinions of her for so long that she believed herself stupid and incompetent. Once the subject was raised, Mary easily grasped the concept of affecting a concerned vigilance without raising suspicion.

"I cannot express enough gratitude to you, Aunt Euphoria, for releasing Mary from Lady Wickham's employ. You will certainly have no cause to regret it, for she is good-natured, courageous, and most devoted. However did you manage it?"

"Will you think any less of me, Niece, if I confess I had nothing to do with the matter?"

"But . . . ?" C.J. was baffled. "If *you* did not convince Lady Wickham to release Mary, then . . . ?" Silence. Clearly, the countess was not willing to divulge the name of the hero or heroine responsible for Mary's arrival in the Royal Crescent. It was the subject herself who revealed the Samaritan's identity when she shyly mumbled a few words about his most handsome and generous lordship.

"Percy!" whispered C.J. Evidently, he had been paying considerable attention to her tirade that rainy afternoon in his salon. Was the man who had rescued the little maid from an aristocratic employer who routinely beat her the very same Darlington who had so vociferously defended the efficacy and inviolability of the English class system? She bade Mary fetch the earl and bring him to Lady Dalrymple's bedchamber.

"How can I properly express the enormity of our gratitude?" C.J. said softly. "Your lordship has done all of us the greatest kindness." She tugged lightly at his sleeve to draw him nearer. "What did you do? Pay the old bat off?" she whispered, curious about the possibility of some sort of sensational form of rescue, through bribery, extortion, or equally devious means.

"Miss Welles, if you and your aunt are pleased that Mary Sykes has come to reside under Lady Dalrymple's roof and will now be in her employ, that is all the thanks I require. Please forgive my unwillingness to discuss the matter any further." Miss

Welles had no need to ever learn that he had paid the greedy old gimp handsomely with a hundred pounds in bank notes, the loss of which did much to further increase his debts on his already overmortgaged estate.

"VERY RESOURCEFUL, SAUNDERS. Very resourceful," Lady Oliver praised, pressing a golden guinea into the servant's eager hand. Suspiciously eyeing her benefactress, Saunders bit the coin before it disappeared into her apron with the speed of a sleight-of-hand trick. Saunders narrowed her small gray eyes in an expression of tacit thanks, with the complete understanding that there might be more guineas that would be freely parted with upon the exchange of such similarly valuable intelligence. She didn't worry about the suspicion that might arise from trying to spend such a large denomination. Saunders had no use for feminine fripperies. Enough of Lady Oliver's guineas, and she could kiss servitude good-bye.

Her ladyship pursed her lips thoughtfully. "How clever of you to keep a small pencil and a scrap of paper hard by so that you may remember such things as they occur. You have been most accommodating, Saunders. And quite observant." She knocked on the bedchamber door. "I shall pay my respects to your mistress and collect my nephew. Clearly, his infatuation is far worse than even I had suspected. But," she sighed, "something will be done about it, and if I have any say in the matter, the sooner, the better."

"I AM WELL ENOUGH to walk on my own!" Lady Dalrymple announced days later, dismissing her chair carrier just outside the Pump Room. C.J. scrambled to keep up with her aunt's morning constitutionals. To ensure Lady Dalrymple's continued recovery, C.J. had confided in Mary, who was now the only one of the household staff on whom C.J. could rely to keep her counsel regarding the dutiful dispensary of her ladyship's "magic pills."

The countess had a renewed interest in life, following C.J.'s directives, not only with regard to the strange little tablets but also to the judicious taking of regular but moderate forms of exercise, which were chiefly borne out in daily visits to the Pump Room, and the taking of the waters both internally and externally, followed by extravagant shopping expeditions.

C.J. made certain that her ladyship drank her prescribed three glasses of water every day; and she herself was finally growing accustomed to the sulfuric odor and taste of the beneficial waters pumped directly into the elegant social hall from the source below and served warm to the patrons. It was quite an acquired taste for the modern palate.

When the crowd was thin, C.J. had the opportunity to admire the atmosphere of the room itself, finding the pale blue, cream, and gold interior restful and pleasing to the eye. But from late morning through the afternoon, the room bustled with the well-heeled *ton* of Bath, who came to the Pump Room every day to see the same circles of friends and cadres of enemies, and to catch up on the latest social scandals—all in the name of healthful pursuit. The quotidian excursions also provided the opportunity for couples to engage in flirtations under the protective noses of the young ladies' chaperones.

The Miss Fairfaxes made excursions to the Pump Room an integral part of their daily routine, with their mother in tow clucking all the while like a hen about Lady So-and-So or Countess Whatnot as though they were intimates. In fact, Mrs. Fairfax appeared to be a repository for gossip, though where she got her intelligence, no one quite knew. Rumors abounded that the woman used the discretionary allowance provided to her by her gentle and amiable husband to cross the palms of several well-situated servants employed by the most influential members of society.

The seventeen-year-old Miss Susanne invariably appeared mortified by her mother's conduct, remarking once to C.J. how unfair it seemed that the behavior of her mother—and her elder sister as well, who took too much after the Fairfax matriarch by vociferously flaunting her ignorance in public gatherings—should reflect upon her father and herself, who surely didn't merit such censure.

Mrs. Fairfax waved to C.J. and Lady Dalrymple, indicating that she and her brood had intentions of joining the countess's party.

"Are you quite up to her company this afternoon, Aunt?" C.J. asked solicitously.

"Heavens!" Lady Dalrymple responded. "The way the woman taxes one's nerves on occasion is a great stimulation to my constitution. Without a proper argument now and again, I feel my brain becoming addled from lack of use. You must look upon it as sport, child. And despite the occasional vulgarity of her manner, one must remember that she is a well-intentioned woman and a devoted mother."

The Miss Fairfaxes were in the midst of an animated discussion of a highly inappropriate nature for public consumption—and of which their mother most emphatically disapproved—when their party approached C.J. and the countess.

"Well, it is a good thing Lord Digby apparently shares my sentiment on the ill effects of education on young women," the matron said, drawing herself up.

"Whatever do you mean, Mrs. Fairfax?" asked C.J., already feeling a lump rise in her throat at the mention of Lord Digby.

"Oh, goodness, I thought *everyone* had heard the news, especially you, Lady Dalrymple, as you are so thick with Lady Oliver."

This time it was the countess who raised a quizzical eyebrow. "Augusta Oliver, whatever her faults, does not traffic in idle gossip," Lady Dalrymple replied smoothly, masking an anxiety that rivaled her "niece's."

"Well," burbled Mrs. Fairfax, "I have it on the best authority that Lord Darlington's estate is overmortgaged and in absolute ruins, and the only way that Delamere can possibly be salvaged is through a highly advantageous match between his lordship and an eligible young heiress. By all accounts, Lady Oliver is quite settled on her godchild, Charlotte Digby."

C.J. felt her heart plummet to the marble floor and shatter at her feet. "But they barely know one another!"

"Quite true. Quite true," Mrs. Fairfax acknowledged, oblivious to Miss Welles's consternation. The matron was beside herself with pleasure at being able to provide intelligence to her social betters. "The Digbys are from Dorsetshire. Their son, Lady Charlotte's elder brother, is Henry Digby, better known as the Silver Captain for the store of gold coins he seized from the Spanish treasure ship *Santa Brigada* in 1799."

"Then why is he called the Silver Captain if he recovered gold coins?" asked the astute Miss Susanne, not one to readily believe her mother's tales.

"Because, my pet, the Royal Navy gave him a share of forty thousand pounds sterling."

Quickly doing the math, C.J. multiplied the figure by a factor of fifty to achieve a rough idea of the sum in third-millennium American dollars. Two million. She made the error of whistling in most unladylike amazement and tried to appear as though the sound had been produced by someone else.

"The late Robert Digby, Henry and Charlotte's uncle, owned Minterne, in Dorset, which he purchased from the Churchill family in 1768. In his will, he left the estate to his considerably younger brother, the present Lord Digby. Henry is quite devoted to his sister and has no reservations about adding to Lady Charlotte's dowry portion with some of his own funds." A beaming Mrs. Fairfax congratulated herself on her awareness of such vitally important matters.

Lady Dalrymple and her "niece" exchanged concerned glances. C.J. found no words with which to reply, stunned to her very core by Mrs. Fairfax's revelation. Could it possibly be true—that Lady Oliver was brokering a match between her nephew and her godchild? And assuming there was any truth to the rumors being spread by the Fairfax matron, was Darlington aware of his aunt's machinations?

And if his lordship had full knowledge of Lady Oliver's matchmaking, why had he entered into an understanding with C.J.? They *had* entered into an understanding, *hadn't they?* Their afternoon of lovemaking had been the most passionate, tender, trusting, and truly beautiful experience she had ever had. And not only had he willingly given her a lock of his hair, but he had made her a gift of the locket in which to protect the keepsake—a pendant that had belonged to his own mother. After such an intimate gesture, C.J. had every reason to believe herself secure in the earl's affections. Surely, she had never been given cause to doubt them. C.J. blinked away tears and turned away from the little party lest her emotions be detected, for in such a case they were sure to become a topic for immediate dissection.

"I would not be so hasty to share that which you are not entirely sure of, madam," Lady Dalrymple replied somewhat tensely. She too would feel like a dupe if rumors of an impending betrothal between Lady Charlotte Digby and Lord Darlington were genuine and undistorted.

Mrs. Fairfax raised herself to her full height of approximately five feet one and gripped each of her daughters by the wrist. She did not like to have her veracity doubted. "We have much to do today and precious little time remaining to dawdle. Come, girls. Your ladyship, it is a great pleasure to see you in such restored health." She nodded civilly to C.J. "Good day to you, Miss Welles."

Miss Fairfax trotted dutifully beside her mother, although C.J. did not fail to miss the touch of the young blonde's fan to her lips as they passed Captain Keats, who honored his inamorata with a subtle inclination of his head and the trace of a smile. Miss Susanne turned back to regard C.J. with a look of sympathetic concern as her mother towed her away.

"Heavens, Cassandra!" Lady Dalrymple looked as though she were about to bite off a corner of her silk fan.

"How could Mrs. Fairfax be telling the truth? Forgive me if I misconstrued," C.J. began under her breath, conscious of her use of understatement, "but I was under every apprehension that it was Lord Darlington and *I* who had entered into an understanding."

Good God! She had made love with the man, and were word to get out, she would be cast out of society, inasmuch as she was a part of it to begin with. The swift downfall of Lady Rose was a testament to the narrow view taken of such behavior. In any event, the repercussions would severely affect her benefactress. Lady Dalrymple had taken enormous risks with her own reputation by restyling a former lady's companion—as far as she knew—as a titled relation and member of the aristocracy.

A familiar presence, sporting a new bonnet of white muslin, came into view. "Bath is getting so very empty that I am not afraid of doing too little."

"Ah, Miss Austen." The countess greeted their visitor with a warm cordiality that showed nothing of the effects of Mrs. Fairfax's news. "Always a wit."

Jane bestowed a kiss on Lady Dalrymple's cheek. "Every neighborhood should have a great lady," she advised C.J. with a wink.

"My aunt so cleverly got the advantage over Mrs. Fairfax just now. Perhaps you saw her departing in haste with her two daughters bringing up the rear like ducklings," C.J. told Jane.

Lady Dalrymple crooked a plump finger at Miss Austen, beckoning her closer. "Apart from her usual vociferous display of her own ignorance as regards the education of women, the matron has just boldly imparted a piece of gossip that concerns your cousin, Lord Darlington. I daresay, it was news to my ears."

Jane screwed up her face in disgust as she regarded the retreating figure of the vulgar Mrs. Fairfax. "She will never be easy 'til she has exposed herself in some public place," she remarked dryly, sending C.J. into a fit of much-needed laughter under the circumstances.

"How remarkably perceptive you are, Miss Austen," C.J. gasped, swallowing hard to avoid the hiccups.

"I must say I challenged the veracity of her tale, following which she left, much insulted, in high dudgeon. I hope the foolish woman's intelligence is false as a mock turtle soup. Oh, my heart," Lady Dalrymple said, placing her hand upon her bosom. C.J. was concerned that Mrs. Fairfax's unwelcome news might cause an undue setback in her "aunt's" condition. She gave her protectress a look of concern, but the countess dismissed her anxiety with a forced smile and a wave of her hand. "Perhaps if we had flattered her ability to acquire such gossip with acuity, rather than doubted her perspicaciousness, she would have departed a happier woman, though I daresay she did not deserve any encomium."

"That woman is fool indeed, who while insulted by accusation, can be worked on by compliments," Miss Austen observed.

"My legs grow heavy," Lady Dalrymple announced. "I had promised Cassandra a stroll along Milsom Street this morning, but I fear I am too fatigued to honor it." C.J. immediately arranged for a chair and saw to it that her "aunt" would be brought home right away.

Jane allowed that she possessed an hour or two of leisure, although her family had learned from an advertisement in the *Bath Chronicle* that a suitable house just opposite Sydney Gardens might be available, and she was eager to inspect it. She was quite pleased at the prospect of having such a restful and verdant spot so close to their rooms.

C.J. pressed her hand into Jane's. "Your company gives me such pleasure," she beamed. Then, drawing her friend closer, she whispered, "Please spare me a moment or two of your time. I have something very particular to discuss with you, and it cannot wait."

Chapter Twenty-One

Miss Austen dispenses advice to our heartsick heroine, and a shopping expedition leads to a nearly fatal disaster.

THE YOUNG WOMEN locked arms and exited the Pump Room, halting just under the arcade, where the shade afforded them a degree of privacy. "Mrs. Fairfax has quite undone us," C.J. began, referring to herself and the countess. "I am quite aware that the woman is a rumor mill, yet she seems to be thoroughly convinced of the sincerity of the news that there will soon be an alliance made between your noble cousin and Lady Charlotte Digby."

Jane was very quiet. She carefully chose her words. "I have not seen it in the papers. And one may as well be single, if the wedding is not to be in print."

"You know as well as I, Miss Austen, that when we last were in company together, in Sydney Gardens, there was an understanding between his lordship and me. You surmised as much. You *saw* as much." With a delicate cambric handkerchief she blotted away the tears that had begun their slow trickling journey down her cheeks.

Miss Austen emitted a commiserating sigh. "*Ohhh* . . . women fancy admiration means more than it does. And men take care that they should." Her tone bore a trace of bitterness. Jane gently placed a gloved hand on C.J.'s arm. "It must be terrible for you to hear it talked of. I think the less that is said about such things, the better; the sooner 'tis blown over and forgot."

"*Forgot?* I don't understand you. Surely you are aware that this transcends the confines of mere *admiration*." C.J. changed arguments. "His lordship does not even know Charlotte Digby. How can he possibly love her? I would hazard that he has never spent an unchaperoned moment in the girl's presence. How can he know her mind? Her likes and dislikes? Her taste in all manner of things?" Her poor square of cambric was by now reduced to a wet rag.

Jane sighed. "Happiness in marriage is entirely a matter of chance. In many respects, it is better to know as little as possible of the defects of the person with whom you are to pass your life."

"But you cannot possibly believe that! When you yourself have always believed in marrying for love or not at all. To avoid knowing anything of import about the man you will marry is never to be given the chance to marry him for love."

Jane turned white.

C.J. immediately realized she had said far too much. Not only had she divulged Miss Austen's deepest personal credo, but she had carelessly disclosed intelligence that the Cassandra Jane Welles of 1801 would have had no cause to know. She flushed a shade of deep crimson.

"I beg your pardon, Miss Austen. I am somewhat overcome at present," C.J. sniffled into the hanky. "My remark was entirely unsuitable and inappropriate. It was beyond the bounds of all decency to be so bold as to make my own conjecture upon your opinions of love and matrimony. Of *course* I would not know your history," C.J. fibbed, "but I came to the presumption that since you have arrived at a certain age of maturity and remain unwed, you place a higher store on the tenderer sensibilities than the need to enter into an arrangement where there was no love on either side—or at least on your own."

Miss Austen's response was itself a confirmation. "I have no notion of loving people by halves," she smiled. "And I'll allow that my attachments are always excessively strong. All the privilege I claim for my own sex is that of loving the longest, when existence or when hope is gone." Her expression turned momentarily melancholy.

C.J. wondered about Jane and Tom Lefroy. "I do believe that men have a greater capacity to transfer their affections from one object to another with equal zeal, while we tend to mourn our loss for a lengthier duration," she replied sourly. The pair of them, she and Jane, had such rotten luck when it came to men. "Darlington cannot be marrying for love, but for money, if he is to marry Charlotte Digby at all," she added emphatically, realizing that Miss Austen had not exactly confirmed the accuracy of Mrs. Fairfax's gossip.

However, Jane issued no denial, and her assessment of her own cousin's behavior bordered on the pragmatic. The sudden acquisition of ten thousand pounds was the most remarkable charm of the young lady to whom he was now rendering himself agreeable, she told Miss Welles, acknowledging her awareness that Delamere was mortgaged to the hilt and that Darlington was under pressure from Lady Oliver to remarry well in order to save the family seat.

"From what I hear, her portion may be considerably more than ten thousand pounds," C.J. added glumly. It translated to a sudden windfall, equivalent to nearly half a million twenty-first-century dollars. Her eyes once more welled with hot tears. "Tell me truly, Miss Austen . . . does he love her?" C.J. held her breath.

"Knowing him as I do, I must confess that his affection originated in nothing better than gratitude," Jane replied, emphasizing the word *affection* with an undisguised tone of sarcasm.

"I am sure he seems practically ancient to the nubile Lady Charlotte. A noble relic," C.J. responded bitterly. In her own era, the man would have been approaching the prime of life. Still, the earl was certainly in high demand, despite Harriet Fairfax's dismissal of his age as positively ancient and the fact that many were aware of his financial entanglements with regard to the mismanagement of his estate. Indeed, there had been no dearth of attention in his direction at the ball in the Upper Rooms. Like a bevy of eager stage mothers, more than a handful of matrons—Lady Digby only one among them—had practically shoved their daughters under his aristocratic nose. And Darlington had behaved civilly, cordially, but as far as C.J. could detect, seemed to award none of the young ladies particular favor, behaving as though he had no wish to enter the marriage mart anew, until he met *her*, C.J. Why, he had *said* as much. Or was that merely a successful ruse to seduce her?

So *that's* what Lady Oliver had been up to at the Assembly Ball. The old bat was playing Pandarus.

"To be so bent on marriage—to pursue a man merely for the sake of a situation—is the sort of thing that shocks me," Jane said, alluding to Lady Charlotte's exchange of several thousand pounds for the right to be mistress of Delamere.

"I had not thought so little of Darlington's character," C.J. sobbed. "I misjudged your cousin entirely."

Miss Austen placed a protective arm about her companion's shaking shoulder. "There are such things in the world, perhaps one in a thousand, as the creature you and I should think perfection, where grace and spirit are united to worth, where manners are equal to the heart and understanding," she said, wiping away C.J.'s tears with her thumb. "But such a person may not come your way, or if he does, he may not be the eldest son of a man of fortune," Jane added, taking the liberty under the circumstances to rather uncharacteristically disparage her own relation.

"Would that his lordship took more after you than his aunt," C.J. replied ruefully, accepting the loan of Jane's handkerchief. "The woman is a veritable gorgon. A dragon at the very least."

"I am mightily sorry that my cousin has done you such injury. But have you no comforts? No friends?" Jane asked rhetorically. "Is your loss such as leaves no opening for consolation? Much as you suffer now," she added, taking Miss Welles gently by the shoulders so she could look her companion in the eye, "think of what you would have suffered if the discovery of his character had been delayed to a later period, if your *engagement*"—Jane selected the word carefully—"had been carried on for months and months, as it might have been, before he chose to put an end to it. Every additional day of unhappy confidence on your side would have made the blow more dreadful."

"I find small consolation in that." C.J. wiped away another wayward tear and offered her companion the return of her linen square, disappointed that the advice she received from the sagely perceptive writer was not what she had hoped to hear. "I am sorry, Miss Austen, for keeping you too long from your appointment at your prospective new lodgings."

But Jane refused to leave her friend in such a state and the young women continued to wend their way along Milsom Street.

"If a man truly loves, then money should be no object. How many love affairs have been terminated because one party or the other has insufficient funds to make a match?" C.J. bemoaned as they paused outside the window of Moore's Universal Toy Shop.

"Poverty is a great evil." Miss Austen was focused on the middle distance and not on her walking companion. Was she thinking of Tom Lefroy? C.J. wondered.

After purchasing a vegetable wash ball from Moore's, which the proprietor assured his customers would prevent the hands from chapping, remove freckles, and whiten the skin, and "was of superior quality to any ball yet sold in this kingdom," the ladies continued their morning progress up Milsom Street.

Madame Delacroix's small salon was crowded with patrons. The Miss Fairfaxes and their mother could be seen through the large window, attempting to bargain with her mercer over the price of a subtly striped silk that would have done little for the coloring of either daughter. Upon seeing Miss Welles and Miss Austen, however, Mrs. Fairfax raised her double chin and ushered her brood out of the shop as though she had no wish at present to be within spitting distance of Miss Welles.

Jane went into raptures and excitedly clutched her friend's arm when they came to the brand-new bow window of Travers's.

She insisted that Miss Welles accompany her inside the emporium while she indulged her passion for bonnets. Confessing under her breath to her companion that she had not the means to afford such extravagances as the outlandish creations on display, she nonetheless spent a good five or ten minutes trying this hat and that, all with a terribly sober expression on her face, as though she wished the proprietor to believe that she was a truly serious customer.

After finally settling on two particular bonnets and modeling first one, then the other in increasingly rapid succession, she placed a hand inside the crown of each, and holding the elaborate concoctions before her in outstretched arms—the better for Miss Welles to arrive at a proper determination on which was the more suitable of the two—Miss Austen remarked with what C.J. could only describe as absolute deadpan, "I cannot help thinking that it is more natural to have flowers grow out of the head than fruit." At which point both young ladies were overcome with such fits of laughter that they could not contain themselves, much to the chagrin and disapproval of Travers's elegant clientele.

The two young women had not been in the milliner's for very long when the door chime sounded and in walked Mrs. Leigh-Perrot.

"What a happy surprise!" she exclaimed upon seeing her niece. She greeted her in the Continental fashion, placing a kiss on each of Jane's cheeks.

"Aunt, you remember Miss Welles," Jane said, and C.J. received the same cordial salutation.

"I must look at the lace," declared Mrs. Leigh-Perrot as she eyed several different options in the case before her. "I hear Mr. Travers has just gotten a new pattern from Belgium that will be just the thing to spruce up one of my caps. And perhaps there will be a yard or two to spare, to add to an old tea gown."

The young women placed their reticules on the counter while they continued to try various bonnets, posing in front of the cheval mirror while they simultaneously wielded a handheld glass to afford the fullest view. Jane then found herself enticed by the different varieties of French perfume atomizers, hand-blown into exotic shapes that resembled genies' bottles. "I cannot say when I have more enjoyed a shopping excursion," Miss Austen remarked, enviously eyeing an ivory satin evening reticule. One day, she hoped, when all of England was reading *Elinor and Marianne* and *First Impressions,* she would be able to afford any of the luxuries Mr. Travers so temptingly displayed. If only she could overcome the writer's block that had plagued her since her family had been compelled to retrench. She had found nothing to recommend Bath until she had made the acquaintance of Miss Welles. Perhaps now she might begin to regain her passion for storytelling.

"I must dash; your uncle is expecting me," Mrs. Leigh-Perrot told her niece as she moved swiftly to the door. But she had barely grasped the brass handle when Mr. Travers halted her progress. "If you will forgive me, madam, please approach the counter."

The middle-aged woman looked behind her.

"No, madam, it was you I was addressing," the shopkeeper said, motioning for Mrs. Leigh-Perrot to return to the counter. "My deepest apologies if I am incorrect," the snooty Mr. Travers added, reaching for Mrs. Leigh-Perrot's reticule, "but I believe that one of your purchases was . . . not accounted for . . . in our ledger." C.J. detected a slight twitch at the corner of the woman's lower lip. "Would you please pass me your reticule," Travers asked, leaving Jane's aunt little choice in the matter. He opened the drawstring and found a small brown paper parcel that contained two yards of Mechlin lace and an additional, unwrapped ecru-colored yard that had been stuffed into an inner pocket of the lining. The milliner narrowed his eyes and looked at Mrs. Leigh-Perrot. "Bartholomew," he called to his runner, "fetch the constable." The small blond boy darted like a sprinter off the block and dashed out the door, leaving the bells above it jangling madly.

"You will be so good as to wait here, madam," the shopkeeper told Mrs. Leigh-Perrot.

The older woman was deathly pale, all color drained from her complexion. No doubt the memories of her months of incarceration and her subsequent trial for shoplifting only the year before—and at which she was fully acquitted—came back to haunt her like a cemetery of spectres.

"I am sure it is all a dreadful error," Jane said, going over to comfort her aunt.

"Ladies," Travers said, addressing the Misses Welles and Austen, "please present your reticules at the counter."

The young women anxiously handed over their purses for inspection.

"It is worse than I had thought!" the milliner exclaimed as his nimble boy reentered the shop with a huffing Constable Mawl in tow. He brandished a mother-of-pearl-backed tortoiseshell hair comb and two jeweled hatpins, which he had fished out of Miss Austen's reticule. Both young ladies gasped. Had Mrs. Leigh-Perrot been surprised, she would have looked at the items with shock, and not turned away from them.

Mr. Travers displayed the contraband before the constable.

"Now, where did *this* one come from?" asked Mawl, pinching the length of lace between dirty thumb and forefinger as though it were a bit of disgusting cobweb.

The milliner blanched when he saw the grimy thumbprint on his unpaid-for wares. "That would be from the madam's purse," he replied disdainfully. "And the hatpins and the comb were found in the reticule belonging to the young lady," he indicated, pointing a pale finger at Jane, who stood trembling in the center of the floor at an uncharacteristic loss for words.

Mawl pawed through the delicate items, muttering figures aloud. He dangled the yard of lace before the anxious face of Mrs. Leigh-Perrot. "How much does this bit of fluff go for, Mr. Travers?"

"A threepenny bit to the yard, Constable," replied the milliner. "Irish lace is tuppence to the yard, but the goods we get from France and Belgium, now that's a horse of a different—"

"I'm not concerned with horses and laces, Mr. Travers. I'm concerned with cost. Now, madam, as this bit here costs less than a shilling, you're a lucky woman. More'n a shilling could get you fourteen years in Botany Bay, as you might remember, mum, from a little incident not much more'n a year ago. You won't be transported to Australia for this offense, but you will have to appear at the next assizes, at which the magistrate will determine your fine. I am writing up a warrant," he said, removing an official-looking leatherbound book from his coat pocket. "I warn you, though," he added, poking a finger at Mrs. Leigh-Perrot's nose, "if you fail to appear, your luck will change considerably."

"Now *you,* missy," he said, turning to address Jane, "I daresay you'd better be learning how to waltz Matilda to 'The Bold Fusilier' and consider that to be a stroke of good fortune. I have no need to ask the good Mr. Travers the sum total of these items, as I can safely assume that dainties like these," he remarked, testing the sharpness of each hatpin, "cost a pretty penny."

"They were imported from France," interjected the shopkeeper, "before the hostilities." He peered over at his own merchandise, currently being sullied by Mawl's large paw, to gain a better inspection. "Let's see . . . the one with the cabochon is . . ." He made a number of quick, muttered calculations. "All told, twelve pounds six."

"What is yer name, miss?"

"Jane. Jane Austen, sir," a pallid Miss Austen replied, her voice trembling.

"Miss Austen, the penalty for having stolen property this dear is *death;* but if yer lucky to know an influential barrister, you might get off with deportation to Australia and fourteen years hard labor there."

Jane reached out her hand to steady herself on the mahogany-trimmed glass display case. It looked as though she might faint dead away at any moment.

"Of course, if your serjeant-at-law is a good-for-nothing,

you'd never need to leave good English soil—that is, until yer feet left the ground!" He laughed raucously at his own joke, but his audience refused to appreciate the humor.

C.J.'s experience with the present system of jurisprudence, which had left her with the distinct impression that it operated on the presumption of guilt rather than that of innocence, compelled her to speak up for Jane. Not only was Miss Austen innocent of blame, for she would not possibly resort to petty thievery, but if she were adjudged guilty, the Jane Austen that the world would come to consider one of the greatest chroniclers of her age would never be born. The Jane Austen who stood before C.J. would either have her life cut short by a hemp necklace or would be forever altered by a sentence of several years' hard labor in an Australian penal colony. She remembered reading that Mrs. Leigh-Perrot was something of a kleptomaniac who escaped such a sentence by the grace of formidable legal representation, as well as a number of character witnesses. And in Mrs. Leigh-Perrot's case, her defense was aided by the disclosure that her accusers were notorious blackmailers. But what would happen to Jane if C.J. did not defend her?

"Miss Austen did not place the items in question in her reticule," C.J. announced. "That is *my* reticule in which Mr. Travers found the hatpins and the comb."

"Yours?" they all gasped.

Mawl squinted his beady eyes and focused on the self-proclaimed culprit. "You! I recognize you, now." He smacked the side of his head with his huge hand. "You're the lightfingers what stole the—"

Once C.J. realized where the constable was headed, she overlapped his speech, saying, "The ornaments in question are—"

Then Miss Austen interrupted. She started to say "mine indeed," and fished in C.J.'s reticule for the money to pay for them, giving Mr. Travers the impression that Miss Austen's actual reticule was C.J.'s purse.

But C.J. could not permit Jane to remain under any cloud of suspicion. "The items that you found in the reticule, Mr.

Travers, are a most particular request from my invalid aunt, the Countess of Dalrymple. As she frequents your emporium with great regularity, I made the assumption—and now I fully comprehend the gravity of my error—that my esteemed aunt had her purchases placed on account at this establishment. I did not realize that you had failed to notate a debit for them in your ledger."

Mawl scrutinized the shopkeeper's face. "Is that true?"

"It is true that the countess maintains an account with Travers Millinery: Domestic and Imported," the proprietor said, struggling to maintain his dignity.

"And I shall pay for the lace," Jane said, removing a coin from C.J.'s purse, "as I am quite sure that an oversight was made and that my aunt simply wished to separate the white lace from the cream." Her voice then assumed a confidential tone. "She is past sixty years of age, you see, and her eyesight is not as good as it once was where it comes to the discernment of subtle variations of color." She offered the money to Mr. Travers and sneaked a stern glance at Mrs. Leigh-Perrot.

The constable now deemed it meet to reassert his authority. "Then, sir, I put it to you: are you willing to accept this payment for the lace and the young lady's request to put her items on account for Lady Dalrymple?"

Afraid to lose further trade, the milliner nodded his head.

Constable Mawl smiled with evident satisfaction. "Then I bid you all a good day." He turned on his heels and strode out of the shop and down Milsom Street, whistling the tune C.J. recognized as "Waltzing Matilda."

Three relieved women departed the milliner's and Mrs. Leigh-Perrot rushed home to the safety of the Paragon.

Jane took both of C.J.'s hands and held them while she studied her friend's face. "You would have done as much for anyone else, I'm certain," she said quietly.

"No," replied C.J. softly, "I daresay I wouldn't." She gave her friend's hands a gentle squeeze and caught Miss Austen's unspoken expression of gratitude.

Suddenly, C.J. was overtaken by a violent wave of nausea.

"Miss Welles!" An alarmed Miss Austen steadied her friend's arm, and with nowhere else in the immediate vicinity to rest, escorted C.J. back to the milliner's and led her to a seat just inside the door. She asked Mr. Travers to fetch a glass of water, which C.J. sipped slowly, feeling quite flushed and more than a little dizzy.

Minutes later she excused herself from Miss Austen's tender ministrations and bolted from the shop in search of a bush behind which she might discreetly purge herself of the beverage.

Jane stood by her companion, a cool hand to the girl's forehead, holding back her ringlets, while C.J. retched uncontrollably, embarrassed to the core. Another bout of nausea sent her to her knees. "Help me," she whimpered. "I must go home."

Chapter Twenty-Two

*Our heroine finally takes the waters; and Lady Dalrymple
strikes a bargain with an uninvited, and not entirely
welcome, guest.*

As the days passed, C.J. continued to assuage
her recurring attacks of nausea by nibbling bits
of candied ginger. She recalled having wondered
when she first arrived at Lady Wickham's town house how she
would find out what to do when she got her period, not knowing
the protocol for such things. But only once had she needed to
avail herself of the rags that Mary kept in a drawstring bag,
tucked away in a cupboard. She had arrived in Bath on the fifth
of April 1801; Constable Mawl would never let her forget that
day. It was now June. C.J. counted on her fingers, calculating the
time. Perhaps her condition was related to anxiety. She had
plenty of that to spare. On the other hand, she had never been
pregnant and didn't know exactly what to expect if she were.
Mary, who had no inkling of C.J.'s secret, was certain that her
condition was intestinal and could be alleviated if she joined
Lady Dalrymple in taking the waters. A lengthy soak in the hot
Kings Bath, followed by a quick plunge into the cold Queens
Bath, should nicely do the trick, she was sure. And so thrice a

week C.J. donned the ugly brown linen shift specially provided by the attendants and took the cure. Each time she went, she held out a hope of seeing Darlington there, but he had never given C.J. any indication of requiring the waters' restorative properties. How she wished to tell him why she believed she needed to take them! How she yearned to see him! She did see many other couples besporting themselves with no heed paid to a ready audience of gawkers. What a horrid location for an assignation! The baths themselves, which resembled modern swimming pools of modest size, were nothing but public germ tanks where invalids of both genders mingled, regardless of infirmity. People with running sores and infections shared the same water as those with common colds, fevers, or contagious diseases such as consumption. C.J. wondered if the water was ever changed or filtered. The stench would have been palpable had not the attendants attempted to ameliorate it by floating pomanders of lavender and copper bowls filled with scented oils. The countess believed that her "niece" had taken to accompanying her of late simply to monitor her progressive return to good health. She was given no reason to suspect that anything was amiss with the girl's own well-being, and C.J. did nothing to disabuse Lady Dalrymple of that notion.

MEANWHILE, IT APPEARED that Cassandra Jane Welles had benefactors in the unlikeliest places. It had been the brainchild of Bath resident John Palmer (the elder) to build a new theatre in Orchard Street to replace the old playhouse that had been erected nearby at the time of Beau Nash's arrival some years earlier. The original theatre, built in 1705, was razed in 1737 (due to poor attendance) to make way for the Mineral Hospital. But Palmer felt that if a new playhouse were to be constructed, residents and visitors alike would throng to see the works of the Irishmen Richard Brinsley Sheridan and Oliver Goldsmith, his fellow Bath neighbors. Palmer was proven correct. His new theatre continued to increase in popularity, not merely with audiences, but among the actors themselves, who became eager to secure an engagement in the spa city that was now one of the most glittering jewels in the Georgian crown. In 1768, His Majesty granted the Orchard Street Theatre a license, and John Palmer's playhouse was henceforth to be known as the Theatre Royal, Bath—such prestige having been previously conferred only on London's fabled Drury Lane.

By the time Sarah Siddons made her debut there in 1778 in Sir John Vanbrugh's comedy *The Provok'd Husband*, the Theatre Royal was already a raging success. It goes without saying that had C.J. Welles known of John Palmer, she would have freely acknowledged him a debt of gratitude for the creation of a most remarkable time-travel conveyance.

At the present moment, another, quite different, conveyance was pulling up alongside the façade of Leake's bookseller's emporium, adjacent to the post office. This one was the not-quite-literal "progeny" of brewer and theatrical manager John Palmer (the younger), who had taken it upon himself to address the issue of postal reform; his efforts resulted in the residents of the golden city of Bath receiving their letters and parcels from London a full day earlier than ever before. This pilgrimage, made by parcels and up to four passengers, took all of a fleet thirteen hours, necessitating a pair of horses, changed every six or eight miles. Each stop was made with equal alacrity, as the mailbags were ready for the driver upon his arrival; and the guard, who rode with the coachman on the box, would deposit the mail sacks from each destination in the boot of the carriage, permitting the driver to retain his position. Thus the journey could be effected with all due speed.

Stepping from the light coach emblazoned with His Majesty's crest was a ruddy-faced gentleman dressed in a quaintly grand manner: his elaborate white jabot foaming like a frothy meringue over his bright green coat and striped silk waistcoat. Puffing and winded from the mere exertion of descending from the Royal Mail, the person in question gave every indication of having once been handsome of face and figure, in possession at one time of a full head of wheat-blond hair—now tending to thinness—while his physique, once trim, had become rather thick waisted and stout. No doubt he had come to take the waters for his gouty left foot.

"Give a hand there! Caution, lad!" he boomed at one of the young scamps who made a penny or two by helping Royal Mail travelers with their baggage. The boy handed the wheezing wayfarer his valise, a weather-beaten brown leather affair that looked to the child as though it had seen as much abuse as its red-faced owner, who, he noted on receiving only a shilling's tip, smelled of gin, tobacco, and garlic.

"Very nice. Very, verrah nice," the man slurred, and one might have thought he was admiring the magnificent Gothic architecture of Bath Abbey, had it not been for the passing dairy maid whose buttresses were nearly as prominently displayed. The Marquess of Manwaring extended his hand toward the healthy young woman to sample her wares, but the girl was too quick for the besotted old sot.

"Just what do you think yer about, sirrah?" she demanded indignantly. "Manhandling a poor girl right out in the middle of the street!"

"Not manhandling, young lady. Man*waring*. I'm a marquess," the would-be violator belched.

"I don't care if yer the bloody Prince of Wales!" the dairy-maid exclaimed. "Yer a gouty old pervert, that's what you are. I'll thank ye to keep yer hands to yerself."

The marquess felt a meaty hand clamp down upon his shoulder. "That's my good coat," he protested. "And I'll thank you to keep *your* hands to *yourself!*"

"You are addressing a constable, sirrah." Constable Mawl drew himself up to his full height of well over six feet. He loved playing to a crowd.

"Do you not know whom *you* address, Constable Mawl?" the gouty-footed man thundered theatrically. "I am the Marquess of Manwaring."

"You're also drunk and disorderly, your lordship," asserted

Mawl, taken down a peg by the realization that the marquess might have an influential friend or two who could easily put in an ill word, triggering the loss of his constabulary quicker than he could down a pint of ale on a hot summer afternoon.

"I am an actor!" the portly man proclaimed.

"And not a bad one," murmured one of the Royal Mail passengers to one of the impromptu assemblage who had gathered to witness the show. "I saw him play Bob Acres in Newcastle. He's no Garrick, mind you, but he did Sheridan proud."

"His Dogberry in Bristol was well received," piped up another passerby. "Shame his own family didn't catch him in that role. He was never as good before or since."

Constable Mawl, who prided himself on having ears, as well as eyes, affixed to the back of his head, addressed the crowd. "So you've heard of the stinkin' bloke, 'ave you?" He waved his enormous hand in front of his face as if to fumigate the atmosphere. "If 'e's as well known as you say he is, and being a marquess and all, I'm willing to release him upon his own re-cogni-zance, providing 'e's got somewhere to lodge in Bath. But if I catch you acting like the town drunkard again, your lordship, it's the jailhouse for you. Now go home, Maude," he told the incensed dairymaid, as though she had encouraged the marquess's drunken advances.

Albert Tobias, Lord Manwaring, was in need of a fortifying pint or two before setting off to visit his sister in the Royal Crescent. By the time he reached her doorstep, he practically fell over his own gouty foot, cursing a stone riser for surprising him.

"Here you go, lass," he burped, thrusting a fistful of colorful ribbons at a stunned Mary Sykes, who had opened the door to admit him. The gift to the young serving girl, who he decided at first glance was rather pretty, though a bit too thin for his taste, was only the first of the extravagant tributes he had brought to grease the wheels of his sister's generosity. By the time Collins had shown him to Lady Dalrymple's front drawing room, the marquess-cum-actor, who had given the luggage boy outside the post office a paltry shilling, had bestowed a fistful of crowns upon her ladyship's butler, and was about to present his sister with a bouquet of pastel-colored Belgian linen handkerchiefs, edged in lace tatted by the residents of the Beguinage in Bruges.

Lady Dalrymple was taking tea with Lady Oliver when Collins interrupted their light repast to inform her ladyship that the Marquess of Manwaring desired an audience with her. Euphoria's fury at Lady Oliver's attempt to insinuate a godchild into her nephew's affections in place of Miss Welles had ultimately given way to a desire to confront her formidable opponent. At present, the rift between the two former bosom friends appeared irreparable, with Lady Dalrymple accusing her old girlhood playmate of betrayal, appealing to her own comprehension of such disloyalty by deigning to dredge up Lady Oliver's unspeakable past. As Augusta's own unhappy history was not above reproach, how dare she condemn Miss Welles for having a scandal in her family!

But Lady Oliver, who was not yet prepared to reveal her hand by disclosing the raft of intelligence she had been receiving from her diligent and vigilant spy, Saunders, simply held fast to the unsuitability of a match between the Earl of Darlington and Lady Dalrymple's impoverished soi-disant niece, "Miss Welles."

"The girl has neither fortune nor reputation to recommend her. You cannot, other than in your extravagant flights of fancy, overlook the inadvisability of my nephew's forging an alliance with a young woman who has had neither a proper upbringing and education nor introduction and exposure to society."

"It is to my niece's credit that she is not a pale, overweaned weakling who knows naught but needlework and natters on about bonnets," the countess argued. Seeing that she was making little headway in her suit, Lady Dalrymple elected to aim for her guest's jugular vein. "Rest assured, Cassandra will not make the sort of wife that a man of the earl's breeding and intelligence soon tires of, compelling him to seek happiness in more fascinating pastures."

The countess could have been alluding to any number of

arranged marriages among the aristocracy of the era; however, owing to her own lurid and unhappy past, Lady Oliver was keenly aware that Lady Dalrymple's reference was deliberately targeted at her. Drawing herself up to her full height, she glowered at her hostess. "Please call for my carriage, Lady Dalrymple. There is nothing further to be said between us. Convey my compliments to your cook for an exemplary afternoon tea." Lady Oliver nearly collided with Lady Dalrymple's brother in her haste to leave the drawing room.

A theatrically practiced voice boomed, "The influence of women is only successful when it is indirect. So long as they confine themselves to country houses, the dining room table, the boudoir, and the bedroom, I make no objection. The better a woman speaks, the more embarrassing I always find it. It makes me feel quite uncomfortable."

"Then you did not have to listen at the keyhole," the marquess's sister said tartly, her expression as sour as the lemon juice she was straining into her tea. "Charming words for a man who, in his profession as an actor, spends a good deal of time in the company of the fairer—and soberer—sex. What brings you to Bath, Albert?"

The marquess-turned-thespian assumed a classical pose and declaimed:

"Of all the gay Places the World can afford,
By Gentle and Simple for Pastime ador'd,
Fine Balls and Fine Concerts, fine Building and Springs,
Fine Walks, and fine Views, and a Thousand fine Things,
Not to mention the sweet Situation and Air,
What Place, my dear Sister, with Bath *can compare?"*

"I preferred the panegyric when Anstey penned it," Lady Dalrymple said, calling her brother's bluff. "And Christopher Anstey wrote 'mother,' not 'sister.'"

Manwaring puckered his lips and gave his sister a jovial look.

"Can't even win for trying." When he bestowed a sloppy kiss on the countess's rouged cheek, she could smell the gin on his breath.

"Actually, I'm in a bit of a spot, Euphie," the marquess hiccuped, helping himself to a cup of tea. He produced a silver flask from the pocket of his coat and enhanced the brew with the addition of a dram of whisky covertly acquired from a friend at the newly opened Chivas distillery.

In no mood to spar with her sponging brother, particularly after her argument with Augusta Oliver, the countess deftly removed a savory biscuit from her brother's hand and fed it to an appreciative Newton. "No good. 'E's up to no good," warned the prescient parrot.

"Thank you, Newton." Lady Dalrymple slid open the door of the gilded cage and reached in, so her pet could hop onto her jeweled finger. "When that quack surgeon Dr. Cleland recommended nearly twenty-five years ago that you take up gambling as a distraction from the gout, he neglected to inform you that such a 'cure' might become addictive. Your last episode at the gaming tables has reached the ears of everyone in Bath," the countess remarked to her brother. "A man named Newman, I believe."

"If he had not been cheating at faro, he would not have gone and hanged himself," Albert remarked laconically. "I was not the one who was contriving to win by dishonest means."

"No, not *this* time," Lady Dalrymple replied. "Nevertheless, Mr. Newman's untimely demise has created quite a scandal, regardless of the circumstances. Your role in his sudden departure from this earth has been widely speculated upon. Once again, your behavior has sorely tested your family, which is beholden by both blood and duty to defend your actions."

The marquess tippled directly from his flask and wiped his mouth with one of his sister's yellow damask serviettes. "I believed the man was cheating at cards. I merely pinned his hand to the table with a serving fork and remarked quite pointedly,

'Sir, if you have not a card hidden under that hand, I apologize.'
I believe the unfortunate result quite decided the question."

Ordinarily, Lady Dalrymple was not the judgmental sort.
But Lady Oliver's objection to the marquess as a potential new
father-in-law for Lord Darlington enforced Euphoria's resolve to
remove all impediments to her "niece's" nuptials. She, more
than anyone, would have been quick to acknowledge
Manwaring's unsuitability to mix in polite society, but Albert
was her brother, and therefore bore defending.

The Marquess of Manwaring rested his head in his hands.
"I'm sunk, Euphie," he admitted, then began to sob uncontrollably. "It's not the liquor talking. My debts . . . I can no longer
manage 'em. The creditors have been beating down m'door." He
pointed a stubby finger at his unfashionable green coat. "Even
me tailors. I may have to decamp to the Continent to escape
'em." Albert was about to reach once more for his silver flask
when he caught his sister's disapproving eye and slid it back into
his pocket. "I thought by touring the provinces, I would be away
from London long enough for them to forget. But they won't
have me anymore."

"Who won't, Albert?"

"Bristol. Newcastle. York. Leeds. Not until I sober myself up,
they say. So I've got no income, you see."

"Then perhaps you could take up some more lucrative pursuit in order to discharge your debts," the countess counseled.
"Three years ago Rowlandson found himself in similar straits
when his commissions for portraiture fell off, so he took up cari-
cature. It's one and the same, if you ask me. His watercolor series on *The Comforts of Bath* have made him rather more than
comfortable. I have a set of prints myself. They're quite amusing
if one's sense of humor is as colorful as his illustrations."

Albert looked at the rug and shuffled his feet. Lady
Dalrymple noticed the shabby condition of his brown leather
shoes.

Her ladyship released an exasperated sigh. "Do you expect

me to discharge your debts for you? Portly and I rescued you for years, and never once have you shown an ounce of gratitude. You are everything that is wrong with the aristocracy, Bertie: you're an advantage taker. You take and take and expect that everything you receive is your due."

"Well, I'm choking on that silver spoon now, Euphie."

"I can't say as you don't deserve to."

"I'll make it up to you this time," Albert begged, blowing his nose phlegmatically into one of the linen tea towels. "If you could see your way to lending me a few thousand . . . I'll do anything you ask."

The countess gave her brother a long, hard look. A project was formulating in her mind that she was not yet ready to give voice to. So she gave a little "harrumph" instead, then installed herself at her escritoire and wrote out a draft for a modest amount, blotting the ink dry before handing the check to her brother. "This will see you set up at one of the better hotels in Bath," she told him. "Try the White Hart Inn near the Abbey first. You will be so good as to stay there until you hear from me again."

The marquess gave his sister a sloppy, grateful kiss on her rouged cheek. "You won't regret it, Euphie."

Lady Dalrymple touched her handkerchief to her face with the same motion she had used to blot the check. "I shall see what can be done about putting your thespian talents to use once more," she said. "Good afternoon, Bertie."

Book the Fourth

Chapter Twenty-Three

*In which our heroine attends her second Assembly Ball; a
shocking announcement is followed by one more devastating,
accompanied by a display of extremely provocative behavior;
and an extraordinary demand is made of our reluctant hero.*

"I AM SORRY, MISS WELLES. There has been no
reply," a rather irritated Collins informed Lady
Dalrymple's niece. After learning of Lord Darlington's purported arrangement with the Digbys, C.J. had sent no
fewer than four letters to him requesting an interview. Every
time the house bell rang, C.J. raced down the stairs in anticipation of a response from his lordship to her increasingly urgent
missives; yet on each occasion, she was cruelly disappointed.
Her news, her need to learn where the earl's affections truly lay,
her agitation and anxiety, and the life growing inside her all felt
as though they were increasing with alarming—and exponen-
tial—rapidity.

Lady Dalrymple, who quite fancied a change of venue and
claimed that her health had become markedly improved, thanks
to Cassandra's "exemplary care"—a cryptic reference to her
"niece's" magic tablets—proposed that they attend the
evening's Assembly Ball, suggesting that they would no doubt

encounter his lordship in the Upper Rooms that evening. C.J. eagerly accepted, and they planned to arrive early in the evening so as not to miss the earl should he decide to put in but the briefest of appearances.

C.J. enjoyed dancing, to be sure; and Mr. King, the highly respected Master of Ceremonies, had made it a point at the last assembly to address Lady Dalrymple and offer his compliments to her on the introduction of her niece to the *ton*. Nevertheless, as she dressed for the ball like a vestal virgin in another filmy white gown, which Madame Delacroix had assured her was cut in the daring French fashion and was sure to turn heads, C.J. felt like a fraud. Her hormones were zinging around like electrons and her hot blood and even hotter temper were sooner or later going to get the better of her in some public place.

Now more inured to the habits of the *haute ton*, everything C.J. had read about the cutthroat marriage mart paled in comparison to the actuality. Impeccably turned-out mothers, still attractive and viable themselves, to C.J.'s way of thinking, promenaded their nubile, well-heeled daughters like sirens in a seraglio. Although these young virgins were all demurely gowned in shades of white or soft pastels, the irony of it all was that these dresses were often so daringly cut that some of the better-endowed girls seemed in very real danger of causing a commotion by overflowing their décolletages, especially during some of the more energetic country dances.

And C.J. had never seen such an array of plumage. The ladies' headgear at previous assemblies had been modest by comparison to tonight's display. To be certain, there had been several fashionable silk turbans and short "Brutus" ringlets alongside the linen and lace lappets favored by the elderly dowagers. C.J. wondered if there had been a sudden run on ostrich plumes, for many of the women wore their panaches sprouting from their foreheads, whether on bands or affixed to turbans with ostentatious—and shockingly large—brooches crafted from precious and semi-precious stones. Half the treasure of the South African gem mines must have been amassed in the ballroom that evening.

The dancing commenced at seven o'clock. Having never arrived this early to the Upper Rooms, C.J. did not know what to expect. At her previous ball, her own party had arrived fashionably late, some two hours after the festivities had begun and just before the country dances were about to start. And even then, the gathering had been sparse, to say the least. Tonight there was an aura of the extraordinary, a palpable difference between this assembly and the last.

The Master of Ceremonies opened the ball, and the orchestra struck up the requisite minuet.

"Ever since Beau Nash formalized the rules of conduct at the Bath public assemblies, they have begun with the minuet," Lady Dalrymple whispered to C.J. "I was but a child at the end of the Beau's days. Confidentially," she added, as she raised her eyes above her fan, "—and this does not bear repeating—he was a bit of a dissipate, back then, a mere shadow of his former glory, my mother used to say."

Amid several murmurs, Mr. King led out the Earl of Darlington to the center of the floor.

Lady Dalrymple continued to educate her "niece" on the unfamiliar customs. "At the very beginning of each ball, the Master of Ceremonies leads out two persons of the highest distinction present. The gentleman selected by the Master of Ceremonies dances with the lady whom the Master of Ceremonies chooses, and when the minuet ends, she will be returned to her seat, whereupon the master will lead out a second young lady of rank to dance with the gentleman. And this ceremony will be observed with each gentleman, who will be obliged to dance with two ladies."

A mixer, thought C.J., amused. Her good humor was immediately put to the test. Mr. King offered his arm to Lady Charlotte Digby and presented her to the earl, who stiffly stood all alone in the center of the spacious ballroom.

Lord Digby followed his daughter's dainty footsteps, joining the couple on the dance floor once they were brought together by Mr. King. "Your lordships, ladyships, if I may crave your indulgence . . ."

The movement of fans, quite necessary in the warm early summer evening, fluttered to a halt.

"It gives me the greatest pleasure to share with you the announcement of the betrothal of my only daughter, Lady Charlotte Digby, to his lordship, Owen Percival, Earl of Darlington. We hope that this evening, you will join in their happiness."

C.J. felt as though her throat and intestines alike had been gripped in a vise and were being held fast. Before she felt her equilibrium betray her, causing her to sink to the floor in a dead faint, she glimpsed the ostensibly happy couple in the center of the room and had the surprising presence of mind to note that they were anything but contented. Darlington looked uncomfortable and extremely embarrassed; nevertheless, his stately carriage did not betray any signs of turbulence. Poor Charlotte, who was rather lovely, in a dewy English-rose way, was looking at her intended with an expression more ambivalent than amatory: an innocent, pink-eyed, fluffy-tailed rabbit being led to the sacrifice.

For Miss Welles, her current medical condition notwithstanding, marriage to the earl was a consummation devoutly to be wished. For Lady Charlotte, it appeared to be little more than a daughter's duty.

C.J. thought she saw Darlington glance in her direction when the commotion created by her sudden, though graceful, descent to the floor drew his attention away from Lady Charlotte. Had she imagined that such a delicate flower as her young ladyship detected the look of extreme concern that clouded the earl's handsome countenance and then had firmly pressed a gloved hand onto Darlington's sleeve, preventing him from attending to the fallen woman near the perimeter of the room?

Restored to equanimity by a few Samaritans and a glass of punch, C.J. rested on a chair, surprised to see the minuet still in progress. For the remainder of this interminable formal dance, C.J. found herself biting her lower lip until it bled and she required a handkerchief to blot it. Her distress was not lost on her "aunt," who caught the eye of the Master of Ceremonies just as the center couple was concluding the minuet.

Lady Charlotte was returned to the adoring bosom of her family, and Mr. King approached Lady Dalrymple and her "niece." The Master of Ceremonies offered a stunned Miss Welles his arm. As all eyes were upon her, she could not turn back toward the countess to satisfy her curiosity as to whether Lady Dalrymple had played a part in this turn of events.

What could she possibly say to Darlington? Certainly, propriety dictated—

Damn propriety! Damn it to bloody hell and back!

As Mr. King handed C.J. to the earl, she broke free from the Master of Ceremonies' grasp and made a dash for the long table near the entranceway, leaving a puzzled Percy on his own. She continued to shock the well-heeled assemblage by dousing her body with water from the heavy silver urns, the contents of which had been intended for the purpose of refreshing the patrons' parched lips. C.J.'s flimsy, white muslin ball gown, now soaking wet, clung to her shivering body and undetectable bandeau like the drapery on an ancient Greek caryatid. Her appearance would have been quite à la mode in Paris, where such wetting down had become a custom among the fin de siècle fashionistas, but even the more sophisticated members of the English aristocracy were appalled by her display.

"Heavens! Who does the girl think she is . . . Sulis Minerva?" drawled a dandy whose horizontal-striped silk waistcoat and vertical-striped surcoat made him resemble nothing less festive than a large piece of Christmas ribbon candy. He withdrew a pristine lace-edged handkerchief from his sleeve and dabbed a mirthful tear from his jaundiced eye.

"I think she'd do Sue Em proud," giggled his companion, referring to Miss Welles's current resemblance to the hybrid deity to whom Bath was consecrated—the Celtic Sulis, goddess of the spring from which the healing waters came, and her Roman counterpart, Minerva, goddess of healing as well as of wisdom.

"Bless me, she's making quite a spectacle of herself!" remarked a shocked Mrs. Fairfax, a bit too loudly, to her two daughters, who fought over their mother's quizzing glass, eagerly awaiting whatever the eccentric Miss Welles might think to do next.

"You haven't seen anything yet," C.J. shot back to the gossipy old windbag. She approached the orchestra, and crooking her finger at its leader—who was all too happy to bend down to speak to her, as it afforded a better gander at her spectacular figure—she requested a polka.

The musicians, pleased to depart from the expected stately and, frankly, rather boring minuet, and sensing that something quite out of the ordinary was happening, struck up a lively tune in three-quarter time.

"Now, your lordship," C.J. began, approaching a nonplussed Darlington, who had remained standing like a condemned man in the middle of the room. "Shall we dance?"

The confounded nobleman, not wishing to offend Miss Welles, although her own rather stunningly offensive comportment of the past few minutes had discredited her quite enough, proceeded to arrange his arms in the proper form for the polka.

C.J. felt a perverse thrill take hold of her senses. Knowing full well that the ballroom of inbred aristocrats would not learn the dance for nearly a dozen years, she rearranged Darlington's arms in the configuration that she had been taught back in her own century at one of her dance workshops.

With their hips nearly touching, their left arms meeting overhead in a balletic arch, while their right arms clasped one another about the waist, C.J. talked her partner through the simple boxlike step of an early waltz. The proximity of their bodies, combined with the intense gazing into each other's eyes—as the form of the dance figure left nowhere else to look—generated the gasps of outrage that future historians would chronicle when the daring Countess Lieven was credited with introducing the waltz to London society in 1812.

The ladies who did not faint, or pretend to, so as to distract their respective male companions from the spectacle at the center of the room, fanned themselves furiously and sought to shield their virgin daughters' eyes from the view of the sopping wet Miss Welles dancing virtually hip to hip with the apparently mesmerized Earl of Darlington. He, too, should be scandalized, thought many of his peers, who—if pressed—would have admitted their envy of the nobleman's present position.

Lord Digby was growing more florid than usual. His wife was unsuccessful in trying to put a good face on her morbid embarrassment. Lady Charlotte, on the other hand, found herself somewhere between mildly jealous, awkwardly uncomfortable, and inexplicably fascinated. Part of her wished to tear her betrothed from the siren in his arms; another part wished the siren to teach her the figures.

Darlington regained his senses, after several lilting turns about the floor, when the aghast faces around him finally swirled into focus. "Miss Welles, you must cease this childish behavior," he reprimanded in a tone that he himself realized was an unfamiliar one. "I will accept the responsibility for my own mortification under the circumstances, but can you not see the irreparable damage you are bringing to your character?" He tried to keep his voice low but had to speak louder than he had planned in order to be heard above the music.

"Your lordship, *I* am not the one to blame for the destruction of my reputation," C.J. retorted, her voice rising in pitch. "You are quite concerned for my character when it conveniently suits, but what does your precious society say about the character of a nobleman who encourages a young woman to share his bed, makes assurances that lead her and her esteemed aunt to believe his intentions of matrimony, and then suddenly abandons her—with neither warning nor apology—and immediately becomes betrothed to a woman of means, little knowing—or perhaps caring—that his seduced and abandoned lover now bears his child?"

She had been so focused on her admonishment of the earl

that she failed to note that the polka had ended, and that the shocked musicians sat, bows poised in midair, eagerly awaiting Darlington's reaction.

Upon the horrific realization that her revelation had been heard by all and sundry, owing to the deafening silence—and suddenly mindful of the way Lady Rose and Lord Featherstone had been treated by their so-called equals—C.J. elbowed her way through the crowd and bolted from the ballroom.

The collective gasp upon Miss Welles's stunning exit sounded like the sudden deflation of one of the Montgolfier brothers' hot-air balloons.

Following a shocked silence, the room soon became atwitter with wagging tongues. "What else would you expect from a poor relation? A churchmouse?" And Lady Oliver sniffed, "No doubt encouraged by her aunt to behave with such hoydenish abandon."

Never before had Lady Dalrymple wished that Beau Nash had sanctioned the wearing of weapons in the Assembly Rooms. Were the ironclad rule not strictly enforced, the countess herself would have unsheathed a rapier and made swift dispatch of her former bosom friend. "I have never heard such rubbish, Augusta!" she declared. "And while I have no use for your opinion of my own character, I intend to reveal you to be nothing more than a conniving prevaricator, intent upon destroying the good name of my dearest of kin."

Certainly the girl was within her rights to be heartbroken over Darlington's betrayal, as well as his callous disregard of her attempts to contact him in order to verify the truth of the rumors that he would soon wed Lady Charlotte, and to hear such confirmation from his own lips. That much—that *little*—he surely owed her. There had been a formal understanding forged between the pair of them, Percy and Cassandra, no doubt about it. Whether Cassandra's extraordinary conduct this evening was out of turn was not for Lady Dalrymple to speculate upon. Her "niece" was as she herself had once been called—an original.

And Euphoria was proud of the appellation—and proud of those who flew in the face of conventional behavior.

On the other hand, what if Cassandra truly were enceinte, as the young woman had hinted? Was it then her delicate condition that governed her outrageous performance this evening? The countess was determined to see the girl vindicated. But how?

RULED ENTIRELY by her feelings of shame and humiliation, C.J. had torn through the ballroom and the anteroom, dashing blindly past scads of aghast onlookers and out into the night. The moon was but a silver sliver in the sky, and her eyes had not yet adjusted to the darkness when she stumbled over a loose stone in the road. Down she went, face first, ripping her fine kid gloves, bloodying her palms and bare forearms, losing a slipper, and tearing the front of her gown. She let fly a string of well-known Anglo-Saxon invectives, which she continued to repeat while surveying the damage to her wardrobe and her person. Her bodice and bandeau were past all repair and she had neither shawl nor cloak with which to cover her now nearly bare torso. There was no question of returning to the Assembly Rooms. The only thing to be done was to locate her dancing slipper and limp back home.

DARLINGTON'S ATTEMPT to follow upon Miss Welles's heels as she fled the ballroom had been impeded by his aunt and Lord Digby, as well as by several others in attendance. By the time he was able to breathe the night air, Miss Welles was nowhere to be seen, and there was no trace of her—no dropped reticule or mislaid shawl. Once his eyes adjusted to the dim glare of the street-lamps on Albert Street, he thought he could make out a figure hastily descending the hill. On the other hand, he could have been mistaken. Nevertheless, he increased his pace. If his intuition was correct, Miss Welles was the figure in question. If not, he was prepared to accept the attendant embarrassment of accosting a complete stranger. After all, his humiliation in the ballroom just moments earlier was the least of what he deserved.

The night was so quiet he could hear the sound of his own footsteps reverberating through the narrow lane off the façades of ashlar stone as his boots pounded the cobblestones.

It was a blessing that Mr. King was not as fastidious as his predecessor, Mr. Nash, in checking the patrons in the Upper Rooms for weapons. Darlington placed his hand on the hilt of his *main gauche,* which he had been able to conceal in a custom-tailored pocket within the lining of his dress coat. As far as Darlington was concerned, rules applied to others. There were always exceptions, always extenuating circumstances. For example, should the unchaperoned Miss Welles be accosted on her way to the Royal Crescent, he would be able to offer her his protection. Did he believe himself above the law? Unequivocally. He claimed it as the privilege of the aristocracy.

In that case, the nobleman thought, why had he allowed his aunt to convince him that Miss Welles was unworthy of him? That she had no portion coming to her upon marriage, and that Delamere must be saved at all costs? Lady Oliver had appealed to his sense of honor should it come to the necessity of discharging dozens of tenant farmers and their families. She had prevailed upon his vanity when it came to avoiding the disgrace of bankruptcy and the seizing of his lands by his bankers at Coutt's. Retrenching was unthinkable for someone in his exalted position. Under the present unfortunate circumstances, there was only one option, which was to forge a respectable alliance with a young lady of means: an heiress whose dowry would not only ensure his continued ownership of Delamere, but whose person might produce the necessary heirs to continue the family line.

To be sure, there was a sacrificial lamb, as Lady Oliver had so caustically, even cavalierly, agreed. But Miss Welles would soon get over her disappointment and, if necessary, could be persuaded to accept consolation in the form of a modest financial settlement. The dragon was thoroughly convinced that the eccentric bluestocking who had turned her nephew's head was not only expendable, but perhaps would even be more content to receive compensation in lieu of the match.

And his aunt, who had raised him and to whom he did acknowledge a great debt of gratitude, a woman who had such an unfortunate and disgraced history herself, had always merited his dutiful compliance, though many of his acquaintance firmly believed that as Darlington neared the age of forty, the debt of respect he had thus far accorded Augusta Oliver's opinions and actions had long since been fully paid and that he had long ago squared his accounts with her. Whether or not this was the case, the earl still felt a duty toward the woman despite her ill treatment of him. It was not in his own nature either to stoop to her level or to exact a form of familial revenge simply because his aunt behaved abominably.

Yet Darlington had heretofore considered himself a man who took risks. He came from a line of men who defied convention, who marched to their own fife and drum. The second earl had departed for distant parts to indulge his passion for antiquities after he had indulged his parallel passion for an uncommon, and fallen, woman. However, his lengthy absences from Delamere had been the cause of the estate's demise, insisted Augusta Oliver. The father's abrogation of responsibility now rendered the son a slave to it. Now the third earl must preserve both his family home and name. There was no alternative, his aunt decreed.

Darlington's guilt was unspeakable. And propriety dictated that he honor the formal betrothal that had just been announced publicly to the *ton*. Yet, that did not prohibit him from continuing to care deeply for the welfare of Miss Welles. He did not expect her to ever grant him forgiveness. She had been humiliated beyond—

My God! The full force of Miss Welles's accusation struck him. The young woman had announced right in the middle of the ballroom that she was carrying his child. Could it possibly be true? Possibly, of course. In the one afternoon they had made such magical love, Cassandra could have conceived a child. Miss Welles had never struck him as being a deceitful sort. Quite the contrary, her frankness often astounded him. In fact, Miss Welles was the most honest young woman the earl had ever met.

If her outburst had not been a fiction born of anger, had she been speaking the truth, the girl was exposing herself to the utmost censure as well. Lady Dalrymple's eccentricities were not always understood by the *ton*; if her niece was with child, both women would certainly be cut by society.

And where did that leave *him*? the earl wondered. Would Lady Charlotte wed him after all, whether or not Miss Welles's pronouncement was true? It would make the young heiress appear a fool. Her parents would no doubt wish to extricate her from impending disaster before further ruin ensued. They would claim damages against him and demand a large financial settlement. And he would be responsible as well for Miss Welles's bastard. *His* bastard. Their bastard. Another dark stain on the Percival escutcheon.

He noticed a huddled form by the base of the tree at the center of the Circus and, approaching it, found the object of his search, sobbing, bleeding, and half clad, gazing at the façade of his town house. "Take this, Miss Welles." Darlington unfastened his cloak and draped it over C.J.'s shoulders, gently fastening the garment about her so it would remain closed. He drew away with extreme formality and extended his hand. "Come. I will escort you home."

C.J.'s face was wet with tears. "Is that all? I allow I am not familiar with the ways of the *ton*, nor may I ever comprehend your rules of protocol. But I believed that we had an understanding. I took—and still take—tremendous risks to enjoy your company." She placed a trembling hand on her still-flat belly. "I carry your child, Percy!"

He bore the look of a bewildered parent. Now that they were

alone, it should have been the time to take this woman in his arms and murmur sweet promises of a glorious future together. But he could not. And not for lack of desire, but for having made the decision to adhere to those damn codified societal dictates after decades of throwing them to the dogs. "I . . . realize that anything I say will make me appear a fool, Cassandra—"

"The game still confounds me. Forgive me," C.J. replied bitterly. "I was under the impression that you were no longer permitted to address me by my Christian name now that you have promised to wed another."

It was true, of course. He couldn't even handle *that* simple convention properly. Darlington hated himself for the necessity of forcing this remarkable woman to comprehend his dilemma. "I love you, Miss Welles. I beg of you not to question my regard for you. And were it still in my power to make you my wife, as I intended, I would do so with alacrity. It pains me enormously to be so cruelly frank, but at present I do not possess the capital to restore Delamere to a fully functioning estate. If the property must be sold, who knows what might happen to those who live and work upon my lands, who depend on my stewardship for their livelihood? Crops must be grown; fields must be worked. The tenant farmers live off a portion of what they sow and reap. The shops in the nearest village are dependent upon the tenants possessing the financial means to make their purchases there, or the emporia must close, leaving the shopkeepers destitute as well. The same is true for the tanner, the farrier, the saddler, even the taverns."

He regarded C.J.'s devastated expression and cursed the years of mismanagement and neglect, even assigning blame to his beloved father for bringing his son to this miserable crossroads that compelled him to be so cruel to Miss Welles—the first woman he'd loved since he'd lost Marguerite—and to subject her and their child—if indeed there was one—to the horrors of censure and ostracism. Darlington gave C.J. a desperate, tormented look. "Would that this very minute I could take you to

Delamere so that you could meet for yourself the hardworking men and women and the rosy-cheeked children whose faces, even as we speak, grow pale from malnourishment."

"Then why, at the very least, could you not have responded to my letters?"

"Because I was fighting like the very devil to do my duty, Miss Welles. It would not be considered seemly for me to correspond with a former lover when I have promised my hand to another. But the stringently prescribed rules of society make no allowances for the promptings of the heart, and for that reason, I cannot for the life of me adhere consistently to their dictates. Duty demands that I abjure your companionship, but honor compels me to look to your welfare. Believe me, Miss Welles. I have agonized over this decision. And every fiber of my being aches over having caused you and your aunt so much distress. But my intentions were thwarted by a team of solicitors who impressed upon me the gravity of my financial situation. The full extent of the mismanagement of the stewardship of Delamere was brought to light. I was aware that there were . . . problems . . . but until Lady Oliver arranged for a meeting with our bankers and solicitors, who enlightened me on the severity of the matter at hand and the imminence of the danger . . . I confess that I believed that things would find a way of sorting themselves out. Therefore, with the heaviest regrets, I must marry a lady of means whose portion, added to my own ever dwindling funds, will preserve Delamere."

"Then why did you make me believe that we had an understanding?"

Darlington took her hands in his as though they were broken-winged sparrows. He withdrew his handkerchief and blotted away the blood on her palms, then kissed each one with a great degree of tenderness. "We did indeed have an understanding. The first time I wed, Miss Welles, I did so for love, and counted myself extremely fortunate and exceptionally unusual in that regard. After Marguerite's death, I had not intended to enter the marriage mart again, as I no doubt have mentioned to you. But you so captivated me that I decided to change that decision. I had fully planned to offer for you formally when Lady Oliver made her revelation."

"Why did I suspect that your aunt had something to do with this?"

Darlington seemed unwilling to accept that his aunt's machinations had as much to do with the disposing of Miss Welles as with preserving the family estate. "Once Lady Oliver realized that I had prepared myself to remarry, she acted as she has done for the past several decades: with paramount pragmatism."

"How typical of your aunt," C.J. said, smudging the tears on her cheeks. "That love should play no part."

"Miss Welles, you must truly know little of the English aristocracy, although you were born into it. In most unions, love is never the driving force or guiding beacon. There is something much, much stronger."

"Duty, yes. And have you no duty to *me* after . . . ?" C.J. swallowed hard. "After the time we spent together . . . and the . . . result? If not duty, what could be stronger than love—unless you refer to hate?"

"Money." Darlington helped C.J. to her feet. "I regret, too, that I must see you home, Miss Welles. I am sure Lady Dalrymple is anxious about your sudden departure from the Assembly Rooms and is on her way back to her town house as we speak."

"Take me there," C.J. demanded.

"Where?"

"To Delamere. Not a few moments ago you expressed the wish to show it to me. I need to see what happens there, your lordship. How people live."

"Do you disbelieve me? I swear on my honor—"

"Take me there now, your lordship. I want to see. I must content myself by witnessing with my own eyes what goes into running such an estate."

"I can arrange to drive you there in my carriage, if you are properly chaperoned, perhaps one day next week, Miss Welles. It is a good distance from Bath."

"Now." C.J. was adamant. If she was going to lose Darlington forever and raise their child alone, then she wanted to see the reason for her fate firsthand.

"I cannot bring you there in the middle of the night, Miss Welles, particularly in your current dishabille. You must admit, even in your present state of despair, that it would be unseemly. And, undoubtedly, your aunt is already made anxious by your absence."

"Yes, you've already said as much. Please, your lordship," C.J. insisted, wiping away her falling tears with her filthy gloves. "If nothing else, do me this final kindness, and I will never ask anything else of you. After this night you may forget there ever was a Miss Welles in your life."

Darlington's heart was breaking. He could not bring himself to cause Miss Welles any further distress this night by refusing her, and thus felt compelled to honor her uncommon request. An hour later—torn between duty and desire, and despite his better judgment—the earl commandeered his own carriage and, with C.J. still wrapped securely in his cloak, set forth on the open road for Delamere.

Chapter Twenty-Four

*Containing a revelatory excursion to the English countryside,
following which, our heroine is thrown to the wolves with no
champion in sight.*

IT WAS STILL DARK when Darlington's coach sped up a circular driveway and clattered to a halt in front of an imposing villa in the Palladian style. With no servant in sight, the earl handed C.J. down from the carriage. In the moonlight, she could still make out the impeccably trimmed hedges and manicured lawns that formed the immediate landscape.

"Follow me, Miss Welles." Darlington led the way up the gravel path to the front door and rapped sharply upon it with his walking stick.

It was some minutes before the door was opened. The mobcapped matron who welcomed them rubbed the sleep from her eyes. "Good heavens, sir, is everything all right with your lordship?" She turned around to regard the enormous grandfather clock, which struck three as she spoke. " 'Tis the dead of night."

"My profoundest apologies, Mrs. Rivers. My . . . companion . . . wished to see Delamere and insisted that her visit could not be postponed."

Mrs. Rivers was either myopic or discreet, for she passed no comment on the companion's disheveled appearance. She took a moment or two to puzzle over her employer's remark about the urgency of his call, then a smile crinkled in the corners of her blue eyes. "Ah, then, is this to be the new ladyship?"

Darlington and C.J. exchanged a look.

Mrs. Rivers lowered her head and dropped a shallow curtsy. "Forgive me, your lordship, but with so little activity at Delamere nowadays, I fear the staff has little else to do but gossip."

"I am Cassandra Jane Welles, Mrs. Rivers." C.J. extended her hand to the housekeeper, who, now fully awake, was studying the young woman's strange attire, wondering why she should be swathed in the earl's cloak. "It is my fault entirely. His lordship graciously indulged my thoughtless whim. I am sorry we have disturbed your slumber."

"Charming young lady, sir, if I may say so. So, she is not to be the new mistress of Delamere?"

Darlington sighed. "Alas, no. I . . . promised . . . Miss Welles a tour of the estate," the earl began.

"Not without a cup of tea first," replied the motherly house-keeper. "And you cannot come all this way from town without showing Miss Welles some of the rooms."

Not immune to Mrs. Rivers's gentle powers of persuasion, Darlington agreed to escort Miss Welles on a tour of the main house. C.J. thought of Catherine Morland visiting Northanger Abbey. Carrying lit tapers, up the sweeping staircase they climbed, past full-length portraits of the former earls of Darlington and their wives—including two Gainsboroughs of Percy's parents and a glorious Romney of Percy himself. On the second floor of the manse, Darlington opened a set of double doors onto a ballroom that rivaled the size and splendor of the one in Bath's Upper Rooms.

"I cannot allow as this is proof of financial ruin," C.J. said, admiring the chandeliers of Austrian cut-crystal and the highly polished parquet.

"The only visitors this room has seen in several years are the parlor maids," the earl replied. "We cannot afford to entertain as we once did. The ballroom is of no more use to me now than a fallow field of wheat."

They returned to the top of the staircase and entered the room opposite the ballroom. Where the walls were not lined floor to ceiling with bookshelves, they were hung with richly colored Gobelin tapestries.

"Quite a library you have here, your lordship," gasped C.J.

"My father's. Greek, Latin, Hebrew," Darlington said, pointing to various Moroccan leather-bound collections. "A lot of use they were to Delamere."

"Why do you sneer? Surely you still value his books greatly, because you have so lovingly preserved them."

"They'd be best used for tinder at the moment." The earl sighed regretfully. "My father's cherished volumes do not put bread in the mouths of my tenants, Miss Welles. These scholarly works may be of use one day to a museum, but they avail me little at present. Come, I shall show you the . . . less glamorous aspects of my estate."

By the time they reached the foot of the central staircase, Mrs. Rivers had lit a cozy fire in the parlor off the grand foyer and poured two steaming cups of Earl Grey for the master and his guest, who, having thus fortified themselves, set out to view the remainder of the property.

Once past the pristine confines of the manor house and its verdant terraced parklands, in the dim pre-dawn light the world became a muddy, dreary gray. The coachman cursed while the horses balked, anxious about pulling the carriage over the rutted, slippery ground. After riding for what seemed like miles, they stopped before a large, gabled cottage.

Darlington pointed from the coach window at the trellised ivy façade. "This is my steward's home."

"Quite quaint."

"Mr. Belmont deserves all the charm of the English countryside that we can afford to provide. He works like the very devil to keep our heads above water. After Huggins was discharged, it took a strong leader to take the matters of the estate in hand. You will see what I mean, Miss Welles, as we drive farther along."

On either side of the road, C.J. noticed tremendous stretches of open fields. In the moonlight they looked like giant silver carpets.

"You see?" Darlington remarked, gesturing at their immediate surroundings. "That one was wheat . . . and the one on the right was rye."

"Both fallow?" C.J. asked.

"If the fields were fallow, they would be ploughed and harrowed and we would be able to use the soil next year. No, Miss Welles, the land you are presently looking at is barren. Not enough nutrients in the soil, Belmont tells me."

Soon they came upon a village of sorts, although the streets, such as they were, remained unpaved. C.J. could smell the damp thatch from the roofs of the cottages, which seemed surprisingly cramped together given the tremendous expanses of land encompassing the estate. The noise of the approaching barouche created something of a commotion. Candles, torches, and lamps were lit, and a few curious tenants ventured out of doors, buttoning and tying on their breeches over their blousy muslin nightshirts.

Darlington gave the signal for the coach to halt. He and C.J. descended from the carriage and knocked on one of the cottage doors.

They were greeted by a family of six: the head of the household brandishing a hunting rifle; the mistress, wailing babe in arms, realizing that it was the master who had come to call in the dead of night; and three more youngsters, all of whom seemed to be under the age of twelve. None of them smelled as though they routinely bathed. Their bare feet were callused and dirty. C.J. peered past the doorway into the cottage. In the single room on the main floor of the house, she spied a hodgepodge of hand-hewn furniture, wooden trenchers and pewter mugs left unwashed on a rough wooden table; and in the center of the floor, a homemade hobby horse and a legless rag doll took pride of place.

"Cor, you near frightened the wits out of meself and the missus!" exclaimed the tenant farmer, who replaced his gun in a bracket above the stone mantle. He tugged on his beard.

"My apologies for having incommoded you at this hour—"

"Bless me, it's not yet dawn!" the wife contributed. She turned to the mewling baby. "Hush up, now," she cooed. "Mama will find you somefing to eat."

"You poor child," said C.J. Realizing she had nothing upon her person to give the hungry babe, she reached out sympathetically to the infant, who immediately latched onto her pinky with his sticky little hand.

"Is something the matter, your lordship?" asked the farmer, who had successfully rubbed the sleep from his eyes.

"My . . . companion wished to see Delamere," Darlington added, finally able to complete his sentence. "Once again, I apologize for the earliness of the hour, Mr. and Mrs. Midge."

"I am entirely to blame for the inconvenience," C.J. added hastily, drawing Darlington's cloak more tightly about her person. "It was my idea to come to Delamere on such ridiculously short notice. I had to see the estate for myself. His lordship is entirely irreproachable."

Mrs. Midge appraised C.J. "I would offer you something to eat, but we only had a bit of a light supper ourselves, and the larder is . . . uncustomarily . . . bare." She caught her husband's eye, and C.J. realized that Mrs. Midge was too gracious to say that the family had indeed been rationing their food.

Midge drew the master aside. "A word in your ear, sir, if I may be so bold." Darlington nodded his assent. C.J. strained to overhear their conversation. The farmer pointed to the leavings on his table. "It's gotten so it's my family or the hogs," he said. "In a manner of speaking, sir. Belmont is a fine man, but it is going to take a good deal of work to undo so much neglect. I've been feeding my family the grain that should be for the chickens . . . the missus 'ere is getting to be a regular Merlin in the kitchen with what she makes fit to eat. And getting the young 'uns to swallow it, well, that's another act of magic. Horseflesh tough as leather, bones of the hens that starve to death for soup. But she's superstitious, my Delia is . . . won't eat the meat of a bird what's died of malnutrition."

Feeling dreadfully responsible for the situation, Darlington shook his head and explained that measures were being taken to restore Delamere to its former prosperity.

C.J., who could not continue to feign obliviousness to the conversation, opened her reticule and handed her impoverished host the entire contents of her small leather coin purse.

Darlington swallowed hard in an attempt to mask how touched he was by her compassion.

"Cor! Bless your heart, miss." As though struck with an epiphany, an effusive Mr. Midge stepped back a pace or two and regarded Darlington's companion. "You say *you* are the one to blame for dragging us all out of our beds before dawn because you had to see Delamere right away?" he asked her.

"I am afraid so, Mr. Midge," C.J. replied, wishing there were more she could do for this man and his family—nay, all of Darlington's tenants, were it in her power to do so.

"Then, if I may be so bold, sir," Midge said, his eyes twinkling, "it is all the talk about the estate that your lordship is to take another wife. May I be so bold as to inquire, then, if this kindhearted young lady is to be our new mistress?"

The earl exchanged another glance with C.J. "Alas, no," he replied truthfully. The eager solicitousness of his staff and tenants toward Lady Cassandra amused him to some extent. But for the most part, their immediate high regard for Miss Welles served to reinforce and confirm his own admiration for her and was a most painful and guilty reminder that their union was not to be.

SEVERAL HOURS LATER, Darlington thanked Lady Dalrymple for so graciously receiving him after his public embarrassment of her family at the Assembly Ball. Miss Welles's disappearance was accounted for, and her ladyship was grateful that Cassandra had been safely returned home.

C.J. had learned a good deal from her journey to Delamere. Enough to know that being poor in this society was nothing like she ever imagined it might be. No rustic idylls, but misery, depravation, and squalor, above which even the most honest and earnest could not lift themselves. The sanitary conditions in the cottages were appalling, although Darlington was no doubt doing the best he could for his tenants. Owing to the demands of his estate, however, the earl would not be a proper husband or father to their child, and C.J. no longer held out hope that he would have a change of heart or mind. He had explained himself quite thoroughly on that point. Her wish to know his situation firsthand had quite expanded her mind, and her own future looked nearly as bleak. If she and her babe survived childbirth, no end of struggles awaited them. Cut by society, if she managed to avoid the kind of financial desperation that would lead her straight to an establishment like Mrs. Lindsey's, she would never be more than a shopgirl or tavern maid. Perhaps she would get work as an actress. Actresses were social pariahs already. She dared not rely on Lady Dalrymple to come to her rescue once again. It was too much to either ask or expect, even from the most generous of souls. And she could never live with herself knowing that she bore the responsibility of dragging the poor dowager countess down to hell with her. Everything had gone wrong so quickly. Back in her own era, C.J. might have become the toast of Broadway, however briefly, and be able to provide state-of-the-art medical care for herself and her child. She could live an independent life, relatively free of censure. Instead, she had willingly given it all up, believing that she was beloved. Such thoughts, she knew, were unhealthy for her delicate condition, so she sought comfort instead in the knowledge that Lady Dalrymple's well-being had vastly improved with the combination of the "magic pills," a better diet, and regular exercise.

AFTER A BRIEF AND FITFUL SLEEP, during which her mind was chiefly filled with disagreeable thoughts, C.J. elected to take a constitutional after breakfast, the meal itself an unpleasant event owing to her bouts of morning sickness. She could have gone to the Pump Room, but surmised that her performance at the Assembly Ball would form the primary topic of the day's gossip. It was too much to bear, so she walked all the way to Sydney Gardens and back in the hope of running into Miss Austen, who might offer her the solace of her ever pragmatic perspective as well as a friendly ear.

What a strange look the customarily cordial Folsom gave C.J. upon her return! When he opened the door to admit her to Lady Dalrymple's town house, he practically backed away from her as though she carried leprosy or head lice.

Collins immediately directed her to the drawing room and informed her that she was expected. *Well, of course I am expected; I live here,* C.J. thought.

What she saw resembled a firing squad. Lady Dalrymple, wearing a lace cap that made her look considerably older and more ill, appeared exhausted and confused. She was propped up on the divan while her two pekes yapped at her ankles and a fretful Mary Sykes cooled her with her favorite silk fan. Dr. Squiffers pursed his lips and steepled his fingers in a most sanctimonious way. Saunders and Lady Oliver conferred in a corner. Darlington, wearing a haunted expression, had stationed himself at a window, in nearly the same posture C.J. had found him on the evening she returned to Bath with Lady Dalrymple's medications. And Constable Mawl, looking gruff, dwarfed the settee upon which he was attempting to perch like a gentleman.

Words deserted her.

Finally, Lady Dalrymple broke the silence. "Oh, Cassandra," she wailed.

"Oh, Cassandra," echoed Newton. "Oh, Cassandra."

"What has happened? Have I done anything?" the young woman found herself asking her "aunt's" parrot.

The usually saturnine Saunders smiled.

Finally, Squiffers stepped forward. "Miss Welles," he began, forming his words slowly, as though she were incapable of rational comprehension. "Over the past few weeks, it has become increasingly clear to those in your proximity that you have exhibited abnormal, indeed aberrant, behavior."

"Aberrant?" C.J. questioned. She was indeed uncomprehending.

The doctor removed a small, leather-bound notepad from an interior pocket of his black coat and began to read from a list written in a cramped scrawl. He looked over at Saunders, who nodded her head and rewarded the medical man with a gimlet-eyed gaze. "Perhaps, I should begin at the beginning. Constable?"

Mawl rose to his feet and stepped forward as though he were called upon to testify before the bar. He assumed a pompous stance. "The alleged Miss Welles was apprehended by me, near Stall Street, just after Easter Sunday. She was caught thieving and appeared to be without fixed abode. The minx was thereupon taken to the jail, where she was placed in the care of one Jack Clapham, warden."

"Constable, did this alleged Miss Welles ever tell you at the time you apprehended her, or during her incarceration in the prison, that she was the niece of a noblewoman: to wit, Lady Dalrymple, whom you see seated before you?"

"What is this all about?" C.J. demanded, feeling increasingly ill and fearing the reply. "Why do I feel like I am on trial here?"

"Because you are, in a manner of speaking," Squiffers replied. "Are you or are you not related to Lady Dalrymple? What manner of young woman roams the streets of Bath unchaperoned, with nowhere to rest her head at night? What manner of young woman must steal for her supper?"

"Breakfast," C.J. corrected sullenly. What manner of a nightmare was she caught in?

"If Lady Wickham had been well enough to travel, she, too,

would be sitting here to question the sanity of a young woman who spends weeks in her employ, yet neglects to mention that she is the niece of a countess who lives but a few minutes' walk away." Dr. Squiffers flipped through his little pad of notes.

"The old bat is healthy enough; she's just too cheap to hire a hack."

"Mary!" Lady Oliver gasped at the maid's rudeness.

"Mary!" Lady Dalrymple said, nearly simultaneously, rather proud of the girl's audacity.

"Miss Welles is the dearest, sweetest friend I've ever had," Mary proclaimed, dropping the fan in Lady Dalrymple's upholstered lap and rushing over to protect her champion. She threw her arms around Cassandra and held her tightly. "Miss Welles is not touched. And whoever says so is touched himself!" she insisted, choking back sobs.

So *that* was what was going on. Dr. Squiffers, clearly bolstered by the support of nearly everyone in the room, with the obvious exceptions of Mary and Lady Dalrymple, thought she was mentally unstable. C.J. reflexively touched her stomach as if to protect her child from hearing its mother so maligned. What did Darlington think? Did the man she had fallen in love with now regard her as a madwoman?

Squiffers began to read from his notes. "Miss Welles comes and goes from the house at all hours, often unchaperoned. Miss Welles has been observed wearing the same garments at all hours of the day, not changing her morning frock for a tea gown on several occasions. She seems overfond of a cheap, yellow muslin and a particular blue sarcenet, although her ladyship has ordered many frocks made to her liking and her measurements. Miss Welles undertook to treat her ladyship of a severe illness of the heart, whereupon she procured some medication that was unfamiliar to every apothecary to whom a sample was presented." Mary looked shocked and was about to protest that she had never betrayed Miss Welles or her ladyship and that one of the little tablets must have been stolen from her when the doctor raised his hand to hush her. He continued his recitation of C.J.'s transgressions. "Miss Welles's conduct in prohibiting her ladyship's physician to attend her and to prescribe an acceptable course of treatment is evidence of an unstable mind."

Poor Lady Dalrymple, who had invested so much in her. And who had always trusted her own lady's maid, never suspecting that the witch had her greedy hands in Lady Oliver's purse. How could Saunders have betrayed her mistress? And how could Lady Oliver have so betrayed a bosom friend?

"Mary, ring for Collins," the countess said quietly. "Saunders, you are dismissed from my employ. Collins will see to it that you are packed and out of my house within the hour. You will receive no severance, nor will I provide you with a reference."

The dour-faced servant looked to Lady Oliver, clearly expecting to be rescued, if not offered a new situation outright, but her ladyship was far too canny to openly tip her hand.

Dr. Squiffers steadied his own nerves by pressing his forefingers together as tightly as he could. "Lady Dalrymple, under the circumstances, I have no alternative but to admit Miss Welles to St. Joseph of Bethlehem."

Mary gasped. "Bedlam?!"

The countess fainted.

It was Darlington who came to Lady Dalrymple's side, pouring several drops of cool water from a pitcher onto his monogrammed cambric handkerchief, which he fashioned into a compress for Lady Dalrymple's throbbing temples. C.J. looked at him imploringly. "Your lordship?" she whispered. Her lips trembled. Should her words beseech or berate?

"Nephew, we have nothing more to do here," Lady Oliver remarked sternly. "I should like to call for my carriage."

The earl regarded his aunt. "For years now, I have been willing to see you through rose-colored lenses, owing to the dreadful hardships you endured as a young bride. You never permitted me to forget your own misery, and your bitterness grew like a chancre on a blossom, destroying all hope of its everlasting beauty. The scales have fallen from my eyes, Aunt Augusta. Or shall I say I have ground the rose-tinted glass beneath the heel of my boot. We have nothing to say to each other."

"You will regret it, Percy," Lady Oliver warned. "You will live to regret this day." She lowered her lorgnette and swept imperiously from the room.

"Not half so much as I regret seeing the rest of the world through your jaundiced eyes," her nephew retorted. He made a protective move toward Cassandra, but the physician held up his hand to stop him.

"Miss Welles is going to Bethlehem, your lordship. The documents have been signed." Squiffers produced a set of folded papers from the deep pocket of his coat and showed the earl the autograph that committed her to the asylum.

"You bastard." Darlington had been bested. All it took was a physician's signature, and this one was legal. Would that he could strangle the doctor and take Cassandra with him to the countryside. Flout convention. Blast propriety. Dash the Digbys! He would marry his Cunegonde, Miss Welles, and they would survive if they had to work the land themselves.

Darlington despised the triumphant look in the medic's eyes. "Miss Welles will come with me," the doctor said with finality.

Chapter Twenty-Five

*Concerning the conditions in a nineteenth-century madhouse,
and our heroine's incarceration therein. The Marquess of
Manwaring plays his part to perfection, spinning a fanciful tale
that contains nothing but the truth itself.*

THE RED BRICK BUILDING with the cast-iron gate was forbidding from the outset. Ivy tendrils curled upward from the foundation as if to further shelter the Bethlehem inmates from the view of the outside world.

St. Joseph's of Bethlehem was the sister hospital, C.J. learned, to St. Mary of Bethlehem, the first English madhouse, which opened in Bishopsgate, London, in 1403. The London asylum quickly earned the nickname Bedlam, and the homeless people of the Tudor and Stuart eras were known as Tom O'Bedlam, as they wandered the streets of the city in parti-colored attire begging for food and alms.

Clearly, Dr. Squiffers, convinced by the testimony of Constable Mawl, was certain that this "Miss Welles" was a latter-day street person who in order to survive had spun a series of tall tales, none of which were true and most of which conspired to take advantage of specific members of the aristocracy, doubtless to win their hearts and the forfeiture of their purses.

He lifted the handle of a small, black metal box that hung on the outside gate and rang the bell within it.

Presently an extraordinarily tall, nearly bald gentleman of middling to advanced age came to the gate and unlocked it for the doctor and his charge.

"Squiffers."

"Haslam."

The iron gate clanged shut behind them, the sound ringing in C.J.'s ears.

The lanky giant wordlessly led them along a worn flagstone path, up to a second gate. He removed a large iron key ring from his waistcoat and unfastened the enormous padlock, then opened the oaken door directly behind the portcullis.

Haslam exposed a mouthful of yellowed teeth. "This way madness lies," he grinned, gesturing down a grayish, grim corridor. "You say she's another country pauper?" he asked Dr. Squiffers. "We've got so many of them in here, I've stopped keeping track. Shut yer!" he snapped at a moaning inmate who thrust a bony arm through the bars of a cell. The madman's glazed eyes gave the impression that the human being behind them had long ago died, and that it was merely his starving carcass that had stubbornly refused to give up the ghost.

C.J. stopped in her tracks at the sight of a man in leg irons shackled to the stone wall of his cell. They *dared* to call this a hospital? The conditions were worse than in the prison!

Shrieks, groans, and unintelligible ravings echoed off the walls of the narrow corridor. C.J. would have tried to hold her ears, had not Squiffers a firm grasp of one of her arms.

"I'm John Haslam, resident apothecary in charge here," the gaunt giant told the stunned young woman. "And I run a tight ship. The usual treatment for this one?" he asked the doctor.

Squiffers was about to nod his assent when C.J. stopped and whirled around, planting her feet. "What are you going to do to me?" she demanded, her voice rising.

"Finest care in the kingdom, pretty one," the madhouse

keeper replied. "Regular bleeding, purging, and vomiting. We've got some two hundred inmates who receive a steady diet of water gruel every day for breakfast, porridge at lunch, and rice milk on Saturdays at dinner. Three meals a day! And of course at Bethlehem, we believe that the moral force of the 'eye'—my eye—will lead these mad sinners to God," Haslam gleefully told the physician.

"I am not mad!" C.J. shrieked, and summoned all her force to shake loose from Squiffers's grasp. She raced away from the mad-doctors, down the corridor, heart pounding, adrenaline pumping.

But her freedom was short-lived, as she found herself lifted off the floor by two enormous guards who seemed to have materialized from the ether, men as tall as Haslam, but with perhaps thrice his bulk. They bore her back to the doctors, still attempting to elbow her way out of their firm grasp and kicking her legs as fiercely as she could, given the narrowness of her hem.

When the duo reached Haslam and Squiffers with their prey, the keeper unlocked a cell, and pushed back the door. A huge metal contraption, like a giant black birdcage, hung from a chain of heavy links attached to the low ceiling. The bottom of the cage remained suspended about two feet from the floor of the cell. "This'll keep her from doing injury to herself or the others," Haslam explained. "It will stop her kicking, for sure."

No! They couldn't! C.J. thought. In an instant, she became a living thing inside what nearly passed for a gibbet, the cage barely big enough to contain her slender body. Haslam slammed the door of the cage, rattling it to be sure that the lock held fast. He removed a gold pocket watch from his waistcoat and checked the time. "Ahh. How fortuitous of you to arrive at this time of day, Miss Welles. You are just in time for lunch."

The apothecary turned and escorted Squiffers from the cell and down the corridor, their retreat greeted by a chorus of cries and jeers from the unfortunate incarcerated souls.

There she was, trapped in an iron cage, in a walled cell, in an airless stockade, which itself stood behind two impenetrable gates. All C.J. had left was her mind, which she was sure to lose for real, the more time she spent imprisoned within these walls. So this was where society locked away its undesirable element, its untouchables. Certainly, there were genuine madmen and madwomen in Bethlehem, but how many others had lost their minds *in* the asylum, who had been shut away simply for being homeless or helpless?

And the more she thought about it, the more C.J. realized that the barbarism to which she was currently subject was not entirely unknown in her own century. Too often C.J. had come across headlines of abusive and appalling conditions in mental wards and nursing homes. Her heart had gone out to the victims she had read about and whose stories were played out in the nightly news, but they had always been more or less fictional characters to her. Now she was one of them.

How could she retain her wits and devise a means of escape? How could she convey a message to those who still cared about her? C.J. tried to shift her weight; her legs had already fallen asleep. Even the mound of straw in the corner of the dark cell seemed inviting by comparison.

Something rustled in the dark. For a moment, C.J. thought she saw the straw move. Perhaps she was losing her mind sooner than she feared.

A woman's head, covered with long, matted gray hair, poked through the smelly reeds. The head was followed by a body resembling nothing so much as a sack of potatoes. The colors of whatever garments the lady had been wearing had faded into nondescription. Her breasts sagged to her waist. It was nearly impossible to tell her age. But she fixed upon C.J. with piercing blue eyes. For several moments, the two women simply regarded each other, with more curiosity than wariness. Finally, the other spoke, never releasing C.J. from her bright blue gaze. Her voice sounded like aged whisky. "I've been here twenty years," she said.

"How old are you then?" C.J. asked curiously.

"Nineteen . . . and twenty-three and sixty-five if I'm a day."

This did not seem a satisfactory answer to the new inmate. "If you are but nineteen years old, how can you have been here for twenty years?" she queried.

The haggard woman sat up and began to rock herself, singing a ballad with a lyric of her own devising, set to a familiar tune.

"Alas, Lord Featherstone did me wrong, for to get me with child on a mild midday; my maidenhead died the same day as my father, and . . . look you!" The madwoman staggered to her feet.

C.J. noticed that her cellmate was pregnant, immediately putting her in mind of her own dire plight. "Lady Rose?" she asked, horrified.

"I was once a lovely pink rose, but my bush was pruned," Rose continued in a singsong. She lifted her skirts. *"In for a penny, in for a pound,"* she chanted, displaying her privates. "Oooh, I've lifted my skirt for men much better than you, I warrant."

Rose rubbed her belly and began to cough; it was a dry, hacking sound. "Pray, sir, have you got anything to drink? I am parched with thirst." She looked about the ratty straw until she found a tin cup. Rose stared into the bottom of the cup, wishing it full, then turned it over and demonstrated to C.J. that there was nothing in it. She stumbled over to C.J.'s cage, still clutching her cup and peered closely at her. "Ohh, you're a *lady*," Lady Rose marveled. "I was a lady once."

Rose's arms were rail thin. Perhaps she had eaten nothing during her incarceration. With her swelling belly and skeletal frame, she resembled the photographs C.J. had seen of starving children in Biafra. "Lady Rose, what happened that you should end up in Bedlam?" Should she divulge her knowledge of Rose's recent whereabouts, that the last time C.J. had seen her, Rose was the main attraction at a gang rape masquerading as a bawdy costume ball?

"Curse the day you were born a woman!" Rose hissed. She began to sway to and fro, picking up the thread of her tune.

*Lord Featherstone could not live alone, cut by the ton and his
    family.
A babe on the way fair ruined his day, nor could he repair my
    virginity.*

Lady Rose, shivering, scratched at her bare, scrawny legs.
They were dotted with ugly sores. "Mrs. Lindsey was kind to
me, so kind . . . until . . ." She clawed at her own belly.

"Until she could tell you were carrying a babe," C.J. whispered.

Rose nodded. "I'm cold, so cold. Can you keep me warm,
mistress?"

C.J. searched the confines of her cage for anything resembling a blanket, while Rose, dripping profusely with a cold sweat,
tried to hum to herself to keep her teeth from chattering.

"I'm afraid I have nothing here, your ladyship," C.J. said.
That it should come to this. At least the poor young woman deserved to be addressed properly. The rest of her dignity already
had been stripped away by degrees. "Come to me, Lady Rose."
C.J. crouched at the bottom of the cage and stretched her arms
through the bars as far as she could reach.

Rose crawled over and nestled like an obedient child in the
pungent straw matting while C.J. managed to cradle the head
and shoulders of the unfortunate soul in her arms. Rose began
to rock and sob, in between shivers, and for several minutes C.J.
rocked with her, the cage swinging to and fro.

Rose's flesh then began to grow cold to the touch; her
singing stopped. The only noise C.J. heard was the cacophony of
shrieks and cries from other inmates. To her mortification, she
realized that Lady Rose was most likely at death's door. C.J.
cried herself hoarse calling for the doctors.

"SOMETHING MUST BE DONE!" Darlington raged, as he paced
the carpet in Lady Dalrymple's drawing room.

Lady Dalrymple put three lumps of highly taxed sugar in her

tea. "Not only is Miss Welles perfectly sane, Percy, but she is carrying your child. You did believe her when she announced her condition at the Assembly Ball? Do you wish that horrible Dr. Squiffers to salve your conscience and subject her to further shame by verifying her condition? Heavens! What unmarried young woman would go to such risks? Was it a *mad* thing she did that night—or a *brave* one? My niece loves you, you foolish man. From the moment I saw Miss Welles, even in her ill-fitting servant's garb, I thought that you and she would suit. She has a lively mind, Percy. You need that."

"Well, 'tis true enough that the girl possesses an uncommon spirit."

"One that will be utterly destroyed if she is permitted to languish in that asylum a moment longer. If she dies there, your child dies with her." Her voice choked with emotion and anger. "So help me, Percy, that girl is my happiness—and yours—you damn fool. If we lose her forever, you will never again be welcome in my sight!"

"I am thoroughly aware of my own culpability in this affair. Let me be the responsible party here," Darlington fumed. An afterthought overtook him. "Perhaps I drove Miss Welles to madness by abandoning her when I had all but offered for her."

"Fie, Percy, you give yourself far too much credit! My niece is heartsick; that's what's the matter with her and you did indeed drive her to that, but she is no more mad than you or I, and you know it. I have my flights of fancy, to be sure," the countess continued, aware of the deception she had perpetrated on her friends as well as on the rest of the gentry of Bath. How well she knew that the noblest among us are not always fortunate in having a noble birthright. "They have always served to entertain me . . . and will have to do so even more now that I am alone in the world."

"You're never alone, mum. You'll always have me. I promise it," Mary blurted earnestly. "I give you my solemn word that even if I do become a midwife, I shall see to your care for the rest of my days."

"Midwife?" Darlington and Lady Dalrymple echoed.

"Forgive me for speakin' so; I know it is not my place, but I have always dreamed of it. I have fancies too! Although I know that I cannot have thoughts above my station—and have no proper learnin' besides—I was born on a farm, and babe or calf or foal, I know how to assist a female who is going to be a mum."

Darlington tried to maintain a clear head. These women were plaguing him with the sort of circuitous logic that was peculiar to their sex. Talk of babes and midwifery and flights of fancy—while Cassandra was incarcerated in a madhouse! "Mary, I give you my pledge that if we manage to free Miss Welles from Bethlehem, I will permit you to be present when she is delivered of her babe. But for the nonce, we must see what can be done to effect her release from the asylum."

"Precisely, Percy." The countess rose from her seat and began to pace to and fro, nearly wearing a path in the carpet with her tread. Her front parlor was fast becoming its own Bedlam. "Wherever one wishes to lay blame, I remain certain that Cassandra does not belong in Bethlehem." She leveled a stern gaze at the earl. "To my mind, we have one course yet to pursue, though it unnerves me to think that an inveterate bettor may be the ace up my sleeve."

AT PRECISELY EIGHT O'CLOCK the following morning, a portly gentleman was seen rubbing the sleep from his eyes in the tastefully designed vestibule of the Cadogan House Hotel on Gay Street. Two cups of strong black coffee—Sally Lunn's Gamblers' Blend—had not provided even half the energy he needed to perform the role required of him.

As the marquess had been compelled to sell off his equipage in order to satisfy creditors, which is why he had endured the journey to Bath in the mail coach, Lady Dalrymple had arranged to have her brother's coat of arms painted on one of her own carriages. She had paid dearly to achieve the appropriate effect on such short notice.

Now Albert Tobias, Lord Manwaring, fiddled with the shiny brass buttons on his new coat—a gift from his sister—remarking upon the fact that the glint they made in the bright sunlight produced no adverse effect whatsoever on his head. Perhaps this was the first morning in many that he had not awakened suffering from the aftereffects of too much brandy, wine, or gin. He had not been particular of late when it came to a preference in spirits. Come to think of it, he mused, running a plump hand along his blond, balding pate, this was the first day in many that he had awakened in the morning at all. Ordinarily, Nesbit, an ever faithful valet—and his sole remaining servant apart from the housemaid—would bestir him with a glass of brandy sometime during the midafternoon hours.

A conveyance that looked remarkably like the ghost of his own carriage rumbled up to the portal. It was being driven by the burly coachman whom Manwaring recognized as an employee of the countess.

A plump hand, also quite similar to his own, though bedecked with rubies and opals, gestured wildly for him to ascend. "Get in, Bertie. Heavens, you dawdle!"

The liveried and periwigged footman practically whisked the marquess into the barouche, where he sat facing his sister and Lord Darlington.

Lady Dalrymple fished in her reticule and, after some searching, retrieved a small envelope. She handed the packet to Manwaring. "There are one hundred pounds in here, Albert. I have spoken with my solicitors in London, whom I have authorized to write you a draft for another nine hundred should you play your part to perfection this morning."

It was a bloody windfall. "Oh, Euphie," the marquess slobbered. Tears of gratitude coursed down his florid cheeks.

"Don't blubber, Bertie, you'll ruin your new waistcoat."

Manwaring took his sister's hands in his own, clutching

them so tightly that his palms bruised from the pressure made by Lady Dalrymple's enormous rings. "I always knew you were the kindest, dearest sister a creature could ever hope to have," he continued theatrically.

"You shall see how kind I can be if you do not win the day," the countess scolded. "I hope all the liquor you have consumed over the years has not destroyed your memory. You will need it for what I am about to *remind* you, as it concerns the history and particulars of your daughter, Cassandra Jane."

"JOHN HASLAM, RESIDENT APOTHECARY," the tall, gaunt man said as he extended his hand to Lords Manwaring and Darlington. "Perhaps your ladyship would prefer to wait in our garden—it's quite lovely, very restful—while the gentlemen and I see to business."

"Her ladyship will do nothing of the sort," Lady Dalrymple snorted. "If your conditions here are tolerable enough for female patients, they will be tolerable enough for female visitors." The truth was the countess desperately wanted to be in her brother's company should he require any prompting. Besides, she was curious about the institution itself. From the façade, it seemed no more threatening than an average hospital, but from the fetid smells lingering in the air and the stifled cries that she could hear from where she stood in the vestibule, she surmised that there was a goodly degree of barbarism practiced here. What vile, inhumane things had these monsters already inflicted upon her "niece"? It was too horrible to contemplate.

"And what might bring your lordship here?" the apothecary asked Darlington.

The earl kept a hand on his sword hilt. "Merely an interest in how you treat your patients, Mr. Haslam."

Haslam led the way down the dingy corridor to the cell where C.J. was incarcerated, still in her black iron birdcage, an immobile bundle slumped on the straw below her. Lady Dalrymple gasped. Her hand fluttered to her heart. Her "niece" looked as though she had not had a bath since her arrival, her rosy color had turned pale, her usually glossy dark curls hung limp and life-less about her face. Even C.J.'s eyes had taken on a dull sheen.

"My niece," the countess cried, stretching her arms toward the cell.

By way of greeting, C.J. regarded her with a swollen, tearstained face and pointed at the body lying in the straw be-neath her.

"What is it, child?" asked Lady Dalrymple, her handkerchief to her nose.

"The last act of a tragedy." C.J. quietly wept, the tears cours-ing down her grimy cheeks. "That was Lady Rose. She's dying and no one would come to her aid. They killed her; they all killed her," she muttered. "And her innocent babe as well. A double murder," C.J. added, placing her hand on her own womb.

"*Lady* Rose," sneered Haslam. "She's naught but a lying doxy," he grunted to a shocked Lady Dalrymple. "Claimed she was ravished by a dozen different upstanding members of the *ton*—lord this and earl that—the finest men in Bath. Help *her*? She deserves all the suffering she brought on *them* for blackening their good names!"

"Heavens!" the countess gasped.

"Release my daughter this instant, you quack!" thundered the marquess in his finest theatrical timbre.

"Y-your *daughter,* sir?" Haslam stammered.

"Of course, my daughter, you nitwit. Release her from this barbaric contraption immediately, before I have the law on the lot of you here."

"But, I thought . . ."

"Clearly, when one spends the better part of one's days in the company of madmen, one loses one's own ability to think sanely. Although I have not seen my daughter in some years, that does not alter her birthright or her lineage. Come to me, my child!"

Manwaring opened his arms, striking his most paternal pos-ture, and C.J. saw Lady Dalrymple behind him, beckoning her to go along with the charade. When Haslam unlocked the cage,

C.J. tumbled to the straw beneath her, nearly falling on the inert Lady Rose. Owing to her close confinement, her limbs had all the strength of tapioca pudding. C.J. stumbled to her feet, trying to recover the sense of feeling in her legs. She ran a hand through her tangled hair and tried to make herself presentable. "Papa?" she questioned tentatively. "Papa, is that you?"

"My child, my dearest, only daughter," Manwaring sobbed in a maudlin display that nevertheless had Haslam reaching for his linen pocket square. "I thought never to see you again."

"I-Is this *indeed* your daughter, your lordship? Look closely." The apothecary bent to whisper in the stout man's ear. "If you have not seen your daughter in some time, this young woman could be an impostor."

The rail-thin medic received a swift elbow to the gut for his pains. "Not know my own daughter, you charlatan?! My little Cassandra . . ." Manwaring ran stubby fingers through C.J.'s matted curls. "She has her mother's hair. Look! Her mother's eyes!" He raised his hands to the young woman's face, pudgy thumbs pushing down her cheekbones as if to accentuate C.J.'s brown eyes. "Euphie, the locket," he called, reaching out an arm toward his sister, who was sobbing noisily into her handkerchief.

Lady Dalrymple fumbled with the clasp on her locket.

"Heavens, Euphie," a frustrated Manwaring sighed. "Come forward and show Haslam the resemblance. Is it not remarkable, sir?" the marquess asked when the locket was opened and the portrait revealed.

"Indeed it is, your lordship," the apothecary was reluctantly compelled to agree, as he glanced from the painted miniature to the disheveled inmate.

"And look, she wears the cross that was her gift at her birth from me and my late wife Emma, Cassandra's dear, departed mother. Such a beautiful woman Emma was." Now Manwaring's tears were genuine. It had been years since he'd spoken aloud of his late wife, and it was her untimely demise that had triggered his rapid descent into the hellish depths of drink and gambling.

Compounding matters, he had defiled her legacy to their daughter, having been forced to pawn the engraved silver backing into which the cross had been inserted. The marquess reached for C.J.'s throat and fingered the pockmarked amber talisman. "I'd recognize that nick in the bottom right corner anywhere," he sniffled, practically slobbering on his starched cravat.

C.J. reexamined the cross and, to be certain, there *was* a notch in it. *Lady Dalrymple briefed her brother well*, she thought with a smile. "We have . . . ever so much . . . to discuss, Papa," she began haltingly, but the marquess enfolded her in a paternal bear hug.

"Hush, my pet. There will be time aplenty for swapping stories." He turned to address the apothecary. "First we must get my own flesh and blood released from this pit of insanity," and turning back to C.J., he added, "and get you home, where Mary will fix you a nice hot bath. And," he muttered to himself, "I think, under the circumstances, a brandy would not be remiss."

Lady Dalrymple glared at the marquess, then fixed her stern gaze on the keeper of the madhouse. "I expect that you will release my niece immediately, Haslam," she ordered. "And that you will deliver to me all of your papers concerning her incarceration. You will keep no copies, do you understand?"

The apothecary, cut down to size, merely nodded meekly, then showed the little party the door.

Once safely in the confines of the carriage, Darlington, who had remained a silent, shadowy figure for much of the duration of their visit to Bethlehem, extended his hand to the marquess. "Congratulations, my man. That was well done! Bloody well done!"

Manwaring preened like a peacock. "Nice to know the old boy's still got a sense of improvisation," he crowed.

Lady Dalrymple patted her brother's knee. "I am quite proud of you, Bertie," she smiled. "And you may keep the suit, especially as you sobbed all over the front of your silk waistcoat."

"Would you mind terribly if I returned home today, by the Royal Mail?" Albert asked his sister.

"Just when I was wondering if I'd miss you."

As they approached the city, Darlington gave a command to the coachman to stop near the Abbey so Manwaring could catch the next Royal Mail coach.

"Now don't spend everything I gave you at the taverns, Bertie," Lady Dalrymple cautioned in her most sisterly tone. "My solicitors have the strictest instructions that the funds must be used to pay off your creditors first." Manwaring looked stricken. "It's time one of us grew up, love. Might as well be you." The countess gave her brother a sloppy peck on the cheek and squeezed his arm. "Be well, Bertie."

The marquess turned to C.J. and beamed. "The pleasure has been all mine, Miss . . ."

"Welles. Cassandra Jane Welles, your lordship." She permitted him to kiss her proffered hand. "Garrick would have been proud of you." She winked at Manwaring, who lit up like a Christmas tree.

"Would he now? Well, bless my soul, you are an excellent judge of talent, Miss Welles. May I be so bold as to express the hope that we meet in future."

"I should like that," C.J. replied. And she meant it.

They watched as Manwaring waved a cheerful good-bye at the carriage, and when he thought they were no longer looking, he turned and walked into the nearest pub.

"*Plus ça change, plus c'est la même chose,*" C.J. said, smiling and shaking her head.

"I just hope he leaves himself enough to get back to London," Darlington added. When the carriage stopped in the Circus, the earl stepped out, then reached inside and took C.J.'s hands in his. "Rest assured, Miss Welles, I will visit you when I am able. I hope you understand that there are some matters to which I must devote my most immediate attention."

Oh, how she wished he would have enfolded her in his arms and kissed her, not minding her filthy and bedraggled condition, and then carried her inside his town house and bathed her with his own hands.

"YOU HAVE SUCH LOVELY HAIR, Miss Welles," Mary said admiringly as she poured a pint of porter through her mistress's curls. "And this will make it shine all the more," she added, referring to the mixture of heavy dark beer and water.

"Perhaps it is foolishness to have accepted his lordship's offer at all. To go riding with him, I mean." C.J. inhaled the soothing verbena scent of the water in which she bathed. "For one thing, should we be recognized, Lady Charlotte will pitch a proper fit. For another, I don't expect that many ladies in my . . . condition . . . would ever think about getting astride a horse."

"In my village, we were too poor to have horses. The beasts fetch a dear price. My mother rode our donkey while she carried a babe within her, and she was delivered of six of us, bless her soul. I lost my four brothers," the maid said matter-of-factly, "but it had naught to do with ridin'."

C.J. gently placed a wet hand on Mary's arm. "I am sorry about your brothers."

Mary shrugged off the touch. She was hardier than C.J. imagined. "I should not have spoken of my brothers. Forgive me, Miss Welles. We do not want to hex the babe."

It was quite possible to lose the baby, C.J. knew. An excursion on horseback was tempting the fates, but stillbirths and the infant mortality rate were also extraordinarily high, even among the aristocracy. Not to mention dying in childbirth. She shuddered and tried to lower herself farther into the hip bath.

"I have been thinkin'," Mary said as she rinsed the beer from her mistress's hair, "that I should like to apprentice myself to a midwife so that I may learn how to deliver your babe, Miss Welles. But I know it would never do. A girl like me is lucky enough to have a situation as a lady's maid, and were it not for your kindness—and that of his lordship and her ladyship—I would not even have that."

"Mary!" The notion was a bit overwhelming. C.J.'s eyes began to brim with tears. And this was the timid child who not too many weeks ago refused to use the word *pregnant*. What a long way *she* had traveled!

"I wanted a way to thank you for everything you have done for me. You have taught me my letters, got me to think for myself . . . and this is one of my thoughts!"

C.J. regarded the little maid. "Why are you crying, Mary?" she asked gently.

"Because, Miss Welles, I should very much like to have something I can call my own . . . to make myself truly useful in this world . . ." She fought for words. "I want ever so much to learn to be a midwife, but you and her ladyship have been so kind to me, and you are so very dear that I shouldn't want to leave Lady Dalrymple's employ. Servants never give notice anyways, 'less they're gettin' married and goin' away."

"Mary." C.J. raised a sudsy hand to the girl's face and gently touched her cheek. "I am heartily sure that her ladyship—with her unusual opinions—would no doubt be the first to acknowledge that a woman should find a purpose in life . . . and a profession. Imagine! You will be able to earn your own way and be your own mistress!"

The encouragement was bittersweet. "I suppose I want it so much . . . to be a midwife, I mean . . . for a selfish reason. It was you, Miss Welles, what—*that*—put the notion in my head, though I can't say as you knew anything about it. Perhaps," Mary added in a small, hopeful voice, "even after I become a midwife, you will consider engagin' me as the babe's nanny."

Chapter Twenty-Six

*An eventful chapter, in which a pleasant midday excursion
becomes a dramatic ride, with disastrous consequences; while
one young woman languishes, another flourishes; Lady
Dalrymple bestows an extraordinarily magnanimous gift; and
our heroine receives a mysterious note.*

DESPITE THE FACT that she had been arrested, imprisoned, tried, nearly committed to a lifetime of indentured servitude, publicly jilted by the man she
loved, and, most recently, incarcerated in a madhouse, C.J. had
come to feel, in a most inexplicable way, that she really belonged
in 1801. All her life she had felt like a fish out of water. In fact,
her late adoptive father used to call her Guppy. One day he and
his wife had found a confused and frightened toddler wandering
around the streets of Greenwich Village. Years later her adoptive
mother told her that at first she wouldn't speak, so they had
thought she was a mute, or retarded. They had taken her to the
local precinct, where the police looked through all the missing
persons reports but found no match for her. Because Mr. Welles
was so well respected in the community, the state granted his
petition to allow him and his wife to keep C.J. until her birth
parents came forward to claim her. But no one ever did, so after

a few years they legally adopted her. C.J. herself had no memories of anything before she was found by the Welleses.

To be sure, there had been enough mishaps and ugliness to make one question the sanity of her decision to remain in Bath. However, there was the occasional unalloyed delight that had eased her permanent transition into the infant nineteenth century.

On the day after her release from the madhouse, C.J. returned from her morning constitutional to discover draped across her bedspread the most exquisite garment she had ever seen. She held it before her as she surveyed her reflection in the cheval mirror. The deep green velvet was of the finest quality. C.J. opened a large, round hatbox to discover a handsome black veiled riding hat. And at the foot of the bed there was another box that contained a pair of black boots with a sturdy heel.

Trying on the new riding habit, C.J. frowned, lifting the skirt's heavy, lopsided train over her right arm. This could not be right, she thought, as she studied her reflection. She donned the black hat, which sat solidly upon her head at just the proper angle, hoping that it would ameliorate the picture before her. How could a celebrated modiste like Madame Delacroix have made such a mistake?

Oh, God! Her stomach lurched as she suddenly made sense of the strange configuration of her hem. *Of course!* She was expected to ride *sidesaddle*.

Thus it was with no small degree of trepidation that she met the earl, who came to fetch her in his coach to take her to his stables in Bathampton. C.J. resolved to put a bold face on it and not let the earl sense her inexperience. After all, she was an actress—or had been. She would have to feign a familiarity with the sidesaddle, or risk giving herself away yet again. Her fears returned as to whether she was tempting the fates too much and putting her unborn babe at a ridiculous and unnecessary risk, but Mary had made a salient point: in this era, women in her condition often rode. Perhaps she was being overly cautious.

One of the earl's grooms led out a chestnut mare and adjusted the saddle girth.

Darlington grinned. "She reminds me a bit of you, Miss Welles. Her name is Gypsy Lady."

"For her wild spirit or for her nomadic tendencies?" C.J. quipped.

The dapper groom helped C.J. into the sidesaddle, offering his open palm to boost her up. She had seen enough movies to know that she needed to secure herself by hooking her leg over the pommel. It was an awkward position—to face forward while both of her legs draped over the left side of the mare. She hoped that neither the groom nor the earl saw her trembling. And that Gypsy Lady didn't sense her trepidation.

"You look quite elegant, Miss Welles," Darlington called to her as he saddled a huge white mount. He patted the horse's immense yet graceful neck.

"What is his name?" C.J. called gaily.

"Esperance."

"A good name for a Percy, your lordship!" C.J. trotted Gypsy Lady over to Darlington, whose groom was adjusting the length of his stirrups.

He leaned toward her. "One of the most remarkable things about our friendship, Miss Welles, is that I can make a reference to Shakespeare, or mythology, or history without the need to explain, define, or clarify my meaning."

C.J. discovered that she had no trouble maneuvering the reins and her riding crop, although she had not had occasion to use the stick and always deplored doing so. As long as she was going slowly, she maintained her balance in the sidesaddle with ease and enjoyed moving her body in tandem with the mare's loping rhythm.

"I thought you might like to see the view from Charlcombe," Darlington proposed as they rode side by side. The steady clip-clop of the hooves along the dirt road had an almost soporific effect. The air smelled clean and fresh from newly cut grass and hay. "It's a delightful old village; in fact, Miss Austen quite prefers to walk in this area."

C.J. was entranced by the verdant surroundings, the gentle rolling hills, and the wooded valleys dotted with wildflowers.

"We can dismount any time you like, Miss Welles, should you wish to explore any point of interest on foot."

C.J. nodded. In fact, she would very likely find many places of interest but was tentative about alighting from Gypsy Lady, now that she was beginning to gain a degree of ease in the sidesaddle position.

Darlington was looking ahead, pointing to a small village church built of stone in the Norman style. "Cassandra, have you ever read *Tom Jones*?"

"Yes, indeed. Why do you ask?"

"Despite my inquiring, I should not be surprised at your answer. So many young ladies of fashion are actively encouraged not to read novels, as it is commonly believed that the morals they contain may destroy the mind." Darlington stopped in front of the old Norman church. "The church of St. Mary the Virgin. Henry Fielding was married here," the earl remarked, referring to the author of the ostensibly salacious novel in question. "St. Mary's is traditionally considered the mother church of Bath. As a matter of fact, the Abbey used to pay its dues to St. Mary's to the tune of a pound of peppercorns annually."

"That's nothing to sneeze at!"

"Touché, Miss Welles. Shall we ride down into the valley?"

"Why not?" answered C.J., unaware of his intentions.

"Race you!" he called as he spurred his horse into a canter.

"No, I can't, Percy! The baby!" C.J., who had been quite comfortable on Gypsy Lady as the horse walked beside Darlington's mount and had rather liked trotting, now found herself in a situation that she had difficulty managing with any degree of grace or agility. Gypsy Lady was true to her appellation. As soon as Esperance went into his brisk canter, the mare wildly followed, temporarily throwing C.J. off balance.

Her mind was a jumble of thoughts, cautions, warnings. She

was neither a strong nor an experienced enough horsewoman to control Gypsy Lady. Darlington was way ahead of her, cantering apace down the hill, and had not the slightest notion that she was in trouble.

An ordinarily harmless woodland creature darted across the road with another in hot pursuit, spooking the mare. She reared up, throwing her novice rider, whose leg, swathed in yards of fabric, got tangled in her stirrup as she hurtled toward the road below.

There was a thud as C.J. hit the uneven path dotted with twigs and stones. The thud was followed by a terrible silence that seemed to echo through the valley below.

Darlington spurred his stallion back up the hill to find Gypsy Lady, a look of fear in her huge brown eyes, standing obediently by the prostrate body of her rider: a heap of grubby green velvet lying in the dust. A yard or so away, Cassandra's new black riding hat bounced away, its sheer tulle veiling caught by a breeze.

The sun gradually descended toward the horizon while Darlington sat by Cassandra's immobile form along the infrequently traversed road. Finally he was able to hail a passing cabriolet to request assistance. The coach's owner insisted on turning from his intended route; and, after helping Darlington lift Miss Welles into the carriage, they made the briefest stop at the stables, alerting the grooms to retrieve the earl's horses, which had been temporarily tethered to a stile. This done, they raced posthaste for the Royal Crescent. The carriage's owner, one Captain Keats, saw that Miss Welles arrived as safely as possible, given the alarming circumstances.

DARLINGTON'S DEEP BLUE MORNING COAT rested on the back of his chair. An otherwise perfect cravat was crumpled and stuffed in the pocket.

"Perhaps you should take a walk, Percy. Stretch your legs," Lady Dalrymple whispered, as she entered her "niece's" bedroom with a cup of tea for the earl. "It is daybreak and you have been sitting here for hours, without respite. You must allow Dr. Musgrove to administer his treatments."

"Bloody tractors." Darlington was about to condemn Americans again, as it was a Yankee Doodle doctor, Elisha Perkins, who had invented the curative instruments that bore his name. Although the earl still found the application of Perkins Tractors to be outright quackery, he had no alternative now but to place his trust in the eminent Dr. Musgrove's restorative methods. Still, four days had passed, and Cassandra had yet to stir. Darlington needed someone to blame for her condition. If Dr. Musgrove was an honest medic, then such blame must be assigned to himself for having insisted on such a foolhardy venture: encouraging a woman with child to indulge him in a horse race.

As soon as Miss Welles had been transported back to the Royal Crescent, Dr. Musgrove was fetched upon the instant. He chastised both Darlington and the captain, explaining that the young woman should not have been lifted from the road and thence conveyed along rocky thoroughfares, lest she had suffered a broken neck in her fall.

Captain Keats, a man of few words who had seen too many of his compatriots fall in battle, acknowledged that he had, on more than one occasion, tended to a wounded companion in similar straits to Miss Welles's and informed the physician that at the time he believed there was no alternative.

Lady Dalrymple admitted the young physician to Cassandra's room.

"The young lady's condition remains unchanged," Darlington volunteered before Musgrove could form the question on his lips. The pleasant-looking man, perhaps a half-dozen years younger than the earl, opened a large, black leather satchel and removed a pair of metal rods resembling the divining rods Darlington had seen in his youthful travels to the East. Dr. Musgrove stroked the rods over his patient's skin.

Mary, who had been quietly standing by her mistress's bedside when the doctor paid his daily calls, had become intrigued by the practice, and finally grew bold enough to inquire as to the application of the rods.

The young doctor affected his most assured and professional demeanor. "Perkins Tractors are commonly employed to cure epilepsy—the falling sickness, in common parlance—the gout, and inflammations. Miss Welles took a nasty fall, and as a result has broken her ankle joints, which twisted when she came into contact with the ground. Thus, it is for the inflammation that the tractors are applied."

"Might I, sir, if I may be so bold?" Mary asked him with sweet simplicity, and all were quite surprised when the doctor permitted her to step between him and his patient. With the gentlest of touches, she felt the tender area about C.J.'s ankles, her face intent as though she were listening to her palpations for some sort of sound. "There is no break here," she finally said with grave solemnity. Her voice bore a tone of experience not a soul in the household had ever before heard from her.

"Mary!" chorused the others.

"I was born and reared on a farm in Hereford, sir," Mary said, addressing the doctor with polite deference but without apology. "And although Miss Welles is neither calf nor foal, I am no stranger to broken limbs. You see, sir, if you place your hand just above and below the bone thusly . . ." She demonstrated, gently guiding Dr. Musgrove's thumb and forefinger to C.J.'s right ankle, "you will feel that there is no space—that the bones are fused quite properly. I cannot speak for the usefulness of your metal rods, but I am quite sure that Miss Welles has suffered no broken bones in her ankles."

The assemblage watched the girl with stunned admiration. Lady Dalrymple beamed as proudly as if the little maid were her own daughter. What fools the gentry were, the countess thought, to assume superior knowledge in all things, claiming it as a birthright.

"Did you ever think to check for broken bones before you began to apply this ridiculous contraption, Dr. Musgrove? Tractors!" scoffed Darlington. "I should not root about your fancy medical societies boasting of your latest cures when you have been shown up by your patient's maidservant!"

Dr. Musgrove, rather than resenting Mary's intrusion and the earl's outburst, stroked his bare chin and regarded the servant girl curiously. After some moments, he said, "I suppose the reason one refers to my profession as the *practice* of medicine is that one can always learn something new about it." The company laughed at his attempt at levity and his ability to smooth away a potentially unpleasant situation. Such response emboldened the young medic to beg a favor of the countess. "If it pleases your ladyship, I should be grateful for the opportunity to consult with . . ." He cocked his head toward the lady's maid.

"Her name is Mary. Mary Sykes, Dr. Musgrove."

"Much obliged, your ladyship. I should very much appreciate the opportunity to converse with Miss Sykes regarding other medical matters of which she may have some degree of understanding."

Lady Dalrymple was much amused by the look in the young doctor's eyes. Portly's favorite spaniel, Troilus, had possessed just such a look. Sweet, slightly sad, expectant. "I suppose I can spare Mary for an hour or two, but only if the girl herself expresses a desire to comply with your request. Mary, would it please you to speak to Dr. Musgrove?"

"Oh yes, your ladyship!" the maid answered eagerly.

"Show the doctor to the drawing room then. I shall be in presently to chaperone you."

"Thank you, your ladyship." Mary curtsied.

Dr. Musgrove made a slight bow. "I am honored, your ladyship."

A grinning Darlington shook his head. "Not merely allowing, but *arranging* interviews between a lady's maid and a man of medicine. Lady Dalrymple, I daresay you *are* an original."

Mary led Dr. Musgrove from the chamber and was followed soon thereafter by the countess, who lingered to bestow a kiss upon her "niece's" brow. She laid her own rosy cheek against the

young woman's pale one. It much concerned her that Cassandra
had yet to regain consciousness after more than half a week.

Miss Austen, upon hearing the terrible news, had made daily
pilgrimages to Lady Dalrymple's to inquire as to the health of
her friend. Even the redoubtable Lady Oliver had seen occasion
to pay a call, although her appearance consisted mostly of dire
warnings to her nephew that he would soon lose his looks if he
did not get some sleep. She rebuked him for ignoring Lord
Digby's repeated attempts to reinforce his daughter's betrothal,
despite the mortifying incident in the Assembly Rooms, and
had not ceased to remind him that he would suffer the most vi-
cious censure if he reneged on the arrangement.

The earl blamed himself entirely for everything that had befallen Miss Welles. She had been an innocent, a pawn in a
sophisticated game of financial chess played by the titled aristocracy. He despised his aunt for persuading him to violate his
understanding with Cassandra, and worse, to so publicly commit to another. He despised himself for permitting it. Darlington had always prided himself on his integrity and his fierce
resolve to make his own choices. True, Aunt Augusta had raised
and cared for him and for Jack, his younger brother. But after all
these years, he was finally asking himself when such an obliga-
tion was to be considered paid in full.

Darlington had vigilantly watched over Cassandra, sung to
her, stroked her brow, caressed her cheeks, held her hands, even
read to her from Shakespeare's sonnets, but nothing availed.
Every so often her delicate eyelids would flutter, but they had yet
to open. He wondered how he had let matters get so out of hand.
The young, pale, trusting woman who lay before him deserved
more. He had been determined to demonstrate this in every way
still open to him; and even at that, he had exposed both his reputation and hers to ruin. Now, as he watched the steady rise and
fall of her shallow breathing, he knew what he must do—must
risk—to set things right. All the time that Miss Welles had lain
abed, he had feared to ask Dr. Musgrove if Cassandra had lost
their child when she was thrown from her horse. *His* horse. How

could he have been so foolish to ask her to ride out with him in her delicate condition?

He tenderly kissed her, feeling the warm softness of her lips against his own. Did sheer exhaustion cause him to imagine it, or did Cassandra seem to kiss him back? He leaned back in the damask-covered chair and blinked to try to keep himself awake.

Not much more than a minute had passed when C.J. opened her eyes for the first time since the accident. She was disoriented, and the sight of Darlington—pale, unshaven, and coatless—seated on the chair beside her bed added to her confusion. "What happened?" she asked, her voice barely audible. "Did someone die?"

She spoke! "No, my sweet Cassandra. No one has died, thank God!" The earl proceeded to explain the details of her accident and how long she had lain so still in the road before someone had fortuitously happened along.

"Would you do me the kindness of helping me to sit up, your lordship?" she asked.

Darlington regarded her dubiously. "If you are quite convinced you are able to do so."

"Nonsense, Percy," she replied softly.

"You sound like your Aunt Euphoria." His heart soared to see her spirits rallying. Treating her with the utmost tenderness, Darlington propped her up against a down-filled bolster. She reached for him and he caught her upturned palm in his hand, kissing it, and pressing it to his stubbled cheek.

"Since I appear to be alive," she said hoarsely, "would you now consider doing me another tremendous favor?"

"Send me to Samarkand for silks, or to Abyssinia for cinnamon, Miss Welles."

Although she immediately discovered that it pained her ribs to do so, C.J. laughed. "There is no need for dramatics, your lordship, unless I *am* dying. And besides, I think cinnamon comes from the West Indies. But," she added, reaching up to stroke his face, "perhaps a shave and a wash might do."

Darlington sat on the edge of the bed and held her. "My

love . . . I am so thankful you are all right," he murmured into her hair. He kissed the top of her head and sat beside her. "That was a nasty spill you took, Miss Welles."

They had been riding. She could remember fragments. A hare darting out of the brush . . . her mount shying, then rearing up. "How is the horse?" C.J. inquired. Her mind was still muddled and her thoughts were jumbled, one atop another.

"Gypsy Lady?"

She nodded. "You did not have to des—" She broke off, unable to bear the notion that the horse might have had to be put down due to her damned inexperience as a rider.

"She is as feisty and fit as ever she was, although I daresay she appeared as concerned for your welfare as I did. Instead of bolting once you had been thrown, she stood still, waiting for me to come and fetch you. When I no longer heard the sound of hoofbeats behind me, I knew something was dreadfully wrong."

C.J. beckoned Darlington closer, then clasped her arms around his neck and clung to him. "Then I have both of you to thank for saving my life," she whispered.

"You wonderful, wonderful girl. Miss Welles has awakened!" he shouted toward the door.

With another jubilant cry, Darlington greeted Mary, who entered the blue room a few minutes later bearing a steaming cup of chicken broth, followed by Lady Dalrymple carrying a bouquet of fresh-cut flowers. "Look! She is sitting up!" He retired from the room, leaving C.J. to the ladies' ministrations.

Mary arranged the bed tray across C.J.'s lap, laying a pretty serviette across its woven wicker surface. "Now you must take some nourishment, Miss Welles," she said sagely. "If not for yourself, you've got the babe to consider."

"Am I . . . still . . . ?" C.J. feared giving voice to the thought that had just clouded her mind. Mary, who had seen no sign of blood on Miss Welles's linen undergarments following her brutal accident, or any stains on the bedsheets during Miss Welles's recuperation, nodded her head. "For aught I can tell, your son . . . or daughter . . . is unharmed." Availing herself of one of Lady Dalrymple's flowers, Mary filled a graceful silver bud vase with one perfect rose in a shade of palest apricot. "I'd been thinkin' myself that you might like to have somethin' pretty to wake up to, but seein' as you are quite awake, you can enjoy it all the sooner," Mary added, dropping an efficient curtsy.

"With your ladyship's permission," she said, turning to the countess, "I have been asked to assist at the birth of Mrs. Jordan's babe. Dr. Musgrove has arranged for me to apprentice to Mrs. Goodwin, the midwife. Imagine *me*, your ladyship—at the bedside of such a great lady! She's lyin' in at the town house the Duke of Clarence gave her in Sydney Place."

Lady Dalrymple waved a jeweled hand. "Heavens! How could I possibly deny such a request. What prestige, Mary!" The countess dabbed away a falling tear. "How soon they leave the nest!"

"Bless you, your ladyship, for your great kindness," Mary gushed, practically dropping to her knees in genuflection before retiring from the room.

Hardly a moment later there was a knock on the door, and Mary reappeared with a calling card on a silver salver. "Your ladyship, Captain Keats has come to call again," she whispered. "Shall I admit him?"

Darlington appeared in the doorway. "Now that Miss Welles is awake, I am certain that she would care to thank the captain for his assistance following her nasty spill the other day."

The officer entered quietly, took a chair beside Darlington, and inquired after the invalid's health. C.J. gave him a puzzled look; then a glimmer of recognition dawned, and a smile crept across her pale features. "Captain Keats. The very man I have meant to speak to," she said weakly. "Kindly convey my good thoughts to the Fairfax family, with particular commendation to Miss Susanne. I am quite fond of the girl."

"In point of fact, Miss Welles, I was on my way to pay a call upon the Fairfaxes when I encountered you in such danger. I shall pass on your felicitations to the family, and to Mrs. MacKenzie upon her return from Scotland."

"Mrs. MacKenzie?" C.J. was completely baffled.

"Four days ago, Miss Welles—the day of your dreadful accident—Miss Susanne Fairfax eloped to Gretna Green with Major Kenneth MacKenzie of the Seaforth Highlanders. I had just heard the news and was on the way to see the family when I saw Lord Darlington kneeling by something in the center of the road, and stopped my carriage."

C.J. was dimly aware of the journey she had taken in the officer's coach, lying across as much of the cordovan leather seat as possible, with her head resting in Darlington's hands, drifting in and out of consciousness. "I cannot thank you enough for your chivalry, Captain Keats. Were it not for your assistance, I dare not think where I might be today. You have indeed been our knight in shining armor."

The officer smiled proudly. "I am the third son of a baronet, who bought my colors for me, despite Mrs. Fairfax's confidence that I am nothing but a poor churchmouse, or a scurvy fortune hunter."

C.J. brightened. "See. And I *knew* you to be a gentleman."

The captain bowed. "I am pleased that my brief visit has been able to cheer the patient. My heartiest congratulations on your recovery, Miss Welles," he said before leaving her chamber.

A plan was forming in Darlington's mind. If the decidedly parvenu Miss Susanne Fairfax could flout convention and risk the ostracism of her family's acquaintances to marry the man of her choice, why then could not a peer of the realm wed the woman who was his heart's desire? Perhaps he would have to sell off a portion of his property—even lose Delamere and need to retrench—but events of the past week had forced him to face his future. He would formally offer for her not to extricate her from the situation in which he had placed her, but because he could not imagine living out the rest of his days without her, a lifetime plagued with regret and recriminations. His happiness, he now knew, rested in the bed but a few feet from him.

He rose from the chair a changed man. "Miss Welles, if you will permit me to leave your bedside, I have every intention of making you a happy woman." Cheered to the core by her expectant glow, he added, "I am off to my barber's!" The earl departed C.J.'s bedchamber to the silvery sound of her laughter. Never had he heard music more delightful.

"And not a moment too soon!" quipped the countess, who availed herself of the vacant chair by C.J.'s bed and took her "niece's" hands. "I have been tardy in properly thanking you for saving my life, Cassandra."

"There was no other alternative, Lady Dalrymple. No thanks are necessary." C.J. swallowed the last of her hot broth.

"Nevertheless, I have been remiss. But have taken the steps necessary to rectify it."

C.J., still finding it difficult to maintain an unmuddied thought process, gave the countess a curious look.

"Some weeks ago, I visited my solicitors," Lady Dalrymple began. "At the outset of our interview, Mr. Oxley and old Mr. Morton were quite convinced I was addled, since, apart from my dearly departed Alexander, I have no other children and yet I had come to them with the express purpose of discussing my heir. After my illness, and yet again since your accident, I was reminded how precious is the gift of our time on this green and gilded sphere. I know no other way to thank you, Cassandra, for the joy you have brought to me since our paths had the good fortune to cross. I instructed Oxley and Morton to draw up formal papers of adoption, naming you as my heiress. After my death, although you will be unable to become Countess of Dalrymple, you will inherit my wealth and my personal effects, including the emerald ring I have oft caught you admiring. And as no records can be produced stating that you are *not* Bertie Tobias's only child, the solicitors agree that your inheritance of his possessions is unchallenged. My brother is quite fond of you, Cassandra. I feared I would have to bring him 'round to the wisdom of my view, but once the papers were drawn up, I am told that Albert signed them with a characteristic dramatic flourish. Everything is now legal and binding."

C.J. regarded her benefactress with a widening stare of dawning comprehension. "Aunt Euphoria . . ." Her voice cracked with emotion.

" 'Tis no less than you deserve, Cassandra. And though he is capable of finding a more than adequate conclusion to his current conundrum, your new status has the happy effect of relieving the Earl of Darlington—if he is astute enough to realize it—of the agony of being forced to choose between love and duty."

"I—I don't know what to say, Lady Dalrymple—other than thank you. This is indeed the most generous thing anyone has ever done for me," C.J. said with stunned appreciation. Her eyes welled with tears.

"Where my brother and I travel next," the countess said simply, "we shall not require town houses."

The two women embraced, C.J. feeling warm and secure in the dowager's arms. "I love you not for what you have done for me, but for who you are, Aunt Euphoria."

"I could very well say the same about you, Niece." Lady Dalrymple kissed Cassandra's forehead, then smoothed her hand over C.J.'s brow with a maternal caress. "Cassandra Jane Welles, you have undergone more travails since the day you arrived in Bath than most young ladies experience in a lifetime. I grow quite fatigued myself just thinking on it. Now let us both take some rest," she whispered, then left the bedroom, closing the door quietly behind her.

As C.J. finished the last of her broth, she noticed a folded note placed under the saucer. Curious, she opened the unfamiliar seal and read its brief contents.

There was no alternative. She must travel to London by the very next Royal Mail.

Chapter Twenty-Seven

Wherein our heroine embarks upon an eye-opening tour of London town and is reunited with one of her benefactors.

THE GLEAMING, pale yellow mail coach rumbled along the outskirts of Bath bound for London. C.J. had not counted on how sore she had become from lying abed for so long. Her ankle joints were still somewhat swollen, and her spine from stem to stern, as well as her rib cage, ached with each bump in the uneven road. Every rut over which the carriage wheels clattered at their breakneck pace was the father to a fresh spasm of pain. Compounding all, she continued to suffer from the ill effects of morning sickness, and her stomach lurched every time the coach did.

Having charmed the driver into permitting a fifth passenger, as she was quite slender and traveled with naught but a carpetbag, C.J. found herself wedged between two rather taciturn gentlemen, a nephew and uncle, apparently, on their way to London to visit their hatters and tailors.

On the opposite seat, it was another story. A husband and wife, who had evidently been married for some years, began their quarrel at the crack of the coachman's whip outside Leake's booksellers and had not ceased squabbling since. He

complained that she used rouge to paint her face in a fruitless effort to appear youthful. She parried with a gripe about his thrift.
Had they a carriage of their own, they would not be forced to endure intolerably cramped quarters with strangers. The husband
riposted: had she less of a penchant for bonnets, jewels, and
other finery, they would have a tolerably fine equipage. And so it
went, for several miles. C.J. pretended to be asleep, which was a
shame because the Wiltshire countryside was lovely to behold.
The verdant scene outside the unshuttered window offered an
uninterrupted view of grazing sheep and cattle enjoying their
quotidian existences unconcerned with the rush and bustle that
necessitated the Royal Mail's haste to traverse their pastoral do-
main.

As they neared Salisbury Plain, the uncle, a Mr. Carlyle,
raised a gloved hand and gestured out the open window.
"Stonehenge," he said to his nephew. "Coming up ahead. It's a
vista not to be missed at this time of day."

The nephew, who would have had to lean over C.J.'s body to
partake of the view of the prehistoric megaliths and lintels,
glanced at his pocket watch. "Why, we have several hours to go
before sunset."

"Sunset, bah!" commented his uncle, reaching for a pinch of
snuff. "This is the time when the sun casts the finest shadows."
He leaned as far back against the rear of the coach as he could.
"Here you go, miss," he said, offering C.J. the chance to look
past him out the carriage window.

Although her glimpse of Stonehenge was but brief, C.J. was
measurably affected by its power and mystery. Though the sun
was now high in the sky, it had rained early that morning and the
smaller inner stones, because they were still wet, appeared to be
blue, lending the awesome circle an even deeper magic. "It is . . .
truly breathtaking, sir. Thank you kindly." Her enjoyment of
Stonehenge, however cursory, temporarily relieved her mind of
the anxious thoughts that beset her and what she might do upon
her arrival in London.

The Royal Mail coach reached its final stop sans further incident, and C.J. gave the outrider the address that had been written on the cryptic note. He was quite insistent that she not achieve her destination on foot as it was not in the city's most savory location and assisted her in acquiring the services of a reputable hackney to bring her to Whitechapel High Street in the heart of East London.

Shortly before dusk, C.J. was helped to dismount from the hackney and immediately stepped in a mudpie. At least she hoped it was mud. The driver did not fail to remark upon her obvious unfamiliarity with the surroundings in which he was depositing her—not merely the copious quantities of mud and manure, but the confluence of urban stench and filth in one of the oldest districts in London.

Assuring the hackman that she was well provided for, C.J. began to wander about the bustling—and odiferous—center of commerce, searching for the mysterious address.

"Gone?!" Lady Dalrymple exclaimed, examining the state of C.J.'s rumpled bedclothes. "When did you last see my niece, Mary?"

"Not for several hours, ma'am," the girl replied, fearing retribution for her inattentiveness. "As she needed her rest, I thought it best not to disturb her. Clearly, I was wrong," she added, her eyes welling with tears. Almost reverentially, she began to smooth the sheets and counterpane. "Holy lamb of God!" she cried, discovering the crumpled note amid the bedclothes. "Miss Welles has gone to London!"

"Mary, how do you know?" asked the countess incredulously.

"It's right here, in this note. The one that came to the door so early this mornin'. I brought it to Miss Welles with her bowl of broth when she woke." She handed Lady Dalrymple the scrap of paper. "It says somethin' about Miss Welles's amber cross and a mystery to be solved." There was a shocked pause as the countess regarded the lady's maid with great astonishment.

"Miss Welles taught me my letters," the girl said, with a mixture of pride and sadness at the sudden departure of her beloved mentor.

"She must have gone to this address," Lady Dalrymple reasoned, turning the parchment over and over in her hand. "Mary, ring for Collins. We must prepare to travel to London. I shall dispatch a note to Lady Chatterton and inform her that if we locate my niece, we shall be able to attend her masquerade at Vauxhall Gardens after all. You shall help me see to our disguises, Mary."

"If I may be so bold, ma'am, should not his lordship be informed as well, as regards Miss Welles's disappearance? For certain he will be quite concerned. I can run to the Circus with the note," Mary offered helpfully. There was little time to lose.

DAVIS, THE EARL'S ANCIENT MAJORDOMO, was surprised at his lordship's insistence that the tiny serving girl be shown up to the library rather than be asked to leave Lady Dalrymple's note at the door.

Mary's arrival had caught him preparing to depart posthaste for Canterbury to obtain a costly Special License from the archbishop. He had already wasted enough precious time, and the dispensation would eliminate three consecutive Sundays of reading the banns, during which his aunt would undoubtedly waste no time in registering her own objection to his marriage to Miss Welles. Lady Oliver had fumed enough when Lord Digby, in a remarkable volte-face, had told her that his wife and daughter were quite undone by all the embarrassment and gossip following the announcement of Lady Charlotte's betrothal, and thus had agreed with alacrity when Darlington requested to withdraw quietly from their arrangement.

"I do not know this address," Darlington told Mary, studying the handwritten note. "Clever of its author, though, to pose a rhyme."

"Will you come with us to London?" the maid asked. "Her ladyship said something about a party at 'Vox-ill' something—a fancy dress ball."

"Do you mean Lady Chatterton's ball at Vauxhall Pleasure Gardens?"

Mary nodded. "Yes, I think that was it. Sounds about right to me."

"My aunt and I were invited as well. I had not intended to leave Miss Welles's bedside while she was still infirm; yet honor and duty now impel me to ride to London in search of her. Ordinarily, Lady Chatterton's midsummer masquerades are not to be missed. It gives her an opportunity to exercise her passion for Shakespeare. Every guest is exhorted to arrive in costume, dressed as his or her favorite Shakespearean character."

"Then is Lady Chatterton an actress, your lordship? Like Mrs. Jordan or Mrs. Siddons? Miss Welles is very fond of Mrs. Siddons," Mary added, tearing up at the woeful thought that she might never again see her beloved mentor.

Darlington smiled and offered the maidservant a linen handkerchief. "Lady Chatterton is a great patroness of the arts who once had aspirations in that direction, I believe. But it is not seemly for a noblewoman to appear upon the stage, so she contents herself with entertaining those she would consort with, in addition to lavishing upon her favorites extraordinary sums of money to ensure their welfare and their livelihood."

He would have to postpone his journey to Canterbury. Locating Miss Welles before she fell prey to the more unscrupulous and unsavory of London's residents took precedence over his petition. Darlington rang the damask bellpull. "Whether or not my aunt Augusta wishes to join us is of no concern to me," he muttered. "But Miss Welles's safety and well-being are of paramount importance. Mary, tell your mistress that I will offer my coach-and-four for the expedition," he said, and seizing upon an alternative plan, added, "and if we cannot find Miss Welles in advance of Lady Chatterton's masked ball, no doubt there will be plenty of my acquaintance in attendance whom I can enlist to aid in our search."

Mary nearly threw herself at the earl's feet, thanking him profusely. She knew he would be their champion, just like the ones in the stories about the Middle Ages that Miss Welles used to tell her. With her heart now somewhat lighter, Mary scampered back up Brock Street to give Lady Dalrymple the good news.

"GARDY LOO!" a woman shrieked at the top of her voice, just before the steaming, reeking contents of a brass chamber pot were emptied into the street below. Those who seemed to have taken notice, stepped away from the sidewalk, such as it was, and moved toward the muddy street, only to be nearly overrun by a small child pushing a heavy wheelbarrow laden with nuts.

Never before had C.J. experienced anything like this teeming flood of humans and beasts, of cries and shouts of commerce and of consternation, and of smells both pleasant and assaulting to the nostrils.

At the side of Gun Lane, a young girl baked potatoes over a coal stove that threatened to roast her in the summer heat, while a carman shouted at her, "Stand up, there, you blind cow! Will you have the cart squeeze yer guts out?"

Singing samples of his wares, a ballad seller knocked from door to door of the crowded buildings, best described to modern sensibilities as tenements, while in perfect harmony a tinker cried, "Pots to mend!" banging on a kettle with a hole in its dented bottom.

In Spitalfields Market, as the afternoon drew to a close, merchants, keen to close out transactions and rid themselves of their stock before nightfall, called out bargains on carp and pickerel. "Two for a groat! Four for sixpence! Mackerel here!" A man in black gabardines and a skullcap bought some carp. "For mine wife," he said to the vendor in a lilting accent. "By you, she says, it's always good."

The stench of tanned leather displayed on wooden dowels in makeshift open stalls, combined with that of fish, fresh or otherwise, nearly caused C.J. to retch until the pungent aroma of strong, hot brew from a nearby coffeehouse overpowered the competing odors.

"Knives to grind!"

"Pots to mend!"

"Buy my flounders!"

"Buy my maids!"

A painted ancient announced the availability of her human wares as a well-turned-out wench, full of face and figure, reached for a gentleman's sleeve. "Come, milord, come along. Shall we drink a glass together before sunset?"

Amid this hurly-burly stood a do-gooder atop a soapbox struggling to be heard above the din. "Gin is the principal cause of the increase of the poor, and of all the vice and debauchery . . ."—he paused to eye the whore, her fresh prey now fully within the grasp of her lacquered talons—". . . among the inferior sort of people, as well as of the felonies and other disorders committed about London!"

As if to prove his point, the general cacophony was shattered by the cry of "Stop thief!"

C.J. looked up to see the old Jew who had purchased the carp take off through the market after a slip of a lad, but he was no match for the child's age and speed. Down he went, his precious package trod in the mud by a dozen passersby, eager to catch a good view of the show. "My watch!" the man cried, pointing after the boy, who had slipped into a narrow alley, probably gone forever.

Would no one else help this man? C.J. was amazed at how such a crowd could gather for the spectacle, and yet not one of them offered him a helping hand or a sympathetic look for his plight.

"It's just a dirty Jew," a man of roughly the same age said dismissively when he saw the victim's gabardines. The good Christian spat in the dirt.

Surprisingly unflinching, the robbery victim retorted by releasing a series of epithets in a strange, foreign tongue. She offered her hand to the man, who was trying in vain to brush the dust from his garments. "May I help you, sir?"

The gentleman looked as though he was not particularly keen on taking a woman's hand. "I am well enough," he said, getting to his feet on his own. "But I am appreciative of your courtesy. In this town such things are not expected."

"I have just come to London this afternoon."

"You'll learn," the Jew said bitterly.

Unthinking, C.J. extended her hand again in order to introduce herself. "Cassandra Jane Welles."

The man looked kindly at her now, but still refused to touch her. "Moses Solomon."

"Perhaps you can help me, Mr. Solomon." C.J. recited the address she was seeking.

"Hmmm." Solomon tugged at one of his *peyos*, the long curls that he had wound around his ears. "It's in Old Jewry Street. You're not far from there. But then again, you're not near." He gestured down the road. "To the south and to the west. Cheapside. You don't know where you're going, do you?" C.J. shook her head. "Probably where the little pickpocket went with my watch. Mathias ben Ezra's. It's a pawnshop. But ben Ezra does his business under the name of Mathias Dingle." Solomon stroked his beard. "A wolf in sheep's clothing, he thinks he is. He's fooling no one. What, you don't take my meaning, miss?" Receiving another uncomprehending reply, Mr. Solomon elucidated further. "He's a Jew. Like me. Dingle," the man scoffed. "He's no more a Dingle than I am a Digby." His reference to the Digbys caused C.J. to wince. "You're not as lost as you think. Walk with me, Miss Welles. I'm going only as far as the shul, but you'll be halfway there. I hope you're a good walker. By sundown, ben Ezra—*Dingle*," he snorted, "will be closed for Shabbos."

Moses Solomon led C.J. through the narrow streets of

Whitechapel and Spitalfields, the old Jewish Quarter of London, amid the babel of several tongues being spoken at once, street musicians plying their trade on pipes and tambourines, the toll of churchbells, and the cries of vendors purveying hot and cold foodstuffs of all varieties. At a muddy intersection, a youth set off something like a bottle rocket, and as the flare shot into the darkening air of early evening, an assembled crowd cheered him on, begging him to ignite another.

Mr. Solomon halted in front of an unimposing façade tucked into a narrow lane. "This is Bevis Marks, where I take my leave," the Jew said. He pointed toward the end of the lane. "That is St. Mary. Follow the street south to Leadenhall. As you walk toward St. Paul's Cathedral, Leadenhall becomes Cornhill, which becomes Poultry—in Cheapside. From Poultry, a little street you'll find if you turn north toward the old London Wall. This is Old Jewry. The address you want is there. And now, I bid you *yom tov*."

As Solomon entered the synagogue, C.J., repeating the Samaritan's directions in her head, hastened toward her destination.

Alas, although she walked as quickly as she could manage, she did not reach Old Jewry Street until dusk, and Mathias Dingle's pawnshop was shut tight. Through the dusty leaded panes she could see an array of assorted bric-a-brac: seven- and nine-branch candelabras, musical instruments, gold pocket watches, porcelain snuffboxes, strands of pearls, and brooches encrusted with precious gems. Above her head hung the pawnbroker's symbol, the pyramid configuration of three balls, and a painted sign reading DINGLE'S.

Frustrated and exhausted, and straining from too much exertion so soon after her accident, C.J. continued to walk toward St. Paul's in the hope that she might find a place to rest. It seemed that the logical next step was to find someone who might have heard of her "father," the Marquess of Manwaring. C.J. remembered that he lived in London but knew not his address or whether he was even in town. She stopped at the cathedral to sit for a while and to soak in the restful ambiance. After the clamor of Spitalfields, she craved a more meditative pace. Had she felt heartier, she might have climbed all the way up to the Whispering Gallery.

At least this time, C.J. had arrived with money in her purse. Close by, in Fleet Street, she sought a pub that seemed pleasant and safe enough. In an attempt to blend in, she ordered a drink. As C.J. nursed her glass of ale, praying that the few sips would produce no ill effect on her pregnancy, she scoured the room for faces she might find familiar, portraits from histories read in her other life now appearing in the flesh. Who were the yellow journalists of the day, she wondered, who noisily regaled each other with war stories in the crowded wooden booths?

"All alone tonight, miss?" the publican inquired.

To dispel any assumption that she was an unsavory trollop, C.J. replied, "I am looking for my father, the Marquess of Manwaring. I am told that he . . . frequents this establishment," she lied. All C.J. knew of Albert Tobias's habits was that he was a great habitué of taverns, so she hazarded a guess that this might be one of them.

"Not here, I'm afraid," the barkeep said. "Not regularlike. But just down the road at the dram shop—" He scratched his head. "This here, The Broken Quill, this is for li-te-rary folks. But your da, he likes to raise a glass with the theatricals at The Blue Ball or over at the Nelly Gwyn."

"Naw, 'e's 'ome in Lincoln's Inn Fields, nursing 'is gouty foot, 'e is." A scrawny man at the far end of the bar piped up and joined the conversation.

"I have not been to London in so long," C.J. said truthfully. "I wonder if you might direct me to him."

"Go to it, Timothy! Used to carry hack chaises in his younger days," the bartender told C.J. "Knows these streets like the back of his sorry hand."

Eager to be of service, and after treating C.J. to her ale, her new drinking companion escorted her to the street, then pointed the way up Chancery Lane to the Stone Buildings. "You take

care now, there's a good lass," the lonely tavern rat said, a bit sad
to lose his new acquaintance so soon.

"My daughter!" the marquess cried joyfully, enfolding C.J. in
his arms, to the perplexion of his maidservant, Mimsy, who had
never heard tell of such a person. Manwaring limped down a
dimly lit corridor that opened onto a room of modest proportions. "Miss Welles, isn't it?" he added, after the maid's departure. "Such an extravagant surprise! What brings you to
London? Wait—don't tell me just yet—we must discuss it at
great length over adequate refreshments. Might I interest you in
a brandy?" he asked, pouring a healthy dose of the amber liquid
into a crystal snifter. He rolled his hands around the bowl of the
glass and handed it to his "daughter," then refilled his own glass
and motioned for C.J. to sit beside him.

She drew up the leather ottoman. "I received rather a curious note . . . *Papa*," C.J. began. "It seemed to indicate that my
amber cross has a past—a history—in which the writer of the
note, who did not sign his name, feels I should take a keen interest. Have you ever heard of Mathias Dingle? Or Mathias ben
Ezra?"

The marquess crooked his right forefinger and took a pinch
of snuff. "A Jew?"

"I have no idea. I have never met the man. But he appears to
be the proprietor of a pawnshop in Old Jewry. In Cheapside."

"My dear child." Manwaring sneezed. "Excuse me." He withdrew a large white handkerchief from the deep pocket of his
banyan and blew his nose loudly. "My dear child, I have been acquainted with so many shylocks in my lifetime—onstage and
off—that I cannot rightly say offhand if the name rings a bell.
Dingle won't be open for business again until Monday morning—the Jews are not permitted to open their shops on our day
of rest—but don't look so crestfallen, my dear. What say you
make the best of it and provide a poor soul with a couple of days
of your delightful companionship?"

"Well, it's certainly a pleasure to see you once again," C.J. said, pretending to sip the liquor.

"We've got quite an extravaganza to attend tomorrow night at the Vauxhall Pleasure Gardens." Manwaring rang the little silver bell that rested on the table by his elbow. "Mimsy," he said when his maidservant appeared, "run to Lady Chatterton's with a message from me. Inform her ladyship that my daughter, Cassandra, has just arrived from Bath, and that I would be a rude mechanical indeed to attend her masquerade without the company of my long-lost child."

The compliant and extremely energetic Mimsy sped out of the house like a squirrel after a November acorn.

"Quite a woman is Lady Chatterton," the marquess told C.J. "Extremely generous patroness. A widow. Just turned forty but still has all the bloom of youth. Has had an eye for me for some time now." He winked at his "daughter" and took another pinch of snuff. "What's the matter, child? Don't think I can still attract the ladies, do you? I'm barely fifty. Clementina once traveled to Bristol to see my Dogberry. Says she'll do anything for me. Except marry me—until I've got my reputation back, she says. Drink up, now."

"I'm sorry, Papa. I'm unused to brandy, and while I'm sure it's of the very finest quality, I fear that it's a bit too strong for my taste."

"More for me then." The marquess downed C.J.'s brandy and immediately refilled his own glass to the heart of the bowl.

Manwaring stood at his sideboard and sighed like a man in love. "There haven't been many, Cassandra, who would sully their character by hobnobbing with the likes of me, but Clementina—Lady Chatterton—has always been in my corner." He sank back into his chair and patted his large belly. " 'Course, whenever she invites me to one of her soirees, it's always to be a *masked* ball," he laughed.

THE FOLLOWING MORNING an engraved invitation was deliv-
ered to C.J. at the Stone Buildings. " 'Dress as your favorite
Shakespearean character,' " C.J. read. "Whatever shall I wear?
Who are you going to be, Papa?" she asked the marquess.

Manwaring puffed out his chest. "In the role for which I was
greatly renowned in the provinces . . . in my soberer days. I shall
go as Bottom the Weaver." C.J. laughed. "I was verrah, verrah
good, I'll have you know," he retorted, thinking his "daughter"
doubted his fine thespian talents.

"I do not disbelieve you. On the contrary, I was thinking it
was perfect casting," C.J. rejoined, smiling. "But who shall I be?"

"I think you should go to Lady Chatterton's Midsummer
Night's Masquerade dressed as a dutiful daughter. What think
you of some very attractive seaweeds? You would be quite a
fetching Miranda."

C.J. wrinkled her nose. "Ugh! Miranda is far too insipid for
my taste."

"She's a good daughter, though," Manwaring protested.
"Then what about Cordelia? Now there's a loyal daughter for
you."

"I'll be hanged first," riposted C.J.

The marquess led C.J. to a roomful of costume pieces and
accessories, a veritable treasure trove of satins, silks, and velvets,
of ruffs and cuffs and farthingales, of caps and helmets, staffs
and swords of all variety. "I'm a bit of a hoarder," Manwaring explained. "Many years ago, when you would have been but a very
little girl, I did a season with the great Siddons. She gave me this
piece as a gift for my collection. Said she was having a new one
made, anyway, for her Rosalind."

C.J. gasped and held out her arms to receive the purple velvet doublet. "*Siddons* wore this?" she said breathlessly.

"The very one. She was much thinner then," the marquess
said, appraising the size of the luxurious garment.

"Oh, may I really wear this?"

Her "father" nodded.

"Then it's all settled. I shall go as Rosalind!" C.J. exclaimed, continuing to marvel over the opportunity to wear a costume that once belonged to the greatest actress of the day.

SEVERAL HOURS LATER, Mimsy opened the door to her master's apartments at the Stone Buildings and gasped in amazement at the sight before her. Familiar with some of the personages in the doorway from his lordship's theatricals, she found herself in the presence of Cleopatra and one of her handmaidens wielding an enormous ostrich- and peacock-plumed fan, most effective for chasing the city stench from the royal nostrils of the rather plump Queen of the Nile; an extremely statuesque—and aging—Titania; and a man in a filthy loincloth dripping with plants that resembled seaweed, but who appeared to be extremely fit and handsome under all the "dirt" that he had smeared across his bare chest, arms, and legs.

"May I help you?" Mimsy asked, recoiling from the live snake entwined around Cleopatra's fleshy upper arm.

"I am the Countess of Dalrymple. Is my brother at home?" demanded the redoubtable personification of Egypt.

"Ohhh. Gone off to Vauxhall already. His lordship and his daughter. They took the boat over, as his lordship thought that the young ladyship would find the conveyance that much more entrancing, your ladyship."

"She's *with* him . . . Miss Welles, I mean," said the slender Charmian, in her excitement about to forget her station entirely by tugging on Caliban's sleeve. Realizing she had nearly touched his bare skin instead, Mary drew away in horror and wrinkled her nose. "You're so *dirty,* your lordship," she whispered.

"Caliban's not dirty . . . he's misunderstood," replied Darlington. "Besides, this horse is a bit long in the tooth to play Romeo."

"Good heavens, I hope *Romeo's* not your favorite Shakespearean character. One should never die for love," Lady

Dalrymple exclaimed. "Particularly a man of your parts and years. One must *live* for it."

"We are wasting time on airy persiflage," proclaimed the formidable Queen of the Fairies, brandishing her gemstone-encrusted wand as though it were a mace. "We must go after them!"

"First we must learn how to recognize him, Augusta. What is my brother attired as?" asked Lady Dalrymple, subduing her slithering armlet with a gentle stroking gesture.

Mimsy dissolved into peals of laughter. By way of explanation, as she was too overcome with mirth to form a proper sentence, she began to pantomime the configuration of Manwaring's elaborate headdress. "An *ass!*" she finally replied, convulsed with giggles.

"How appropriate," remarked Lady Oliver tartly, dismissing the maid with her wand. With great haste, the foursome donned their black domino masks and returned to Darlington's coach for the ride to Vauxhall Pleasure Gardens.

Chapter Twenty-Eight

*Containing the stunning denouement of our adventure and a
revelation beyond anyone's wildest imagination.*

THE ONLY PERSONS not in Shakespearean costume
were the liveried staff, and even they were all attired like servants of the Sun King, Louis XIV, in
powdered periwigs and pale blue coats embroidered in gold.

C.J. was helped from the small swan-shaped boat at the
bankside and stepped into a fragrant fantasyland. Even the illu-
mination was magical. Paper lanterns were suspended from the
tall trees that were planted in neat rows, forming an arboreal arcade open to the clear night sky above.

"Some prefer the newer Ranelagh Gardens," Manwaring told
her, "but I'm still partial to Vauxhall." He gestured toward the
pavilion, drawing C.J.'s attention away from the laid-out walks
paved with tiny pebbles of golden-colored gravel and the marble
statues and tableaux cleverly tucked into lush groves.

"You must first meet our hostess," he said, leading C.J. into
the pavilion, designed to look like the enchanted palace of a
genie. In the center of a 150-foot rotunda sat an orchestra of perhaps a hundred chairs engaged to play minuets and mazurkas,

polkas and pavanes throughout the night, while guests danced or chatted away in the tiers of boxes that ringed the room.

The murals on the walls took C.J.'s breath away.

"Oh yes, those are Hogarth's work," Manwaring said, admiring the paintings. "Best man for the job, if I do say so myself."

"I imagine he got paid handsomely to satirize what we do here," C.J. mused. "And thoroughly enjoyed himself in the process."

"*Ahh,* our hostess." They approached a blond woman, delicate and diminutive, dressed fittingly as Titania, Queen of the Fairies. "Welcome, players all," said Lady Chatterton, bestowing a kiss on each hairy jowl of the beast that stood before her.

"Greetings, your ladyship," boomed the marquess through Bottom's heavy headdress.

"Manwaring! How delightful!" replied Lady Chatterton in her silvery voice. "I would recognize thee anywhere."

"And this is my daughter, Cassandra."

C.J. doffed her velvet cap and made a leg. "The pleasure is all mine, Lady Chatterton."

"Is she an actress?" inquired the hostess of the marquess. "Verily, your daughter has the legs for the trouser roles. Is it Rosalind or Viola?" Lady Chatterton asked C.J., waving her beribboned wand, cleverly configured to serve a double duty as her mask.

C.J. thought for a moment, then answered, " 'Believe then, if you please, that I can do strange things. I have, since I was three years old, convers'd with a magician, most profound in his art, and yet not damnable.' "

"Rosalind it is then!" Lady Chatterton exclaimed, delighted. "How clever you are! And 'tis indeed since you were about three years old that you last saw your father, isn't that so?"

Uncomprehendingly, C.J. smiled politely, pretending to take Lady Chatterton's meaning.

"Dance, drink, and be merry, my friends, for tomorrow the servants will clear away the traces of tonight's revelry," their hostess exhorted. "A pleasure, my dear, to see you reunited with your father," she added, as she was whisked away by Mark Antony.

The marquess watched the retreating figures and wondered if the Roman general was a rival for the attentions of his love. "I go in search of some punch, my child. Feel free to stroll about at leisure," he told C.J., leaving her side for the allure of intoxicating elixirs.

"OH YES INDEED, Lady Dalrymple. I conversed with your brother not several minutes ago. And what unalloyed joy to see you again in London," Lady Chatterton told the dowager countess. "And Lady Oliver, of course." The two Titanias regarded each other with masked hostility. "Why, Darlington, how . . . brave!" the hostess exclaimed when the earl removed his mask to greet her.

"How fortunate it is that we are having warm weather," the nearly naked nobleman remarked airily.

"Albert is Bottom the Weaver tonight," Lady Chatterton informed them. "And quite a fine Bottom too," she added with a wink at her old bosom friend Lady Dalrymple.

"The ass is far too burdened for my taste," said Lady Oliver sourly.

"We must find them," Darlington said, ill disposed to waste precious time in pleasantries. "I believe it will be best if we all pursue different directions." Like a general, he dispatched his troops. "Lady Dalrymple and Mary, go that way to seek his lordship. Aunt Augusta, you search the pavilion for him. He is no doubt to be found not far from the punch bowl. I shall look for Miss Welles out here among the groves."

It proved a daunting task indeed to find the Marquess of Manwaring. Just as there was more than one Titania in attendance, Bottom proved to be a favorite as well among Lady Chatterton's guests. "Aha!" cried Lady Dalrymple, only to embarrass herself at having grabbed the wrong ass. In the excitement of having learned of her presence, no one had thought to ask how Cassandra was costumed. Lady Oliver thought they should look for a Lady Macbeth or perhaps Katherine, the shrew, while Lady Dalrymple was convinced her "niece" was sure to be a spirited Beatrice or the loveliest Juliet in the gardens.

Darlington commenced his search along the gravel footpaths. The paper lanterns cast a rosy glow on the already golden way beneath him. "Cassandra!" he called into the secluded groves. "Miss Welles!"

Having traversed the length and breadth of the gardens for some minutes without finding success in his endeavor, he leaned against a tree to catch his breath.

"You look fatigued, Caliban." The voice came from a youth seated on a marble bench nestled within a cluster of trees.

"Who's there?" Darlington asked, and the youth adjusted his mask to preserve his anonymity.

"A friend," answered C.J., attempting to disguise her voice by pitching it in a lower register.

The earl regarded the lad in his doublet and hose of amethyst. "*Ohh,*" he sighed. "What a fortunate youth you must be. You are far too young, *sir,* to know what anguish it is to break a lady's heart."

"In truth, I have not broken a lady's heart . . . that I know of . . . but indeed, for all my tender years, too well I know what it is to have one's heart broken. Come, sit beside me. If you have such a tale of woe, you will find my ears amenable to the hearing of it." C.J. motioned to the space beside her on the bench.

"The sad saga is not mine own," Darlington began, "but that of a bosom friend," he continued, quite sure of his intimate familiarity with the shapely legs of the "youth" at his side.

"Pray confide it, if you may," C.J. said, secure in her personal knowledge of the musculature of the half-bare man seated next to her. He had not thought to disguise his voice, or, perhaps in his haste to leave Bath to find her, remembered to remove his signet ring.

"It is a cautionary tale, good youth." Darlington sighed. "I had a friend who used his lady ill. He loved her from the depths of his soul for her beauty and her clever wit, and for the generosity of her person in so many bountiful ways. They had an understanding between them, which afforded my friend the delectable opportunity to gain the most intimate knowledge of his lover's body. Never before had he experienced such rapture—he told me—and was certainly ready to offer for her and to make extravagant wedding plans."

In the dark C.J. bit her lip. "What happened?"

"My friend learned the truth about the destitute condition of his estate and the attendant devastation upon the lives of his tenants. Against his judgment, he permitted himself to be persuaded by his aunt to break off the understanding and enter into a formal betrothal with an heiress who was his aunt's godchild."

"How cruel! Did he make amends to his jilted lady?"

"Not nearly what she deserved. And for all that, he learned that she was carrying his child. He was torn between love and duty. Or more aptly put, love and money."

"Pray continue, Caliban."

"He realized how grave an error he had made when his love was injured in a dreadful riding accident. While she languished twixt our world and the next, he made plans to extricate himself from the betrothal and then journey to Canterbury to request a Special License from the archbishop so they could marry, posthaste, wherever they chose. When he discovered that his love had most suddenly departed for London, he followed her trail, thus obliged to postpone for a day or two his expedition to Canterbury."

"He threw over the heiress?" C.J. asked breathlessly.

"My friend had no alternative. He could not bear to lose his love, and to see her suffer alone raising their child, shunned by polite society, knowing that he was the cause of their mutual misery but lacked the courage to remedy the situation. So he risked his own nearly guaranteed ostracism."

"That is quite an extraordinary tale, sir. How does it end?"

"That remains to be seen, good youth. My friend now agonizes over whether his lady—should she learn that he fully in-

tends to marry her with all the pomp and circumstance accorded his station—would accept his humblest and deepest
apologies for all the pain he caused both to her and to her esteemed aunt. He desires to know whether his mistress would
consent to his suit after all the unpleasantness that has passed
between them. And naturally, my friend wonders if this lady is
too angry to accept him now, and if she still loves him as he
does her."

"I should hazard a guess," C.J. began, "that once your
friend's lady hears his account and is convinced of his unswerv-
ing devotion to her for the remainder of their days, she might be
exceedingly pleased with his decision to reunite and to join their
bodies and souls in holy matrimony." She angled her body
toward Darlington's. "If you will permit me to try a little exercise, I can demonstrate to you just how grateful—how *happy*—
your friend's mistress would be."

C.J. climbed onto the earl's lap, straddling him. As she
gripped him with her legs, her lips met his in a deep kiss.
Tingles of sensation exploded along her spine like thousands of
tiny Roman candles. For the briefest moment she prayed that
whatever body paint the earl had smeared all over his bare torso
would not smudge the great Siddons's velvet doublet. *Oh, well.*

In the distance a crowd had gathered to watch a parachutist
jump from a hot-air balloon and descend softly with his gossamer canopy, as if on a cloud, to the ground below. The lovers
could hear the boom, crackle, and hiss of Lady Chatterton's fireworks display.

C.J.'s practiced hand slid under the folds of Darlington's
loincloth. He emitted an ecstatic groan when she touched him.
She began to readjust her position to kneel before him.

"My lady must be pleasured first," whispered the earl,
pulling her legs back around his waist. He slid C.J.'s violet-
colored hose over the firm globes of her buttocks and down past
her thighs, feeling the heat of her bare sex pressed against him.

"Will you touch me . . . *there?*" she asked, widening her legs
for him. "I want to see the colors again."

Darlington slipped two fingers into her soft wetness. "Ohhh, Cassandra, my dearest Cassandra. Will you marry me?"

"Aren't you supposed to be on your knees when you ask me that?" C.J. teased, her eyes glazing over with bliss.

"I can stop doing this and go down on bended knee if you would like me to," the earl said, reaching the most sensitive core of C.J.'s sex.

"Later," she gasped, tears of mingled joy and satiation coursing down her cheeks. "I want to give myself to you," she whispered huskily, feeling herself open to him even farther as she spoke the words.

Darlington was ready for her and eased inside, burying himself to the hilt in her heat. Like one body the lovers moved with a slow, undulating rhythm. C.J. could feel every inch of Darlington's flesh; each pause he took caused her to crave his reentry all the more. She trembled with the anticipation of each renewed stroke and the full union of their bodies that it would bring.

"I feel so alive," C.J. murmured, flinching slightly from the electricity Darlington's touch produced when he slipped his hands underneath her doublet and linen and caressed the bare skin along her back. She placed her hands on his shoulders, arching away from him as she came, allowing his strong hands to support her. "Pink. I saw pink," she said breathlessly. "What does that mean?"

Darlington gently touched the base of her spine, causing C.J. to shiver with pleasure. "The first level of the chakra—red, and sometimes it can seem pink—is the grounding seat of *Kundalini*, the creative life force."

"Only the *first* level?" C.J. joked, tugging her tights back into place. "The first time we made love, I saw green. I've regressed!"

"But now you carry the creative life force within your womb—our child. Red is where it all begins."

"I want to make you see indigo," C.J. whispered, darting her tongue in and out of Darlington's ear. She found him again with her warm hand. "Indigo—and violet."

There was a shout and a whistle, and the sound of crunching gravel announced the approach of intruders upon the lovers' idyll.

"God in Heaven—my nephew has taken to drowning his sorrows with *boys!*" exclaimed a horrified Lady Oliver. "And at a time like this! To be caught *in flagrante!*" She nearly fainted from the shock. "Our family will be ruined forever! Percy! Rouse yourself immediately from this pastoral torpor!"

"If that's a boy, I'm more of an ass than you already think, Augusta," said the marquess, highly amused by the scene before him. Still, he would have found more to smile at had one of the amatory combatants not been his "daughter." Hadn't he troubles aplenty without the apple of his eye falling so near to the tree that ostensibly bore half the responsibility for bearing her? All his careful wooing and repeated assurances of his reformation had come to naught, for Lady Chatterton would surely refuse his suit now.

The hostess herself and an elderly man dressed as Prospero stopped short at the sight. "I have been wondering all evening when someone would take advantage of our Arden," Lady Chatterton said with surprising gaiety. "Shall we allow them a moment or two to . . . compose themselves?"

Lady Dalrymple, huffing and puffing down the gravel path, with Mary in tow—desperately trying to keep pace with her mistress while simultaneously cooling her off with the ridiculously large feather fan—joined the rest of the search party, who by now had discreetly turned their backs while C.J. removed herself from the earl's lap.

"Well, it appears that Darlington has found my niece," the countess remarked with a wink at her brother. Manwaring moaned with paternal misery. At least his sister had been spared the brunt of their shocking discovery. It was not the activity itself that appalled him, rather that the indiscretion had turned it into a nearly public display. Who knows how much further his "daughter" might have taken things, swept away as she was by her passions? Evidently, Cassandra had a lot to learn about their society—and Darlington should have known better. For the first time in his life, he found his views aligned with those of Lady Oliver, who was busily overdosing herself with smelling salts.

"Cupid's dart hath the surest of aim," said Lady Chatterton, giving Bottom a friendly spank on his posterior with her wand. "And without any more ado, ladies and gentlemen, I bring you Shakespeare's most powerful magician." She gestured grandly at the extravagantly attired "wizard" beside her.

Manwaring peered out from the eyeholes of his headdress. "*Now* it rings a bell. I believe that's the shylock m'daughter was speaking of but yesternight!"

"Look closer, your lordship," said Lady Chatterton dryly. She directed the tip of her wand toward the bearded man's opulent robe covered with ancient signs and symbols. "This is no Shylock, but 'tis *Prospero*."

Prospero, in the person of the pawnbroker Mathias Dingle, retrieved a small blue velvet pouch from the folds of his voluminous robe. "If you please, your ladyship," he said addressing their hostess, "would you be so good as to shine your lantern on this pouch."

Lady Chatterton obliged, and the pawnbroker removed an odd-shaped piece of silver from the pouch and handed it to C.J., who was now seated beside Darlington on the marble bench. She was still blushing an unflattering shade of carmine from their having been discovered as they were. "Can you read it?" Dingle asked her. C.J. peered at the metal object. "Please hand her the lantern, your ladyship. Now, can you read the inscription, my child?"

C.J. squinted at the tiny print. "It is inscribed with the initials C.J.W.T. and bears the phrase 'from her loving parents, Albert and Emma.' What is this about?" C.J. asked in an astonished whisper.

"The cross, child!" exclaimed Manwaring excitedly. "Is this the mystery?" he asked the pawnbroker.

C.J. extracted the amber cross from where it lay beneath her doublet. She matched the piece of amber to the oddly shaped bit of silver.

"What means all this?" Darlington asked, still averting his eyes from the others. Bad enough that *he* had been found in such a compromising posture, but had not poor Miss Welles been made to endure enough censure through his attentions to her?

"It fits—just barely," C.J. said, attempting to insert the cross into its silver backing.

"Bertie." Lady Dalrymple regarded her brother. "There must be an explanation."

"As I told Cassandra, I have had the unhappy occasion to consort with a number of shylocks over the years who have crossed my palm with silver. I cannot rightly recall a transaction with Mr. Dingle, though I confess his face is one I do remember."

"If I do not bespeak my modesty too much, I have a good memory for details. And a better one for figures," the pawnbroker said. "Since I opened my business nearly fifty years ago, I have recorded every transaction from each client who has entered my shop. I have just given Miss Welles the piece of silver backing into which the very same amber cross she now wears was set, the entirety given to her at her birth. The marquess removed the silver backing and pawned it with me decades ago in order to satisfy a gambling debt. Truth to tell," Dingle added, removing his conical hat and scratching an itch under his skullcap, "with my clientele . . . the buyers . . . I don't get much call for a piece this shape. Besides, it's too small and the value of the silver is worth bupkes. It was only good for scrap, and wouldn't fetch much because it is not much more than an inch long, and hollowed out to make room to set the cross. But the marquess brought me a few items at the time, and so I gave him a guinea for it. His wife had just died and he had a young daughter to raise alone. My heart went out to him."

C.J. was stunned. "But how did you remember you had it after all these years?"

"Remember I didn't. It was her ladyship who remembered."

"I cannot take that credit, Mr. Dingle," replied Lady Chatterton in her lovely, silvery voice. "Several weeks ago, I had occasion to visit my solicitors, and was ushered into Mr. Oxley's office to wait while Mr. Oxley and Mr. Morton were engaged with another client. The walls are not as thick as one might imagine, even for such accommodations in the Strand. I beg you to forgive me, Euphoria, but I chanced to overhear some of the discussion about your niece's inheriting your brother's property as well as your own wealth and personal effects. I remembered that the marquess had lost his daughter when she was a child of about three years old." Lady Chatterton regarded Manwaring with the utmost compassion. "I have always believed in my heart that his lordship has not deserved the ignominy accorded to him for this past quarter century."

"Ha!" snorted Lady Oliver. "He's naught but a dissipate drunk and a degenerate. An actor!"

Lady Chatterton ignored the interruption. "His wife died giving birth to their only child. What deeper sorrow can one possibly imagine? And how hasty everyone was to condemn him for his subsequent decline. I daresay it would take nearly inhuman strength to overcome such tragedy without some loss of dignity. Lady Dalrymple's conversation with her solicitors gave me the notion to embark upon a quest. Over the years, the marquess had occasion to confide to me his overwhelming feelings of guilt and remorse over the unfortunate loss—or should I say 'misplacing'—of his young daughter. He agonized over having pawned the silver from the cross given to her at birth, cognizant that he had no right to do such a thing with an item not only not his own, but the sole property of his innocent babe. I thought at the very least, I might be able to locate and reacquire the bit of sterling so that Manwaring would have something to remember his daughter by. And a few weeks ago, when I learned quite by happy accident that Lady Cassandra was alive and well and living under her aunt's protection, I thought to help reunite father and child. And what pleasure it would afford me if the marquess could then restore the pawned item to its rightful owner! Aware that his lordship had divested himself of nearly all the material particulars of his estate, I visited every pawnshop in London, and at long last I came upon Mr. Dingle's emporium. He most obligingly showed me his ledgers. I perused every entry under Manwaring's name and when I spied the record with regard to the bit of silver backing, I asked Mr. Dingle if he would be so good as to send a note to Lady Dalrymple in Bath, addressed to the attention of her niece."

Manwaring removed his heavy headdress and placed it on the ground beside him. He was sweating profusely and accepted the loan of the Jew's large white handkerchief.

"What are you saying, Lady Chatterton?" C.J. asked. Her heart pounded against the walls of her chest.

"I am saying that it appears that you have been reunited with your family after all these long years of absence."

A stupefied C.J. glanced speechlessly from Lady Chatterton to Manwaring to Lady Dalrymple.

"The T is for Tobias, of course. And the W on the inscription was for your mother's maiden name—Warburton," murmured Lady Dalrymple.

"Siddons," Manwaring said slowly, regarding C.J. in the great tragedienne's velvet doublet. "It was that season . . . yes . . . you were no more than three years old and I had taken you traveling with the theatre troupe throughout the provinces."

"After Emma's death, Albert insisted on taking care of you himself. He swore you were all he had left in the world and would not even permit me to raise you," Lady Dalrymple said, still absorbing the stunning realization that the lie she had invented to protect Cassandra had indeed been the truth all along.

"We were in rehearsal at the Theatre Royal in Bath," the marquess recalled. "It was a very popular melodrama that was on the bill—*De Montfort*. I was assigned a small, but rather significant role, if I do say so. A character named Friberg. He's the chap who gets to introduce Jane de Montfort for her grand entrance. That was Siddons herself, and all eyes were upon me as I spoke my lines. Cassandra had been a good little tyke, amusing herself backstage with the props and the costumes and so forth, but as this was my big moment in the drama, I could not keep watch over her. Just as I spoke my line—I remember it to this day—it went"—he stepped forward and struck his most theatrical posture—" *'It is an apparition he has seen or it is Jane de Montfort,'* Cassandra went toddling across the entire width of the stage on her sturdy little legs, and disappeared into the wings. We looked high and low for her after the rehearsal, but we never saw her again."

Lady Oliver narrowed her eyes. "Highly irregular! Highly irregular, indeed! How do we know for sure, amid all this theatrical folderol, that this young woman is indeed who you claim she is and not an impostor?"

"If I recall correctly, my daughter had a little birthmark on the inside of her left thigh," the marquess said. "Shaped a bit like a tea kettle."

"A tea kettle? How preposterous!" sniffed Lady Oliver.

"I can verify that information for you if you wish," Manwaring retorted.

"You'll do nothing of the sort," replied Lady Chatterton and Lady Dalrymple in tandem.

"I think not, old chap," interrupted Darlington, staying the marquess with his hand. "I shall undertake the task."

"I'm surprised that you do not remember," C.J. whispered into the earl's ear.

"I do, actually. And it happens to be true. But why squander such a delicious opportunity?" He guided C.J. to her feet, and they began to disappear behind the cluster of tall trees.

"On second thought, perhaps it was on the sole of her right foot—," the marquess said ponderingly. "Bless me, it's been so many years, I cannot remember . . . I need a drink."

Darlington and C.J. emerged from the grove. "Remarkably like a tea kettle, your lordship." The earl winked at Manwaring. "And one of Staffordshire's finest—I believe the mark most resembles a Wedgwood."

Mary threw her arms around C.J.'s neck, weeping tears of jubilation, then an emotional Lady Dalrymple embraced the couple after first removing her serpentine accessory and handing the snake off to a terrified Mary, who immediately dropped it amid the golden pebbles. "So, my niece," the countess said, "it would certainly appear that you are indeed the very person I have claimed you to be all along." Lady Dalrymple joined her hands with those of Darlington and C.J. "And here is your heiress after all, Percy."

"God grant you joy," said Lady Chatterton, waving her wand over everyone who was in any way reunited with a loved one during the past several minutes. "But I think you need it most of all," she added, blowing some sparkly pixie dust at a glowering Lady Oliver.

Her head spinning from this most extraordinary of revelations, C.J. sank down onto the marble bench. So this *was* where she belonged; her every instinct about her visceral connections to this world had been accurate. In fact, she had been transported into the *future* when, so many years earlier, she had disappeared into the wings at the Theatre Royal, Bath. Now, she had come *home,* to continue to live the remainder of a life begun in the eighteenth century.

"I am astounded, Clementina, that you went to all this trouble for me." Manwaring bestowed a kiss on Lady Chatterton's delicate fingers. "I am touched beyond all measure. Behold me, an unworthy suppliant at your feet," he declared, dramatically prostrating himself before her.

Outside the pavilion, the fireworks began anew, sending showers of silver and gold into the treetops and down again.

Mathias Dingle removed his conical hat emblazoned with stars. "Our revels now are ended," he said with a smile to Lady Chatterton.

Darlington slipped his arm around the waist of his future wife, drawing her to him. "On the contrary, my dear sir," he exclaimed, "I'll wager they have barely begun!"

C.J. COULD SCARCELY WAIT to return to Bath to share the news of her good fortune with Miss Austen, informing her when they met three days later that Lady Dalrymple had named C.J. as her heiress and would settle an income upon her.

Jane gasped with delight at her friend's great fortune. "An annuity is a very serious business."

Then a beaming Darlington announced for the benefit of his cousin, "And the young lady lately known as Miss Welles has consented to do me the great honor of becoming the Countess of Darlington. I had thought to postpone my entreaty to Cassandra to do me the ultimate honor until I had the proper documents in hand, but once I saw her at Vauxhall, I found I could not contain myself." He discerned a distinct blush on his fiancée's cheeks. "I have just now come from Canterbury so as not to add a moment's more delay, although the elaborate wedding preparations I have in mind—which will accord Lady Cassandra the fullness of the honors she deserves—will take a good deal of time and effort."

Miss Austen emitted an exasperated sigh. "Why not seize the pleasure at once? How often is happiness destroyed by preparation, foolish preparation?"

"As though I have not waited long enough," C.J. replied with a light laugh. "You need not go to extremes on my account, Percy."

"Is not my Cassandra the most charming girl in the world, Miss Jane?" Darlington said, a besotted smile on his lips.

"It requires uncommon steadiness of reason to resist the attraction of being called the most charming girl in the world," Jane teased.

"I shall endeavor to keep my head then," C.J. replied, as the two young ladies exchanged an impish glance. "But you must allow, Jane, that your cousin is quite charming when he is smitten. Quite a contrast to how studious he looks with his spectacles on! And I daresay I cannot number many men among my acquaintance who have as thorough a knowledge and understanding—and passion—for the poetry of Shakespeare, as well as a rather wicked art collection."

Jane ruffled her cousin's hair. "His friends may well rejoice in his having met with one of the very few sensible women who would have accepted him, or have made him happy if they had."

His lordship took his leave just as Mary appeared in the doorway. "Lady Dalrymple wishes to know if you and Miss Austen might join her in the front parlor for tea, your ladyship." C.J. replied that they would be delighted to accept her aunt's offer, particularly if there were rosewater biscuits to be had. She noticed an unusual brooch pinned to Mary's livery and inquired after its provenance. "A gift it was from Mrs. Jordan and His Highness, to thank me for assistin' in the delivery of her babe. A boy, it was. In the pink of health."

"Goodness!" C.J. exclaimed admiringly. "Then did you actually meet the Duke of Clarence?"

Mary shook her head. "Oh no. But Mrs. Jordan herself pressed this into my hand."

"Mrs. Jordan was up and about so soon after giving birth? I pray that I may be as fortunate," said C.J., lovingly caressing her abdomen.

"Oh, she's had so many babes, she says they practically pop out by themselves now," Mary replied. "She told us she just summons the midwives to entertain her in her hours of labor so she should not have to endure them alone. Why, she was even doin' speeches for us from the theatre while she was pushin' out the babe. And Mrs. Goodwin asked her to do Pickle," Mary added, referring to the role for which Mrs. Jordan had gained the most renown.

Astonished, C.J. clapped a hand to her breast. "I pray, too, that I may have her humor under the circumstances!"

Epilogue

AND SO, DEAR READER, they were married. In the quiet parish church of St. Mary the Virgin, where Henry Fielding recited his vows, the third Earl of Darlington married Lady Cassandra Jane Warburton Tobias, only daughter of the eighth Marquess of Manwaring. Miss Austen's "foolish preparation" was dispensed with at a small ceremony attended by the couple's intimate friends and family.

Lady Oliver was conspicuous in her absence.

Following tradition, the groom handed his bride up into the open carriage, then climbed in beside her. The newlyweds tossed coins to those who had come to wish them well, then spurred their steeds toward the city. As they rode along Stall Street, headed for Darlington's town house in the Circus, the new countess asked her husband to have the carriage brought to a halt. She alighted in front of an apple cart, took a good deal of care in selecting a particularly fragrant specimen, then removed a gold crown from her reticule. "For your pains, Adam Dombie," she told the stunned costermonger.

The following March, as the vernal equinox was celebrated with great relief that the dark days of winter had once again drawn to a close and the crisp spring air promised warmer and gentler breezes to come, Lady Darlington was delivered of twins by Mary Sykes.

William, the boy, had his father's dark curls and lapis-colored eyes; his sister, Nora, younger by a quarter hour, was possessed of the same deep blue eyes, but her hair was as fine and fair and golden as her mother's had been when she was a newborn.

Their godmother was Miss Jane Austen.

Both babes demonstrated a remarkable, and rather immediate, inquisitiveness and shared a stubborn reluctance to go to Mrs. Fast, the wet nurse. On the afternoon following the births, Mary presented Lady Darlington with a small packet wrapped in tissue. Inside it was the cameo that had been bestowed upon the apprentice midwife by Mrs. Jordan.

"Mary, how can I possibly accept this?"

"It is the least I can do for your ladyship. Had it not been for you learnin' me my letters and his lordship relievin' me from my situation at Lady Wickham's, I should never have made anything of myself, and now—"

"Mary, side by side we have scrubbed the rust stains from roasting pans, dyed used tea leaves black for smouch, and slept in the same bed. I cannot permit you to call me 'your ladyship.' I beg you to use my Christian name."

"Oh no, your ladyship. Will you never learn? You are a countess and I am but a midwife. It is not at all proper."

"Well then, you must at least permit me to address you as Mrs. Musgrove in future. And may I offer the deepest felicitations from Darlington and me." Mary blushed a deep crimson. The twins' godmother reappeared, bearing a tray of refreshments. "How astonishing I still find it," C.J. remarked to Miss Austen, "that after all my peregrinations, Bath is my home after all."

Jane smiled, and taking Cassandra's hand in hers, pressed it to her cheek. "A heroine returning, at the close of her career, to her native village, all in the triumph of recovered reputation and all the dignity of a countess . . . is an event on which the pen of the contriver may well delight to dwell; it gives credit to every

conclusion, and the author must share in the glory she so liber-
ally bestows."

An ending thus became a beginning, as Lord Darlington had
so presciently predicted. And for the remainder of their days
together, Lady Darlington remembered fondly her Aunt
Euphoria's advice and danced for her husband—with great regularity.

Acknowledgments

MANY THANKS TO my wonderful agent, Irene Goodman, who valiantly championed this book through its myriad revisions, and to my terrifically incisive editor, Rachel Beard Kahan, who took a chance on it and went well above and beyond her editorial duty by giving me a grad-level crash course via e-mail in the laws of primogeniture. Plaudits also to Shana Drehs for taking up the editorial baton without missing a step. Recognition is also due to William Richert, who was there the night "Amanda" was born; to Michele LaRue for being the most patient fan of this novel; to M. Z. R. for the magic bullet, and to Miriam Kriss for the graphic; to the generous, kind, and supportive members of the Beau Monde for their raft of encyclopedic knowledge; and to d.f for his continual, and enthusiastic, encouragement. A bouquet to Laurie Peterson for hiring me to play Jane Austen in *The Novelist* and to Raffaele A. Castaldo for making me believe I really was in Jane's parlor in Steventon. Finally, a special nod to the magical city of Bath; every time I visit, I feel as if I've come home.

By a Lady

AMANDA ELYOT

A READER'S GROUP
GUIDE

An audition for a plum role in a play about Jane Austen becomes an unexpected adventure for New York actress and unabashed Anglophile C. J. Welles. Upon exiting the stage following her final audition, C. J. finds herself inexplicably transported to Bath, England, at the turn of the nineteenth century. Alone in a strange place, at first C. J. is frightened and confused, and barely succeeds in fitting in without betraying the truth of her origin. But she grows increasingly comfortable after she meets the delightfully eccentric Lady Dalrymple, with whom she forms a special bond. A budding romance with Owen Percival, the dashing Earl of Darlington, fosters her increasing affection for the earlier era, especially when C. J. finds out that Darlington's cousin is none other than Jane Austen—one of C. J.'s literary heroes.

But C. J. remains desperately torn between the two centuries. She longs to return to her own time but faces the difficult decision of leaving behind her new friends and the irresistible Lord Darlington. Then, in the midst of a remarkable turn of events, C. J. makes a startling discovery, uncovering a secret about her past that may explain why she wound up in Bath in the first place.

By a Lady is a marvelous fish-out-of-water historical drama, laced with comedy, romance, and mystery. This guide is designed to help direct your reading group's discussion of Amanda Elyot's delightful novel.

Questions for Discussion

1. Before you read *By a Lady*, had you read any of Jane Austen's novels? If so, what are some themes common to Austen's writing that appear in *By a Lady*? Do any of the characters in *By a Lady* resemble those in Austen's works?

2. At the book's opening, the author includes this quote from Jane Austen: "The novels which I approve are such as display human nature with grandeur—such as show her in the sublimities of intense feeling—such as exhibit the progress of strong passion from the first germ of incipient susceptibility to the utmost energies of reason half-dethroned—where we see the strong spark of women's captivations elicit such fire in the soul of man as leads him . . . to hazard all, dare all, achieve all, to obtain her." Do you think *By a Lady* lives up to the standards Austen sets forth in these words? Why or why not?

3. Do you share an affinity for another era? If so, which one and why?

4. Austen's *Pride and Prejudice* opens with this line: "It is a truth universally acknowledged, that a single man in possession of a good fortune must be in want of a wife." How does this sentiment hold true in *By a Lady*?

5. The author describes the acute class differences in Georgian England, as well as C. J.'s intense feelings about this disparity. On page 134, Lady Dalrymple says to C. J., "I do not condone the behavior you just witnessed, nor do I agree with it, but my dear, that is the way of the upper crust." On page 177, Darlington says to C. J., "The English class system has been ingrained for centuries, Miss Welles, and everyone knows and accepts his place with alacrity. That is the way of the world." Do you agree with the sentiment that a tradition should be upheld for no other reason than its continued existence? Where in the modern world are there similar disparities in economic and/or social classes? Why do you think this kind of inequality has endured? Do you think circumstances in these societies could someday change?

6. *By a Lady* is full of rich period detail—clothing, sights and smells, societal customs. What were some of the more surprising aspects of Georgian life you became familiar with through this novel?

7. "Every time C. J. thought she had gotten a handle on their mores or manners, these Georgians threw her a curve. A proper lady did not address the servants as equals, and yet she drank her tea out of the saucer!" (page 111). Discuss other points in the book where such inconsistency in manners is displayed by members of Bath's society.

8. In Chapter Three (page 32), when C. J. is brought in front of the magistrate, she learns the origin of the phrase "rule of thumb" as it applied to a case of a man accused of abusing his wife with a stick. In Chapter Ten (page 124), she is horrified to discover the quite literal meaning of "putting on the dog." Are there other colloquialisms from the Georgian age enduring today that you know of? What are they and what are their origins?

9. "Nearly everyone here danced around his or her intentions, cloaking them in nuance, riddle, and understatement," C. J. observes on page 137. What are the benefits of a polite society like that of Georgian Bath, where custom prevented expression of candid thoughts and ideas? Would you prefer this type of polite society, or a more liberated society where people were free to express their opinions? Why?

10. "Despite the fact that she had been arrested, imprisoned, tried, nearly committed to a lifetime of indentured servitude, publicly jilted by the man she loved, and, most recently, incarcerated in a madhouse, C. J. had come to feel, in a most inexplicable way, that she really belonged in 1801" (page 315). Were you surprised at C. J.'s decision to remain in nineteenth-century Bath? Did you see her decision as a foreshadowing of the novel's subsequent plot twist?

11. Did the book's ending surprise you? Why or why not?

12. Who are your literary heroes? Who would you like to befriend in another life?

Also by Amanda Elyot

Written as a memoir, this lush, compelling novel of passion and loss tells the story of Helen of Troy and the truth about her life, her lovers, and the Trojan War. This is the tale as she would have told it—her legendary beauty still undimmed by age.

$13.95 paper (Canada: $18.95)
0-307-33860-6

FICTION   Elyot, Amanda.
Elyot
          By a lady.

$14.95

DATE			

4/06

BAKER & TAYLOR